THE

SANDBOX

THE
SANDBOX

A NOVEL

DAVID ZIMMERMAN

Published in the United States in 2010 by
Soho Press, Inc.
853 Broadway
New York, NY 10003

Library of Congress Cataloging-in-Publication Data

Zimmerman, David.
 The sandbox / David Zimmerman.
    p. cm.
 ISBN 978-1-56947-628-4
 1. Iraq War, 2003—Fiction. 2. Soldiers—Fiction. 3. Americans—Iraq—Fiction.
 I. Title.
 PS3626.I49S36 2010
 813'.6—dc22

                              2009043994

Book interior by Elyse Strongin, Neuwirth & Associates, Inc.

Paperback ISBN: 978-1-56947-916-2

10 9 8 7 6 5 4 3 2 1

I talked to one of the local hajji leaders during a routine traffic patrol. His car broke down at the intersection where we'd set up shop. I'll never forget it, he told me, the saying of these times is: everything is true, nothing is permitted. Some medieval prince said it, and now they're saying it again. I kept thinking about it all day. I still think about it now.

—Interview with Iowa National Guard Infantryman, 2007

Nothing is true; everything is permitted.

—The Old Man of the Mountain, Leader of the Hashishins

For my wife Tina and the twenty-nine kisses.

ACKNOWLEDGMENTS

I owe a debt of gratitude to a great number of people: Scott Yarbrough for his tireless reading of manuscripts and stalwart friendship, Steve Pett for his endless encouragement, Deb Marquart whose continuing belief kept me plugging away, Charlie Kostelnick, Matthew Miller and his keen perspective, Jon Billman, Joseph Thomas, Eva Talmadge for her excellent editorial suggestions, Patty Pace who helped shape my concept of story, David Starnes who helped shape my concept of life, Dennis Thompson, Imad Rahman and Tamara Guiardo for their determination to keep me from staying on the ground when I fell, the Wisconsin Institute for Creative Writing, Jesse Lee Kercheval, Jack Gantos, Val Helmund, Laura Hruska and the rest of the Soho Press staff for their patience and superb editorial advice, the Iowa State University ROTC program, Kami Hinojosa for her great story about the M.I. interrogation, Mike Tate for his advice on Army lingo and blogs, Dave Marshall for his great stories of Army life, as well as Ted, T.F., Henry, D.K., Little A, and all the other soldiers who wished to remain anonymous, Patrick Zimmerman for his sharp reading skills and all the rest of the Zimmerman and Amalfitano families, especially my beloved feral nephews and nieces Parker, Jack, Hannah, Mark, Luke, Leah, and Emma, and finally for my greatest ally and friend, Tina.

THE
SANDBOX

1

The body of the naked child lies in the center of the highway. Except at first I don't know it's a child, or even a body. The whole convoy stops. From our position in the trail vehicle at the rear, Rankin and I see only a small white mound, like a fallen bird. To Rankin the kid looks more like a lump of shortening melting on an iron skillet. If we hadn't heard what it was over the radio, I'm not sure I would have noticed it until we passed, and maybe not even then. This road is strewn with trash. Some of it deadly, most not. Empty plastic sacks, crumpled paper, flattened packs of Miami cigarettes—the harsh national brand—broken car parts, dead mules, and now unwanted children. Heat distorts the air above the blacktop, bending the horizon. The thermometer on the dashboard reads 118 degrees. The body of the child seems to quiver in the sunlight.

I squint and try to see what might have killed the kid. Car accident? Shrapnel? I have yet to see a natural death in this place. No one dies peacefully in his bed any more, unless it's because he got hit in the head by a stray while he was sleeping. From here, the child looks like it simply got tired and lay down in the middle of the road. We sit in the third Humvee in a convoy of three and wait. Rankin asks me to roll him a cigarette and sets his pouch of Bugle Boy on top of the steering wheel. He's missing the last joint of his pinkie finger: an accident on the firing range at Basic. A fuckwit from suburban Atlanta forgot he had a round in the chamber and Rankin had the bad luck to be beside him. The pink stub shines as though he's polished it.

Someone, it looks like Gerling, gets out of the first Humvee to take a look. After a moment, he walks back to the second vehicle and knocks on the window. They parley. Earlier this week, one of the guys shaved Gerling a Mohawk. It flops around each time he moves his head, like the comb of a giant rooster. Rankin groans and adjusts the air vent. Every once in a while I glance up and watch Gerling wave his hands around and move his mouth like he's trying to chew his way into the Humvee. Then I stop paying him any mind. Instead I focus on the sticky flakes of tobacco. After two months in Transarabia's Six Zone, a body on the road, even the body of a child, no longer holds my attention. When I think about this, it makes me unhappy, so I try not to. There will be plenty of time to think about it when I get home, I tell myself. Right now it is too dangerous to obsess about such things. It will only make life harder, and life is hard enough as it is. So I put this child in the small cigar box I keep hidden in the back of my head, close its cardboard lid, and snap a couple of rubber bands around it to keep it tightly shut. Just like I've done with the rest.

Rankin and the radio talk, but I focus all of my attention on the pinch of tobacco and the rolling paper. I try as hard as I can not to think about anything else. This is how I will get through my war. Work on one thing at a time and only think of that. Then go on to the next thing. But Rankin shouts something, and I'm forced to stop doing my one thing.

"Huh?" I ask, irritated that he's interrupting me.

"Jesus," the radio squawks. It sounds like Lieutenant Saunders, the Military Intelligence guy everybody hates. "Just send another gobstopper to look at it. Why the hell do you want me to go? Send Hazel or Greer, he's the Goddamned medic. It's too fucking hot out there. Either that or tell one of the villagers to go check it out when we come back."

I hate it when he calls us gobstoppers.

"What?" I say finally, because Rankin keeps giving me this look of disbelief.

"I said, holy shit," Rankin says.

Rankin is tall and thin with a short uneven afro and an Adam's apple the size of a golf ball. We enlisted on the same day at the same recruiting office, a dinky little place in a strip mall on the south side of Savannah. Two desks, a computer, and a few tattered posters of heroic soldiers hoisting flags. When the recruiter asked why we wanted to sign up, neither of us had much to say for ourselves. "I'm bored," Rankin told him, and I nodded in agreement. It was the truth, but even then it didn't seem like enough. The recruiter thought it was plenty. They always do. Just one more box to be ticked off. We shared a bunk bed in Basic, and although we don't have a lot in common besides timing and geography, we get along fine.

"Holy shit, what?" I ask.

"Didn't you hear what he just said? Shit, man, you're always off in la-la land." Rankin punches a button on the FBCB2, the Force XXI Battle Command, Brigade and Below, which is a fancy name for the ugly green in-board computer bolted to the dash. It contains a GPS locator and shows us a map of the general area and our grid coordinates within it. In the old days, before HQ stripped down the base and took all the good stuff away, an operator back at the Communications Trailer used it to track movements of friendly and unfriendly troops and send us info about them both. The screen would show a little red triangle wherever they thought the enemy was located, and a sexy female voice would say, "Warning! Enemy in the Area!" Rankin and I called this voice Miss Hilton.

"Man," Rankin says, flicking the FBCB2 with his finger, "this thing's practically useless. Where's Paris when you need her?"

Lieutenant Saunders steps out of the lead Humvee and walks across the asphalt with his head ducked down. The heat distortion makes his body seem to sway. Gerling and Kellen follow him. Kellen is the smallest man on base, possibly the smallest soldier I've ever seen. That he managed to get around infantry height requirements is baffling. Rankin, as always, has a few theories. One includes a famous general and a beautiful female pygmy. Kellen's a cheerful guy with a shock of hair the color of mayonnaise and a face stained brown with hundreds of tiny freckles. Even from here, I can see that he's grinning. What the hell about? Maybe he can't turn it off. Gerling continues to wave his arms around like he's trying to signal a passing helicopter. After some discussion, Lieutenant Saunders kneels down beside the child's body. I wonder where this child came from. If maybe someone threw it out of a passing car, like a cigarette butt. We're traveling along a section of the Turkish highway, so named because the Turks used this route to invade several centuries ago. Not much else happened here until we arrived. My Army map calls it Highway 6A. Judging from the grid map, we're almost exactly thirty klicks south of Kurkbil, the only settlement in a fifty-klick radius. We've stopped in a landscape of jagged brown boulders and pus-colored dust. No water, no plants, no people. Even the goat herders, who go everywhere, don't come out here. Someone, I think, had to have brought the child to this place on purpose. The idea makes me very uncomfortable. Into the cigar box it goes.

"Can you fucking believe this shit?" Rankin gives me that goggle-eyed look again. He seems frantic. I look around but don't see much reason to get upset.

"What?" I ask him.

"It's a white girl. Somebody shot her in the head and dumped her."

"What?" I repeat, not sure whether he's feeding me a line of bullshit.

"You heard me."

"Goddamn, that *is* fucking weird." I sit up and peer through the dust-coated windshield. Now that I know what it is, the little white lump in the road looks completely different. The girl's body is as white as a milk tooth, bright against the crumbling asphalt. This doesn't make any sense. Why would— "Are you sure he said a white girl? Maybe he made a mistake. These women are covered from head to foot their whole lives. I don't expect they ever get a tan."

"That's what the man said. You better believe this will stir some shit up. A white girl? Damn. Remember what I'm telling you, man, when—"

Before Rankin can finish telling me what to remember, there is a flash. Then the Humvee rocks with the shock waves. The windshield cracks. Sand and dust blow over us. The explosion is so loud that it becomes something felt rather than heard. It pushes against my chest and makes my ears pop. One moment Lieutenant Saunders is leaning over the child, the next moment he's gone. Gobbets of flesh and gravel rain down on our vehicle. Oily smoke drifts between the cars. One of the other soldiers from the first Humvee—it looks like Gerling—stumbles backward, holding his stomach with both hands. His face is painted with gore. I can't see the other man who got out of the car with them. Kellen. I don't know either of them very well. They've only been on base for about a week and a half. Nobody talks to the FNGs—fucking new guys—for at least two weeks, sometimes even longer.

My first instinct is to put us into gear and drive through the kill zone, like they taught us in Basic. But Rankin hops out and heads toward the blast site. Without a word, I jump onto the road and follow. Nevada and Hazel get there first. Hazel turns and vomits on the gravel shoulder. He seems to be saying something, but I can't hear him. My ears are humming like a broken refrigerator. "You're still alive." I chant this to myself. "You're still alive." Kellen wobbles out of the black smoke and stops in front of me, swaying back and forth. His tiny hands are pressed together, as though he's praying. He holds a severed hand between his palms. Even though it's nearly twice the size of his own, there's so much blood on his face and his uniform that it takes me a moment to see that this isn't his. I look from his hands to the blast site. I don't see Lieutenant Saunders anywhere. Kellen holds the largest piece of Lieutenant Saunders left. I can't quite absorb this information. Kellen blinks and leans forward. I reach him just before he drops.

"I caught it," he tells me as he falls.

"Medic!" I shout.

I lean Kellen against the tire of the lead Humvee and search his body for shrapnel wounds. Blood soaks his shirt and drips purple onto the asphalt. Something must be seriously wrong. A bullet pings off the bumper of the Humvee to my left. I look up, confused for a moment.

A second round pops off the pavement beside me and ricochets into the windshield. A star of powdered glass appears between the cracks caused by the blast. My first impulse is to turn and run away as fast as I can. I blink and swallow hard. The feeling doesn't go away, but I push it aside as best I can. There is a rattling sound just beneath me. It's my foot, jittering in the gravel.

The man at the wheel of the Humvee beside me yells, "Where are the shooters?"

I scan the horizon, but they could be in any of a hundred different crevices beside the road. Piles of broken rock and scree litter the landscape for miles. Some of the boulders are as large as tanks. I try to breathe slowly, but I can't.

Kellen squeezes my fingers.

"Stay with me, Kellen," I tell him. "Don't you dare pass out."

Without quite meaning to, I glance down at the severed hand lying beside his leg. A gold band on the second finger shines in the sunlight. Lying on the pavement this way, separate from its body, it looks more terrifying and human than the face of a corpse.

Kellen lets out a groan and tries to say something, but only manages to cough. Flecks of blood spray my arm. They are the same size and shape as the freckles that cover his cheeks. When he speaks, his voice is ragged and wet. "It's a remote detonator. Look for the wire." His face is white beneath the blood. There are bits of flesh caked in his thick blond moustache. I wonder how he knows this about the detonator.

Our combat medic, Doc Greer, sprints over, and I scan the gravel shoulder for the remote wire. Rankin squeezes off several three-shot bursts from between the Humvees. He looks exactly like the illustration for "Firing from a Kneeling Position" from our rifle manual in Basic. He chews his lip and fires again. I have no idea what he's aiming at. A bullet hits the door of the Humvee just beside him with a loud clink.

"I've got to get another triage kit," Doc Greer says. His face is twisted, angry. "Goddammit. We're running out of fucking everything."

Lieutenant Blankenship shouts at us from behind the middle Humvee. "Look to the muzzle flashes. Don't fire willy-nilly." He leans over the hood of the vehicle with his sidearm drawn, although it's almost useless from this distance. When I turn back to Kellen, Doc Greer is gone. I have no idea where I put my rifle. An infantry soldier's worst nightmare. Panic makes my mouth go dry. Then I see it lying just beneath Kellen's arm. I nearly cry with relief. I can't remember taking it off my shoulder.

"I got a line on you now, hajji motherfucker," Rankin shouts, clicking his rifle onto automatic with his thumb. He rakes the hillside in a slow zigzag pattern, emptying his entire clip. "Goddamn chickpeas."

"Controlled bursts," the lieutenant shouts, "controlled bursts."

"Fuck that," Rankin mumbles, slamming another magazine into his M16.

2

My watch seems to believe it's only been eleven minutes since we stopped to check out the dead girl's body. My watch and I, we often disagree.

Behind the second Humvee, someone pants and wheezes. "Fuck," they say, "Goddamn." I wipe my face with my sleeve and peer up at the line of broken boulders on the rise above the road. Nothing moves. Not even the air. Okay, I think, let's get this shit finished and get out of here.

"I'll be back in a couple of mikes." I squeeze Kellen's hand, but he doesn't respond. Shit. His eyes are closed. A fresh trickle of blood runs from his ear and drips once, twice, three times. For a long moment, this is all I see. These slow drops. I fight the urge to wipe the blood away. "Listen, you fucker, don't die on me."

He groans. I let out a long breath.

I duck-walk over to the blast site, careful to look out for any potential second improvised explosive devices—IEDs—hidden in the trash along the gravel shoulder of the highway. This is a famous trick. Attract with the first blast, kill with the second. Daisy chains, they're called. But it's hard to see much of anything. The sunlight stings. Somewhere between here and the Humvee, I lost my sunglasses. Goddammit. I get down on my hands and knees and crawl, hoping I don't draw the sniper's attention. I'm looking for something like a speaker cord. I should be traveling overwatch, the standard squad formation where each man covers the rest as they move ahead, but I just want to get this done with. Blood from the pavement soaks the knees of my pants. It has already turned tacky. Sometimes I feel small bits of flesh under my palms. My hands make a nasty smacking sound each time I move. If I think about what I'm crawling over, my mouth fills with spit and my throat tightens up. One thing at a time, I tell myself. Find the wire. After a few very long moments of scanning the roadside, I start to worry they might have used a cell phone as a detonator, that there isn't a wire. We've heard this is common in the capital now, but I've never seen it out here.

And then something I don't see starts it all up again. Behind me, several men fire their rifles in bursts of three. My ears continue to ring from the explosion, so the reports sound far away, but they're still as sharp as snare-drum pops. Bap, bap, bap. Bap, bap, bap.

"Motherfuck," someone says in a slow, distinct voice. "All I wanted was to snag some Goddamn toilet paper from the PX."

I look up over my shoulder. Nevada squats in the back of the lead Humvee with the Ma Deuce. It's an old .50-caliber machine gun we jury-rigged to a wooden crate and ratcheted down to the truck bed. Another example of making do with fucking trash when they don't send us the right equipment. He doesn't fire. He just squints up at the rocks.

I keep on crawling. Right when I decide to quit and move back behind the Humvee, I see it: a thin yellow cord snaking up into the gravel. I whistle to Rankin and hold it out for him to see. He gives me the thumbs up and runs behind the line of vehicles to where I'm taking cover behind a rock. Another soldier, anonymous behind the smear of blood on his face, follows Rankin. It might be Boyette, but I don't take the time to puzzle it out.

The wire twists up between the rocks to a massive egg-shaped boulder on the rise above the highway. I give it a flick, so we can see where it leads. Rankin indicates with hand signals that we should run for the next group of rocks. I suck in a breath and nod. Rankin fires off three rounds. I look up just in time to see a small figure in a blue windbreaker throw something before falling back behind the boulder. Whatever it is, it thuds into the sand on the other side of our rocks. He must be out of ammo, I think, if he's chucking stones at us. Two things happen almost simultaneously—on the ridge above us, someone cries out; and just as I'm standing to get his position, I'm knocked backward by an explosion.

3

"How you doing, Durrant?" It's Rankin, standing above me with the sun behind his head. He's just a fuzzy silhouette. "You all right, Big D?"

I try to sit up, but the world goes gray and I decide to stay where I am for a while. My pants feel warm and heavy and wet. Shit, I think, they're filled with blood. I wait for the pain. It doesn't come. I must be in shock. I guess I'm going home.

Doc Greer holds up three fingers. "How many fingers, Durrant?"

"Three," I tell him, feeling around with my mind for the pain. "I think I got hit in the stomach or the leg. I'm bleeding all over the place. Can you see it? Is it bad?"

"Oh, man," Rankin says, smiling.

Somewhere in the middle distance I hear Lieutenant Blankenship shouting. Another voice yells back in fast, jittery Arabic. On the pavement beside me, Lopez changes a tire. His mouth is pinched tight, and his thin black eyebrows are bunched up like angry inchworms. He seems annoyed, but all of his movements are measured and precise. Every once in a while, he glances up toward the rise where the shooters had been. I think we got at least one of them. Rankin grins at me.

"What?" I say. "What?"

"You ain't hit." Rankin says.

"When the grenade went off," Doc Greer tells me, smiling now too, "you voided your bladder. It's not an uncommon response."

Rankin nudges my leg with his boot. "Phooey. From the smell of it, he voided more than that."

They both laugh now. Lopez frowns at us and shakes his head. Even in the harsh sunlight, I see where his constant ironing has made permanent crease lines in his desert fatigues. I notice he's made one of his little black crosses on the waist of his pants. Lopez draws a black cross in indelible ink on everything he owns—rifle, helmet, shirt, boots.

"Don't you have something to do, Rankin?" Lopez says, his mouth a tight line of disapproval.

"Shit, man," Rankin says, laughter still in his voice. "We got them. Lighten up, little Fobbit."

Lopez doesn't respond, but I know he's irritated. Fobbits are what we call soldiers who try and escape the hairy missions by finding ways to stay back at the Forward Operating Base. The FOB. Lopez isn't really a fobbit, but it entertains Rankin to call him one because it never fails to get his goat.

"I pissed myself," I say. "I fucking pissed myself."

Rankin gives me a long, slow nod. "You sure did." He pulls out his tobacco pouch. "Nothing like a good smoke after a firefight. Don't you think?" He raises his eyebrows at me.

"Let me sit up first," I tell him. Our base has been out of ready-mades for almost two weeks. Along with toilet paper and coffee filters and about a dozen or so other basic necessities of life. I quit smoking before I left the States, right after I found out my girlfriend was pregnant, but I relish the smell of unlit rolling tobacco and the sticky residue it leaves on my fingers.

"Give him a second, Rankin," Doc Greer says. "Let him catch his breath. Poor guy just pissed himself."

They laugh again.

Two soldiers crunch by on the gravel, carrying a stretcher. The sun obscures their faces, but I get a good look at the guy on the stretcher. It's the hajji in the blue windbreaker. He has the face of a twelve-year-old boy. Every few seconds he convulses with pain, clutching his belly and whimpering like a kicked dog. The hajji and I look at each other as he passes. His eyes are the same warm brown color as rolling tobacco.

"What happened?" I ask them.

"When he jumped up and chucked that grenade at you, I popped a few off and hit him just above his pelvis." Rankin tosses the pouch and papers onto my stomach. "Right about there. I didn't know he was just a baby."

"Shit, man, I'd rather get hit in the head," Doc Greer says, making a face. "At least it's over quick. A gut shot can take days to kill you. The kid doesn't even look like he's got pubes."

"I bet you'd have a good time finding out," I say. "If you hurry, you might even have time to play pop-goes-the-weasel before they put him in the back of the Humvee."

"Don't ask, don't tell," Rankin says.

We laugh. All of us, that is, except Lopez.

Lopez stands and brushes the dust off his knees. "That poor *kid* killed Lieutenant Saunders and he just about killed Durrant here with a grenade. I hope the wound does kill him. I'd like to go over and finish him off with a pop in the head." Lopez does the obligatory finger against the temple gesture. "It'd serve that little so-and-so right."

"So-and-so," Rankin says and laughs. "Man, you crack me up. So-and-so. You talk like my meemaw."

"If you hadn't of shot that poor *kid*, he would have killed both of you. He was holding another detonator. Look, Hazel and the hick are getting rid of it." Lopez points to the other side of the road, where Hazel and Boyette are tearing ass across the gravel.

"Fire in the hole!" Hazel shouts.

The earth erupts behind them, making the cracked windows in the Humvee behind us rattle. The sound rumbles up through the asphalt and into my vertebrae. It seems to go on for a very long time. Dust rises above the blast site and floats across the landscape in a dense yellow cloud. I realize I've been holding my breath. This seems to happen a lot lately; I'll suddenly notice I've been holding my breath. I'm not sure when it started. This bothers me obscurely, so I push it out of my head and exhale slowly. Someone, probably the wounded boy, begins to make a high-pitched keening sound that rises and falls like a civil defense siren.

"Shit," Rankin says in a soft, almost apologetic voice. "You know that's got to hurt."

"Shut up," Lopez says, his face purple and clenched like a fist. "Just shut up."

4

My head clears quickly, but even so, Rankin insists on driving back to the base. He tells me the rest of the story as we go. After I blacked out, the other hajji held us off with an AK-47 for a few minutes until he ran out of ammo. Then he tried to run away. Boyette caught him with a flying tackle and dragged him back. "There was hardly any hajji under the robe," he told Rankin. "After I scared the shit out of him, all that was left was a beard and bones." Rankin said the older insurgent looked like he might be the boy's father or uncle. The old guy spat on Boyette, so he chucked him into the back of the Humvee like a spare tire. Rankin thinks they'll send a helicopter down this afternoon to pick them up along with Kellen and Gerling. They can't do it now because there's a sandstorm between us and HQ. I don't say much to all this. I keep looping the moment Kellen squeezed my hand and made that sound. It isn't so easy to cram that one in the box.

Our original mission for the day, the whole reason both lieutenants came along, was to drive a few hours south to Inmar, the capital of the South Western Department or, as the military calls it, Six Zone, and have a meeting with the local tribal sheikhs. It was a bullshit detail, and everyone knew it except Lieutenant Blankenship. The real purpose of the trip was to trade GameCube games with some of the men at division HQ and try and snag a few cases of toilet paper and cigarettes. Lieutenant Saunders loved his video games even more than the enlisted men. Myself, I was hoping to score some Turkish Cassandra whiskey, the kind with the sexy harem girl on the label, or at the very least a bottle of arak, a fiery homemade liquor they make here. It tastes like licorice, which I hate, but it'll fuck you up something fierce. Strictly off-limits, but the noncoms let us get away with the occasional nip as long as we're quiet about it and they don't actually see us drinking.

Since none of this was on the up-and-up, the only one who didn't know the real score was Lieutenant Blankenship, the same one who'd probably end up taking the heat for this little trip turning into a soup sandwich. Lieutenant Blankenship's a West Point ring-knocker, five months in-country and strictly by the book. In fact, he carries the book around with him. The seven-dash-eight, the infantryman's bible. He's a couple of years younger than I am, twenty-two or twenty-three. When I first arrived, we had a captain running the show. But after HQ decided to scale down operations, they left Lieutenant Blankenship in command of the forty-five men who remained on base. Lieutenant Saunders didn't show up until later. This reduction was supposed to be a temporary situation, no more than a week or two. Just until they decided whether to close the base down or nudge it up to battalion strength and turn it into an operational center. It's gone on for quite a while now, nearly a month. The lieutenant's in command limbo. No one really knows what's going on. Least of all him. I almost feel sorry for the guy, but not enough to set him straight about the real reasons for going to Inmar.

I wonder what effect Lieutenant Saunders's death is going to have on the leadership of the base. Before this, the two lieutenants had shared an uneasy balance of power. Now Lieutenant Blankenship will be the sole commanding officer, along with First Sergeant Oliphant, the man who really runs the day-to-day operations. Sergeant Oliphant's the oldest man among us, a grizzled old-timer in his forties with a gray-streaked buzz cut and arms as hard and thin as hickory ax handles. If you want something done or you want to talk with Lieutenant Blankenship, you go to Sergeant Oliphant. His relationship with the lieutenant goes beyond suction. In all the ways that really matter, Sergeant Oliphant leads and the lieutenant follows. Even Lieutenant

Saunders deferred to him. As far as rank, the third in command will now be Sergeant Guzman, who is easily the most popular NCO on base. Sergeant Guzman's a huge Puerto Rican guy in his late twenties, born in Queens and raised in Atlanta. Maybe six-foot-five or -six with gigantic muscles. He has biceps each the size of a normal guy's thigh and a beautiful singing voice. On some nights, Rankin and I can hear Sergeant Guzman singing old Spanish ballads in his Conex about a hundred yards away. Although he's got a temper that comes on so fast you'd think there was a switch on the back of his head, he's the NCO most of us go to first if we're in trouble. He'll listen. Right now he heads up my group, but with this new leadership shuffle, I worry that this might change. I look over at Rankin and consider asking him about it, but there's really no point since he won't know any more than I do.

Rankin sings softly to himself as he drives, tapping out the time on the steering wheel and looking over at me occasionally with a concerned expression. Before he let me climb into the seat, he covered it with a tattered oil rag. He doesn't say anything about my piss-soaked pants, but I'm still embarrassed. The silence is almost worse than if he'd ragged on me about it. It won't last long. Once I get back to base, I'll never hear the end of this.

My stomach gurgles and throbs. I think back to my last meal. A chili Meal, Ready to Eat, or MRE. These are the modern version of C-rations, but to hear tell of it from Sergeant Oliphant, not a whole hell of a lot tastier. It doesn't seem to be sitting too well. I close my eyes and try to think about something else. My girlfriend. How she looks when she's getting dressed, picking up her bra off a chair and smiling at me as she reaches around to hook it into place. Or the kind of vehicle I want to buy with my hazardous-duty pay when I get back. A blue Ford F-150 pickup with—my stomach gurgles again, much louder this time, and the muscles spasm. It feels like someone's jabbing me in the belly with a fork. My mouth fills with spit.

"You all right?" Rankin says, peering at me over the tops of his sunglasses. "You got that same green look you got when you ate those bad oysters back in Savannah."

I can't respond. I'm concentrating on keeping the chili down.

"D?" Rankin asks, raising his eyebrows and bunching up his lips. "You hear me over there in la-la land?"

"I'm fine," I say.

"Then why are you holding on to your belly like that?"

I hadn't even noticed I was doing this, but he's right. At some point, I'd started cradling my stomach with both hands.

"You best not be puking in this vehicle, D. The smell will never come out."

"I'm fine," I say, trying to sound as if it's true.

Rankin clucks his tongue at me, but leaves it at that.

The landscape drifts past. A single smudge of dark yellow below an angry blue sky. Rocks protrude at random here and there like carious teeth. The sandbags on the floorboards shift each time we bounce over a bump in the road and fill the cab with extra dust. We do not pass a single vehicle. Out south of the base, the land is mostly flat and treeless. An occasional boulder or a clump of dead weeds are about as much variety as you get on this bleak plain. Driving here can make you feel as though the whole world is blasted and burned and you are the last humans left on the planet. But as we approach the base and the small village of Kurkbil, a series of lumpy purple hills appears on the horizon. They are the only geographic feature of note between the capital city and Inmar. In the local dialect, they are called the Noses because of their sloping triangular shapes. They are rumored to harbor small bands of resistance fighters. The area is riddled with caves and narrow box canyons. The only way in or out is by mule or helicopter.

The convoy moves slowly. One of the bullets has damaged our lead Humvee, and we can only move as fast as our slowest car. A dozen or so klicks from the base, we approach an abandoned factory. The grounds take up a space about the size of a Wal-Mart parking lot and are surrounded by an eight-foot mud-brick wall topped with rusty strands of razor wire. Inside, there is a sprawling complex of low cinder-block buildings covered with peeling green sheets of corrugated steel. At the very center stands a larger building, maybe two and half stories tall, with double rows of windows just below the roof. On clear days, the factory is visible for almost twenty klicks because the owners originally painted the walls a vivid scarlet. Over the years, the paint has faded into a bright Pepto-Bismol pink. The factory once produced stuffed animals for children and novelty items for adults: cigarette lighters shaped like pistols and fake teeth that chattered when you wound them up. It's been abandoned since the invasion. The three brothers who owned it packed up as much of their inventory as they could and fled the moment they saw our tanks. The road to the capital is still strewn with dusty pink rabbits and purple bears. According to Rankin, who had to pull guard detail at this place a while back, the machinery is still in good condition; but even from the road, the pockmarks from machine-gun fire and RPG blasts are visible on the main building's sides, and the wall surrounding the factory grounds has crumbled in many places.

Rankin looks over and raises an eyebrow. "You look bored, D. Maybe you should take up a hobby."

"Like what?"

"Well," he says, putting on his thoughtful face, "like speed cigarette-rolling. Stateside, it's really catching fire. I hear ESPN2 even has a show. You could time yourself and see how fast you finish a sack. Here, give it a try." He digs into the front pocket of his fatigues and throws his pouch of tobacco into my lap. "But D?"

"Mmm-hmm."

"Careful you don't get it too close to your pants."

"I was waiting for this shit to start."

"You got to mind your hygiene out here, D," Rankin tells me with a straight face.

I shake my head and start to twist one up. I'm glad to have something to distract me from my stomach cramps. They've gotten worse. Each time we hit a bump in the pavement, I think I'm going to spray the Humvee with half-digested chili.

As I'm lighting the cigarette for him, the Humvee in front of us rolls to a stop.

"Goddammit, Greer, what is it now?" the radio squawks.

"Uh." Greer whispers a quick question to someone in his vehicle before talking into the radio again. "A nobby, sir."

This is our base's radio code for a flat tire. Since we use these crappy toy-store walkie-talkies for foot patrols and the radios in our Humvees operate on a standard civilian band, the lieutenant worries that the insurgents are capable of monitoring our radio transmissions. Most of us are of the opinion that these new codes do more to confuse us than the enemy.

"Goddammit," the radio says. I imagine the lieutenant spraying the dash with spittle. His voice is painfully loud.

Rankin reaches over and turns the volume down a notch, and I thank him. I hand him the cigarette and lean back in my seat. This stop might last a while. I take shallow breaths and hold my belly with both hands. Every few seconds, the muscles in my stomach clench up and pointy little fingers of pain jab at my insides. A vulture glides down into the rubble-filled yard of the factory. Then another. I wonder what has crawled in there and died. Lopez and Nevada and two others hop out of the first Humvee to set up a defensive perimeter. Hazel mans the second vehicle's .50-caliber and scans the factory's rooftop with binoculars. He looks as bored as I feel. Doc Greer gets out too and opens up the back door so they can get the jack. I catch a quick glimpse of the older hajji huddled back there. Doc Greer slaps his foot to get him to move it. He's none too gentle. Their lips move, but I can't make out what they're saying. Nevada points to the tire and lights a cigarette. Lopez pulls a face, but he kneels and starts cranking up the jack.

Rankin laughs. "Fucking Lopez."

My stomach squeezes itself into a ball and stays that way. Little BBs of greasy sweat pop up on my forehead and my throat constricts. I close my eyes and try again to think of something else. It's no good. I'm going to puke. I have to get out of this Humvee. Rankin glances over at me but doesn't say anything. Sweat drips down my cheeks and beads on the tip of my nose. I lean out the window to spit.

"Rankin," I say through my teeth, "I'm going to yurp."

Rankin frowns.

"I've got to move, man. You know I hate to have people watch and—"

He turns and looks me full on. "This ain't the time or place for this kinda shit. There could be a sniper up there. Pull yourself together, D. Just lean out the window. I'll close my fucking eyes."

"No, really. You know I can't do it out there in front of—"

Rankin rolls down his window and looks around. "Jesus Christ, D."

"I got to go. Radio ahead, if you want. I won't go far. I just have to—" A bit of vomit comes up into my mouth and I'm forced to swallow it down. I close my eyes and unsnap my seat belt. My head spins. For a moment, I'm not sure which way is up and which way is down.

"Shit." Rankin chews at his lower lip and gives me the stink-eye. "You're going to get us both in trouble." All the same, he flicks his fingers at me like he's shooing a fly out of the car. "It's your ass."

I open the door and jump down. As I run around the rear of the Humvee, I can hear Rankin complaining. "You owe me for this, man. I expect five hundred smokes."

I am recognized as the best roller of cigarettes on base. I make them plump, tight, and even. Nevada is a distant second, but Rankin and Nevada don't get along. Rankin would smoke a hundred loose, crumbly cigarettes before he'd ask Nevada to roll him one. Nevada grew up wild in New Orleans in a project near the number two St. Louis Cemetery, and Rankin was raised in a middle-class black family in south Georgia who sent him to community college in Savannah. They might as well be from different countries. A week back, the two of them almost came to blows over a rap Nevada made up about Rankin trying to lighten his face with Clorox and Q-tips. Then Rankin reminded Nevada who it was that joined the Army because a judge gave him a choice between Basic or three to five up at Angola State Prison. It took five guys to pull them apart. Rankin and Nevada exchanged hard looks for a few days, but then it blew over. They still won't play video football together.

I lock my gun and run across the road. Puke rises in my throat and some of it dribbles out of the corner of my mouth as I go. Doc Greer shouts something I can't quite make sense of. I keep running. Up to the gate and in. Feeling my way around with the tip of my rifle. Just after I turn the corner, I let it all out. Gallons of it. The sound of liquid hitting the ground makes me retch twice as hard. I dry heave until bitter strings of bile drip onto the dirt. Behind me on the road, someone shouts my name over and over again. My throat stings and my eyes fill with tears, but I feel better almost immediately. I spit several times and slump back against the wall, trying to catch my breath.

When I straighten up to wipe my face on the sleeve of my uniform, I see a brief flash of movement on the far side of the main building. The factory yard is filled with all manner of construction waste and general debris: piles of broken masonry, tangles of rusty wire, chunks of rebar-studded cement, and waist-high patches of dry weeds full of wind-blown cans and wisps of weathered paper. My eyes are bleary and I might have been mistaken. It feels like a fuse burned out somewhere deep in my head and, in the sudden dark, my brain stopped working right. Still and all, I'll be damned if something didn't move over there.

I make sure my M4 is locked, load a round into the chamber, and start backing out of the factory yard, scanning the windows and mounds of trash for movement as I go. I'm used to the heavier M16, so I find myself constantly checking to see if I've forgotten to load my clip. A squadron of flies has already discovered my puke. The buzzing of their wings seems unnaturally loud and grating. And then I see it again. Something purple flits between two piles of broken brick. I blink and look hard, but whatever it was, it's gone now. Maybe a jackal. I've heard they get pretty big. I take a step back. Pebbles rattle behind a nearby heap of gravel. Then the little purple creature zips one mound closer to the factory's main door, one mound closer to me. It looks like a small woman or a boy. A long rope of tangled black hair bounces on this miniature person's back as it runs. Immediately, I think of it as a her. Not even teenage boys in this country let their hair grow past their shoulders. Whoever it is doesn't seem to have a rifle, but she could be packing a small handgun or a grenade. I consider firing a warning shot, but that would bring the entire squad over here. They'd pound every inch of this place with lead before I had a chance to explain, and then my ass would really be toast. Back on the road, someone shouts. It's unintelligible. My ears still ring from the IED blast, but it isn't really noticeable until I try to make sense of people's speech.

It's time to move. The lieutenant's probably pitching a fit back there. I take a quick glance over my shoulder to measure the distance I'll have to run until I have decent cover. A good dozen yards or more. Just as I'm bracing myself for the dash, I spot her again. Without a sound, she appears, perched like a purple sparrow on a stack of broken brick. I freeze. We stare at each other for a very long moment. I'm no longer positive it's a female. Angular, dirt-smeared features and waist-length hair that even from twenty yards away looks matted and ratty and infested. Hunger has made the child's eyes huge and its body UNICEF-thin. It's very hard to tell ages here, but this one can't be older than thirteen or fourteen. The kid's dressed in what looks like a collection of knotted purple rags. Maybe it *is* a girl. The sex of young children is often impossible to figure out in this country, a fact that fucks with the head of many a soldier when he first arrives.

"Hey," I say, letting my rifle strap slide so the barrel points toward the ground. I hold up my hands.

The kid hisses. Her eyes narrow. And then she bolts away like a feral cat, leaping over the puddles of broken glass and the rusting clumps of rebar. I want to give chase, but out on the highway, Lieutenant Blankenship shouts something in a tone of voice I can't ignore. I heft my rifle and jog back to the convoy. A fifty-yard dash. My heart rate increases when I see they've already finished changing the tire and loaded up the jack. Nevada smokes a cigarette and points his rifle at the factory. He grins at me as I jog across the highway and then points to his ass.

Before word one, I knock off a crisp salute. I've found that making my salutes as straight-backed and formal as possible sometimes has a soothing effect on the lieutenant. In this case, it doesn't help.

"What in the fuck all was that?" Lieutenant Blankenship shouts through the window of the lead vehicle. His face is gray and strained, and I immediately wish I'd listened to Rankin. "If you've got to take a shit, you know the appropriate defecation formation. Two armed men as escort and no more than ten yards from the convoy. You could have—"

For a moment, I think of lying, but I'm caught off balance by what just happened. Seeing the girl has got me feeling something I wasn't prepared for, something I can't quite name. "I'm sorry, sir," I stutter. "I had to be sick, and then I saw a child and—"

"A child?" he asks, incredulous.

Behind him, Lopez glares at me as he gets into the Humvee. I want to flick him off, but I'm in enough trouble as it is. Lopez is soon to become a sergeant and officially outranks me, something he never lets me forget. He and the lieutenant are chess buddies. They like to quiz each other on regulation minutiae and regimental nicknames.

"Yes, sir," I say. "A little girl, I think."

He rewards me with a thoughtful frown before turning to look at the other men in the Humvee. "Did any of you see a child back there?"

"No, sir," they sing.

"What the hell would a child be doing out here, Durrant? Use your fucking head. If there was one here, and I'm very far from believing such a thing, she'd be out to set us up. Get your ass back in your vehicle. We've got wounded men. If someone so much as fires a BB gun at us, I'm blaming you. This is a perfect place for an ambush, you stupid—"

"Yes, sir."

I turn and run before he can finish. My face is hot. He's right. I had no business running off like that. Gerling looked pretty bad, and I know Kellen got hit in the leg with shrapnel.

"Man, he's pretty fucking P.O.'d. You should of heard what he was yelling on the set," Rankin says, tapping the radio with the thumb of his cigarette hand and knocking a worm of ash onto the dashboard. "He'll have you stirring shit for weeks."

I groan. Stirring shit is what we call burning the waste from our homemade field latrines. It is possibly the worst detail there is. The ashes are greasy and leave marks on your uniform, and the smell of burnt shit sticks to your clothes and hair. Since we don't have enough water to wash our uniforms more than once every few weeks, it means you reek like that for quite a while. Oddly, it smells like burning meat. Haul a hotplate out to a Porta-John and fry some beef jerky until it burns and you'll get some idea of the smell. Usually we pay one of the local hajjis to do it.

Rankin puts the Humvee into gear and we lurch forward. "At least you blew off some of the stink while you were out there running around."

"But be honest. You saw her too, didn't you?"

In the rear window of the Humvee in front of us, Hazel holds up his hand as though to wave at me. Then he pretends to crank down his fingers with his other hand until only the middle one is left, all the while grinning his lopsided grin and shaking his head. With his other hand, he holds up a twisted piece of metal, probably shrapnel from the artillery shell they used to make the IED. Hazel loves to collect the bits of metal left over after the enemy tries to blow us up. If he doesn't find some after an attack, he tends to freak out. Hazel has this desert voodoo notion that his collection will protect him from mortar attacks while he's sleeping.

"Huh?" Rankin says, giving me a sidelong glance.

"That little girl." As I say it, I crane my neck and look out the rear window to see if I can spot her again. I know I didn't imagine her. I was almost close enough to smell her. I saw a girl. Or a child. You don't hallucinate something like that. I wish she would come out again for a second, just long enough for somebody else to see her.

"I didn't see nothing." He squints at me again, concern crinkling up the skin at the corners of his eyes. "Just a broke-down old factory and a seriously pissed-off officer."

"Don't fuck with me, Rankin. Please. I'm serious."

He gives me a long, slow shake of the head. "You really got thumped back there, didn't you? We best get you checked out when we get back to the Cob."

5

The Cob. The old Corn Cob. Or, as it's known on paper, Forward Operating Base Cornucopia. A 300-year-old fortress constructed of mud bricks and undressed stone blocks. At sunset it resembles a huge golden-brown corn cob laid on its side. It was originally built by the Khalifa Omar Rahman to defend himself against attacks by his younger brother Mohammed Rahman. For a time at the end of the nineteenth century and the first few decades of the twentieth, it served as a prison. Then, in the nineteen eighties, some enterprising government official converted the compound into a cement factory. Now we have it.

The actual fort stands in the center of this enormous, empty space about the size of eight football fields, which in turn is surrounded by a thick brick wall. We only use eight or so of the stone rooms at the front of the fort, but behind this there are dozens and dozens of smaller rooms and crumbling corridors. We call this unused space the old fort. Underneath it is a dungeon, which I've heard stretches out beneath the entire base. We reinforced the original fort with cinderblocks and it became the motor pool, armory, and supply facility. Directly across from the fort is a cement factory, which was built around a flimsy steel frame and covered with corrugated fiberglass sheets, half of which have blown off. The only thing we use it for now is to house one of our latrines. The Army put up the rest of the base pretty quickly, which is to say shittily.

To the west of the fort, several rows of enlisted men's tents stretch out in the dirty yellow sand; to the east, there are the two common tents for recreation and the mess tent and kitchen. To the east of the cement factory are the command and communications trailers and the officers' Conexes, big steel prefab boxes about the size of railroad shipping containers with two-man living quarters built inside. All of these buildings combined occupy less than an eighth of the space inside the Cob. It feels like a small settlement on a large plain.

Whenever I pass in through the Cob's front gates, I always feel a little of my anxiety lift away. The perimeter walls are nearly fifteen feet thick. Although the bricks are crumbling and rotten in places, it would still take a pretty mean artillery attack to breach the walls. The base is self-contained and has a rough sort of comfort. Although I never forget I'm in a war zone, once I get on base it's nice to know the bad guys are locked outside. On hard nights when I feel rattled, I try to imagine we're as secure as jewels in a strong safe. Every once in a while this actually works.

When I first arrived here, we had almost three times as many soldiers and twice as many tents and trailers on base. Once the Army decided this area was pacified and secure, they trucked or airlifted all the decent buildings off to Inmar, including the Porta-Johns. Now all we have left are a smattering of two-man tents pitched above wooden pallets, a few office trailers and Conex units, a random assortment of canvas-covered structures, and forty-two active-duty soldiers. During a sandstorm the month before I arrived, the mess tent literally blew away during breakfast. The roof broke free of its stakes, flapped around in the wind for a while, and then fell in on itself. One soldier broke his arm and another one almost suffocated before they dug him out. After that, we stabilized everything with sandbags and two-by-fours. The office trailers look like tiny Gothic cathedrals with flying buttresses made of PVC piping and guy wires.

One of the worst aspects of base life is the latrines. They promised to bring us new Porta-Johns when they trucked off our old ones. You'll see them in a week, HQ said. They lied. We built a few groups of two-man latrines the next morning out of scrap plywood and two-by-fours set above old fuel drums. At first there was only a back wall to lean up against when struggling with the infamous MRE constipation. Every passing Joe got a view of your knobby knees and red straining face. For pissing, we have white PVC tubes that drain directly into the sand (regulations state you can't mix Number One and Number Two; the Army even likes to control your bodily functions). After a week of this sorry situation, somebody, probably Hazel, strung up pieces of oil-stained canvas around the latrines, shower curtain–style. My theory is he wanted a little privacy for his stroke mags.

For some reason, when they carted off half the base, they left behind an artillery battery, but they didn't leave anyone trained to use it. Rankin thinks they just forgot about them. And us, I told him.

For the most part, we feel safe here. Or at least as safe as anybody can feel in a place where half the population wants to kill you and the other half hates you. Once the Army took over the Cob, they set up floodlights and guard towers and a minefield. Ribbons of concertina wire curl through the sand. We've got M60s and wire-guided missiles, .50-caliber Ma Deuces, Eagle Mount 240 Bravos, and plenty of M4s and M16s. Nevertheless, there's one thing that's never far from any of our minds, especially on those nights when the wind whips up from the desert and the stars disappear and mortar rounds start dropping into the compound. The Khalifa's brother took the fortress in a single night, and in the morning he stuck Omar's head on a pike.

6

The storm appears at the far edge of the plain as we reach the outskirts of Kurkbil, the village just below the base. A bulging wall of dark and dirty yellow that stretches from the floor of the plain to the upper edge of the sky. It moves as quickly as a tank at top speed and seems to obliterate everything in its path. This beast sweeps across the desert like the Hand of God. The way it looks, I can almost imagine it as a living creature, a huge and malign force bent on swallowing the world from horizon to horizon. Nothing escapes the storm. And once it engulfs something—a house, a tree, a boulder, a road, a man—it seems to have vanished forever. A sandstorm looks like the end of the world.

7

Even before we reach the base, Lieutenant Blankenship is shouting orders over the radio. He's out of the Humvee before it comes to a full stop, swinging a green metal lockbox and yelling for stretchers. His teenager's face looks pinched and serious and we work quickly to do what he asks. The insides of the Humvees are smeared with blood. Everyone looks pale and dirty. Faces blur. Boots beat the sand. Voices are raised. We hustle, for our wounded and for ourselves. Nobody wants to be outside when the storm hits. Already we can hear the winds. They shriek and rumble as though the storm is scraping the desert down to bare rock.

Studdie and I carry Kellen to the clinic. Doc Greer gave him a shot of morphine on the drive back to the base and Kellen doesn't open his eyes until we settle him into a cot. Even then his eyelids only flutter briefly, showing just a narrow arc of white before they close. Studdie wasn't on this run to Inmar, and I can tell from the breathless way he questions us about it that he's sorry he missed the fight. Doc Greer won't answer him. In fact, he turns his face away from each question, so I end up laying it out for him. Studdie's a tall guy with broad shoulders and thin, sandy hair. He grew up in a military family, went to an academy high school, and enlisted the day he turned eighteen. His grandfather woke him up that morning by telling him he could enlist today or leave the house. Until he'd done his service he couldn't take part in the family business, a turpentine plantation just outside LaGrange, Georgia. But Studdie says he would have done it anyway, and I believe him.

I run from there to help secure the motor pool and tell Ahmed to head home to the village. Ahmed is a local guy who works on base most days, filling sandbags, unfilling sandbags, burning trash, helping Cox in the machine shop, and cleaning vehicles. Basically, he does the shitwork. As scrawny as he is, Ahmed can heft a good bit of weight and always seems to be busy even when he's not doing anything, a skill I'd like to learn. I think he's in his twenties, despite the wrinkles on his forehead and the thinness of his hair, but he could just as easily be thirty-five or forty. When I find him, he's listening to an old Walkman Cox gave him and messing about with a pile of screws. As soon as Ahmed sees me, he pulls back his yellow-and-white-checked headscarf and smiles, making his eyebrows meet above his nose, but he doesn't waste time with his usual chat and gets the hell out of here after I tell him the news. Everyone respects a sandstorm.

Just after I finish winding down one of the bay doors, I hear the crunch of sandy boots on concrete. It's Lopez. He stands in the doorway beside supply room number two and watches me. The wind ruffles the collar of his uniform. Behind him I can see the storm swallowing the highway leading into Kurkbil. It looks like a moving wall of night. I briefly imagine standing alone before the full force of the storm, allowing it to sweep me away. Lopez steps through the doorway.

"What were you saying to him?" He gestures behind him with his thumb.

"What?" I ask, honestly having no idea what he's referring to. I'm still thinking about the storm.

"Ahmed. What were you talking to him about? The IED?"

"No," I say, "I told him to get home before the storm arrives."

"Right." He spits the word out. "He couldn't see it coming on his own."

I clench my jaws to keep from saying something smart.

"Not inside the motor pool. No."

This seems to stop him for a moment. In the gathering darkness, his eyes seem very shiny, like wet black rocks. He steps forward, and for a second or two, I think he's getting ready to punch me. His face looks so grim and determined. I glance around him to see if anybody else can see us. There's no one on the parade ground, and Specialist Cox, the mechanic, has already left the motor pool. We're alone. Lopez takes another step forward and screws up his face as though he's about to shout.

"What, Lopez?" The storm is close enough for me to have to raise my voice. "What do you want?" The look he's giving me is starting to get on my nerves.

"I know what you're up to, Durrant."

"Yeah, what's that?" This whole conversation is creeping me out. He seems to be on the verge of confessing some terrible secret I am certain I do not want to be privy to.

"I know why you ran into the factory today." He pauses and gives me a meaningful look. "Did you sabotage the tire, so we would have to stop there? I found a clean cut on the tire. Only a knife would make that."

"No, what the fuck is up with you, man? How the hell could I make a tire blow out just when I wanted?"

He scrunches up his face into this exaggerated expression of disbelief. Now I really want to punch him. I realize I'm clenching my fists and force myself to jam them in my pockets, which are still slightly moist. I reek of piss. With the storm coming, I didn't have time to change. This makes me even angrier. Remember what happened the last time, I tell myself. Don't be an idiot.

"I know what you're up to," he says again, and then he points to his eye, like a warden in a second-rate prison movie. "I'll be watching you."

I want to say, that's right, man, that's exactly where my fist will land. Instead, I just stand there and stare at him like my head is empty. He takes two steps backward before turning to walk away. Asshole.

8

I make a mad dash to the Comm Trailer. I figure everyone else will be battening down the hatches and I'll get a little extra time on the satellite phone. I'm not sure it'll work when the storm hits, so I need to move fast. It's nibbling at the edge of town as I duck in. The sun looks like a dirty penny.

Sergeant Guzman is in the process of shutting everything down. He pulls the cigar out of his mouth and groans when he sees me. The sergeant is way too big for his uniform. In fact, it looks as though his uniform is stuffed with the bodies of two men and topped with a single, miniature head. There are a lot of big guys in the military, so this should tell you something.

"I'll be fast," I say.

"The hell you will, Joe." Sergeant Guzman calls everyone Joe.

"How about rock, paper, scissors? I lose, I'll shine your boots, clean your rifle, and roll your smokes for two weeks."

Sergeant Guzman is a notorious gambler. I've heard guys say he'll bet on the length of time it will take to grow a moustache or how many puppies a stray dog will have. I don't know about that, but I did see him bet on how many times Lieutenant Blankenship would refer to the seven-dash-eight handbook in a single morning briefing. He won with a spread of twelve to nine. I've heard him call in football bets to his bookie in the States. The man has never missed wagering on a scorpion fight. Today is no different. The sergeant doesn't hesitate.

"Make it three. And you only get five minutes. No more."

"Deal," I say.

We knock fists. One, two, three. I hold out paper. He holds out rock.

"You better make it fast, fuckwit," Sergeant Guzman says, "because I am not, I repeat, I am not riding out the storm in this shithole trailer."

"I'll be quick," I say and give him the number I want to call.

"Goddamn right you will, Joe," he says and shakes his head.

The phone rings six times and just as I'm getting ready for the machine, someone picks up.

"Hello?" I say, and then after a half-second, I hear what I just said in the earphone again. This stuttering seems to happen every other time I use the phone. It throws me off balance and makes it hard to concentrate on what I'm saying. Static hisses and swirls down the lines. I imagine the route my voice takes—beamed up into orbit and then down to some satellite tower on the East Coast, into the phone lines and out across a string of creosote-soaked pine poles to a little brick apartment building on the south side of Savannah.

"Toby?" the small tentative voice says, and my heart turns into warm pudding. It's my fiancée, Clarissa, soon to be the mother of my child.

"Oh, baby, am I glad to hear your voice."

"How much time do we have?"

"Ten minutes."

"Five fucking minutes. Tops," the sergeant says, tapping his watch.

"I better get to it then," Clarissa says

"Get to what? I was the one who called you."

"I've been thinking about what I wanted to say the next time you called. Last time we got cut off before we really said anything."

A million worlds away on the other side of the ocean, Clarissa's lips brush up against the mouthpiece, but she doesn't say a word. I take a deep breath and stretch my neck until it cracks. I don't like the way this conversation is going and we've barely said a dozen words.

"How's our little Herman?" I ask, after a long moment of awkward silence.

"Toby, I never agreed to name him after your grandfather." She swallows and I can hear her throat make a dry click. "We don't even know if it's a boy."

"But that night you said—"

"I was drunk. You can't count that."

"Damn right I can. We were also drunk the night we made Herman, and that sure as hell counts."

"That's what I'm calling about."

"No, I called y—wait, is something wrong?" My chest tightens. "Did something happen at the doctor's?"

"Nothing happened. It's just that . . . well . . . I . . ."

A horrible thought occurs to me, one every soldier with a girl back home has at least once a week. "Did you meet someone else? Is that what this is about?" I don't really believe this. Can't, in fact. I'm not sure why I said it.

She breathes. I squeeze my eyes shut and try to picture her face. All I come up with is her left hand. The one with the small J-shaped scar below the thumb. I would polish Sergeant Guzman's boots for a month if I could kiss it right now.

"What is it?" I say after a long silence. "I'm sorry I said that— well—it was—it's been a bad day." I want to tell her about the IED attack, but I know she'll never understand. I tried before. She got frightened. I got frustrated. There's no way to explain something like this to people back home. There just isn't.

She breathes loudly into the mouthpiece.

"We're talking in circles here," I say, although we're not really talking at all. "I can hear it in your voice. Something's bothering you. Is it your parents?"

"Toby." There's an edge to her voice. I wish we could start the conversation over again. It always takes a little while for both of us to relax and really talk to each other when I call, but today is different. It's much worse.

"I just didn't want—"

"Stop, Toby. Just listen to me for a second. Listen." She pauses again, even longer this time, and I think I hear traffic sounds in the background. A radio.

"I'm listening."

The satellite phone's receiver hisses like a leaky tire. The storm is blowing my voice away. Oh, shit, I think, please don't cut off now.

"Here it fucking comes," Sergeant Guzman says, watching from a window in the office. He taps the glass with a finger. I'm not sure if he's talking to me or to himself. "This looks like a mean one."

"What?" Clarissa says. Her voice suddenly sounds very far away and it's not just the faulty connection. "I can't hear you. Maybe you should call back. This is killing me. I don't—"

I force myself to modulate my voice with limited success. "Don't what, honey, don't what?"

"Never mind. I'm sorry. I'm just having a bad day, too. Maybe we should try this another time when we're both in a better mood. Why don't you call me tomorrow? Oh, yeah, I forgot, you only get so many calls each—"

"Look, I know it's hard." I don't want to hang up yet, so I try a different tactic. "It's about killing me, too. If I could leave right now and come home, I'd get on a plane tonight. But I can't. Like you said, we've already talked about all this." I hear the pleading tone in my voice and it sounds fucking pathetic. I stop to clear my throat. "I'll be back in ten months. I know I promised eight, but I got extended, and there's not a hell of a lot I can do. They've got you, body and soul, as soon as you sign the paper. You can wait ten months, can't you? Come on. This is the best thing that's ever happened to me. You. This baby."

"I miss you so much. But sometimes I'm not sure if I can do this any more. If it got any worse, I'd—" She stops suddenly.

You'd what? I wonder. But I can't ask that. I'm not sure I want the answer. But then again, I'll never stop thinking about it if I don't. I can't seem to help myself.

"What are we talking about here? Are you saying you'd—"

I don't even have to say it. She knows what I mean. And I'm not sure if this should reassure me or scare the hell out of me. Somehow it does both.

"No, no, don't be silly. You're my fiancé," Clarissa says, but she doesn't sound so sure about it and this worries me worst of all. "It's just . . . it's harder than I thought. Being apart. Sometimes I have to look at a photo to get your face straight in my head. It's weird. And I'm really scared about the other thing." There's a long pause. I want to bang the phone against the wall. "I'm worried about how I'll—I don't want to be like my mother."

"What are you talking about? You'll be a great mother. The best. You can't think this way. It'll only bring you down. You—"

"Toby. Wait. Let's not talk about this now. I know you've got a lot of stress. You don't need this too. The next time you call, I'll be in a better mood. Today just isn't . . . good." Her voice becomes ragged with tears. I feel my eyes fill. Shit. I look around. Sergeant Guzman stares out the window with a vacant expression on his face. Probably wondering how to beat me next time we play rock, paper, scissors. I mash my eyeballs with the heel of my palm.

"I love you, honey. We'll get through this. It's tough, I know, but just think how happy we'll be. You and me and Herman. Or not Herman, but . . . the baby." I keep on like this for a while before I realize the line has gone dead. It's the storm, I tell myself. It's the storm that did it. I stand holding the phone pressed to my forehead.

The sergeant looks over at me. "You done, Lover Joe?"

"Yeah," I say, "the line went dead."

Sergeant Guzman gives me a sympathetic look and a slow shake of the head. I know he thinks I'm lying and it makes my face get hot. He's a career man, like most of the really good sergeants I've met. His round, almost girlish face fills with wrinkles and he runs a hand over his Marine-style high-and-tight haircut. He can't be more than a couple years older than I am, but the way he acts you'd think it was ten. Sergeant Guzman's got two kids back home in Atlanta, and you can tell being a daddy has somehow aged him on the inside.

"Don't take it too hard, Joe," he says, giving me a gentle shove toward the door. "Whether I want to or not, I listen to these calls every day. Jody problems are always the same."

Jodies are men back home who steal soldiers' girlfriends and wives. We sing songs about them when we march. We joke about them as we eat. But lying in our cots at night, we fear them. They will steal your future just as surely as a bullet or a bomb.

"It's not like that," I tell him, hoping it's true. "The storm knocked out the connection."

"Okay, Joe," he says, and then flicks a switch and the lights go out.

9

It takes me thirty minutes to find my tent. Usually it's a two-minute walk. The sand scours my hands and cheeks. It finds every bit of exposed flesh and tries to grind it away. I think about Clarissa. She said she had to look at a photo to remember my face. I know she can't have forgotten the first time she saw it. I remember that day as clearly as anything that's ever happened in my life, and I know she must still remember too. She has to. It was a few months after my grandpa died. I'd bought a new parachute for a trip with my jumping buddy, Frick. We drove all night to a famous bridge in West Virginia, one of the best base-jumping spots on the continent. The perfect bridge. This was my farewell trip. By then I'd already failed out of college and signed up for the Army. We took turns throwing ourselves off that huge bridge. It was beautiful. Early May. A sky as blue as the ocean looks when you're a child. The new leaves still had that bright neon green color. We took drags from a one-hitter painted to look like a cigarette before each jump, but I would have felt high without it. My body burst into song each time I chucked myself into that gorge.

It was on my third jump of the day that I saw her. Clarissa said I looked like an angel. My new chute was white with golden stripes, and in bright sunlight, it could almost blind you. I saw her the moment my chute opened. Somehow, she'd gotten separated from her friends. They'd been camping for a couple of days in the state park. That morning she got up before the sun rose and the others were awake, and went out alone to see the river, and got lost. Clarissa wandered through the trees for hours. When she finally reached the river, she followed it downstream, hoping to find a bridge. And then, who should appear but an angel.

My pal Frick had work, so he went home that evening. But not me. I had a new pretty parachute and a grateful girl. So of course I stayed on with Clarissa. We ate SpaghettiOs out of fire-blackened cans, drank Wild Turkey, and spent the night making love in the back of my Toyota 4Runner. By daybreak, I knew I wanted to spend the rest of my life with her, or at least move in with her. Corny, perhaps, but such stories almost always are if you're not personally involved. We found her friends around lunchtime the following day, sitting on a log singing Tori Amos songs and snuffling over their lost pal. Three hairy-legged girls in Swedish sandals. They took an immediate dislike to me. I felt so love-drunk, I hardly noticed.

A week passed before I managed to get up the nerve to tell Clarissa I'd already signed on for a hitch in the Army. I took her to Forsyth Park and sat her down by the big fountain. It was a beautiful Tuesday afternoon. A storm the night before had washed the sky clean. You could smell the ocean all the way upriver in Savannah. At first she thought I was joking around, but when the grim look on my face didn't go away, she cried. Then I did.

In the year before I deployed, I saw Clarissa every chance I got. By this time, I'd already run through most of my inheritance, but I used the rest on plane tickets and sparkling rings, taxicabs and tasty meals. Her parents thought I was a chunk of crusty shit scraped off the rim of a truck-stop toilet. On the night I met him, her father threatened to eviscerate me with his thumbnail, a yellow horny thing he kept longer than his other nails so he could use it as a tool. Her mother patiently explained that if she found I'd molested her daughter in any way, she'd hunt me down and nail my member to the floor with carpet tacks. A direct quote. That Sunday morning when I broke the news in the dining room of Lady and Sons restaurant that we would soon be three, her father pushed over the table, jumped across the spilled cheese grits, and choked me until I passed out. When I came to, he gave me a cigarette and we took a walk around the block. Her father spieled off a long list of actions that would cause my early death. At the end, he looked me in the eye and asked if I understood, not whether or not I agreed with him, but whether or not I understood. I nodded. "Good," he said, "I hope your neck's all right."

Clarissa told my fortune with tea leaves. She made me boxer shorts out of six pairs of her own panties. She took a picture of each of her toes and sent them to me in an album she made out of flattened Orange Crush cans and cardboard. She wrote me a poem for every day we were apart. She poured gasoline in the shape of a T in her parent's backyard, so when she woke up and looked out the window she would think of me first thing. She invented a lively dance called the Toby-Toby and performed it in Forsyth Park one glorious Saturday evening in our special spot by the fountain. She tattooed my name on the inside of her lower lip, so we could kiss perpetually. She sang me Stevie Wonder songs on my answering machine. Each time she saw me again, Clarissa would kiss the inside of my left wrist before she said word one. Clarissa was twenty-two the day I met her. She turned twenty-three the day we conceived our child. My love for her swept through me like a forest fire. If it goes out, she'll leave behind miles and miles of hard black stumps.

10

I sit on a cot in Common Tent Number 2 and roll cigarettes. For a tent, it's fairly large, bigger in fact than my apartment back home, but on days like this the extra space only makes it seem emptier, somehow, and shabby. Pinned up on the west wall is a collection of centerfolds, mainly from copies of *Jugs* and *Barely Legal* sent through the mail from friends back home. Pornography is strictly against the rules, but the NCOs put up with it as long as there aren't any female soldiers around, and there haven't been since the base was split. The rest of the tent's space is filled with a beat-up old TV, a ping-pong table that no one uses because the balls are all gone, ten or so folding camp chairs, a cot that Cox rigged up like a couch, and a couple of coffee tables made from ammo crates.

The sandstorm has swallowed us. It's almost impossible to go outside, which is a relief because I'm waiting for the lieutenant to send for me. I've heard from two people now that he's looking for me, but for the time being I've decided to play stupid. I'm not sure, but I think it's possible the lieutenant could give me an Article 15 for what went down today. The wind outside sounds like a crowd of hajji women at a funeral. It shrieks and moans and pulls at its hair, which sets all of us on edge, but no one talks about it. Sometimes dust whispers through the sandbags and under the wall of the tent, creeping over the cement floor like smoke from a forgotten cigarette. Sand gets into everything, no matter how carefully you wrap it up and pack it away. Rifles are the worst. You have to clean them twice a day, and that's when the weather's nice. I can feel the grit at the back of my throat when I swallow. Sand crunches between my teeth and my eyes feel like they've been blow-dried.

A few chairs away from me, Lopez cleans his rifle for something like the tenth time today. He hasn't said a word since we spoke in the motor pool, but occasionally he looks over and glares at me. Anger pours off of him like a bad smell. On the other side of the room, Nevada and Cox play the video game Guitar Hero, a favorite around here. Each player takes turns flicking their thumbs and punching buttons on a fake plastic guitar in time with a variety of heavy metal arena anthems. Cox is working his way through a Black Sabbath song. He's a cheerful, stringy-looking guy who grew up on a truck farm outside Macon, Georgia, and if it's mechanical in nature, he can fix it. His tent is littered with oily machine parts, tools, and dozens of jars filled with the desert insects he likes to collect. Salis sits in the far corner hunched over his laptop. He has his headphones on and whatever DVD he's watching makes him crack up every few minutes. Soldiers here watch DVDs more than they work, sleep, or fight.

Doc Greer, the more sociable of our two combat medics, comes into the room with a Coke, checks out the game momentarily, and then sits down. Immediately, everyone eyes the Coke. According to Sergeant Guzman, we ran out of them last week.

"Do I smell piss in here?" Doc Greer asks me with an innocent look. He rubs a hand over his dull black flattop. A bit of dust puffs up with each stroke.

"Hilarious," I say.

"Wanna hear some weird shit?" he asks me.

"No," Lopez says, not looking up from his rifle. A few days ago he shaved his moustache, probably because Nevada kept calling it his dick tickler, and now there's a light spot on his upper lip the size and shape of an index finger. "None of us want to hear any of your stupid Joe rumors."

Joe rumors are those rumors spread around by grunts in the field. Usually false, and often pathetic. We're being shipped back to the

States in a week. They're sending down some Deltas to run a mission with us. We're getting an Internet café. The best cure for monkey butt is a mixture of Bugle Boy, mayonnaise, and gunpowder. Joe rumors might not be true, but they're a pretty good indicator of morale among the enlisted guys.

"Was I talking to you, Limp Dick?" Doc Greer says. "I think fucking not." Greer can talk this way to Lopez because they're both in the same E grade. Lopez pulls rank more than anyone I've ever met.

"Goddammit, that fucking solo gets me every time," Cox says, passing the plastic guitar over to Nevada. In Nevada's hands, it looks even more like a toy. He may be a relatively short guy, but his hands are huge.

"What's so weird?" I ask Doc Greer, licking the rolling paper and twisting it up. There, twenty. I stuff them into an old Marlboro box. That ought to keep Rankin satisfied for a while. I still feel bad for making him radio the lieutenant at the factory this afternoon.

"One of my pals from training, he works down in Inmar now, directly under the new general." Doc Greer grins. "Get this. When that first guy took over the country as head ambassador, he had the reconstruction funds shipped over in cash. Dollars."

"What?" I say. "That's like millions of dollars."

"Try *billions*, Bubba. They wrapped it up in blocks of ten, twenty, and fifty thousand dollars. In blue cellophane, like shrinkwrap."

"That much cash would be like a mountain of paper," Nevada says, the mention of money having gotten his attention. "No joke, you could fill up a couple of swimming pools."

"Or a couple dozen C-130 transport planes," Doc Greer says.

"Jesus," I say, "where'd they store it all?"

"At first, they kept it in that big old library downtown in the capital, but here's the weird part: it's all gone."

"Gone," Nevada says, as if he knows where it is.

"Gone?" Cox and I say.

"And they don't know where eighty percent of it went. Seven billion dollars." Greer shakes his head.

"You've got to be shitting me. How could someone steal seven billion dollars? That's got to be like the biggest heist in history," Cox says. "I don't believe it."

"No, it wasn't stolen outright. A little went here, a little went there. And when I say a little, I mean millions. It got paid out to politicians and tribal chiefs. Like here, Sheikh Shish Kabob, take ten million and build a road. Here's a bag of ten million, Sheikh Dishcloth, go fix that school we bombed. But the rub is, no one kept track."

"Some of that shit's got to be floating around out there someplace. Ain't no way they spent it all *here*," Nevada says. "Man, I wish—"

"What a waste," Lopez says, "what a disgusting waste. If it's even true."

"Oh, it's true, all right," Doc Greer says. "My pal heard it from the grand poobah himself."

"Then why hasn't it been on the news?" Lopez asks, making a face.

"It has. We just don't get it out here in chickpea land," Doc Greer says. He looks triumphant.

"I wouldn't touch it," Lopez says.

"You mean to tell me you wouldn't want just a little of that money if you found it?" Nevada raises his voice in disbelief. "Just enough to buy your mama a house?"

"No," Lopez says, folding his arms across his chest.

"Then what would you do with it?" I ask.

"Give it back to the government," he says, baffled that I would even ask.

We all laugh.

"So they can lose it again," Doc Greer says.

"I don't believe any of this, this bull malarkey," Lopez says.

As you might imagine, this gets a laugh.

"You want to hear something else strange? It's been a strange day all around." Doc Greer flashes me a conspiratorial grin.

"What?" I say, waiting for the joke.

"That girl we found?" Doc Greer gives me a sidelong glance. For a second I think he's talking about the one I saw at the factory, and

I feel a strange elation. "The one they covered with lye to make her look like a white girl?"

"Yeah?"

Cox turns from the TV screen to listen. He didn't go out with us today, but I have no doubt he's heard about what happened. Word travels fast here. Doc Greer notices and shifts slightly, so he can address both of us.

"Well, when we got back, the lieutenant sent over to check and see if anyone was missing from the village."

"And?"

He shakes his head. "Nada."

"Where else could she have come from?" I lick the grit from my front teeth and spit into an empty artillery shell lying on the crate beside me. Someone's been using it as an ashtray and the ashes fly up into my eye. "There isn't anywhere else."

"Somebody's lying. That's what I think," Cox says, moving over to a chair near the cot. The sand has made his hair, normally the color of orange soda, look like a helmet made from old pennies. "They don't want us to know they're involved."

"I don't know," Doc Greer says. "Who shoots their own daughter or sister in the head and wires her up like a bomb? Even a hajji wouldn't do that. Somebody else's kid maybe, but not their own."

"They blow themselves up all the time. It don't make a fucking bit of difference to them." Cox points at the roof of the tent. "Going home to Allah."

"I don't buy it," Doc Greer says, running a thumb along the scar on his neck. It zig-zags down from the base of his ear all the way to his collarbone. Rankin says it's a shrapnel wound from a tank shell, but I've never actually asked him. "They're not as bad as all that in the village. They're mostly just normal people. If a kid was missing, everybody'd know about it."

Outside, the wind whips into a frenzy, making it impossible to speak. The air inside the tent fills with millions of tiny particles. Cox coughs and coughs. The lightbulbs develop blurry yellow haloes. It feels like trying to breathe flour. This big blow only lasts a minute, but in that time each face tightens, each of us sinks a little deeper inside ourselves.

I spit a mouthful of yellow mud into the artillery shell casing. "Well, maybe they're worried that if they tell us which of the bad chickpeas took her, the ones who did it will come back and take another one." I'm not sure I believe this. I'm just throwing something out there. Sometimes silence is worse than aimless chatter.

"No," Lopez says, snapping the stock of his rifle into place with a heavy click and laying it down on the crate in front of him. The rest of us flinch. He treats us to a smug grin. "She wasn't from the village. You're looking in the wrong direction."

"So, General Bull Malarkey, where should we be looking?" Doc Greer asks. It's difficult to tell whether he's being sincere. This is often the case with him. I'm not even sure *he* knows when he's being serious.

"If they were up your ass, you'd know where they were," Nevada says.

I snicker. It's not very funny, but I can't seem to help myself.

"There's a battalion of insurgents up in the Noses just waiting for the right moment." Lopez glares at me. "They'd do something like that. They're all a bunch of sickos."

"Bullshit, Lopez," Cox says, irritated. "If there was a battalion up there, they would have shown up on satellite by now. That's just a ghost story."

"Satellites can't see into caves. You've been up in the Noses. There's a cave every ten feet. Enough to hide half a dozen battalions. Some of those caves even have water, underground springs." Lopez looks around the circle, pleased with our reaction. "Right now, they're probing our defenses, seeing how well we hold up. It's just the beginning. Things are going to get worse." He thumps his chest with a fist as though the idea invigorates him.

"I don't know, man." Doc Greer shakes his head. "Sounds farfetched to me. They've been lobbing the occasional mortar at us since I got here last spring. Probably just a handful of hotheads from Kurkbil with a crate or two of shells. They never fire off more than one or two a night."

"Just wait and see," Lopez says.

Even Nevada's listening now. He joins us, lighting up a cigarette and peering at us through the smoke. Lopez has cooked up some serious bad vibes. They fill the room with a smell like ozone. I don't like this kind of talk. It's no help, and it starts the kind of thinking you can't shut off. It creates a sort of paranoia feedback loop. I roll a finished cigarette between my fingers. The craving to light up is almost overwhelming. As I reach for a book of matches on the table, the outer flap of the tent rattles open, and even though the inner flap is shut tight, yellow tendrils of dust come snaking across the floor. I drop the matches. Boots thud. A muffled conversation goes on out in the vestibule, a little canvas hallway set up at an angle from the inner flap to keep the dust from blowing straight into the tent. I look over at Doc Greer, who is chewing at his tongue and staring hard at the floor. Everyone's waiting to see who's coming in.

"How's Gerling and Kellen?" I ask him, hoping for better news.

He stops chewing at his tongue and looks over at me with a pained expression. "Gerling's lost a shitload of blood. A chunk of shrapnel went clean through him. It grazed his liver. I'm almost sure of it. Dyson and I got him stabilized the best we could, but . . . at least he's unconscious. Not hurting. I just left him with Studdie and Dyson. We're waiting on a medevac, but until this storm lets up. . . ." He nods his chin toward the ceiling and makes a puffing sound of frustration. "The fuckers should have sent us a chopper just as soon as it happened. They had plenty of time to get in and out before the sand started blowing. It doesn't make sense to me. At least Kellen's pumped full of morphine and feeling no pain. He just got his ticket home."

The flap slaps open and Sergeant Oliphant trudges in, looking from face to face until he finds mine. Everyone stiffens. White skin circles his eyes, but his cheeks are powdered with sulfur-colored grit. A cloud of dust comes in behind him. It tastes like talc and stale cumin. He points to me.

"Durrant. Outside." He shakes his goggles. "Grab your eyepro and a mask."

Lopez grins at me.

11

The winds blow in every direction. Even with the protective earplugs, the sound is enormous. It feels as though it might lift you up. There are a thousand notes inside of it—a deep rumbling like a diesel tank engine, the squeal of tearing metal, a hollow moaning, a multitude of voices. I do not mean people speaking words. It sounds like singing. Or crying. Visibility is cut down to four or five feet, sometimes less. The sergeant and I follow a trail of emergency lights on plastic sticks that run from building to building, blurry blue shapes that pulse and wobble. The air heaves and shifts around us like a solid thing. When I look down at my arms, the hair is standing straight up. Static.

12

Lieutenant Blankenship sits at his desk, drinking what appears to be fruit punch out of a Little Mermaid souvenir glass. He's a thick-necked man with steel-rimmed reading glasses and dark brown hair cropped to less than half an inch. Old acne scars pepper his jaw line and dot his long narrow nose. Although he's younger than I am, he sometimes acts like he's in his late middle age. I've only been in this trailer office a couple of times before. Usually when I do requisitions forms and whatnot for the lieutenant, we meet in the storage Conex. Sandbags are stacked neck-high all around the office trailer and piled on the roof. It looks like an igloo. But inside it's more like something you'd find parked in the muddy lot of a construction site. A water cooler, an overworked window AC, worn green linoleum on the floor and fake wood paneling on the walls. Walk ten more steps, open the pebbled glass door, and there's another room, pretty much the same. The lieutenant sits behind a standard issue green metal desk between a filing cabinet and a bookshelf loaded with manuals. The only other piece of furniture is Sergeant Oliphant, behind me, who smells like a dirty sock filled with chopped onions. He's close enough for me to feel the moist heat on my neck when he breathes. I stand at attention for a good ten minutes while the lieutenant flips through a folder. I can only assume it's mine, and it's not too hard to imagine what he's looking at:

NAME: Tobias Jacob Durrant.
RANK: Private E2.

HEIGHT: 5'11".

WEIGHT: 160 lbs.

EYES: Green.

HAIR: Brown.

DISTINGUISHING MARKS: Tattoo of a seahorse on left shoulder.

NEXT OF KIN: None.

HISTORY: Two juvenile arrests: public drunkenness and disorderly conduct. A six-pack after a football game and a fight on Broughton Street during the St. Patrick's Day parade. Three semesters of college at Armstrong Atlantic University in Savannah, GA. Scholastic probation. Three months as an ice cream truck driver. Six months working for a locksmith. Enlisted in Army. Data Analysis course. Accepted to Airborne School. Dismissed for assaulting a fellow soldier. Entered Language Institute and studied Middle-Eastern Languages. Dismissed after several months for missing classes. Then on to mobilization at Fort Polk and a flight to the sandbox.

"Tell me again why you got out of your vehicle today, Durrant?" He flips a page, pushes his glasses up on his nose.

"I got sick and I didn't want to—"

"You should have just leaned your head out the window."

"Yes, sir." There's no point in arguing or trying to explain something I don't really understand myself. It'll just sound like a lie. And then he'll wonder why I'm lying.

"Is that the real reason you left the convoy?"

"I wasn't thinking straight, sir. The grenade explosion had me feeling whacked out. All I knew was I had to get away and be sick." I pause for a moment. "Sir."

"Even so, it was an exceptionally stupid thing to do."

"Yes, sir."

"And that was the only reason? You didn't perhaps—" The lieutenant stops speaking suddenly and studies my face. He's looking for something there, and I get the feeling it's something very specific. I wish I knew what it was he wanted to hear, so we could end this game. I'm not sure if I'm supposed to answer him, so I remain silent. The air in the office feels dense. I want to unbutton my shirt or even take it off.

"H'mm." He picks up a silver mechanical pencil and taps my file with it.

"You said something about a kid, Durrant. What was that all about?" This comes from just behind my right ear, from the sergeant. Instinctively, I turn my head. He cuffs me lightly with the back of his hand and I straighten to attention once again.

"So?" the lieutenant prompts, raising his eyebrows. "What about this kid?"

"I saw a child on the factory grounds, sir. That's pretty much it."

"A child?" He smirks.

"Yes, sir."

"Let me make sure I understand you. You say you saw a small child all alone in an abandoned factory about twenty-five klicks from the village. Is that what you're telling me? And this child wandered out there all alone? To do what? To play?"

"When you put it that way, sir, I realize it sounds a little odd, but—"

"A *little* odd?"

Sergeant Oliphant permits himself a chuckle.

My face feels hot. It takes all my self-control to keep from bolting, just getting the hell out. I force myself to think back to that moment in the factory grounds. I puked. I saw a flash of movement, and then I saw the kid on top of that brick pile. I can picture the kid. Long black hair, a dress made of purple rags knotted together, scabby little stick legs. There's no way I could have imagined all of that. I remember the child too clearly. And then the nastier part of my brain starts to pick at it. Well, your eyes were still blurry from puking. The sun was bright. Broken glass can throw all kinds of crazy reflections. You'd just gotten knocked out by the concussion from a grenade. There's a chance you just might have imagined some—no, Goddammit, I saw her. I know it.

"You realize," the lieutenant says in a quiet voice, "I have to punish you for this. Do you understand why this kind of behavior is a problem?"

"I put my fellow soldiers in danger, sir."

"You left the patrol without permission."

Sergeant Oliphant coughs and shifts his feet behind me. I wonder if this is a signal of some kind. The lieutenant looks up and then back at the file.

"Outside of this incident, I've had no problems with you."

I almost say yes, sir, but stop myself.

"You will be assigned to the latrine burning detail for a month."

I make a sound deep in my throat. It is involuntary. My mouth wanted to form the words, *one month*, and I caught myself just in time. Instead, I force out a cough to cover it.

"Do you have something to say, soldier?" For a moment, in the dim green glow of the desk lamp, the lieutenant looks like a twelve-year-old boy. I wonder what the sergeant thinks about taking orders from him. This is obviously the lieutenant's first time in combat, maybe even his first leadership position, while the sergeant is an old warhorse. If it bothers him, he hides it well. I wonder, not for the first time, what it is that connects these two men. The bond they've formed seems to go well beyond their professional relationship.

"Just clearing the sand out of my throat, sir."

He glances up at me over the rims of his glasses. "Yes, well." Then my file takes up his attention once again.

Behind me, the sergeant shuffles around. Lieutenant Blankenship sighs and looks over my shoulder at him again. He purses his lips in disapproval. The wind shrieks outside the window, which usually looks out on the parade ground. Right now it looks out on dark swirling grit. He gives me an appraising look and points to a folding chair in front of his desk.

"Sit down."

I do.

"You've been working as a clerk." It isn't a question. Most of this work I've done has been for him. "You did a Data Analysis course and some Language School. How good is your Arabic?"

"I can speak about as well as a four-year-old. But the local language is harder, sir."

"Yes," he says, staring at my face without making eye contact. It isn't a comfortable feeling.

"Would you be able to tell if a translator was doing a reasonably accurate job?"

"That might depend, sir."

"On?"

"How fast the subject spoke, the dialect he used, the level of vocabulary—"

He breaks in. "But you could tell whether the translation was an outright falsification." His eyes narrow and his voice goes very flat. I can feel Sergeant Oliphant scrutinizing the back of my head.

"I think so, sir, yes." I watch his face to see if this is the correct answer. The lieutenant gives nothing away. Something odd is going on here. Most of what we've gone over is information he already knows. I can feel him leading me up to the real question. But I haven't a clue what that might be.

"Very well." He pushes up his glasses and rubs his eyes with the heels of his palms. Then he shuts my file. "Do you think you can get back to your tent without the sergeant's guidance?"

"Yes, sir," I say, feeling both irritated by the lieutenant's implied insult and unaccountably relieved to be leaving. I'm not sure I want to know what he's really after.

"You are dismissed."

When I turn, the sergeant holds the door open for me. He smiles. Smug, crafty, amused. "Good night, Durrant."

The door shuts with a click. I walk to the end of the trailer's front room and stand for a moment. Lieutenant Blankenship says something I can't quite make out, but the frustration in his voice is unmistakable. I pause. The sergeant answers. It is a neutral sound. I take three steps back. Careful. Heel to toe. Then another three.

"It didn't even happen in the right fucking place." The lieutenant's words come out in a harsh rasp.

"It's not your fault, sir. You signaled to them to move away," the sergeant says.

"I feel bad about Gerling and Kellen," Lieutenant Blankenship says, and it sounds as though he means it. "It was unnecessary. Those fuckers had their instructions and—"

The entire trailer shudders and sways. An empty metal can thunks into the window screen. I flinch. The sandstorm's many noises synchronize into a single piercing peal of pain. As the wind blows harder, the sound rises in pitch. Without quite knowing why, I brace myself for something horrible to happen when this shriek hits its highest note. And then, as quickly as it came together, the sound unravels into a hundred sobbing voices. My face is slick with sweat. I shift my weight and prepare to leave, but then I don't. Something inside the office shatters. The lieutenant curses. Another half a minute can't hurt.

"If this storm doesn't let up," the sergeant says, "I don't see that we have any choice. We've got to at least give the appearance of—"

Lieutenant Blankenship mumbles something.

"He'll work just fine, sir. With a little guidance, of course."

They both laugh. It is anything but lighthearted. The lieutenant has never taken me aside and spoken to me like he did tonight, and I'm unnerved by it. Usually he ignores me, and this is exactly how I like it. Sweat is slowly turning the grit on the back of my neck into mud. It's time to go. I put on my eyepro and head out, closing the outer door as carefully as I can.

13

Rankin engages in his post-mission ritual back in our tent. After every safe return, he washes his face and hands with soap. Not just a splash, a thorough washing. He fills the metal cup we were all given along with our rucksacks and desert uniforms and the rest of our basic infantryman gear just before we left Fort Polk, moistens his hands, coats his palms with Lava soap, and gives them a furious rubbing. My grandfather told me that back during his war, he used his helmet to do this kind of thing. Now we just get a cup. Once the suds have formed, suds thick enough to shave with, he massages them into his face and neck. Finally, with a small green handkerchief his grandma monogrammed and sent over in his first care package, he dabs away the soap and rinses his face. The whole procedure lasts a good twenty minutes. He does it slowly and with great precision. With all this sand and grit blowing around, I know it can't be pleasant. Rankin gets these little bumps from shaving, so rubbing sand into them must sting like hell. When I first saw him doing it, he just said, "Being a soldier is a dirty business. You got to keep clean."

We also have a pre-mission ritual. Five minutes before go time, we meet at the mobilization spot. Rankin lights up, and even though I've quit, we both take a big drag, hold it a moment, and as we're exhaling, we repeat the words, "This is not our time, this is not our time, this is not our time." Always those words. Always three times. I can't remember exactly when we started this, but we've been doing it so long now, I'd feel naked and uncomfortable out on a mission if I didn't. The hope is that whatever bad luck we've been infected with will blow away with the smoke.

All of us have these little rituals, and some of us keep talismans. If back home someone had told me I'd be doing this kind of thing and doing it with utter seriousness, I would have said bullshit and laughed it off. But once you're in-theater, luck becomes a serious business. Theories abound. There's one school of thought here at the Corn Cob that basically goes like this: we all have a certain set amount of luck, and once that's used up, there's nothing you can do. You're literally shit out of luck. A soldier can use up his luck in a number of ways, but the biggest is the near miss. Any time the enemy throws lead at you and the bullet or shrapnel comes close enough to tear your uniform or hit something near your body or land in a space you recently inhabited, a chunk of your luck goes with it. Because of this, for some soldiers good luck is almost as terrifying as bad. Boyette has told me on numerous occasions that he'd rather have a flesh wound than a near miss. And this is because the same school holds with the idea that a minor injury preserves luck. But there are many other theories about how to stem the flow of good luck and how to inoculate yourself against bad luck. As many, in fact, as there are men.

And yeah, I'll admit it, I've got my own fetishes too. Just before I left Fort Polk, Clarissa cut off a lock of her hair for me. A soft little snip from just behind her left ear. It's my favorite ear because there's a tiny scar on the lobe from the time her puppy nipped her when she was four. I was supposed to get this cool titanium vial to put it in, but I didn't have time, so I wrapped it in a square of tin foil. The other thing, well, it's a bit more embarrassing. When I went AWOL from the Language Institute after I found out Clarissa was pregnant, I made her take another one of those drugstore pee tests, just to see the results with my own eyes. The whole experience got me so excited that I wanted to memorialize it somehow, so I plucked the plastic test wand out of the trash and cleaned it up. I wrapped this in tin foil too, and now both ride in the cargo pocket of my pants on every mission. My family.

14

The sun does not rise. When Rankin shakes me awake, I find my blanket covered with a thick layer of dust and sand. We both slept with our earplugs in. Rankin even wore his goggles. I wish I had. My eyeballs feel as though they've been scoured with steel wool. The storm continues to howl outside. If anything, it sounds worse than yesterday.

"MREs for breakfast today," Rankin says. He looks unaccountably happy.

"What's got you so cheerful?"

"It's like a snow day in Savannah."

I laugh.

When I thump my boots for critters, a large black scorpion comes rolling out. It's nearly the size of my palm.

"Damn," I say, lifting up my boot to mash it.

"Wait, D, wait." Rankin dumps a pile of letters out of a Tupperware container and uses this to trap it. "She's a beauty. I don't believe I've ever seen one this big."

"What in the hell do you want with it?" I ask.

"I think you might just have found a way to get our money back from Nevada."

Suddenly I understand, and it makes me laugh so hard that I cough up sand.

15

Kurkbil is the village a klick or so away from the base that we are supposedly keeping secure. It lies on the main north-south highway that runs from the capital down to Inmar. The Turkish Highway. Route 6A. I doubt if there are more than a thousand citizens all told. Strung along this one paved road is the business district, as the lieutenant optimistically calls it, which consists of a six-table café, a butcher shop, a garage that literally uses one of the town trees as a hoist for engine blocks, a drygoods shop, and a public fountain. Calling it a fountain is a bit misleading. It's really just a rusty spigot that dribbles water into a shallow concrete trough.

The only buildings that aren't constructed from mud bricks are the café and the dry goods shop, which are made of cinderblock and corrugated green fiberglass. Packed dirt paths wiggle off from the paved road like earthworms after a rainstorm. This is where the town's inhabitants live, mainly in single-story mud huts surrounded by fences made of sun-baked bricks or woven palm mats and rows of planted cacti. Each family seems to own at least a half dozen chickens and a goat. The more prosperous among them have a donkey or some sheep. Kurkbil's animals outnumber its humans by nearly three to one.

The town's most prized possessions are its five trees. The largest is an ancient fig tree growing beside the fountain. The townspeople refer to it as Grandfather. This confused me at first because whenever someone gave me directions, Grandfather always figured in. For a while I imagined an impossibly old man who had sired everyone in town.

The citizens were happy to see us at first, but now they don't pay us any more mind than they would one of the countless pariah dogs that patrol the town. When they do take note, it is usually to cross the street when they see us coming or to dart away into the maze of paths behind the shops. This is especially true of the women. All of them, even the teenage girls, dress in dark clothes and keep their faces covered. The young women used to giggle when they saw us walking into town; now they hunch their shoulders and scurry off onto one of the side paths. The men stare at us until we turn and notice, then they pointedly look away. On my first area patrol, Sergeant Guzman told me to remember that someone is always watching, no matter how late the hour or how empty the town looks.

Part of the problem, aside from the fact that we've rousted a couple dozen of the town's families out of their beds in the middle of the night and thrown all their belongings on the floor as we looked for non-existent weapons caches, may be the Middle Eastern Visual Language Survival Guide. These helpful booklets, which are made of laminated cardboard and fold up like gas station maps, were sent out to us about a month ago from CENTCOM. On one side there are cartoon-strip–style drawings of bearded suicide bombers with deranged facial expressions, several of whom appear to have fangs. Coincidentally, one of these cartoon villains bears a striking resemblance to the town's mayor. As you might imagine, that didn't go down too well. For a good week after we started using them, much of the populace was frightened and bewildered, fearing we planned to assassinate the mayor, Rashid Hamid, who went into hiding until the lieutenant himself showed up and guaranteed his safety. On the other side of the guide there are basic phrases in English printed next to translations in Arabic script. For example, "Where can I find a latrine?" Or "Where is the man with the gun?" Whenever one of us whips a survival guide out, it invariably causes more confusion than communication. Whichever hajji we are trying to communicate with will almost always get distracted by the colorfully depicted deaths of cartoon soldiers and immediately protest his innocence, when all we want are directions to the nearest latrine.

Or land mine. Even the children have become wary and hostile. A couple of weeks ago, Hazel got hit in the neck with a clod of donkey shit thrown by a tiny girl in a Backstreet Boys T-shirt. On Monday, the day before the IED attack, a small boy wearing nothing but a pair of patched-up red shorts told me, in perfect English, "You are my bitch, faggot."

16

The insect pit is a large cardboard box that once held MREs. In order to keep it stable, the outside of the box is completely covered with duct tape; and for that natural desert look, someone has sprinkled an inch of sand inside it. There is a huge crowd of spectators this morning. All enlisted Joes. The tent is nearly full. Sergeant Guzman came and placed a bet, but he left before the fights started. He can't risk getting caught in here during the match, but neither can he bear missing the chance for a little gambling action. Somehow Doc Greer convinced Lopez that the lieutenant wanted to speak with him. Now that the tattletale's gone, we can all relax and enjoy ourselves.

Doc Greer makes book. His K-pot overflows with damp wads of bills. Boyette pours out cups of homemade Tang wine for all comers. After every sip, he shouts, "Up went the devil." I decline. It smells like he brewed it from his dirty skivvies. The last time I drank some, I was hung over for days. Usually these death matches are held behind the motor pool because they are so strictly forbidden. No one is really sure why. Oddly, Cox, who loves insects, could care less about the fights. His only complaint is that camel spiders aren't really spiders. It irritates him that we have the classification wrong.

The reigning champ is Nevada's enormous camel spider, Fangella. Rankin and I have lost a substantial amount of money betting against her. Her record stands at 6–0. Also in the lineup are Dyson's spider, Lindsay Lohan; Boyette's scorpion, Daffy; Sergeant Guzman's scorpion, Cream Puff, handled by Cox; and our monster, just now dubbed Uday.

Each time I look over at Rankin, he's giving the Tupperware container gentle shakes to make Uday irritable. When he sees I'm watching him, Rankin flashes me a mad grin. It pleases me to see him in such a good mood. Last night, he didn't say more than two words. This is true of the whole crew. The storm has left everyone feeling on edge and antsy. Yesterday, around 2000, Nevada broke a chair and Salis punched Doc Dyson in the back of the head for no reason. However, you'd never know how jammed up they were yesterday looking at them now. Someone I can't see is giggling like a girl.

"Who the hell is running the base?" I ask Boyette.

"What's to run? Not even the sand nigs are crazy enough to come out in this shit storm." His cheek is puffy with dip. He makes a production of spitting, allowing the brown glop to drip slowly into the empty shell casing he's holding.

"Who's on guard duty?"

"You're looking at him, hoss."

"Jesus," I say.

"Don't worry, Durrant," Boyette says, edging closer to the pit. "If the bad mens come, I'll protect you."

The rules for spider fighting are relatively simple. The bell, in this case an artillery shell casing, rings and each handler lets his creature loose in the pit. If the fighters don't act suitably aggressive, two neutral helpers will push the creatures together with sticks. The winner is the one alive at the end of the match. There has been a lull in fights over the past couple of weeks because no one has felt confident enough to send up a contestant against Nevada's Fangella.

After the first match, Cox sidles up next to me and asks if I'll roll him a smoke. I sigh and take his sack of tobacco. He came into the tent in the middle of the first fight.

"What kept you so long?" I say.

"Sergeant Guzman had me in the Comm Trailer helping him. They can't get the satellite phone working, the radio is all static, and the land lines are down again. I told him it was the fucking storm, but he made me go through all the systems checks anyway. We haven't had contact with HQ since just before the storm."

"And it didn't work?"

"Hell, no," he says, disgusted, "I knew it wouldn't."

"That's a sort of lonesome prospect," I say.

"The El-Tee was going fucking ape shit. Finally, Oliphant showed up and got him out of there. I could barely work with him hunching over my shoulder."

"I don't blame him," I say. "Doc Dyson told me Gerling's getting worse. He thinks somebody should take him out by truck if they can't get a helicopter in."

"No," Collin says, "it's more than that."

"What?" I say, holding out his finished smoke. A perfectly rolled beauty, if I do say so myself.

He looks around, hesitates, and then lowers his voice. "Sergeant Guzman spotted a group moving along a ridge two Noses back from the base. Yesterday, just before the storm hit."

"A group? Like a fire-team–sized group? So what?"

"No, bigger."

"Like how much bigger?" I feel my asshole pucker.

"He counted thirty-seven, but he thought there might be more."

"Shit," I say.

"Yeah," he says, "shit. But also, there's something going down with Intel. They're sending a replacement for Saunders."

"That makes sense."

"Maybe, but I got the feeling the El-Tee thinks they're coming to investigate him about something. He kept telling the sarge 'I got to find out who they're sending. Then I'll know for sure.' That's when Oliphant pulled him into the hall. Like he didn't want me to hear what that was all about."

The room goes up in a cheer and I miss the rest of what he says. Our match has started. It looks to be going well. Uday has Fangella cornered. She's moving in an awkward crab-like fashion and raising her forelegs. Uday makes feints with his stinger. I wonder if he's already nicked her with a little venom. Fangella's moving much more slowly than usual. Suddenly, they engage. The spider has to fight the scorpion off from two sides, pincers and stinger. Uday snips off one of the spider's legs. Rankin pumps his fists in the air. His face is a mask of joy. Cox nudges me and hisses something. He points to the doorway. It's Lopez. He's dusting off his fatigues and still has his goggles on.

"Uh-oh," I say.

Cox just laughs.

Lopez doesn't make sense of the situation right away. He blinks and watches Rankin do a little victory dance, rolling his shoulders and wiggling his butt. The room is in an uproar. No one but me and Cox has noticed he's here. I glance back at the pit and find that we've won. Nevada kicks a chair. Rankin ululates like a local woman and swings his fist around his head. Lopez frowns, then scowls.

"What the hell is going on?" he shouts.

The room goes quiet. Someone, it sounds like Doc Greer, says, "Eek a bug," and chucks a dead scorpion at Lopez. He makes an odd, squeaking sound and brushes frantically at his shirt. Several people laugh. It is well known that Lopez is frightened to death of scorpions. The story goes he was stung by one on the head as a child and nearly died. This might be apocryphal, but his fear is genuine.

"I can't believe you all are doing this," Lopez says. He looks utterly flabbergasted. "Shouldn't some of you be on—"

It is then that the first mortar hits. A dull thud that makes the crate beside me rattle. From the sound of it, the shell lands somewhere near the front gate, but it is difficult to tell because of the storm. Then another one. This one closer. I look down at my watch. It is 1030, still morning, but it feels much later. A third lands close enough to make my teeth rattle and my inner organs slosh in my belly. I hit the ground.

17

"Because we lost Lieutenant Saunders yesterday," the lieutenant tells me, pacing back and forth behind his desk, "some things around here are going to have to change. A shifting of responsibilities." His voice is flat, expressionless. He waits, glancing over at me for a moment as though I might be somehow responsible. "Do you know what his duties were?"

I just look at him.

My eyes burn and my shoulders feel as though someone's been beating on them with a rubber hose. It is 1900 hours. Hazel had come and fetched me from Tower 4. I'd been up there since midmorning, long enough for the blowing sand to scour my watch face so badly I can barely read it. Just after the mortars started dropping, Sergeant Guzman ordered me and Boyette out to the tower to stand guard. "Fire off an occasional grenade," he told us, "even if you can't spot anything out there. We can't allow them to start thinking they can get away with this kind of shit scot-free."

Boyette and I couldn't see a damn thing beyond the railings, and if I took a couple of steps away from him, I could barely see him. The wind blew so hard, we had to put our mouths right up against each others' helmets and shout to make ourselves heard. Boyette being Boyette, he still managed to pack his cheeks with Skoal. Every so often, a glob of dip spit would spatter my arm. When I'd tell him to spit in the other direction, he'd grin like a monkey and pretend not to hear me.

Boyette is the youngest of five brothers born in a trailer up on Tiger

Ridge, a tightly knit community just northwest of Savannah. This small group of families was famous in the early part of the last century for robbing travelers and stealing their women. In Savannah it's common to joke about the closeness of their eyes and their penchant for romancing their siblings. Soon after meeting him, I decided to keep those kinds of jokes to myself. Boyette has hair the color of dirty sand and thin arms gnarled with hard muscle. His eyes look like dull nickels, and when he levels them at you, you get the feeling he doesn't much give a shit about anything, including himself. Boyette's the kind of guy that runs toward gunfire when he hears it. I wouldn't call myself Boyette's best pal, but I felt bad leaving him up there alone. He didn't seem to mind. I'm almost certain Hazel was supposed to stay and replace me, but he acted like he didn't understand me when I asked him. It pissed me off a little bit. The two of us got lost on the way back to the parade ground and somehow found ourselves near the front gate. The metal doors looked as though they'd been rammed by something. It took almost an hour to get to the office trailer, normally a five-minute walk, if that.

The lieutenant coughs. "Look, I know you're tired, but stay with me here. It's important."

"I know—" I clear my throat. "I know Lieutenant Saunders sometimes did interrogation, sir."

"Well, there's a little more to it than that, but you're in the ballpark. The point is that we still have the same tasks to complete. I spoke with HQ just after we returned yesterday and they don't know when they'll be able to send helicopters in. In fact, they don't even know when they'll be able to bring us up to normal troop strength. If you can call what we had 'normal troop strength'." He pauses. A long pause this time. The lieutenant scrutinizes me. His eyes are the wet brown color of used coffee grinds. I worry the sand on the back of my teeth. I wish I could spit it out. The lieutenant seems to be waiting for something. The wind picks up and makes a sound like a dying cat.

"Sir," I say, a neutral statement I've found to be safe in most situations involving officers.

The lieutenant lets out a breath. He looks down at the folder again.

"We need you to speak to the prisoners," he says, staring at my face without making eye contact. He does this every time we talk, and it never fails to make me extremely uncomfortable. "You think you can handle that?"

"I'm not sure what 'that' means, sir."

"Lieutenant Saunders was investigating something." He glances over my shoulder at Sergeant Oliphant. "He didn't have a chance to discuss it with me before he died. We planned to talk about it in Inmar, but I—"

Behind me, the sarge coughs.

"Anyway," the lieutenant continues, "we believe something's coming up. There's been a lot of activity out in the Noses. These prisoners are obviously from the same group that attacked us this morning. They might know what's going on." He takes a deep breath and winces, as though what he has to say next pains him. "I've watched you since you've come here, Durrant. You get along with most people. At least I haven't heard of any recent fights." He stresses the word 'recent.'

Because he stops again, I say, "No, sir."

"I've also noticed people seem to like to talk with you, tell you things. Perhaps we can make use of this skill."

"Sir, like I said yesterday, I'm not that proficient an Arabic speaker and—"

"You'll work with a translator. We have two. One's better than the other, but—"

"We have two terps, sir?" This comes as something of a surprise. I know about one, a guy everyone calls Baba. His real name is something much longer, but he doesn't seem to mind this abbreviation, even though in the local slang it means a thief or a generally seedy character. He's an older guy with a thick pelt of hair on his arms and a face as round and shiny as a pie tin. Maybe in his forties. Recently, he moved onto the base, supposedly for his own protection. I don't doubt it. Hajjis working with the Army have a short life span.

"The mechanic's assistant speaks English, doesn't he?" The lieutenant points toward the window with his thumb.

"Ahmed?" I'm skeptical, but then again I've barely spoken to the guy. Ahmed looks to be about my age. Cheerful. Quick to laugh. "A little, sir. I guess."

The lieutenant glances over my shoulder again. "Right," he says. I'm not sure whether he's talking to me or the sergeant.

"I don't mean to be disrespectful, sir, but I have no training in interrogation. I wouldn't know where to start. Perhaps you should ask—"

Lieutenant Blankenship smiles, showing me a row of white, even teeth. It looks about as genuine as a plastic squirt gun. In fact, it looks as though he's trying to maintain his composure while someone jabs him in the leg with a safety pin under the desk. I bet he has caps. His teeth seem unnaturally white, like they might give off light in a dark room.

Sergeant Oliphant places a hand on my collarbone and squeezes. I clench my jaws. A little more pressure and he'll snap the bone. I want to say all right, I get it, let go. After a few seconds he loosens his grip, but he doesn't take his hand away.

"We need an interrogator, Private." He says the word 'private' as though it's something unpleasant he has to scrape off of his tongue. "Ours has died. Until a replacement comes, you're it. You write the best reports and you're very creative with requisition forms. That shows promise. Think of these interrogations as tricky requisition forms. Got it?"

The sergeant's hand comes to life and applies pressure.

"Yes, sir."

I am released.

"Good."

"May I ask a question, sir?"

The hand readies itself with a gentle squeeze. The lieutenant and I have a rare moment of eye contact and I take this as permission to go on.

"What kind of questions do I ask the hostages, sir?"

"Prisoners, Durrant, prisoners. We're not trying to extort money from the native population."

Sergeant Oliphant laughs, but it is a polite, meaningless sound. I feel my face burn. What the hell is wrong with me?

"I'm sorry, sir. I—well. What questions should I ask them?"

The lieutenant gives me a disgusted look. I'm wasting his time. "Who are you? Where do you come from? What are your plans? Use your head, Private."

"Maybe I should write some out," Sergeant Oliphant says. It sounds as though his mouth is right beside my ear. "Perhaps we should check and see if Lieutenant Saunders left behind any material that could help us."

"Yes," the lieutenant says finally, "right. Durrant, go find Baba and report back. We'll have a list of questions for you then."

Something bothers me about this. And not just the fact that I don't know the first thing about prisoner interrogation. We may be shorthanded and we may be a small isolated base, but I've never heard of a private doing this kind of intelligence work. In the past, we've always shipped prisoners to the capital to be sorted out by the CIA or MI or whoever. But that's not all. I'm not even the obvious first choice. Or the second. There are several other soldiers I can think of right away that would be much more qualified to do this. The lieutenant, for example. This doesn't make sense on any level. It feels like I'm being told to descend a long and tricky staircase while blindfolded. I'm worried about what I'll find at the bottom.

"Now, sir?" I ask. My soul droops.

"When else? This sandstorm isn't going to protect us forever."

By the time I stand up, Sergeant Oliphant has opened the door. He gestures toward it with his hand. "Buck up, fuckwit," he whispers as I pass, "or I'll make sure you're burning shit for the rest of your tour."

18

Baba is gone. And so, says Nevada, is the treasured hoard of *Jugs* and *Hustlers* he keeps in his locker. Nevada had a good forty or fifty of them. All winnings from the insect pit. Outside of DVDs and video games, jacking off is one of the few forms of recreation on the base. The theft of the porno library is an enormous loss to everyone, but to Nevada most of all. He is in a rage bordering on psychotic. When I find him in the mess hall, he looks very near to throttling Doc Dyson to death, although, unless I miss my guess, he'd be the last one to swipe porno mags. He is small, however, which is probably why he's suffering Nevada's wrath. Nevada is not the only one worked up. Hazel paces around the camp tables, locking and unlocking his weapon. He doesn't look at me or answer when I greet him. I stand up on a bench.

"Has anyone seen Baba?"

At first no one replies. There are only six or seven men sitting at the tables, crunching despondently on their sandy T-Rats. I point at Dyson. "Nevada, let him loose."

Nevada stops actively choking poor Dyson, but he continues to rub his fist against Dyson's scalp. No one else pays me any mind either. I whistle as loudly as I can. "Did anyone see Baba leave? His tent is empty, and Sergeant Guzman says a Ma Deuce is missing. Did anyone see him during the attack?"

"That fat fucking hajji," Nevada says, "has just pinched my last nerve. If I find him . . . Goddamn. He must want me to pop him one.

He must really fucking want his ass kicked out through his mouth."
Nevada stops his ranting and looks to the door. Something else seems
to have occurred to him. He lets loose Dyson, who immediately
scrambles to the other side of the tent. His face contorts. "He best not
of taken that too."

"What are you talking about?" I say.

"He was in Number 2 tent after the mortars hit," Nevada says.
"I left my K-pot in there and went to grab it. I saw him playing the
GameCube like nothing was the matter. If he's taken that, I—" There's
no need to finish.

Nevada and four others drop their meals and head to Common Tent
2. I trail behind, dreading yet another trip through the blowing sand.
The sun looks as though it is finally burning out. It's turned an orange
so dark it's almost brown. The winds have died down somewhat. I can
make out the vague shapes of the officers' trailers. A light blinks on
and then off again. The blue emergency lights embedded in the gravel
paths between the buildings flicker, go out, and return.

I hear Nevada scream, "Fuck, fuck, fuck," even before I get in the
outer door of the tent. The GameCube is gone too. Shit, I think,
this doesn't look good for Baba. He'll be shot on sight. My only
consolation is that with him gone I probably won't have to interrogate
the prisoners right away, because Ahmed went home to the village
before the storm hit the base.

19

"What do you mean 'gone,' Private?"

"Vanished, sir," I almost say, into thick sand. "Along with some reading material and the video game console."

"Reading material? What the hell does that mean?"

"Uh," I say, glancing over at Sergeant Oliphant, "girlie magazines, sir."

"Are those allowed?" the lieutenant asks Sergeant Oliphant.

"Not exactly, sir," he says, his face expressionless, "but I've allowed the men to bend the rules as long as there are no women on base. We have an exigency plan if that ever happens."

"Which is?"

"A small fire in an empty fuel drum, sir."

I guess the lieutenant hasn't visited the common tents for a while. And that bit about women seems odd. There hasn't been a female soldier here since we were operating at full strength, and even then they only came out here on transport operations. As truck drivers and the like. In for a night and out the next day. Surely no one, not even the lieutenant on his most optimistic days, still believes the base will ever be that big again.

The lieutenant groans. "I don't have time for this now."

"No, sir," the sergeant says.

"Have you searched the whole base, Durrant?"

"Yes, sir." This isn't strictly true, but I'm sure Baba's gone. "I doubt he'd stay on base, sir, after taking those items. The men are very angry."

This is something of an understatement. Homicidal is more like it. Boyette, after being relieved of guarding the sandstorm, went into a fit of rage upon hearing about it. The effect was so satisfying to watch, Nevada ignored the stream of racial slurs that poured out of his mouth. He finished by telling us in a voice so loud you could probably hear it over in the mess tent, "I'm going to shoot that fat-ass dune coon or kill him, one."

"How did he get out, Durrant?" the lieutenant asks. "Wasn't the gate shut? Who had sentry duty?"

I think about the insect fight. Shit, nobody was on sentry duty. This could turn out to be a monumental fuckup if the lieutenant finds out.

"I don't know, sir, but I'm almost certain the gate was closed. It's been damaged by a vehicle and will not open at present."

"What?" he yells.

"I reported this to Sergeant Guzman, sir."

"Goddammit."

"Here, Durrant." Sergeant Oliphant hands me a sheet of paper. "Memorize these. You can't read the questions off the paper while you're interrogating the prisoners. It appears as a weakness."

"But—"

"I sent Specialist Cox to find Ahmed when I learned you couldn't find Baba."

My face must have fallen, because Sergeant Oliphant glares a warning at me.

"Yes, Sarge," I say.

Someone knocks at the office door. The sergeant cracks it and looks outside. He turns and smiles.

"Looks like we haven't lost all our natives, sir."

Standing in the doorway behind him is a dusty-looking Ahmed with a yellow-checked cloth wrapped around his face. Cox stands beside him. He mouths the words, "GameCube." He must have just found out. It looks as though he might burst into tears.

"I thought you went back to the village before the storm came," I say to Ahmed.

He grins.

"He got trapped in the cement factory," Cox says in a weary voice. "I found him in the mess tent, begging for food."

I turn back around. The lieutenant beams at me across his desk.

"I'll brief you on the way to the holding cells."

I must look confused because he goes on.

"The basement of the old fort."

"On your feet," Sergeant Oliphant says, but he says it very quietly, his voice just above a whisper. This startles me more than if he'd shouted. I stand and follow him into the hall. He elbows me in the ribs and gives me a meaningful look.

"Memorize the list," he says.

20

Prisoner Interrogation:

1. Determine prisoner's name, age, and place of origin.
2. If possible, determine militia group or organization.
3. Discuss recruitment techniques used and the prisoner's personal reasons for joining.
4. Military hardware?
5. Training?
6. Location of org.'s HQ?
7. Determine whether the prisoner has had previous contact with U.S. intelligence officers. (This last is underlined several times in red ink.)

21

Ahmed looks over and grins at me as we make our way down the crumbling mud-brick corridor. The lieutenant leads. I've never been in this part of the old fort. When I first arrived, Sergeant Guzman told me to keep out of here. "The walls are falling down," he said, "and the place is full of scorpions. It ain't a playfort, Joe."

This is the only time we've held on to captured insurgents for more than a day and, I figure, the lieutenant must not know quite what to do with them. Lieutenant Saunders always dealt with this sort of thing, and before him there was another first lieutenant who assumed responsibility for prisoners, who were in any case usually taken away by helicopter within hours. But then again, helicopters usually come to the scene of an IED attack if we sustain casualties. Everything about this feels wrong to me. I know the sandstorm is causing all manner of havoc, but still.

The walls look like they might tumble over with a good kick. We round a corner and go down three steps. The ceiling drops several feet, and the lieutenant, who stands about six-three, hunches over as he walks to avoid knocking his head against the crossbeams. When my shoulder brushes a wall, it comes away muddy. The air down here feels surprisingly damp, but it's pleasant after the dry, dust-choked air outside. The clattering echo of our boots sounds like half-hearted applause. Ahmed nudges me and points. A large rat scuttles away. What the hell does it eat down here? The flashlights make a bouncing pair of yellow balls on a wall at the end of the hallway. Lieutenant Blankenship hands me a small tape recorder.

"Talk to the older one first," the lieutenant says. "The other one's upstairs with Dyson."

"Aren't you going in?"

"The manual says it's best not to overwhelm them during the initial interview." The lieutenant pulls a folded booklet out of his cargo pocket and flips through it. He stops and follows a passage with his finger.

"What's that, sir?" I ask.

"An interrogation manual. Saunders left it behind. I think the CIA worked it up." He continues tracing the words with his index finger. "Here we go." The lieutenant mumbles something, and I lean in. "It says here, they're more likely to confide in you if, after a period of solitary confinement, you attempt to establish a camaraderie. In other words, try and make friends with him."

"Friends?" I ask.

Ahmed laughs. "He not your friend, sir."

I wonder where Ahmed picked up this "sir" business. I've certainly never heard him say it until today.

"Also." The lieutenant unclips a canteen from his belt. "Give him a drink when you take off the hood." He gestures toward the tape recorder with the canteen. "Do you know how to work the machine?"

I nod.

"All right then. Come back to the office trailer when you're finished talking with them."

"You're leaving?"

"Jesus, Durrant." He looks up at the ceiling with a pained expression. It's only a few inches above his head. I could swear he shudders, but it's dark down here. I can't be sure. "I can't hold your hand on this one. We've already been hit once today. I'm needed—" He points to the ceiling. "—up there."

"Fine," I say, "sir."

"It's the one with the pink tape on the top." He hands me a ring with three keys. "Just get it done."

I salute. Ahmed offers a limp imitation. It's difficult to tell whether or not he's mocking us. The lantern swings when Ahmed turns and lifts his hand. Our shadows hunch and stretch, hunch and stretch, like a shadow-play version of evolution. The lieutenant raises a finger and opens his mouth as though to say something. No one moves or speaks. The silence is as loud as a bomb blast. Something scuttles in the dark behind us. We whip our heads around and point flashlights, but it's nothing we can see. Finally, he turns on his heels and marches off. His boots make a very lonely sound.

I take a breath of musty air. Ahmed puts his hand on my arm. This does not reassure me.

"Let's do this thing," I tell him.

"This thing," he says.

He shows me his oddly perfect teeth and tries to raise his left eyebrow, a gesture I know he's picked up from working with Cox. On his face, the effect is disconcerting, to say the least. Like hearing the national anthem sung in Chinese. I unlock the door. It's new, or newer. A large steel door with a Judas hole about the size of a quarter. It hangs crooked on its hinges and complains loudly when I open it. I wonder if we installed this when we renovated the fort. The smell inside is so strong, I can taste it. A shiver of nausea ripples up from my belly. I spit. You will not throw up, I tell myself. Not in front of Ahmed.

"Shit," Ahmed explains to me, tapping his nose.

"Thanks," I say, "for clearing that up."

"You are welcome." He smiles again.

I prop the door open with a fallen brick. A bulb hangs from the ceiling, but I don't see a switch. Ahmed sets the lantern on the floor. Lowering it those few feet makes a considerable difference in the lighting. Huddled in a corner is the older insurgent. He is curled up with his knees pressed against his chest. His hands and feet are bound with plastic flexcuffs and his head is covered with a black cloth hood. Jesus, I think, it's not as though he could escape. Why did they leave him like this? I try and remember who it was that brought the prisoners in. I can guess. Either Boyette or Lopez. The man's pants are soaked through with urine and liquid shit dribbles from a pant cuff when he moves. I pull the hood off, trying not to touch him.

The man's face is deeply grooved and pitted and looks surprisingly similar to the landscape around the base. His skin even appears to have a yellow cast. He blinks in the lantern light and licks his lips. A white flaky substance is caked into his beard, especially around his mouth. It looks like someone rubbed dry instant mashed potatoes into his chin. Behind me, Ahmed unscrews the cap of the canteen and I reach back for it. Instead, I hear him taking loud wet gulps.

"Ahmed," I say, "give some to him."

"This I can do," he says.

He steps over and pours half the canteen on the man's face. The old man sputters and coughs but still tries to drink as much as he can catch. He laps at the water with his tongue like a thirsty dog. The sight nauseates me, even as I wish it didn't. I want to feel something more than that. Angry. Compassionate. Something. I think of Kellen squeezing my hand. It doesn't work.

"Stop that," I say, "you'll choke him."

"He has dirty smell. I don't want to touch him."

"Well, just—" I start, but then decide it isn't worth bickering about. I have to work with Ahmed. Work. Jesus.

I take my Gerber knife out and unfold the blade. As I'm bending down to cut the flexcuffs, Ahmed squeezes my shoulder. "Don't," he says, in a strange guttural voice.

"Why? He's just an old man."

"They have tricks," Ahmed says.

Fine. I stand up. My knees pop. "Ask him what his name is." I turn on the recorder.

Ahmed speaks so rapidly I cannot understand a word. So much for gauging the accuracy of the interpretation. I am certain of only one thing: he did more than just ask the man's name.

The old man stares back at us, silent. His eyes resemble dollops of dirty motor oil resting atop egg yolks. He shivers and blinks. It is immediately apparent to me that this man is very ill. We wait for a moment. Ahmed yells something. I catch the word family. Is he asking the guy's family name? The old man arches his back until it cracks. Nothing. He closes his eyes and smiles. At first I think the door is creaking shut behind us, but no, it is the long whine of a fart. It sounds like air escaping from the pinched lip of a balloon. I take a step back. Ahmed moves forward and slaps him full in the face.

I open my mouth to complain.

Ahmed speaks first. "This is terrible insult to you. It cannot escape my punishment. Only worse one if he touches you with foot."

"Don't do that any more." I sound about as authoritative as a seven-year-old girl. "Ask him what insurgent group he belongs to."

Ahmed shouts something at him. The volume startles both me and the old man. We go through the list of questions. He responds by closing his eyes. Finally, I squat down, so the old man and I are face to face. I experiment with a smile.

"Sick?" I ask in Arabic. "Medicine?"

The old man coughs. It comes from deep in his chest and sounds thick and wet. He clears his throat. I wait for him to say something, raising my eyebrows. Nothing.

Ahmed speaks softly. I assume he's translating the words into the local dialect. The old man smiles. Ahmed smiles. It's contagious. I smile too. Now we're cooking with gas. I shuffle over a little closer. Ahmed speaks again. His voice sounds very gentle.

"Good," I say, "much better."

The old man spits on me. A gob of mucus the size of a Susan B. Anthony dollar. I figure he's been saving it up for some time since this is the first thing to come out of his mouth. It lands on the sleeve of my blouse. Ahmed and I watch as it slides onto the floor. It has the texture of chicken liver and holds its shape after it falls.

"I can kick him. Would you like?" Ahmed looks more than happy to oblige.

"What did you say to him?"

"I tell him, your mother has hairy nutsack and your father shit you out of hole in his ass."

"Why on earth did you say that?"

"I thought maybe more talk would come out of him."

"All it made come out of him is spit." I want to wipe my sleeve on the back of Ahmed's shirt. Instead I smear it on the wall. Jesus. "Please don't do that again."

"Nasty man." Ahmed shakes his head in disgust. "All these people nasty man. If you want, I can kick him with my hand. Right in nut sack." He grins and makes a fist.

"No, we can't do it that way."

"It work better. This I promise to you. That is all these people understand. A kick." Ahmed spits on the floor.

I've had more than enough spitting for the day. "What do you mean, these people?"

"Furdu. All the Furdu are nasty people."

"Furdu?" The word sounds familiar to me. I try to place it but cannot. "You mean insurgents?"

"Yes." He looks at me for a long moment. Half a dozen possible expressions move across his face. Finally he settles on the most obvious look of scheming I've seen in some time. "Insurgents, Furdu. These are same thing." He slaps the backs of his hands across one another.

I chew the tip of my tongue and give the old guy an appraising look. So much for developing a feeling of camaraderie. He gives me the look right back. The deep wrinkles around the corners of his mouth make it difficult to read his expression. I could almost swear he's smiling at me. This guy isn't going to tell me any secrets. Even if I let Ahmed get rough, this sad old fuck would probably have a heart attack and die before he had a chance to spew out enough lies to make us stop. I can't believe the lieutenant didn't know this from the start. And if he did, then I'm not sure what the hell we're doing here.

I have a thought.

"Tell him we're through with him," I say to Ahmed. "Ask him where he wants us to drop him off."

Ahmed looks appalled. He sputters something about nasty people.

"Just do it," I tell him, doing my best angry Sergeant Oliphant impression.

Ahmed asks. It sounds like he's grinding the words out with his teeth.

The old man breaks into an honest grin and shakes a finger at me. You naughty boy, this business with the finger seems to mean. I'm not as stupid as you think. He clears his throat again and Ahmed and I both take a couple steps back.

Instead, amazingly, the old man speaks.

"What?" I say, more than a little surprised to have gotten something more than mucus out of him.

Ahmed raises his hand to give Uncle Insurgent here a slap, but I catch him by the wrist.

"He say, it not matter. You will all be dead soon."

"That's all? He talked for quite a while just to say that."

Ahmed sighs. "Nothing words."

I continue to stare at him.

Ahmed shrugs. "He say your officer know all about it. He say for you to ask your officer."

"What the hell does that mean? Ask him to explain."

Ahmed babbles a bit. The old man sits up and looks at me, speaking quickly.

"What?" I ask. My hands are suddenly slick with sweat. "What?

"He say, I have ten guns and you call me bandit. You have million guns, so they call you soldier."

"That's all?"

"Yes."

"Nothing about the first thing? Ask him to explain again about my officer."

And Ahmed does. He tries the question out in several different versions. No doubt he adds a bit of color on his own initiative. But this is all we get. I'm sure he's only trying to sow dissent among the ranks, not a particularly original technique, but his answer unsettles me. Ahmed blathers on and on. After a while, the old man stops looking at us. His eyes lose focus. If I hadn't have heard him speak just now, I'd believe him to be catatonic. He's retreated to a place deep inside his head where we can't follow. And then he simply shuts his eyes.

"All right," I tell Ahmed, "that's enough."

But Ahmed makes one last valiant effort. He raises his voice and even shakes his fist a bit for dramatic effect. Nothing doing. The old man turns and faces the wall. I take the canteen from Ahmed and slosh it around. There's still a bit of liquid in it. Before leaving, I unscrew the cap and set it on the floor at his feet. Our shadows bob and sway as I step into the hall. I close the door. The metal squeals when I turn the lock.

"What did you say there at the end?" I ask.

"I tell him we come back again."

"That's all?" I no longer believe anything this man says.

"And." Ahmed gives me a hopeful look. "I tell to him, listen, Uncle, I know a little trick with a knife I could show you."

22

The boy prisoner is on the upper level in the complex of half-collapsed rooms behind the machine shop. Although not as cool, the air here smells fresher and the room is clean. Doc Dyson has been looking after the boy's gunshot wound. Dyson appears in the doorway, startling the hell out of both me and Ahmed. There's a smear of blood on his forehead. It makes his thin blond hair look very white. As he steps toward us, he frowns and pulls off a pair of purple surgical gloves. He gestures with his chin toward the hallway and I follow him. Ahmed steps into the room.

"Greer brought him in," Doc Dyson says. "He did a decent job with the field dressing, but from the way he slammed the kid around, I could tell he was too pissed off to take care of him. I hope you're not going to fuck with him."

"No," I say, "just ask him a few questions."

He gives me a hard look, or at least as hard a look as he can manage. Squints his eyes. Tilts his head. Tightens his jaw. I notice he's got a purple bump the size of a prune on his cheekbone, probably Nevada's doing. Our Doc Dyson grew up in a little papermill town south of Savannah, but the Joes think he looks like a miniature California surfer boy. Nevada calls him Boogie Board. I've never asked his age, but I wouldn't be surprised to hear he gets carded for R-rated movies. Doc Dyson's our best combat medic, but I sometimes find it difficult to take him very seriously because he gives the impression of a kid dressing up in his big brother's fatigues. Nothing irritates him more than to be reminded of this, so of course we do it all the time.

"Once they're in our custody, they're our responsibility. They get the same care as one of ours." He holds up his hand as I start to speak. "I know what he did. It makes me fucking angry too. But he's just a kid. He must know a little English because when I asked him how old he was, he flashed thirteen fingers."

"Look," I say, "I didn't ask for this detail. All I'm going to do is ask him a few questions. I'm not going to waterboard the little shit."

"I wouldn't let Greer take care of him. And I'm not about to let you fuck with him." He folds his arms across his chest. "He's gutshot."

"Yeah?" I make a face. "And Saunders is dead."

"And the boy's not doing very well either." He gestures with a thumb over his shoulder. "We're only equipped here to prep wounds for the hospital at HQ. If we don't fly him out soon, he's going to bleed to death. Greer said . . . never mind. This kid's been punished enough. I'm going to stay in the room and make sure he can handle your—" He gives me a sour look. "—questions."

"Don't be an asshole, Dyson," I say. "Lieutenant Blankenship told me it was only supposed to be me and the terp."

He gives me his tough guy squint again. "Fifteen minutes. No more. And I'm going to be—"

Inside the room, someone shrieks. Doc Dyson and I rush in. Ahmed stands in one corner looking sheepish, smiling in a crooked way. The boy wails again.

"I didn't do. The boy just make a sound."

Doc Dyson glares at Ahmed and moves to the boy's side. He lifts a bandage and takes the kid's pulse. This is the first real look I've gotten of him. His hair is matted and dusty and his arms look painfully thin. I step over and smile at him. He has the delicate features of a girl. High cheekbones and long lashes. I'm reminded of the evening my grandfather hit a deer on the two-lane road up to Statesboro. I knelt in the grass and stroked its forehead while my grandfather got his pistol out of the glove compartment. The doe had long, black eyelashes like these and an expression in its eyes that rattled me. The kind of eyes that ask a question you have no answer for.

"That fucker did something," Doc Dyson says, pointing at Ahmed with a bloody piece of gauze.

"This fucker did nothing," Ahmed says with finality. He folds his arms across his chest.

"Let's just get this over with," I say.

"I'm holding you responsible if anything happens," he tells me.

"Yes, yes," I say, rubbing my eyes with my thumbs.

Outside the wind rises to a crescendo. Dust snakes in from the hallway. Then, just as quickly, it dies down again. Dyson walks to the door and stops.

"Fucking storm," he says. "I wish I could shoot it. Herodotus says in his *Histories* that one of the Pharaohs had his army attack a sandstorm and—"

"Great, guy," I say, leading him into the hall by his elbow, "you can tell me the whole story later, but how about right now I just get this thing done."

I shut the door behind him.

I pop a fresh tape in the recorder and set it on the metal stand beside the boy's bed. I state the date, time, and object of the interview. Then I nudge Ahmed with my thumb. "Ask his name," I say.

Ahmed, looking chastened, speaks slowly enough that I can understand.

"Efraim Karsh," the boy says, just above a whisper.

"See, a Furdu, just as I say," Ahmed crows.

The boy begins to speak without prompting, quietly at first and then with greater strength and volume. I look at Ahmed, but he seems to be captivated by the boy's words. I start to ask him to translate, but he holds up his hand. Never once does he look away from the boy's face. After several minutes, the boy stops. He swallows hard and blinks. The effort has visibly exhausted him.

"So?" I say.

"The old man is big uncle. Father's father's brother. Family make the boy come and do this thing. He does not want to go. This, I think, a lie. He is saying, they are not waiting for you, but someone else. The boy, he is saying, he make mistake. The uncle very mad. Then you shoot and so they shoot back. Lie, lie, lie." This last he says with vehemence, spittle flying from his lips as he speaks. "Someone tells him to be saying these things, a made-up talk for you and the sirs. This I know."

"How?"

"His mouth. It is hard, just here." He taps his upper lip. "When a man makes a lie, it stays like this, hard." Ahmed shows me by tightening his lips into a ridiculous scowl.

"Ask him who the girl was."

Ahmed asks.

"He does not know. Again, a lie. His eye, you see it. There is also a lie living there." Ahmed points. "A lie."

The boy begins to cry very quietly.

Ahmed clenches his fists and grimaces. "Lie," he shouts.

The door flies open and Doc Dyson rushes in. His face is bright red. "Enough. Enough. Out! Both of you."

"I'll have to come back, you know," I tell him, forcing myself to speak as softly as I can. "And I'm still going to have to bring *him*." I point to Ahmed, who stares at Doc Dyson with a fearful expression. As small as the Doc is, he can make a big noise when he wants.

"I don't care," Doc Dyson says, looking as though he might cry as well. He turns away and takes a breath. "This storm is driving me fucking crazy." He gives Ahmed a hateful look. For a moment, I think he might attack him.

Out of the corner of my eye, I see the boy make a strange, furtive gesture. He curls his hand into a loose fist and taps his down-turned palm with his fingers.

"Go on back to the garage, Ahmed. Thanks," I say. "I need to talk with the Doc here."

Ahmed leaves and Doc Dyson lets out a long, ragged breath. I close the door.

"I want to talk with this man." The boy has a tiny voice, like a mouse at the bottom of a well.

Doc Dyson and I swing around in surprise. The boy smiles at the reaction he's gotten.

"Did you know?" I say to Doc Dyson.

He shakes his head.

"Don't worry, mister," the boy tells Doc Dyson. "I need to talk alone."

"I'm warning you," Doc Dyson says, but he leaves.

"You speak English," I say.

"I learn some in school. Then after the war comes again, an English doctor he give me a book."

"It must have been a good book."

"Yes," he says and gives me a long, cautious look. "I do not kill your friends with purpose."

"How do you mean?" I say, surprised.

"That man, he's . . . I do not know the English word. Gashtu."

"Gashtu?"

"A different . . . um . . . family. He is right. I am Furdu."

"Like Shiite and Sunni."

"No, we are all Sunni here. Different families. We have our own war inside the big war. Our war is older. That man, he says to me, I will kill you. Then he pushes me here." He points to his bandage.

"I'm sorry," I say.

"It is fine for me. I want to kill him too. The bomb, it is for him."

"The one on the road? It was for Ahmed?"

"Maybe not this Ahmed, but for one of them. They are getting ready. In the hills. They will come soon. You may not trust this man. He is bad man. His family wants to kill everyone. Furdu, American, English. They hate everyone."

"What?" I say. My voice rises.

"It is better if you put him in room under floor. He is here to learn your weak places. They make tests." He points to the door. "The rockets that fall on your cloth houses. They are his. Tests."

"How do you know this?"

"He does not remember my head, but I remember his head. When I see—" The boy points to his eye and winces from the movement. "—I think, yes, I know this ugly head. It is Gashtu head. He and his brothers. They attack my village." He looks up at the ceiling and thinks for a moment. "Two days before this week."

"Then who was the girl on the road?"

"It is my cousin. We put a Gashtu scarf on her head to trick them. Yellow scarf with white spots. You see it?"

I think about it for a moment. Maybe I saw a yellow scarf. I can't quite remember.

He goes on. "It is the father's idea. The mother does not like, but he say, her ghost with Allah now, but the body she can still help. We all cry then." The boy's eyes roll back, showing only whites, and he closes his eyes. I wonder if I should call Doc Dyson. He remains silent for so long, I assume he's unconscious; but after a time, he coughs quietly and opens his eyes. We look at each other. When he speaks again, his voice is a dry rasp. "But, then, I am sorry." His eyes become wet. "It is this person's fault." He taps his chest and winces again. "I am nervous and when I see the men in road, I push the button. I am far away and I think you are Gashtu. My uncle, he is very angry. But when they shoot, we must shoot, he says to me, or they kill us."

"Jesus," I say.

"That man with ugly head." He points to the door. "He has many brothers, many cousins. They all wait for him in the hills. It is very dangerous. You should go to other place. Not here."

"Go?" I say. "Go where? Up in the hills and find them?"

"No," the boy says, horrified. "They are too many. Leave this place."

"We can't leave," I say, taking a knee beside the bed, so our heads are on the same level.

"They come soon," he says. He taps my wrist with his finger.

"Don't worry. You won't be here. You'll be in a hospital."

"No," he says, looking me in the eye, "I will not."

"You can't think like that—"

The door swings open. Doc Dyson marches in with a hypodermic needle and a determined look. "All right, Durrant. Leave him alone. That's enough for now." He finds a joint in the boy's IV line and slowly injects the fluid. "This ought to make you feel better."

The boy nods, his forehead creased and sweaty. He takes rapid shallow breaths. They have the sharp, harsh sound of paper being slowly torn to pieces.

"Are you going to forget English now that I'm back?" Dyson says to the kid and stops fussing with the IV line to watch him. The boy smiles. His features soften and his eyes lose focus.

"No," he says, "you are not an Ahmed."

23

When I report back to the lieutenant, he seems even more distracted than usual. Sergeant Oliphant is elsewhere. The room is lit only by the desk lamp. His shadow looms on the wall behind him like a dark, unhappy doppelganger. I stand at attention for quite some time before he decides to acknowledge me. On the floor beside his desk are stacks of papers and piles of dirty camos. All of the blouses are rumpled, so I can't make out rank or name tape. I wonder if they're his, and if so, whether it means he's living out of his office now. Near the leg of his chair there is a framed photograph of Lieutenant Saunders and a woman. They are young and smiling. Now I understand. Someone's gone through Saunders's trailer. The lieutenant looks up at me and frowns. A look of confusion flits across his face, as though I've only now materialized in his office and, even worse, he has absolutely no idea who I am.

"The interrogations, sir," I say. "I finished them."

His frown relaxes, but only slightly. It's replaced by a look of mild annoyance. "So?" He stares at me fixedly and places his hands down flat on the surface of the desk.

"I've brought the tapes, sir. Would you like me to debrief you?" I hold out a sack with the tapes and the recorder.

He waves this away. "Give it to Oliphant."

We look at each other.

"Go on, then," he says, taking a folder from a stack on the floor. "In a nutshell."

I clear my throat and give him a concise run-through of what happened. The lieutenant shuffles papers. He turns through them too fast to do more than just identify them and move on to the next one. Maybe not even that much. During the time I'm in his office, I notice the sweat stains under his arms and around his neck spread several inches in each direction. I'm not sure he's listening to me at all. After I finish, I offer him the tapes again. He stands and takes the satchel, puts it in a desk drawer, and locks it. All of his movements are very precise and formal, as though he's practiced this many times. I have a strong feeling that he has no intention of looking at them again. It doesn't make sense. We stand in silence for several minutes.

"Is there anything else, sir?" My stomach whines and gurgles.

"H'mm?"

"Is there anything else you would like me to do? Should we decide something about Ahmed? I mean, it seems like he might be—"

"Look, these groups are always infighting. I'm sure they're just saying that to cause trouble for one another. You must sift the information, Durrant. If I'm suspicious of anyone, it's that Goddamned Baba." He turns a page.

"But, sir—"

He doesn't look up. "You're dismissed."

I get up and go. As I'm closing the door, he says my name.

"Yes, sir?"

"What did the prisoners say about the last question?"

"Last question, sir?"

"The one about contact with American intelligence. You did ask them both that question?"

"Yes, sir," I lie, wanting more than anything just to get the hell out of there. This whole day's felt haunted, and now the lieutenant seems like one more ghoul. "They said nothing about it, sir. Nothing at all."

"Did either of them mention anything about soldiers doing digs out in the desert near their village? Or soldiers hiring workers or guides?"

I get the feeling he meant to ask this question all along and is trying to make it seem like it just occurred to him, that this is the real reason he wanted me to interrogate the prisoners.

"No, sir," I say, trying to keep my expression neutral. "Why?"

"No real reason. Just something I had an idea about. Not important."

Right. Not important. Bullshit.

24

"You need to watch your back around Lopez, man," Rankin says.

The fabric of the tent turns everything a muted golden color. The sun drifts toward the horizon, hazy, indistinct, weary. The day has grown old. We sit on our cots and clean our rifles. Rankin dug up some graphite to use as a lubricant instead of oil. He says it will keep the dust from sticking. The smell reminds me of elementary school, sharpening pencils after school as a punishment.

"Yeah," I say, not really interested. I can't seem to stop thinking about the wild girl living in the abandoned toy factory. I keep trying to remember what it was that made me think the kid was a girl in the first place. But then again, what the hell difference does it make?

"You listening to me, Private Durrant? Return from la-la land." Rankin thumps me on the leg with his rifle stock. "I mean it. Lopez is up to something."

"I don't understand why he has such a hard-on for me."

"What?" Rankin snorts. "You mean to tell me you forgot already? At the time, you were weeping and moaning to beat the band."

"What are you talking about?" I say, laying the barrel of my rifle on a cloth beside me.

"Since you're having trouble, let's go step by step. How'd you get kicked out of jump school?"

"I punched that little shit Reyes in the face."

Rankin taps his nose with a finger.

I'd spent only about two weeks in Airborne training before I lost my temper and, in a moment of weakness, popped a fellow soldier one in the jaw. I was on a flight back to Fort Stewart the next morning. The sole reason I'd joined the Army was to jump out of planes, and I'd blown it all in thirty seconds. At the time, I'd considered deserting.

"So what?"

"I can't believe you don't know this shit, man. Reyes is Lopez's half-brother."

"Goddamn. Nobody told me that. Why didn't you?"

"I'm telling you right now."

I give him a look.

"He's out to fuck with your shit, man." Rankin squirts a bit of graphite into the barrel of his rifle and rams a brush in after it.

"No kidding."

"I found him in here this afternoon going through your bag." He clicks the stock of his rifle into place and sets it on his lap.

"What the fuck?" I say. "That asshole."

"He says to me, 'Durrant took my K-pot by accident during the mortar attack. I thought it might be in here.'"

"Bullshit." I pace from my cot to the inner tent flap and back.

"That's what I told him. Bullshit. I said to him, next time I catch you fucking around in here, I don't give a good Goddamn if you outrank me or not, I'm going to kick your ass. He hustled his self right out of here."

"Man, you're right. He's up to something. That sneaky little fucker." I tell him what Lopez said when he cornered me in the garage after the IED attack. The whole business with him pointing to his eye. Rankin laughs. I pace another circuit of our cramped tent.

Rankin stands up and puts his hand on my shoulder. "Don't let him rattle you, D. I'm going to ask around. We'll figure out what kind of shit he's stirring up."

"It's me that'll be stirring shit. For the next month. I got the shit-burning detail."

"For the factory thing?"

"Yeah."

Rankin shakes his head and mumbles something.

"What?"

"This whole place is fucked up. We're down here with barely enough guys to field a fucking football team, and if the boy is right they're gathering up in the Noses, waiting and watching. Breeding like cockroaches. Yesterday somebody told me they spotted like forty hajjis over by—aw, fucking forget it. Since they carted off half the FOB, you can't trust anybody."

"But me," I say.

"Yeah," he says, "like I said, you can't trust anybody."

We both laugh.

I stand there staring at my cot, wondering what the hell Lopez was looking for. I run a list of my belongings through my head. There's nothing here that could get me in trouble. I finished off the last of my Cassandra whiskey a couple of weeks ago and buried the bottle in a sand dune behind the garage. Nothing else comes to mind.

"We'll be cleaning this shit up for the next month," Rankin says, upending his go bag and shaking out the sand.

I stand at the door of the tent for a moment and listen.

"I'll be damned," I say. "You hear that, Portis?"

"Don't call me that." Portis is his first name, his mother's maiden name. An old tradition in the South. "What?" He stops fussing with his gear. "I don't hear nothing."

"Exactly," I say, "no wind."

"Shit, man, you're right."

I open the tent flap. A heavy breeze still blows across the parade ground, piling sand in drifts against anything vertical, but it's nothing compared to what it was an hour earlier. I step outside. This is the first time I've seen the Comm Trailer from my tent since the storm started. Waist-high dunes of powdery dirt have collected on the southwestern sides of the trailers and Conexes. Common Tent 2 leans at a precarious angle, sagging under a load of sand. The guy wires droop. As the storm recedes, it leaves a filmy golden-brown mist hanging thick in the air. The wind smells like unwashed hair. The broken rocks of the Noses draw lines of purple shadow across the plain, and even here in the desert there is the sound of birds. I'm going to get that fucker, I tell them. They don't seem to care one way or the other.

25

I wake in the night and can't go back to sleep. Rankin snores and mumbles in his cot. I've gotten used to his night sounds. In fact, I find them soothing now. He sleeps on one side with his hands tucked under his neck and his mangled pinkie stuck in the corner of his mouth like a pacifier. The only time I ever mentioned this sleeping habit of his, Rankin stormed out of the tent.

The air feels warm and moist from our mingled breath. Instead of hanging in the air, the dust from the storm now sticks to everything. When I accidentally brush the wall of the tent with my elbow, I find it's coated with a damp paste. I sit up and rub my eyes. They're still sore from the blowing grime. Something bothers me about the captured boy's story. I keep turning it over in my head. It doesn't make sense that he'd confused our three Humvees for a convoy of tribal thugs. Their overlook hadn't been more than fifty yards from the highway. Not only that, how could he know there were insurgents massing up in the Noses and that they planned on attacking us in large numbers sometime soon? If these two tribes are enemies, it seems very unlikely the boy's group could get such specific information. Perhaps the lieutenant is right. Maybe they are spreading disinformation. On the other hand, the boy seemed sincere. Hunches, however, aren't always so easy to explain to your commanding officer.

The wind has risen again during the night, and I have to move from tent to tent in order to find my way over to the motor pool without getting lost. Someone has turned the emergency lights out.

The steel door on the south side is blocked by sand. I have to climb in through a half-collapsed hallway in the rear of the old fort. When I turn into the hallway leading to the makeshift prisoner clinic, I hear a soft throbbing sound. I can't quite make sense of it until I reach the door to the boy's room. Doc Dyson sits slumped against the wall with his head in his hands. He's sobbing so loudly, he doesn't hear me approach. A jolt of electricity races from my stomach to my throat.

"Doc," I say.

Dyson looks up at me and blinks. A string of snot stretches from his nose to his knee. For a moment he doesn't recognize me, and then, suddenly, he does. His expression sours. "What the hell do you want?"

"What's happened?"

"They're dead." He wipes his face with his sleeve.

"They?" I say.

"Gerling and the boy."

"How did it happen?"

"How do you think?" he says. "They got shot, bled out, and then died. If it wasn't for this fucking storm, they'd still be alive. They didn't have to die from those wounds."

I keep thinking about what the boy said about Ahmed.

"Dyson," I say, trying not to yell, "did anything seem strange about the way they died? Could someone have made it happen tonight on purpose?"

Doc Dyson stares at me, his eyes blank and uncomprehending.

"Could it?" I ask, my voice rising.

"Come here," he says. It takes him a long moment to stand. His knees pop like snapped sticks.

I follow him into the room. The boy lies naked on the steel gurney. His bandage has been removed. There is a hole the size of a dime in his lower abdomen, just above the hip bone. Dyson gestures for me to come closer. He rolls the body over. I suck in air and fight the urge to run from the room. In his lower back, there's a ragged wound about the size of the boy's own fist. I try to swallow but can't. My throat is perfectly dry. If Rankin's shot had been just a little bit higher, the bullet might have hit him in the heart and he would have bled out on the spot; and if Rankin had aimed just a little to the left, the boy might still be breathing. But this is one of the most dangerous games you can play as a soldier. It never leads to anything good, and so I force myself to stop. One thing at a time. Focus on the task at hand.

"How the hell did that happen?"

"These bullets are designed to roll once they hit. More stopping power."

"Goddamn."

"Don't give me that shit, Durrant. You know what these weapons do."

"It's just—" I stop. I don't know what it just is.

"When I came to give him a shot for pain, it was too late." Doc Dyson makes a choking sound, which he tries to disguise with a cough. "He'd torn off his bandages. It was a mess. The kid must have been squirming all over the place. I should have gotten here sooner, but the fucking wind started up again. A gutshot is about the worst pain you can imagine. He must have pulled the sutures loose, rolling around. By the time I'd gotten here, he'd already bled to death."

"You think it was an accident?"

"If you call getting shot in the belly an accident."

"I mean, you didn't see any footprints in the blood or—"

"This isn't fucking CSI Kurkbil, Durrant. The kid got shot. He died."

"What about Gerling?"

"Studdie sat with him all night. His body just gave out on him."

"Could anybody else get in here?"

"You did, didn't you? The kid didn't need a guard. He couldn't even walk."

I try not to look at the body, but I find it impossible. My eyes keep getting sucked back to it like water to a drain. The boy died clenching his fists. I wonder if he was fighting someone off. Blood pooled on the surface of the gurney drips onto the floor. Near the doorway, I see a long red smudge. Like a shoe might make. This means nothing, but still I think of Ahmed, how he pushed on the boy's wound while Doc and I were out in the hall talking.

"Shit," I say.

"Very eloquent." Doc Dyson presses his eyelids closed with his pinkies. "Would you please just get the fuck out of here?"

I do.

26

We hold a brief service at dawn. Most of the base assembles on the parade ground. It is at moments like this that you really see how badly undermanned we are. Thirty-nine men stand at attention facing west. Up front, someone has set up the wobbly card table from Common Tent 2 and draped it with a green piece of canvas. Two pairs of boots. Two rifles with fixed bayonets pointed down. Two helmets balanced atop the gunstocks. I can just make out the name Saunders stenciled in black on the left helmet. The lieutenant walks to the front and looks out at us. It is so quiet I can hear the canvas snapping against the table's leg each time a breeze rises. Sweat pours down my face and into my eyes. I try my best to blink it away. We stand at attention, so I cannot wipe it off on my sleeve. I close my eyes. Doc Greer stands to my immediate right. His stomach makes a loud gurgling sound.

The lieutenant clears his throat and asks us to sing "The Star-Spangled Banner." Usually we sing "Amazing Grace," which none of us really likes. Today we sing with gusto, at least until the end of the second verse. After this, fewer and fewer soldiers know the words. Here is a song I've heard so many times, it's been reduced to a gray mush. This morning it becomes something utterly new, something shiny and pure, but then we lose track of the words, start mumbling and it turns right back into mush. For a moment, I thought this service might be something special, so when it isn't, the disappointment feels worse. The wind sucks each note from our mouths and whips it away.

Across the parade ground, above the mud brick walls, and up into the dark purple hills.

Finally, when it becomes obvious that we're all just mumbling, the lieutenant holds up his hand. Every back I see is soaked with sweat. Hazel is right in front of me. His shoulders quiver. The lieutenant bows his head and mumbles a prayer. Then he speaks about the two lost men. It is a short speech and it deals mainly in generalities. Loyalty, bravery, courage. While he babbles on, I do my best to really think about them.

The last time I spoke with Gerling was during a poker game. I took every cigarette he had with three jacks, an ace of clubs and a king of hearts. He joked about it, but I could see he was pissed off. Now I wish I'd just let him win. Gerling was the kind of guy that could shave three times a day and still have a shadow on his cheeks. Thick black hair curled up over the collar of his shirt. Doc Greer liked to call him "Guerilling." I know he had a brother in high school. He loved the loud, fast guitar work of Metallica. What else? Not a hell of a lot. He hated beef enchilada MREs, so he always gave them to me. Gerling didn't talk much about himself, or anything really. And Lieutenant Saunders. About him I know nada. Not even his home town. For some reason, this saddens me. These men have been knocked right off the surface of the earth. And at any moment, this could happen to me. There's only one person who would be left to remember my face. Clarissa. That's it. My child wouldn't even remember me. It feels selfish to mourn my own death at a time like this, but these thoughts push themselves into my head. Like a broken faucet, they drip, drip, drip their way into my mind no matter what I try to think about.

Sergeant Oliphant presses PLAY on the battered little boom box from Common Tent 1. A shrill, tinny version of "Taps" squawks out of the speakers. An honor guard shoulders rifles and fires off a volley of salutes. Then, just after the last shots die away, the CD player skips. The final measures of the song hiccup and judder. The trumpet makes a series of blats. The sergeant jumps forward and swats the player until the song stops. We are dismissed.

27

The helicopter arrives at noon. The sky is the color of a nicotine-stained finger. We hear its engines long before it arrives. A dozen of us gather near the pad, hoping it brings good news, but the sand blown up from the rotor wash is so bad that we have to duck inside the garage to escape. We had all hoped for a few helicopters, but they've only sent us one. Cox and I unload crates of ammo and machine parts. More armor kits for the Humvees. This news raises a small cheer among the loitering Joes, although we've heard rumors that they aren't worth a shit. And for some reason, ten cases of strawberry gelatin. Strangest of all are the boxes of expensive Oakley sunglasses. Sergeant Guzman tells us there's one for each man. Back home, these babies sell for about $250. No cigarettes, no toilet paper, just some crappy dessert and overpriced sunglasses. But we do get a new Military Intelligence guy. He's a man in his early thirties with a nail-brush moustache and his own pair of expensive orange-tinted wraparounds. When he appears, the dawdlers melt into the background. No cheer for him. Thirty seconds on the ground, and already he's about as popular as a wet fart. He does not acknowledge our salutes as he steps out of the chopper. When Lieutenant Blankenship salutes him as he comes across the parade ground, it provokes a half-hearted hand movement from the new officer. It's only then that I notice his captain's bars.

"Do you think we have a new CO?" I ask Cox.

He just shrugs.

On my fourth trip back to the helicopter, I hear some shouting.

Nevada and Boyette carry a black body bag toward the trailers. At first I think it must be Gerling. They set it down near the steps and both the lieutenant and the new MI captain come out and inspect it. The lieutenant nudges it with the toe of his boot and Boyette unzips the bag just enough to expose the face inside. It's the boy's uncle. Shit, I think, this ain't right. Both prisoners dying in the same night?

As Nevada passes on his way back to the clinic, I call him over. "What happened?"

"The old hajji did himself."

"How?" I ask, incredulous.

"Hung himself with his pants." Nevada sticks out his tongue, cocks his head to one side and holds up an imaginary rope. "Yup. I cut him down myself. Godawful-smelling little fucker, but crafty, I'll give him that."

"He chewed through his flexcuffs?"

"Fuck if I know. He sure as hell got them off somehow. And it ain't an old wives' tale what they say about hung people."

"What do you mean? What old wives' tale?"

"He was giving me the tent-pole salute when I found him." Nevada makes a face. "Ugly old dwarf left this earth a squirting his business out both ends. He must of saved it up for some time, cause—"

"All right, Nevada," I say, waving him off. "Jesus."

Nevada heads back to the clinic, snickering. I don't believe it. There's no way that old man could have gotten out of his flexcuffs. They're hard to cut with a Gerber knife. Ahmed. That's what I think of first. Maybe getting rid of people who could identify him. But I don't see how the hell Ahmed could have gotten a key to the cell. I bend to lift another crate and notice Lopez standing outside the office trailer with the new MI guy. He's talking and making big, frantic gestures with his hands. After a moment, they both stop and turn my way. Lopez raises his arm and points toward me. Shit.

28

My fatigues are soaked through with sweat and my armpits feel chafed and sore from moving crates in the blowing sand and 115-degree heat. The cool air beneath the fort feels nice at first, but then I start to shiver. After I spoke with Nevada, I realized I had never given the lieutenant back the key with the pink band. I want to see the cell again, so I slip away after the helicopter is off-loaded and leave Dyson and Studdie to strap Kellen in for the ride back to the hospital at HQ. I feel a pang of envy when I hear the engines power up and take him away. I'm careful to make sure no one sees me go into the old fort.

My flashlight flickers, and I pound it against the heel of my palm until it settles. Its light is dim and failing and so is the daylight too, so I jog down the stairs and make my way along the corridor to the holding cell. The door looks even worse than it did the last time I was here. I have to put my weight on the key just to turn the lock. It nearly snaps off inside. The hinges are pulling away from the crumbling brick and the door scrapes the floor when I drag it open. A deep arc has been gouged out of the packed dirt. The smell inside is as bad as I remember. I see the damp outline of the old man's body in one corner and a puddle of murky liquid in the center of the room. A shred of fabric hangs from a beam in the center of the ceiling. It is a good nine feet from the floor. I try to imagine how the old man, once free from his cuffs, could have managed it. I go back to the door and run the beam of my flashlight along the hinges. The metal around the screws has been scraped shiny, as though someone took a knife to it, and the screwheads are flattened and misshapen. Stripped. There's a hammer mark in the metal beside the middle hinge. Someone took the door down. But here's the rub: this door is very fucking heavy. It would be impossible to hold it up and screw the hinges back to the frame at the same time. This is a two-man job. At least.

Behind me, someone coughs and boots scrape in the hallway. My heart wriggles in my chest as though it's trying to escape. I shuffle through my worn stack of excuses but don't come up with anything plausible. I find myself hoping it's Lopez, so I can thump him one and get it over with. The man who appears surprises me completely.

"Private Durrant," the new MI guy says, "right?"

"Yes, sir," I say, saluting.

"Lieutenant Blankenship tells me you interrogated the prisoners." His sunglasses, I'm glad to see, are pushed up on his head, but it's hard to see his eyes in the murky light. Even so, I can feel them scrutinizing me.

"Yes, sir."

"You'll have to brief me on that some time." He pulls a package of Marlboro Reds out of his shirt pocket. "Smoke?"

"No, sir. Thank you, but I quit."

"Too bad," he says, cupping his hand to light one. His eyes are a watery, washed-out blue and completely blank. "Do you like it here on this base, Durrant?"

"No, sir," I say.

He laughs and steps back into the gloom of the hallway. I follow. The beam of my flashlight twitches. So do my hands.

"Unhappy with the leadership here? Is that the problem?"

"No, sir," I say, baffled by the direction this conversation is taking. "Not at all." I can't believe he thinks I'm going to rat out my commanding officer. Even if I hated his guts, which I don't, I would never do that. This man is either extremely disingenuous or extremely naïve.

"It's all right to tell me, you know."

"Really, sir, I have no complaints."

He sets the pace. We walk a few steps, pause, walk a few more. Somewhere above us, a soldier shouts orders.

"What about the other men? Are they like you, unhappy here?"

"It's a war, sir," I say, bristling a bit. "No one wants to be here."

"Of course it is."

He leaves it at that and I say nothing more. Up a few steps the corridor twists around on itself. My flashlight goes dead. Obscenities bounce about inside my skull. I have a sudden urge to thump the captain on the back of his head, and, as if he senses this, he swings around to look at me. Water drips in the darkness ahead. He shines his flashlight in my face. I sense his eyes moving over my features. They feel like roaches skittering across my skin. He turns without a word and moves on. As we mount the stairs toward daylight, he flips down his sunglasses. I realize I don't know his name. At the landing right before ground level, he stops again to scratch under the band of his hat. I can hear the sand scrape against his scalp.

"We've been getting strange reports about this base, Private," he says. His voice sounds bruised and hoarse. "If you can think of anything you might want to tell me about that, I'd appreciate it. It might save you a bit of hassle further down the road."

This is vague enough to be intimidating, although I genuinely have no idea what he might be referring to. This whole war seems strange to me, as it must to every soldier in every war, but this is something new. I step past him into the sunlight. It feels like a blessing.

"I really can't think of anything, sir," I say in a false, cheerful voice.

"Has he ever spoken to you about his home life?" His tone is flat, like he's reading from a note card. "About his religious upbringing, his family history?"

"Who, sir?" I ask.

"Lieutenant Blankenship. I think you know what I'm talking about, soldier."

"No, sir," I say.

He can look it up in the lieutenant's personnel file if he wants to know this shit. I don't much care for the lieutenant, but I don't want to see him run down by some creepy Army spook either. "I can't say that he has. He's very careful about fraternizing with the enlisted men and all that. Lieutenant Blankenship is strictly by the book. A seven-dash-eight man all the way."

"H'mm," he says. "Yes. Well, if something occurs to you, come find me. I'll always make time for you, Private."

"Thank you, sir," I say, although thankful is the last thing I feel.

"You'll thank me later on," he says. Behind their orange lenses, his eyes flick about like a lizard's. "When this is all over."

"Durrant," someone shouts in an angry voice, and I happily run to meet it.

29

It's my talk with the MI captain that does it. I start wondering about the reasons for all of this. What the fuck are we doing here? That kind of thing. Usually, I try to quash this line of thinking before it goes too far. It ruins job performance. Today this thought sneaks in like a cat burglar and starts stealing my attention. Not only that, it brings along some buddies. Now, don't get me wrong, I'm a patriotic guy. I love my country. I stand up and put my hand over my heart during baseball games when they play the anthem. I vote. Well, sometimes. I got all riled up when the towers fell just like everybody else. But that's not the reason I enlisted. My life wasn't going anywhere. Each day seemed duller than the last one. I'd pissed away the money my grandpa left me, and the rest was locked up in investments I'd been told would take months to turn into cash. As it turned out, I got it three days after I'd signed my life away. My recruiter thought this was a laugh riot. He busted a gut when I told him the news. But I needed money pronto and the Army offered a signing bonus. My landlord had threatened to evict me, they'd turned my cable off, and I started each day by picking cigarette butts out of my overflowing ash trays just for the little hit of nicotine in them. The only skills I had were base-jumping, beer-swilling, and bullshitting. I looked in the paper and saw I had a choice between working at Arby's or trying to get a union card for the docks. Shitty or shittier. I was tired of being Toby Durrant, this broke nobody without a family. A sad sack. A loser. At the time, I'd thought that if I were a part of the best army in the history of the world, I'd be somebody. I'd know my place in the world. I'd belong to something important.

Basic sucked. Someone tells you they enjoyed Basic, they're either lying or brain-damaged or a drill sergeant. But when I came out of it, I felt pretty gung-ho. I was proud to be an infantryman, and I wanted to do a good job. A new concept for me. The only activity I'd ever truly tried my hardest at was base-jumping. So I actually studied weapons manuals and the seven-dash-eight before I went to bed. And the weapons training gave me a serious hard-on. Even after I was kicked out of jump school, I still got a thrill each morning putting on my desert cammies. And when they shipped me over to the sandbox, my attitude was simple: This is my job. I'm going to do the best I can. I'm a soldier, not a politician, so I'm not going to worry about what the suits and ties are doing. Maybe there are WMDs out in the desert. It's a big place. Who am I to judge? But over time, this place wears on you. You start to wonder. You try to swallow your doubts and get on with your work. Or at least I do. I did. I don't know. It's not the hajjis that make me wonder, it's our leaders. The hajjis don't want someone else's army occupying their country. That I understand. Neither would I. Since I've been keeping track, our reasons for coming here have changed five or six times. No one even knows what a victory over here means. Doc Greer likes to say we'll leave when Kurkbil is a Burger King town.

Most of the guys don't question why we're here, but the ones who do seem to do it every day. It'll paralyze you and I know it, but today I just can't stop. I pick at these ideas the way you would a fresh mosquito bite. It's one of the worst things a soldier can do while still in-theater, because it'll kill your will to fight. And it's true. I've seen it. For a while, it almost ruined Hazel.

It happened like this. Some piece of shiny brass up the chain of command decided we had someone on the bad-guy list hiding out in Kurkbil. This was fairly early on in my time here. I'd only been at FOB Cornucopia for a few weeks. Before I came to the Cob, I was temporarily stationed in the capital, and I saw more action there than some soldiers see in their entire tour. The Cob was still at full strength. At least five platoons. One night, early, maybe 0100, they sent a couple of squads out to the village in four thin-skinned Humvees. We didn't even have armor kits yet. Those wouldn't come for some time. Our named area of interest was a house on the edge of town. A ramshackle old place plastered over with yellow stucco, but big. Practically a palace, in this part of the country. It belonged to the Habib brothers, the ones who'd owned the toy factory; but by the time we came calling, three families of squatters had since moved in. We set up a perimeter around the house in silence. I came with a weapons squad and carried a squad automatic weapon, a SAW, a big old breechloader that can throw out enough lead to chop a tree in two. We stacked left and right along the outer wall, blew the gate, and hit the front door with a battering ram. Nevada carried the ram and bitched about how heavy it was the whole time. Boyette and Salis watched the other point of egress, the back door, just in case somebody tried to rabbit. This was the first time I'd gotten to use night-vision goggles, and I was pumped to the gills with adrenaline. At one point I realized I was shouting and didn't know how long I'd been doing it. It was that kind of raid. Hazel and I and a few others cleared rooms on the first floor and looked for our target. Shouting, stomping, waving rifles. All we found were women and children. The women cried. The children cried. The babies howled. Some of the guys were none too gentle with these people's belongings. Glass crunched under our boots and cushion stuffing drifted around in the air. The only men in the house were either graybeards in their fucking dotage or kids too young to shave. I remember seeing this one guy named Jackson, long since transferred, bitch-slap a middle-aged woman who wouldn't stop shouting. Hazel saw it too. I had to thump him on the back to get him moving again. He didn't seem all that worked up about it, but it's hard to read a man's expression when he's in full battle rattle.

The intel they'd given us was shit, per usual, but that was none of our concern. Later we found out from bits and pieces of other people's stories that the guy we were looking for wasn't even in Kurkbil that night: he was in a three-star hotel in Jordan. None of this mattered at the time. We were there for a smash and grab. Period. Somebody else could worry about the rest of it. But it was clear to everyone there that the whole op had gone tits-up. This made for hard feelings all around. Again, not so unusual, but frustrating nonetheless.

"All right," the lieutenant leading the charge said, a young guy named Cavanaugh who has since been shipped off to some other FOB. "Tell the rest of those swinging dicks in back to load up. Maybe we can get a little rack time tonight after all."

Hazel followed me around the house. I could see something wasn't right. At some point he'd lost his NVGs. Night-vision goggles. Each time a woman inside the house screamed, he'd twitch his shoulders. And there was a good deal of screaming. I stopped and gave him a close look. His eyes were off somehow, and this worried me. They rolled around in their sockets the way a scared horse's will.

"Durrant," he said, "how long before doing this kind of shit turns us into the bad guys?"

I had no idea how to answer this question, and I told Hazel that.

"Is it too late?" he asked me, pulling on the sleeve of my fatigues. This annoyed me.

"Hazel," I said, "knock that shit off and listen to me. Let's just round up the rest of them, so we can go back to base and rack out. I don't have the energy for this shit right now."

But he couldn't let it drop and I really didn't want to hear it. My eyes burned from lack of sleep. We'd already pulled two night missions that week and three full missions earlier that day. It was only Tuesday. I felt like I was about to collapse and my patience needle had dropped into the red.

"Are we already the bad guys? Doing this kind of shit makes me feel like a Nazi, like, you know, in those old movies where stormtroopers are kicking down doors looking for Jews—"

"Listen, Hazel, these *are* the bad guys we're looking for. Terrorists. Not Jews. Don't be stupid."

I could see Hazel was on the verge of a freakout. His eyes had stopped rolling around, but now he had that wide-eyed, crazed look soldiers will get when they're up to their necks in something hairy. I'd been in that place enough times by then to recognize the look.

"Hazel," I said, "listen. This isn't the time to think about it."

Then he started shouting, "When *is* the time to think about it, huh? After it's all over, after we've done all this bad stuff and we can't take it back?"

I understood how he felt, but it wasn't going to help anybody if he lost his shit now, while we were still technically out on an operation.

"It's not as though we shot anybody, guy."

"Nevada just about lit that kid up on the second floor. You saw that. And Howley knocked the fat woman on the head with the butt of his rifle when she wouldn't get down fast enough. And then Jackson—"

I cut him off. "You're right. That wasn't cool. All I'm saying is, lock it up until we get back. This isn't the fucking time or place to discuss it."

"When?" he shouted, pounding his clenched fists together. Spittle flew out of his mouth with the words. "When *is* the time?"

"I don't fucking know," I yelled back at him. "Now calm the fuck down. We have orders to do this and we're going to finish it. End of story."

"Orders?" His voice broke. We looked at each other. Him panting. Me about to drop with exhaustion. Without once breaking eye contact, he lifted his rifle over his head and laid it on top of a broken refrigerator beside the compound wall. He started unbuttoning his shirt.

"What's that supposed to mean?" I asked him. "You quit?"

Right then, we heard a couple of pops. Small-arms fire on the other side of the house. Hazel just stared at me. Goddammit, I thought, wake up. I slapped him. Not hard. Just enough to get his attention.

"Pick up your fucking rifle," I told him, trying to keep my voice level. "Now."

Hazel did, his eyes still wide and weird. We rounded the house, shouting "Friendlies, friendlies," so they wouldn't shoot us by mistake, and found Boyette hunched over by the back gate, laughing his ass off. This other guy, I can't remember his name now, had shot a cat. He thought it was a mad bomber crawling through the bushes. Salis was laughing so hard, he had bent himself in half over his knees. At first I thought he was puking.

"Hey, guy," I said to Salis, "can I ask you a question?"

"Shoot," he said, still wheezing from his giggle fit.

"What the fuck?"

On the ride back to base, Hazel put his face right up next to my helmet and whispered to me. His breath smelled like wet catshit. "Don't tell anyone about that. Please, Durrant. I just sort of bugged out for a second. It won't happen again."

I told him not to worry. Everyone lost it sometimes. Mum was the word. But what he'd said back there had stirred something up in me. He'd muddied up my thinking. I felt furious, but I couldn't quite figure out where to direct my anger, an aimless anger that made my head feel like it was going to explode.

And now I've got that feeling again. I recognize it, but I can't name it. My hands are sweating so much that I leave a handprint on everything I touch, and my tongue feels like beef jerky. There's nowhere to put it. The cigar box won't take abstractions.

30

Someone calls in a distress code. An attack on a civilian contractor's convoy. They're out past the toy factory on 6A. Maybe twenty-four klicks away. Sergeant Guzman tells us he's taking weapons squad out to provide security until the heavy machinery arrives on the scene. Before we leave, he explains that HQ in Inmar is sending out a few gunships, Kiowas, but they need boots on the ground, now. We take three Humvees. I wish we'd had time to install the armor kits.

As he straps in, Rankin says, "Finally there's something to do around here."

"Careful what you fucking wish for," I tell him.

He just winks and lights up.

But it's true. This is the first bit of action we've had for a while, with the exception of the IED attack. Most of our time's spent waiting for something to happen. You eat, you do bullshit details, you police the FOB, you clean your rifle, you masturbate, you eat again, you clean your rifle, you masturbate, you watch the DVD of *Platoon* for the fiftieth Goddamn time, you go to sleep. Wake up and hit replay. It gets to where most guys break into a smile when they hear a mortar shell fall. At least something's going on.

Whoever it is that attacked the convoy chose a strange ambush location. This part of the Turkish Highway is completely flat. There's no cover for miles. Rankin glasses the horizon as we pull up, moving from sector to sector in his methodical way.

"They got out fast," he says, rubbing his upper lip with the nub of his pinkie. "I don't see a soul."

Pulled up along the shoulder are ten sixteen-wheelers. A couple of the trucks pull two trailers behind them. One of the trucks lies on its side, blocking the highway. As we approach, I notice something strange. I nudge Rankin.

"Is that blood?"

The asphalt is covered in something orange. It looks as though an exotic mold has sprouted up all over the blacktop.

"Nah, that ain't blood." He cracks up. "It's Cheetos."

Sure enough, when we jump out and look for someone to give us a situation report, a sitrep, Cheetos crunch under our boots. They're everywhere. Bags and bags and bags of them. Rankin picks one up and opens it.

"Don't get your trigger finger all gummy," I tell him.

He waggles the bag with his right hand to show me it's safe. "Way ahead of you, D."

Sergeant Guzman shouts and we run to set up a perimeter.

What happened, or what they *say* happened, is this. The driver of the trail vehicle, the last truck in the convoy, thought he saw a flash beside the road and overcorrected to avoid it. Somebody shot at him, he says. The truck went out of control, tipped over and dropped salty snack items all over the asphalt. I'm standing right next to the guy as he tells his story. He's big, sloppy fat, with a beer belly that pooches out over his belt. The guy hasn't shaved in a couple of days and probably hasn't bathed for longer. Stringy brown hair pokes out from under his hat at funny angles. I can smell the liquor on him from ten feet away. I pull Sergeant Guzman aside.

"There's no fucking shooter, Sarge. This guy's shitfaced."

"I know it," Sergeant Guzman says. I can tell by the way he's clenching his jaw that he ain't amused either. Not one bit.

Even so, we search the area, sweeping out into the desert in our Humvees. A complete waste of time. All the other drivers stick to their friend's story.

The cab of the truck reeks of whiskey. Little slivers of glass sparkle on the floormat. Rankin and I investigate, hoping to find a bottle we can salvage. No luck there. We hear the choppers coming long before we see them. That distinctive thud, thud, thud that Kiowas make.

"Shit," Sergeant Guzman says, shading his eyes. "I'll let these guys deal with it." He turns back and looks us over. "Joes," he yells, "get ready to move out."

"What about the truck, Sarge?" I ask him.

"We can't do anything about that. They're sending over some heavy equipment to drag it off. HQ radioed to say they'll be here soon. I want you to be ready to go as soon as their boots are on the ground. I'm sick as hell of looking at this." He stares at the lardo who crashed his truck while he says all this. When the sergeant isn't talking, the muscles in his jaw bulge and tense like he's chewing gum. I thank God it wasn't me who made this mess.

"Hey," Rankin says, as I'm walking back to our ride. "We can't leave without a little booty." He's still munching from his family-size bag of Cheetos.

He's right, I think. It's only fair.

I pull our Humvee up a few yards and we load as many bags as we can. Frito-Lay galore. Every flavor of Doritos from cool ranch to salsa verde, Fritos, Funyuns, Lay's potato chips. We make out like snack bandits.

"Shit," Nevada says, when he sees us unloading back at base. "Why didn't I fucking think of that?"

31

We burn the shit in a rock-strewn field half a klick from the base. Usually, this is a four-man detail, two to keep guard and two to burn the shit, but we're shorthanded today because of the sand cleanup and it's just me and Ahmed. The last guy to get this detail hid about a dozen barrels of shit in a back room of the cement factory, so we've got about twenty barrels to burn. It's hot, filthy work and neither of us says much. The burning fuel oil and the sun combine forces to toast us. Sweat wicks away as soon as it seeps out of my skin. The air doesn't move. The sun sucks the color out of everything except the burn's huge column of black, greasy smoke. It smells distressingly similar to burnt barbecue. I cover my mouth with a bandanna, but I can still smell it, and if I'm smelling it, as my high school biology teacher once pointed out, I'm tasting it. Clumps of ash come floating down and land in my hair. The barrels are filled to the brim, of course, so we end up getting sloshed with shit as well. Ahmed pukes up his breakfast.

I try and ask Ahmed about his family. He grunts and nods. I ask if he's heard about the death of the old man, the prisoner we'd tried to speak with. He looks mildly surprised. Nasty man, is all he says. When I ask him where Baba went, he slaps the backs of his hands together and leaves it at that. Although he's not as cheerful as usual, this doesn't strike me as odd, considering the fact we're burning shit in the middle of the desert. Ahmed seems no more suspicious to me than he did before the boy told me what he'd told me. Our conversation about massing insurgents and spies seems almost preposterous here in the bright, unrelenting light.

When we finish, Ahmed flashes me a tired grin. We share a CamelBak of lukewarm water. The soft, shoulder-slung canteens can hold up to three liters, and we gulp it nearly to the bottom. Ahmed wets his yellow-checked scarf and covers his head with it. I squeeze the last finger of water out of the clear plastic drinking tube and onto my hair. Almost without wanting to, I feel that camaraderie that comes from working hard with another man.

On the drive back to the village, Ahmed asks me if I like girls.

"Yes," I say.

He thinks this over for a moment. "I, too, have a like for girls." When the truck bounces over the ruts in the track, he stutters. "But I do not have a like for the shit."

Before I drop him off at his house, I ask Ahmed why he doesn't choose to live on base like Baba did.

"My family will protect me," he says. "It is very big."

32

The toy factory is utterly still. I park the truck just inside the gate and hope it isn't too visible from the highway. I take out my binoculars and scan the broken windows. Nothing moves. I jump down. Stop. Listen. Something large, maybe a buzzard, flaps up and over the factory. I whistle the opening bars to the song "At the Car Wash," that funky chugging bass line. Somewhere inside the factory, a brick falls, producing an enormous echo in the large empty space. I've brought four MREs, including my favorite—beef enchilada. I walk the length of the factory wall before I go in, following the line of cover, scoping out potential dangers. I click off my rifle's safety. Inside, my footsteps sound huge, like the stomping paws of a monster.

"I have food," I say. My hands sweat; I know she's watching me. I say the word "food" in the local dialect. Still she stays hidden.

The place has been cleaned out, for the most part. All the machinery is gone. Scattered around the cement floor are rusty lengths of wire and twisted iron rebar, pipes and cracked cinderblocks. A pile of headless pink bears rots beside a far door. Broken glass crunches under my boots. The factory floor is twice the size of a high-school gym. At one end, there are large piles of splintered wood and empty crates and oil drums so rusty they look like tubes of dark red lace. A rock bounces off the floor beside me and hits my leg. It doesn't hurt, but someone definitely aimed it at me. A huge smile cracks my face in two. I didn't imagine her. I'm not going crazy with battle fatigue. I can't wait to tell Rankin.

"*Salaam aleikum*," I say and then in English, "I won't hurt you."

I see a flash of movement along the far wall. But I still haven't seen her. Come on, I think, just let me get a glimpse of your face, show me just enough to prove you're real.

"Are you hungry?" I say, trying to make my voice non-threatening.

Something tumbles off the stack of wood at the back of the room and lands with a giant boom. I set the MREs on a window ledge. Before I left the base, I took out the heating packs. The kid won't know how to use them and I don't want her to poison herself by mistake. Just below the window is another pile of rotting teddy bears.

I stand for a long time. Very still. The summer my parents died, I came to live with my grandpa. The two of us tamed a herd of deer by scattering seed corn in a trough at the edge of the wood behind our house. After a month, I could stand and watch them eat from ten feet away. Occasionally they'd raise their heads to look at me before going back to crunching corn. They had huge dark eyes. I gave several of them names. Just before the leaves fell, my grandpa shot the largest of the bucks. I cried when I saw it. He had to trick me into thinking it was hamburger before I'd eat it.

The child remains hidden. This saddens me, and I'm not sure why. I don't doubt I'd do the same if I were in her place. After all, why should she trust me? There's a reason she's hiding out alone in this factory. Twenty minutes pass. Finally, I must go. Somebody will get suspicious if I keep the burn truck away from the base too long. I dropped Ahmed off at his house almost an hour ago. As I'm getting into the truck, I see the MREs disappear from the ledge. Then a small, dirty face appears. We stare at each other for a long moment before I turn the ignition and back out of the factory yard. The child's eyes seem abnormally large in her shrunken face and as black as a night in the desert. She's real.

33

The first mortar knocks me out of my cot. It must have been close. My ears ring. Rankin is on guard duty, so I'm alone. It must be around 0300. I pull on my pants and boots. Two more land on the other side of the base. I feel the explosions in my feet. A siren shrieks. Two men pass my tent at a dead run, heading toward the bunker. Another mortar lands. This one closer. They're so Goddamn loud. Sergeant Oliphant shouts orders on the other side of the parade ground. I grab my rifle and move.

The mortars are coming from two directions, so it's hard to know which areas to avoid. I run in a zig-zag pattern toward the officers' trailers.

"Durrant," someone shouts.

It's Rankin. He waves me over to a Humvee, and I jump in. Boyette rides shotgun.

"I've been looking all over for you," Rankin says. "We're supposed to take the—"

An explosion near the old fort makes the windows rattle.

"Fucking dune coons—" Boyette starts.

Rankin cuts him off with a look. He has about thirty pounds on Boyette, but I wouldn't count Boyette out in a fight. I once saw him take on a giant back in Basic and whip his ass soundly. Even so, Boyette shuts up.

"Oliphant wants us to send some grenades their way," Rankin says, turning in his seat to look at me.

"Goody." Boyette rubs his hands together.

Rankin catches my eye in the rearview mirror and shakes his head. He mouths, *Fucking Boyette.*

By the time we reach the perimeter wall, the mortar fire on the far side of the compound has stopped. We climb the tower with our rifles swinging from our shoulders. The night has gone silent. The only sound in the entire world is the clickety-clack of our weapons tapping the ladder. Studdie crouches on the platform at the top, his rifle pointed up at the hills. He's hunched over, and in the dark he resembles a beanbag chair. I lean against the railing so I can snap my night-vision goggles onto my K-pot and click them on. Luckily, I scrounged up some new batteries this afternoon. One more thing we're running low on.

It's a clear night and the moon is fat. Plenty of ambient starlight. When the sky is overcast, the NVGs aren't worth a shit. I scan the hilltops, looking for movement. On this side of the base, the perimeter wall is built right up against a series of low rocky hills, which gradually become steeper until they run into the Noses.

Although it's a nuisance to have these hills just beyond the base wall, they provide very little cover for anyone trying to attack us. Except for a few sparse clumps of thorny bushes, almost nothing grows here, and the inclines are covered with loose purple shale that has a tendency to slide. No one likes going on patrols in this area, because the chunks of shale can be sharp and the rock is rotten and unstable. Perfect for ankle-twisting. The good grazing land starts about ten klicks to the north, so we rarely see anyone walking around out here; if we do, it's almost certain they're up to no good. I give the horizon a quick sweep. Nothing moving. Rankin nudges me with the butt of his rifle and motions for me to get down. On the other side of the base, someone fires off a quick three-shot burst. And then another.

"What took you so long?" Studdie asks Rankin. His eyes are wide and worried. This surprises me. Studdie usually comes off as being gung-ho. Only a couple of days ago, I heard him telling someone in the mess tent that he couldn't wait to bag his first hajji. I try to remember if I've ever seen him in a firefight. I haven't.

Rankin shrugs and flips on his night-vision goggles.

"Why aren't you firing, Combat?" Boyette demands. He packs his cheek with a thick wad of Skoal, and when he spits for the first time he lets the long line of saliva stretch in the breeze until it sticks to Studdie's arm.

"Shit, man, you're getting your snoose juice on me."

"How 'bout you get started with the bang bang, hoss." Boyette makes a gun with his finger and thumb and pokes Studdie in the belly each time he says bang.

"I don't want to draw attention with tracer rounds."

"What the fuck?" Boyette says. "Is this a war, or ain't it? Jesus Goddamn fucking Christ." He shoulders his M4 and clicks off the safety. "You're useless, Combat. Sit your sorry ass down over there, so you don't get in the way of real soldiers."

"Wait," I say, putting my hand on the stock of Boyette's weapon.

"You too? Jesus, Durrant."

"No, wait until they fire, so we can get their position. Otherwise we'll just be wasting ammo."

"Get their position from what? A fucking mortar tube?" Boyette says, his face crumpled in disgust.

"The sound will carry," I say.

My NVGs choose this moment to go on the fritz. Images shudder and go blank. These things are great when they're working, but all you have to do is drop them once and they're done for. And I've been babying mine ever since I got them. Damn. I toss them in a corner.

Studdie points to the northeast. "Up there on that hill. Down about a hundred yards from the top."

Just as he finishes speaking, we hear a pop and then the familiar whine of an incoming shell. Boyette swings around and fires off a few triple bursts. Rankin does the same. I fire two HEDPs in quick succession—high-explosive dual-purpose rounds that have the same destructive force as a grenade.

"Get some," Boyette yells. "Get some."

The explosions from the grenades light the hill just enough to show a group of five men scrambling up the rocks for better cover. I grit my teeth and fire another round. The incoming mortar lands about fifty yards away, throwing up gouts of sand and shaking the tower. My first grenade hits the hill a dozen yards below the men. If I'm lucky, one of them might have been nicked by a chunk of flying shale. The second grenade disappears without a sound. A dud.

"I can't see shit," I say.

"There's some flares in that box under the radio." Studdie points but doesn't move away from the corner.

Rankin cracks the lid and hands me one. We take off the caps and screw them onto the detonators. I slam mine into the metal railing as hard as I can. Pop. Rankin follows. Pop. One green, one red. The entire hillside seems to shift and tremble in the swaying light of the flares. They drop slowly, rocking beneath their parachutes. Up at the top of the hill, several men head toward the cover of a large rock. I shoulder my M4 and throw another HEDP round at them. Boyette fires his rifle. Tracers flit through the dark. Long red lines that seem to hang in the air. When my grenade hits, one of the hunched figures on the hill is flung backwards several feet. We hear a distant shout.

"Fucking A!" Boyette shouts, thumping me on the back. He nudges Studdie with his boot. "You don't even deserve to be called combat. You're more of a stinky little fobbit."

"Shut up," Studdie says, but his voice sounds as if he's agreeing with him.

The three of us continue to fire at the top of the hill. I load and shoot as quickly as I can. Thud, thud, thud. There is a ferocious beauty in the lines of fire traced across the sky and the bright bursts of orange and white. The flares paint the hillside green and red. I am mesmerized, no longer thinking in terms of bodies and blood. For a moment, it is all just light and sparks. Studdie shakes my pant leg.

"Incoming," he shouts.

This one sounds close. Studdie hops over Rankin's back as he kneels to reload, skitters to the ladder, and starts down. Halfway to the ground, the mortar hits. It lands about three yards away. A bit of

shrapnel clangs off the metal railing. The tower teeters. I'm sure it's
going to fall. I clench my jaw and prepare to crash. Boyette grunts and
goes down on one knee, wheezing and clutching his chest. Studdie
loses his grip and falls nearly fifteen feet, landing flat on his back. It
sounds exactly like someone punching a baseball glove.

"You hit?" Rankin kneels beside Boyette.

"My arm. I'm okay. Shoot the fuckers, combat. Don't mind me."

Rankin and I fire off grenade rounds. I didn't realize he had an
M203 launcher on his rifle. Then I see it's Studdie's. He must have
left it when he ran. One of the grenades hits just below the tight knot
of men crouching beneath a large rock at the very top of the hill.
The second blasts into the rock above them. Their screams carry on
the crisp night air. Rankin fires again. And then shouts that he's out
of rounds. I hand him my assault pack of grenades because he's a far
better shot than I am with the launcher, a clumsy weapon at best and
almost useless from this distance. It's amazing we've done so well. He
fires twice more. The men have dispersed, but he manages to hit their
cache of mortars.

The hill bursts into brief flame. Even from here I can smell the
bitter, burnt-plastic smell of Iranian-made mortars. The large rock
near the crest of the hill slides, then tumbles down into the ravine
below. The last round is a white star cluster. It does nothing more
than light up the sky, a very expensive bottle rocket.

"Shit," Rankin says.

"I should have told you," I say. "I put one in the bottom of the bag."

He shrugs.

"Nice shooting, combat," Boyette says, grinning and pressing the
heel of his hand against his shoulder. "They're standing around up
there wondering where their assholes just went."

I suddenly remember Studdie. Oh, shit. I jump across Boyette's
legs to the other side of the tower. Studdie still lies flat on his back
about five feet from the ladder. Legs stretched wide and arms akimbo.
It doesn't look as though he's moved since he landed. I can't tell if his
eyes are open.

"Studdie," I shout down, "are you all right?"

I wait, staring down at his sprawled form. There's no response. I look over at Rankin. He shakes his head. "Fucking Studdie," he says softly.

"What the fuck was he doing climbing down the ladder in the middle of a firefight anyway?" Boyette asks. His voice breaks. I'm shocked to see he's crying. He turns his face away and looks out toward the Noses.

And then.

"Feeeeeeet." It's Studdie. He makes this sound until his voice cracks.

"Can you move?" I yell down to him.

He doesn't answer.

Boyette and Rankin move to the edge of the tower and look down with me.

"Feeeeeeeet," Studdie shouts again.

"I'm going down," I tell them. "He probably just hurt his foot."

When I get to the ground, I flash my light at him. His eyes shine red like a roadside raccoon's. I take a knee, put my hand on his shoulder. Studdie watches without a word.

"Do you hurt?" I ask him.

"I don't feel a Goddamn thing." Tears make bright streaks from eye to ear, carving clean lines into the grime on his cheeks. "It's like somebody cut off my body."

"Can you move anything?"

"I've only slept with one girl in my whole life." He blinks furiously. "One fucking girl. That's all. One fucking time. The week before I left for this shithole. It was the best thing I ever did. Ever."

"Studdie, man. Don't worry. It might just be a pinched nerve or something. Doctors can do all kinds of crazy shit now. They'll fix you up. Good as new."

We look at each other and quietly consider this lie.

"Greer wants to know, do you need a stretcher," Rankin shouts down.

Orange pinpricks on the hill. A bullet clangs off the ladder. A couple of distant pops. I duck.

"Tell him," I shout, "tell him bring a backboard. Fast."

"One fucking time," Studdie says. "And now I'll never do it again." Snot bubbles in his nostrils. I wipe it off with my sleeve.

34

Here's a filthy, dirty little secret that combat vets will almost never tell a civilian. And truly, anyone who's fired a weapon in combat wouldn't even stop to consider something so obvious. It's like getting excited over the sudden discovery that humans need air to breathe. This is it: we love doing this shit. Guns, blood, grenades. All of it. As good soldiers, I know we're supposed to pretend we only fire our guns and blow up stuff out of duty, and that really killing a man and destroying his family's home is something we only do out of awful necessity. But that's a lie. It just isn't true. We love this shit.

Those shrill women on afternoon talk shows are right about the reasons for this. And it shouldn't really surprise anyone who gives it more than a moment's thought. This is going to sound like such a greasy whopper of a cliché that I'm almost embarrassed to bring it up, but it's the truth: I've been trained since birth to love what I do. I've been playing with guns since I was three years old. One of my first post-toddler toys was a squirt gun. I shot the hell out of that thing. Later, I got a pellet gun. And then a .22. The blood may sicken us, the pain and misery of those afflicted may horrify us, the noise and destruction might strip the insulation right off our nerve wires, and yet. And still. I relish the sound of small-arms fire. The hiccup of an M16. The smell of cordite gives me a hard-on. There's nothing better than the thwock of a grenade coming out of my launcher and the big orange boom when it hits. I fucking love to blow shit up. A firefight is the kick to end them all. Every single one. My body thrills to it even as my head shouts, get the fuck away before you get hit. The world takes on an intensity it never possessed before. I suppose it's traditional to compare this feeling to sex or religion, but to be honest I never felt anything close to this in bed and certainly never in a pew. Before going into battle, I never realized that a cooling engine block contained so many sounds, that dirt could be that yellow, that blood could be that red.

All of us, down to the last swinging dick, have a little of the Boyette in us. At the oddest, scariest times, I'm surprised to find a weird joy creeping up on me, slipping in through my ears, in through my eyes. In a firefight, time goes back to feeling the way it did when I was eight. The moments s t r e t c h. Merely living in a combat zone will do it. Even when I'm not fighting, days last months and months last years. And this is why: I am here. Right in the center of my life. I am occupying this moment and then the next in a way I've never done before and will never do again. Even on the dullest days—and believe me, most days as a soldier are dull—time transforms.

And the reason for this? At any moment, I might pick up my rifle and kill somebody. Shoot some poor bastard right between the eyes. End somebody's life faster than it takes to say the words. Flip that over. I could be killed in an instant, unaware, some afternoon when I've just settled into the latrine for a quick wank. I can say in all honesty that I hate it here. I hate war. I hate what it does to us, what it does to this country, and what it does to the families of civilians who live here. I hate the way it fucks up my head. I'm disgusted by the idea of murdering someone I don't know, for vague reasons that our leaders change each time they appear on TV. But that wouldn't be the whole story. Because even as I'm hating it with every inch of my guts, and I'm talking about the exact same instant, I'm loving it with all my heart.

35

Later that night as I'm spelling Rankin so he can catch a little rack at the back of the tower, I hear somebody mumbling on the Motorola radio Boyette left behind in his assault pack when they dragged him off to the clinic. Doc Dyson had to force him to go. Boyette didn't think the wound was all that bad. A bee sting, he kept calling it. Doc shoved him into the Humvee. I could hear Boyette yelling as they drove off, "I want to do some more shooting." Studdie wouldn't say a word, no matter what Dyson asked him. Rankin and I helped slip the backboard under him and lift him into the vehicle. Studdie's eyes stuck to mine the whole time, as if I could fix it, like there was some magic I could do. It made my stomach shrivel down to the size of a bean. When I asked Dyson what he thought, he shook his head and climbed behind the wheel. Later, we saw a chopper come in. I heard over the radio that it took out two men—Studdie and a guy named Wendell from the other weapons squad. Wendell got hit in the cheek with shrapnel. The chopper caught some tracer fire as it left but kept on going. Rankin and I watched in silence. I'd promised Studdie we'd meet up in the States when I got back, but I think we both knew it'd never happen.

Rankin and I were ordered to stay behind and pull an OP, an observation post, for the rest of the night. The lieutenant has every guard tower manned. The whole base is alert, watching. It seems like a waste. I take out the radio and dial up the volume. It's Salis.

"Yours truly, a satisfied salesman in Wisconsin."

A different person laughs.

"You want me to read you another one? Over," Salis says.

"Roger that, motherfucker." Now I recognize the voice. It's Nevada.

"Dear Penthouse Forum: Last week I had one of the strangest experiences of my life. I am a twenty-three-year-old widow. This past year I was forced to take over my husband's business after he died in a car accident." Salis snickers. "You're gonna like this, over."

"Just read it, over," Nevada says.

Salis continues, lowering his voice for effect. "When most people think of widows, they imagine gray-haired old biddies, but I'm five-foot-one and weigh just a tad over a hundred pounds. My auburn hair hangs all the way down to my waist. I like to keep fit by jogging and yoga. One morning while running, I happened to pass a young man in an Army T-shirt. His muscles—"

Someone in the next guard tower down shouts, hooah.

I turn the radio off. The perimeter of the base has turned into a giant circle-jerk. Jesus.

36

The dark eye of my rifle barrel looks out over the purple hills and keeps watch. Beside me, Rankin shifts under his poncho and mumbles. Sometimes when I'm alone but for some racked-out soldier on duty with me way up on a teetering observation post, I imagine everything I see is from the vantage of that black hole at the end of my barrel. A small circle of delayed threat. I do not look out on the world around me as an American soldier or a man or even a human. I am simply a weapon waiting to go off, and everything that comes into my field of vision also comes into my rifle sights. When I first arrived at FOB Cornucopia, Nevada told me that if you looked into the barrel of your loaded rifle long enough, really stared down into the heart of your weapon, you'd see the place and time of your own death. I laughed it off, thinking he was just giving me shit. Yeah, I said, it'd probably be right then, because it's pretty fucking stupid to look into the barrel of a loaded gun. He pressed his lips tight and shook his head. I wasn't ready for real war wisdom yet. And he pitied me for it.

Rankin snores as softly as a cat. I scan the hills sector by sector. I make sure Rankin is really sleeping. Then I flip my weapon around, eject the chambered round, and click on the safety. The wind is cold enough to numb my earlobes and the tip of my nose. The air smells clean for once, like an ice cube. I tug my neck gaiter up around my ears. The gunmetal feels frosty enough to pull away some skin. I close my left eye and stare into the center of my rifle. I stare hard. Hoping for a comfortable bed and a sleeping Clarissa. This is what I want to see. This is what I'm straining to find. Want to know what I really see? Nothing. The inside of my gun is as black as an empty sky on a cold, dry night in the desert. That's what I see. Nothing.

37

During the burn this morning, Ahmed asks me if anyone got hurt in the attack. I don't like the look in his eye when he asks me. I don't like it at all. So I lie. Nobody, I tell him. Just cuts and bruises. His obvious disappointment is disgusting. More and more, I have to make a real effort not to smack this guy. The truth is different. Studdie is down at HQ in Inmar awaiting a flight to Germany and surgery on his broken back, and Wendell is in a hospital in the capital. Bulletproof Boyette, however, is up and around with his arm in a sling. He's more than willing to show you his wound if you ask him, despite Doc Dyson's attempts to keep him from messing with it. Boyette's taken to calling it his fuck-me wound.

"This is going to make a sick-looking scar. Back home when girls see this, they'll be wanting to fuck me like crazy," he explained to the mess tent this morning.

No one else got hurt.

After dropping off Ahmed, I risk a quick trip to the factory. I whistle the chorus from the song "We Are Family," hoping she'll come out, but the building is silent. Today I bring a plastic bottle of water and five more MREs. I set them down beneath the window and wander back toward the factory office. The door hangs on one hinge. At the bottom there is a foot-shaped hole. I smell something strange and sour I can't identify. The office contains several metal desks and a broken chair. On the wall is a picture of the deposed president. His moustache is as glossy as a terrier's coat, and he looks well fed and content. I thump his forehead with my middle finger. At least we got rid of you, I tell him. The floor is swept clean. On the third desk, I discover a curious collection of rocks and shards of metal and bits of colored glass. They are arranged in the shape of a star. I open a drawer. Someone has laid out a row of feathers according to size. In the drawer below this, I find a necklace made from purple and blue button eyes, strung along insulated copper wiring. I put it back and shut the drawer. I am just about to leave when I notice something in the back corner of the room. At first I think it is a covered body—my heart gallops—but when I look closer, I see it is a bed made from plastic sheeting stuffed with dismembered toy bears. It still holds the imprint of a small body. I bend down and sniff it.

Something hisses.

I wheel and aim my rifle.

She crouches in the doorway and bares her teeth like a hungry wolverine. Neither of us moves. I let go of the rifle and let the barrel swing down toward the floor. She hisses again but with less insistence. I hold up my hands and greet her in Arabic. *Salaam aleikum.*

"I don't want to hurt you," I say.

She takes a step back, glancing over her shoulder. This is the first good look I've gotten of her since that day after the IED attack. Her face is filthy and her hair hangs down in matted clumps. Her makeshift dress appears to be made from the skins of the stuffed animals the factory once made. Her feet are wrapped in rubber tubing and tied onto her ankles with curling loops of phone cord. She smells strongly of wet dog.

"I brought more food. Did you like those MREs?"

She crouches in a defensive posture but doesn't run away.

"What's your name?" I point to my chest. "I'm Toby. Toby." Then I point to her. She flinches, so I pound my sternum with my fist. Once for each syllable. "Toby."

Slowly, she stands upright again, scratching at her head. I expect she has lice. Her knees and elbows are covered in scabs, and one of her eyes is puffy and red. I'm overwhelmed by an emotion I can't identify. Her parents must be dead. No other relatives? The villagers have their own problems. They don't need another mouth. Or perhaps they cast her out. What has she been eating up until now?

I point to her again. "Name?"

She steps back. Something about the way she moves seems distinctly masculine. I can't quite place it. It could be the set of the shoulders. Whatever it is, it makes me think. Maybe she is a he.

"How about I just call you Herman? Huh? How's that sound, Herman?"

Herman yawns.

"I don't have any parents either, Herman. Mine died in a car wreck. My grandpa took me in. His name was Herman too. Then he died. His liver finally quit on him. We're both orphans.

"What awful shit happened to you, Herman? Why are you living here?"

Herman cocks his head to one side and sneezes.

Oh, right, I think, I should give him the candy bar. All kids love candy bars. This particular Snickers came from one of the boxes that fell off the snack truck. The last one. Rankin and Boyette ate all the rest. I dig it out of my cargo pocket. It's flattened and melted looking. Herman flinches at the movement and prepares to take off. I hold it out to him, but he doesn't move. I set it down and step back. Herman eyes me, then the candy bar, then me again. In a move so fast it's a blur, Herman snatches it and vanishes. One moment he's standing in the doorway picking at an elbow scab, and the next he's gone. I walk out onto the factory floor. A board falls at the far end of the room, but he's nowhere to be seen.

At the doorway, I smell something burnt. I follow it to the pile of splintered wood heaped beside the back wall. Behind it, Herman has arranged a circle of broken bricks for a fire pit. The crumpled wrappers from a few cherry energy bars and a stack of half-melted MRE bags lie in a neat pile beside an old plastic bucket. I look inside. This answers my question about Herman's diet. A heap of burnt feathers and blackened bones. I shake it around a bit. Three large rat pelts. I wonder if there isn't some way I could bring Herman back to the base. Maybe I could bribe Ahmed to say Herman is his cousin.

38

Rankin decides I need to go on the offensive. Strike back at Lopez. We've just come in from a sleepless night of area patrols. Someone snuck onto the base just after dinner, around 2000 hours, and torched two Humvees. The lieutenant sent us across the wire to look for them. No luck. We circled the base in thin-skinned Humvees looking for ghosts. I'm so tired I don't even bother wiping myself down with Wet-Naps before falling backwards onto my cot. I get my boots off, barely. Rankin, on the other hand, paces around the tent, tapping the canvas with his index finger as he talks. Oh God, I think, whatever it is you're planning, I'm too fucking beat for it tonight, friend.

"I'm willing to sacrifice Uday," he tells me, pulling out the plastic container where the scorpion lives.

"I don't get you."

"Let me borrow your Gerber knife and I'll show you."

Rankin immobilizes the scorpion by grabbing its thorax with a pair of pliers. Then, very gently, he uses the blade of my knife to trim off the venomous stinger from the end of its tail. He smiles like a dentist. A drop of poison drips from the end. With his lighter, Rankin burns the stinger in an ashtray.

"Now," he says, "it's kiddie-proof."

Then, with a bottle of white correction fluid he's swiped from the Comm Trailer, Rankin paints the unfortunate creature, head to mangled tail, with thin white stripes.

"Why the hell are you doing that? Won't that stuff kill it?" I ask him.

"So he knows it ain't no accident."

"Why the stripes? Why not just paint the whole thing white?"

"You're a white man, ain't you?" He points at his chest with the brush from the correction-fluid bottle. "And I'm black."

39

The scorpion is content to curl up beneath Lopez's pillow and rest. Rankin and I waste no time hanging around: thirty seconds and we're out. There's no doubt in my mind that this will make matters far worse, but I must admit it's extremely satisfying.

40

The new MI captain steps around our tent, sunglasses riding low on his nose. Both of us jump up and fire off salutes. We've been sitting in PX lawn chairs out in front of our tent, cleaning our gear and waiting to hear Lopez scream. How long has this asshole been here listening to us? I do a quick run-through of our conversation. Rankin asked me how I got kicked out of the Language Institute. I'd never told him, because it embarrassed me. But the reason was simple enough. After Clarissa phoned to tell me she was pregnant, I went AWOL so I could go see her. Rankin didn't have to tell me it was a chump move. If it hadn't been for that, I'd probably still be back in Virginia, translating intercepted cell-phone conversations. So, nothing incriminating for the captain's spy file. Nothing he couldn't find out from looking in the official one in the lieutenant's cabinet. The captain cracks a smile.

"Sir," we say.

He returns the salute in a lazy sort of way and sits down on my lawn chair. Rankin and I continue to stand at attention while he glances around at the stacks of stuff I've pulled out to clean. He looks over the contents of our tent as though they're his. I try to catch Rankin's eye.

"H'mm." The captain picks up the book I'm reading, the Harry Crews novel Clarissa gave me just before I left. We try not to stare at him, but Rankin's eyes keep flicking his way. It's then that I notice something funny about this new MI captain, something I haven't ever seen before. In the place where everyone else has a name tape stuck above the front pocket of their shirt, his doesn't have anything. No name, no nothing. The only markings on his uniform are captain's bars. My mouth feels dry.

"Specialist Rankin," he says, after a long examination of our various piles of sandy gear, "if you'll excuse us a moment, I need to speak with your pal here." He draws the word pal out as though it's exotic or funny.

Rankin and I exchange a glance. I know exactly what he's thinking. How in the hell did you manage to get this guy on your case so fast?

"Yes, sir," he says, stepping into his plastic shower shoes and moving off in the direction of the mess tent.

My palms begin to sweat. I wipe them on my pants.

"Think of anything yet, Durrant?"

"About the lieutenant, sir?"

He gives me a pitying look, as though I might be afflicted with some sort of mental disorder. "Yes, about the lieutenant."

"No, sir," I say.

The captain flutters through the pages of my book until a photo of Clarissa drops onto the cot. He examines it. Grunts. Puts it back.

"Mother of your child?"

"Yes, sir." The only one I've told about this is Rankin, and I know he's kept it to himself. The captain must have been listening to our conversation for some time.

"You know, Durrant, you've got a serious enemy on the base. Somebody's trying to nail your balls to the wall. And from what I can tell, he's doing a fine job of it so far. A man who has the lieutenant's ear."

Fucking Lopez.

He gives me a moment to respond to this, but when I don't, he goes on. "This man, he seems to think you sympathize with the enemy. A pretty serious charge."

"Sir, that's a lie, sir, I—"

The captain holds up a hand and presents me with an officer's smile. The one that says, *I own you.* Although evening has drained the day's color, leaving only oranges and browns, his eyes, which watch me over the tops of his sunglasses, look like the desert sky at noon. Bright blue and boiling. He takes out his cigarettes, shakes one up and throws me the pack. Without thinking, I stick a cig in my mouth.

"Keep the rest. In times of combat, smoking helps. Much more satisfying than prayer," he says, leaning over with his silver Zippo. "Quit if and when you get home."

I take a long drag. I'm surprised by how much I relish it. The last time I slipped up and smoked, the cigarette tasted awful. It made it much easier to stay quit. I have no doubt in my mind that this is the first of many cigarettes in my future. The chemicals seem to click into my brain like tumblers in a combination lock.

"Sir, may I—"

"I didn't say I believed any of this nonsense. I'm only telling you so you can see where you stand. On very shaky ground, I don't mind telling you." He lights his own cigarette and blows the smoke at my chest. "I think I can help you, but you'll need to do me a bit of a favor first."

When I swallow, my throat clicks so loudly I'm sure he must hear it. My heart, unfaithful companion that it is, begins to wallop my ribs like a drunken bar fighter. Fast, hard, and irregular. Now I'm really in the shit. The captain has made my life a foreign country.

"Lieutenant Blankenship." The captain compresses his lips with disgust. "He has a lockbox in his trailer where he keeps certain papers: letters, certificates, photographs, and the like. The contents have nothing to do with you. They're nothing special, really."

I want to yell, "Bullshit."

Somehow, the captain has already smoked his entire cigarette. It seems impossible, but I watched him do it. He takes out a new pack and lights another, slowly, carefully. He speaks in much the same way. His intonation is flattened, drained of emotional inflection of any kind but still intense. "At the present time, it would be improper for me to demand that he turn them over in an official context, but they would be extremely useful to me."

"Sir? May I ask wh—"

"No," he says.

"I was under the impression you were here to interrogate prisoners, sir."

"I am, if the need arises. Unfortunately, we have received reports about this base that require me to undertake additional duties, however unpleasant. Believe me when I say that I take no pleasure in this. In order for me to carry out these duties, I must work in complete secrecy. I had no choice but to recruit a confederate, Private Durrant, and this means you are obligated to observe the same secrecy."

"Sir, I—"

"You are not to speak about this to anyone under any circumstances without my express permission. Do you understand, Private? This includes your pal there—" He jerks his chin in the direction Rankin walked off.

"Specialist Rankin."

"Right," the captain says as though memorizing the name, "Rankin."

"Yes, sir, I won't, but—"

"Good." He exhales through his nostrils. "Because if I were even to *suspect* that you had betrayed my confidence, merely *suspect* it—" He draws hard on his cigarette, pulling a quarter of its smoke into his lungs. "—then I would make certain that your enemy here on base succeeded in nailing your balls to the wall." He hammers the air with his cigarette for each of my nailed balls. An ash falls.

I try my best to keep perfectly still.

"Only *suspect*," he says again, sliding his sunglasses to the tip of his nose and glowering at me with his desert-sky eyes. He leans back and crosses one leg over the other, pushing up his sunglasses as he settles on my cot. "Let me explain how we will proceed."

41

Lopez doesn't discover the scorpion until just before roll call. Rankin is polishing his boots with an old pair of boxers. I'm still drowsing on my cot. Lopez's scream carries all the way across the base. I jerk up. Rankin winks. We both light up cigarettes from the captain's pack.

"I knew you wouldn't be able to hold out," Rankin says.

"This is war," I say.

"Fucking A."

42

By the time we reach the burn field, the thermometer in the truck reads 106 degrees, and it's only 0930. Even at this hour, the heat's so intense I have to put on gloves before I touch any metal that's been lying in the sun. I still have a scar on my arm from leaning against the grille of the water tanker one afternoon. The skin bubbled up immediately and Salis, who was standing next to me, laughed his ass off.

As the sun climbs, the horizon loses focus and begins to shimmer. It is far too hot to talk. Ahmed and I take turns dousing our heads with water. I'm careful to keep my CamelBak tucked up under the truck in the shade. The water still gets warm, but at least it's drinkable.

Ahmed seems to sense my tension and keeps a little distance between us while we unload the barrels, sneaking the occasional glance, like I might lose it at any moment and attack him. And he's right to worry: the thought does cross my mind. I came upon him and Lopez chattering away beside the shit truck just before we left to go on the run. I couldn't imagine what they'd have to talk about. I'd never seen them exchange more than a greeting before this. Ahmed kept pointing his finger in the direction of the burn field and making a strange gesture. He wiggled his hand back and forth like a snake. Lopez smiled and said something that sounded like "sleep on it." They stopped talking before I heard anything else, but there's a certain look people get when you come up on them suddenly and they've been talking about you. A sort of unhappy recognition that causes a narrowing of the eyes. And these two had it in spades.

I watch Ahmed pretty carefully as we pour the diesel and start the burn. Something's going on with him. The real question is whether or not Lopez knows about it, and if he does know, whether or not he's in on it. I have a really hard time seeing Lopez as a hajji secret agent, but I suppose other men have turned traitor unexpectedly. Earlier in the morning, I decided to tell the captain I wouldn't do his ugly little chore. I even concocted a self-righteous speech about loyalty. Now I'm not so sure.

The entire ride home, I relish the thought of seeing Herman again. Ahmed manages to ruin this as well. Just as we're pulling up to his house, he gives me a quizzical look, furrows his brow. and purses his lips. It looks rehearsed.

"Where do you go when you drop me?"

"Back to the base." My stomach clenches. "Why?"

"But I am seeing you driving that way." He points in the direction of the toy factory. "Every day I am seeing you. Where are you going every day?"

"Sometimes I like to open the windows and blow some of the stink off before I go back. A little alone time."

"Alone time?" That hackneyed expression of befuddlement appears again.

"Never mind, Ahmed. Good work today. See you later." I force my lips into a grin and give him the thumbs-up, which means stick it up your ass when the hajjis do it. I can tell from his face that he knows I know. He scowls and returns the gesture, jabbing the air between us with violent, little thrusts of his thumb.

Goddammit, I think. One more simple pleasure ruined. I do not visit the factory today.

43

After I give Sergeant Oliphant the truck keys, he orders me to appear at the office trailer at 1800 hours, just after sentry duty. I don't mention it to anyone, not even Rankin, but I turn it over in my head all day. And I know it can't be good when I see Lopez loitering near the trailers. He grins as I climb the wooden steps to the door. I flip him off while scratching my neck.

The sergeant has me wait in the hall outside the lieutenant's office for about ten minutes before they call me in. Doc Dyson steps out. He gives me a worried look that's difficult to interpret.

The lieutenant doesn't ask me to sit after I salute. Another bad sign. I try and calm myself by reading the lieutenant's diploma from West Point. It hangs behind his desk where everyone can see it, right next to a framed photo of the president. He doesn't bother with the pretense of flipping through a file today. Sergeant Oliphant closes the door behind us. For a moment, the only sound is the wheezing of the window AC unit. The lieutenant gives me a hard look.

"Explain your whereabouts in the hours preceding, during, and after the bombs went off in the Humvees yesterday. Beginning at 1400," he says.

"As per Sergeant Guzman's request, I redrafted the requisition forms for medical supplies. I was engaged in this until 1730. Afterward, I went back to my tent and—"

"Wait." The lieutenant raises his hand. He looks behind me. "Are you getting this, Sergeant?"

"Yes, sir," Sergeant Oliphant says from his perch.

"And then?" the lieutenant says.

I give him a precise rundown of the day, making certain to mention every boring detail I can remember: the exact number of pages I read on my break after sentry duty, who I ate dinner with, the number of times I went to the latrine; I begin a joke I heard in the mess tent about a chicken and a nun, but Sergeant Oliphant stops me before I get to the funny part.

The lieutenant pulls at the hair behind his ear and memorizes the tiles on the ceiling. He tells me he's heard a rumor about me putting bugs in Corporal Lopez's cot and that I organized an insect fight in one of the common tents. I deny the first charge. He has no proof. The second isn't exactly true, but there's no point in getting Rankin in trouble too, so I admit it. I'm ordered to continue latrine burning for another month. And then we get to the real reason he's called me here.

"It has also come to my attention," he says, speaking very slowly, "that you were seen speaking to the new MI officer outside your tent. What was it exactly that you were discussing?"

"I am not at liberty to say, sir." I am tempted to spill it, let him know what's going on, but I don't believe he'd be able to protect me, even if he had a mind to, something I'm beginning to doubt.

The lieutenant stands and shouts, "Not at liberty to say? I order you to tell me what went on, Private Durrant." Although I've seen the lieutenant angry many times, I've never heard this tone of voice. He sounds desperate. "Now."

"I'm sorry, sir." I hang my head and give my boots the saddest look I can muster. "But the captain expressly told me not to repeat the discussion to anyone, no matter what."

The lieutenant lets his arms drop but remains standing. I almost feel sorry for him. He doesn't have a chance against the captain. He chews at his cheek and looks up at the ceiling again, as though the answer to his dilemma might be written on the acoustic tiles.

"Did the discussion involve me?" The lieutenant pinches the crease in his pants.

Sergeant Oliphant coughs significantly.

"Oh, well, I . . ." the lieutenant starts, but then sits down heavily on his chair. He looks defeated.

I feel sweat bead on my forehead and upper lip. I nod.

"Durrant? Do you mean—" The lieutenant leans forward and peers at me. Very slowly, so slowly it could be deniable, I move my head up and down once.

There goes the first nail in my balls. I can almost hear the savage thump of the hammer.

"May I ask a question, sir?"

The lieutenant stares at me.

"What is the captain's name?"

"That's . . . I . . ."

"Hasn't he told anyone?"

"Sir," Sergeant Oliphant barks.

"Sir," I say.

The lieutenant scratches the bridge of his nose. Behind me, Sergeant Oliphant lets out a long breath. I wish I could see his face.

"The captain," the lieutenant begins, sounding like the narrator of a nature documentary, dramatic and cheerful, "is here on a special mission that requires anonymity. As commanding officer of this base, HQ has made me aware of the details. That's all you need to know about this subject."

"Yes, sir."

"A fuck-lot of silly pussyfooting around is what it is." He flicks the pen set on his desk. Then, suddenly, his voice changes and becomes authoritative. "Do you know anything about the old man's death? The older prisoner. Have you spoken to anyone about it? You don't have to name names."

"No," I say, meeting his eyes and then looking away, "I haven't talked about it in the way I think you mean, but I don't believe it was a suicide, sir, if that's what you're asking." No response, so I continue. "I can't see how a little old man like him got out of his restraints or managed to get his pants over the beam in the ceiling. The poor guy only had three of his lower teeth. It seems improbable, sir. Someone must have helped him."

"That someone wasn't you, was it?"

"No, sir," I say, barely able to modulate my voice. "Why would I want to do something like that?"

"Oh, I can think of a few reasons." He looks over my shoulder at Sergeant Oliphant, then nods once and closes his eyes.

"Sir—"

"Dismissed."

44

I leave the lieutenant's office at 1900 hours. Rankin and a couple of others are on their way to the mess tent, so I fall in with them, even though I'm not very hungry. Somebody's telling a hajji joke, but I'm not listening, just sort of staring off at the Noses. Jagged purple shapes against a deep blue sky. When I stop to tie a bootlace, I notice a figure running along the wall of the garage toward the back of the old fort. Rankin stops to wait for me, but I tell him to go on ahead, that I have to take a leak and I'll catch up. I lie without thinking and don't stop to wonder why. No one else is on the parade ground. A light burns in the Comm Trailer. Laughter spills out of the mess tent. Once Rankin and the rest of them are several yards away, I sprint over to the garage.

The night is dry and cold. A wisp of cloud races past a three-quarter moon that's rising just above the largest of the Noses. It shines like a brass artillery-shell casing. The sand on the parade ground seems to glow, and the scattered rocks are slick and shiny in the moonlight. My shadow stretches out for klicks, pursuing me like a cartoon villain. When I round the corner of the garage, no one is there.

The fort is sectioned off into two parts. The front, which we reconstructed and stabilized, contains the motor pool and the garage machine shop. Behind this are several large rooms that have been converted into storage areas for food and vehicle parts and ammunition. The original structure was made of large undressed purple stones. The Army added cinderblocks to this, creating an outer shell. Inside the motor pool, they stabilized the ceiling with steel I-beams borrowed from the old cement factory building. The result is extremely ugly but solid and functional. The rear half, what we refer to as the old fort, has two levels and once served as Omar's barracks. The upper level has almost completely collapsed, although here and there it is still possible to make out the original crenellation. The building appears to have been built in pieces over many years, and the walls wander in a strange zigzag pattern for almost a hundred yards. This is where I saw the shadow man. Back where the new storage rooms butt up against the old fort. He was running in quick bursts from one pile of broken rock to another. This is not how an innocent man moves at night.

I stand perfectly still and watch for any movement among the heaps of masonry and crumbling stone. Nothing. Perhaps I made a mistake. The manual we used in Basic advised against staring into the darkness during nighttime guard duty. Too much of this and bushes start to move. Each one becomes a potential enemy. Stare a little longer and you'll find yourself attacking the shrubbery.

Just as I'm about to give up and go back to the mess tent, a brick falls in one of the half-collapsed rooms behind the secure storage area. In the stillness, the sound is huge. Someone mutters. I finger the safety on my M4 and pat my cargo pocket to make sure I have an extra clip. Maybe it's just Cox checking on one of the vehicles. But he would have used the bay doors in front. I grind my teeth and angle my head for a better view. Several twitchy minutes pass. Hazel's donkey laugh drifts over from the mess tent. From where I squat behind the oil drums in the dark, it is a lonely sound. This is a waste of time, I think. But then, even before I shift my weight and take a step, a figure emerges from the ruined room closest to the motor pool's eastern door. His head is wrapped in a cloth. I wish I had some NVGs. I should have brought Rankin. I click off my safety and lead this guy with my rifle. When he comes out into the moonlight, I let the barrel drop. The scarf wrapped around his head is yellow. It's Ahmed. I consider shooting him. In light of recent events, it would be justified. I could just say I didn't see his face and thought he was another mad bomber. But I don't. Instead, I stay crouched behind the barrels until he's about twenty yards away, then I follow him.

Ahmed runs quickly with his shoulders hunched and head down. Every so often he stops, cops a squat and glances around. I drop flat when I see him slow down. His movements are regular and easy to predict. Even the dumbest grunt can tell you this is a foolish way to operate. I'm fairly sure he doesn't see me. When he reaches the northern wall, I think I've got him. Ahmed stops and pulls something from the sack slung over his shoulder. I want to move closer, but I'm afraid he'll hear me. He walks right up to the wall and seems to be punching it. What the hell? Ahmed pushes and shoves the stones with his shoulder, wriggling something as he does it. It looks like he's completely lost his head. But then, slowly, a small section of the wall swings inward like a door. He disappears in the dark space behind it and the wall closes again with a soft scrape.

I wait for a few mikes before I go in for a closer look. It takes me a while to find it. A narrow crack in the wall, edged with metal. I can make out abrasions in the rock at the base of the little door, but just barely. There is nothing around this section of the wall to help me find it again later. I feel around in my pockets. Cigarettes. I place one on the ground at the base of the door and cover the tobacco end with a rock. Unless you were looking for it, it would be almost invisible.

45

Rankin stares at me when I reach the mess tent. I've been gone a hell of a lot longer than a piss should take. I load my tray and sit between Rankin and Doc Greer. Dinner is chipped beef on toast or, as it is more popularly known, shit on a shingle. Boyette takes the bench across from me and slams his tray down hard enough to spatter gravy. He narrows his eyes and looks at his food like he wants to kill it.

"Unhappy about the menu selection tonight, Chef Boyarette?" Doc Greer asks.

"What? This?" Boyette gestures at his tray with a plastic fork. "I haven't ate so good my whole life."

"God help you," Doc Greer says, and seems relatively sincere.

"Fuck, man, I don't care about this shit." He shovels a heap of brown goo into his mouth, chews rapidly, and swallows with relish. "Durrant'll be burning it in a week. No, it's Hazel that pissed me off."

"Why's that?" I ask.

"He says I'm a soldier for fucking Exxon. That's a load of crap."

"He's just giving you shit," I say.

Doc Greer puts a hand over his heart. "I pledge allegiance to the tiger—"

"Shut up," Boyette says.

Rankin lets slip a gruff, "Heh, heh, heh."

"What's so funny about that? I'm fighting for the fucking U. S. of A. I don't give two shits what Hazel says. What about you, Rankin?"

"Poontang," Rankin says.

"The only one I know who actually likes this shit," I say, flicking Boyette on the arm with my sticky spoon, "is the Boy here."

"Hooah," Boyette shouts.

It's loud. We all wince except him.

"What about Salis?" Doc Greer asks. "He re-upped in-theater."

Rankin looks around the table, catching each eye. "When I was home on leave, all I could think about was this fucking place. What you all were up to. What kind of shit was going down. I couldn't even enjoy a movie. I couldn't enjoy nothing. And then I get back here, and all I can think about is getting the hell away from your sorry asses."

"What's that got to do with Salis?" I ask.

"Easy. I can go home and find some other way to live my life. But him?" Rankin says, looking over his shoulder at the man in question. At the moment, Salis is standing on the bench beside Cox, kicking his legs up and flapping his arms like a chicken. "He's a battle-rattle adrenaline junkie. He'd engage a camel if they told him to. After working weapons squad and firing a 240 Bravo, you can't just go home and cook French fries. Salis barely cleared high school. The poor dumb fuck was two months away from his twentieth birthday when they stuffed the diploma in his pocket and made him leave school. Could of gotten arrested for statutory rape those last couple of proms. Then Uncle Sam puts his sad, unloved ass in the infantry. Did they teach him how to work computers or fix engines? Hell, no. The only training he got was how to make pink mist. He ain't going home with a skill he can sell. This is it for him. It's as good as it gets. He may be dumb, but he ain't so dumb he can't see that."

"Yeah," Doc Greer says, "after this, none of us belong anywhere. We're mutants. They don't even know a war's going on at home. When I was back on leave, old men would come up to me in the grocery store or wherever, pat me on the back and say 'I support the troops.' How the fuck do you do that, I wanted to ask, by buying more gas or TV dinners? That phrase doesn't mean shit. It's just a bunch of sounds."

"They don't know what the hell to say to you," Rankin says. "Same as a funeral. Nothing anybody says will make a difference either way. I feel for your loss. I support the troops. Same fucking shit."

But Doc Greer is on a roll. "Well, then they should just shut the fuck up."

"Hooah," Boyette adds.

"Or people'd ask me if I got to fire my weapon," Greer says. His lip curls up on one side so his dog tooth shows. "How can you even talk to people about it when they ask you shit like that? We're no good for normal life now and this ain't no life at all."

"We're war orphans," Rankin says.

"War mutants more like," Doc Greer says.

"Fuck you all," Boyette says, pounding his chest. "I'm a war-yur. Hooah."

"I don't want to hear any more of that hooah shit," Rankin tells him. On this, we're in complete agreement. "Didn't your mama teach you manners? No hooah at the dinner table."

"I'd rather fight them here than back home," Boyette says, throwing out some half-remembered campaign slogan, something he probably saw on TV.

"Not me," I say, "at least that would make sense. If I was fighting them back home, I'd feel like there was an actual reason for doing it."

"Hooah to that," Rankin says.

Doc Greer gives me a bland look. "I wish we were fighting the Canadians."

46

The next morning Ahmed shows up for the burn a half-hour late. He looks like shit—a thumb-sized bag under each bloodshot eye and rough patches of stubble on his cheeks. We didn't bring enough fuel and the shit remains a thick boiling sludge at the bottom of the barrels. There's no way I'm driving all the way to base and back. I make Ahmed suck on the hose to start the siphon I've placed in the fuel tank. His face turns red and his eyes bulge a bit. When the gas fills his mouth, he chokes and then spits several times.

I decide to play stupid.

"Cox wanted me to thank you for returning that wrench last night," I tell him.

"Wrench?" he asks, alarmed.

His discomfort is satisfying to watch.

"Yeah, the wrench. That is what you were doing in the garage last night, wasn't it? Returning the wrench?"

"I am sorry. I do not understand." I notice Ahmed's hand shaking slightly. He stuffs it in his pocket when he sees me looking.

"You all right? Swallowing gas can do funny things to your head. Your hands are shaking."

"It is okay." He wipes his mouth on his sleeve.

"That's some trick you have, getting onto the base. None of the sentries saw you. That could come in handy." I wink at him. A knot of anger hardens in my chest, but this isn't the time to let it loose. "You'll have to show me some time."

"This is no trick. Perhaps the gate man he sleeps. Ha, ha." His laugh sounds like a cough.

"Ah, so you were there." I clench my fists so hard that one of my fingernails breaks the skin on my palm.

Ahmed grunts and looks away. "I am not understanding," he mumbles.

"I'm just fooling with you, bud." I give him a hearty laugh and pound him on the back. Hard enough to make him grunt.

He doesn't smile back. "Yes," he says, "funny fooling."

We don't speak on the way back to the village, but while I'm watching the road ahead, I feel his eyes on me. Usually, I drop him at his door. Today he asks me to stop at the village café. He glances down the track leading to his family's house and then back at me several times in quick succession. I say good-bye, but he just shuts the door and walks quickly to the entrance of the little restaurant, not once looking back. I have to pull into the dirt road in order to turn the truck around. As I'm punching in the clutch, I notice a group of men waiting in the yard of Ahmed's house, which is only a few doors down from the highway. Five grim guys decked out in dusty, baggy-kneed suits and red-checked scarves. They smoke their cigarettes and stare at their feet with a kind of forced casualness. If I was part of a squad today, we'd probably shake them down. They have that look. But I'm alone, so I grind the stick into reverse and drive away. One man takes off his scratched-up, drugstore sunglasses and stares at me through the windshield of the truck. There's a raw pink divot where his left eye should be.

Instead of going straight to the toy factory, I turn onto the washboard gravel road that leads to the base. I drive a couple hundred yards and then stop at a curve in the road where it dips beside a mound of boulders. Here the truck is hidden from both the village and the sentry post. The desert is nearly soundless and the air is heavy and still. I get out and wait fifteen minutes near a patch of stunted brush, hucking rocks at lizards and blowing smoke rings before I climb back into the truck and drive down to the highway that leads to the factory. I can't see Ahmed watching the road much longer than this. His enthusiasm for spying seemed limited today.

I managed to snag a couple of cans of 7-Up along with five more MREs this morning before I left. I'm in a cheerful mood when I park the truck behind the factory gate. The thought of seeing Herman makes me smile. There is a slight breeze now. It stirs the dust and chases bits of paper across the factory yard. Several large dark birds, vultures maybe, drift in the thermals high above me. I see a flash of movement in the window as I'm jumping down from the truck. There's my boy. As I step into the building, I whistle the chorus to "Don't Rock the Boat."

Herman waits in the doorway of the factory office, crouched like a sprinter at the block. I smile and wave. He's changed into a new outfit. The old outfit was ambiguous, but this one is definitely a dress of some sort, constructed from butcher paper.

As soon as Herman sees who it is, he stands up and walks toward me. This bodes well. I set the MREs on the floor and pull the 7-Up cans from my cargo pockets. He must recognize them; his eyes light up and he rushes over to take one from me. After a long sip, he frowns and gestures for me to sit. I do. He brings the can to my lips and tilts it up. This I didn't expect. I almost choke. He laughs soundlessly. Maybe Herman's mute. He gulps the 7-Up in a series of fast, noisy swallows, spilling soda all over the front of his new paper dress.

When he's finished, I motion for him to sit across from me. He hesitates and then sits. I demonstrate how the heating mechanism in the MRE works by pouring the last of the 7-Up into the special plastic bag that comes with the box, but I'm not entirely sure he understands. He tries to drink it and I have to show him using sign language that this would kill him. Maybe I should just let him eat the MREs cold.

"I'm going to have a baby soon, Herman."

He plays with the MRE heating bag. It expands like a balloon as the 7-Up reacts with the granular, black heating agent.

"If it's a boy, I'm going to call him Herman, too. I don't care what Clarissa says."

Herman looks at me in an attentive way. If I didn't know any better, I'd think he understands me. He smiles. Another first.

For the next fifteen or twenty minutes, I tell him stories about growing up in the salt marshes at the edge of Savannah. I sing the theme song to *Sesame Street* and encourage him to sing with me. Herman nods along with the melody but remains silent. I run through it several times before giving up.

"I wish there was some way I could bring you back to the base. Maybe we could get you cleaned up and teach you to work in the kitchen or, better yet, in the garage after I get rid of Ahmed." I don't know why I say this. It doesn't seem possible.

At the mention of Ahmed, Herman leaps to his feet.

"What's wrong?" I pat the floor with my hand and smile. Sit down. His entire body hums with tension. Then he spins on his tube shoes and darts off. I wait for a few minutes, then stand and leave. The mixup with the diesel fuel has made me late enough.

As I'm about to climb into the cab of the truck, he reappears. Tucked under one arm is a package wrapped in the same brown paper he used to construct his dress, tied neatly with pink thread. What I find inside astounds me. Somehow Herman has managed to sew together the parts of several stuffed creatures. The needle work is so neat it almost looks as though it came off the factory line. The plush purple body appears to have once been an elephant's. Sewn to its neck is a pink teddy bear head and attached at the rear is the long fuzzy body of a snake. A red felt tongue flickers at the end. Herman beams at me. I beam back.

"Thank you," I say. My eyes moisten. God, I'm turning into the biggest pussy.

47

Boyette meets me at the gate and tells me I'm late for a general briefing. He's hopping from foot to foot, babbling like a meth freak. "We're finally bringing the fucking war to them, combat," he tells me. As I'm parking the truck, he spots the elebear and smirks, asking if I've got a chickpea chicky hid away somewhere. He leers at me all the way to Common Tent 2. The base looks deserted. Almost everyone must be at this briefing.

The lieutenant glares as I duck in under the tent flap. There's not much interest in my late arrival, so something big must have come up. They've arranged the chairs in rows. Sergeant Oliphant stands at the front of the room with a dry-erase board propped on an easel and a handful of colored markers. Someone has sketched out a crude topographical map of the area. The base is drawn in blue. The hills are brown. A series of red dashes moves out of the base and into the Noses. Scattered here and there among the brown triangles that represent the hills are green squares. Sergeant Oliphant pauses to frown as I come in and waits until I sit before he continues. I slip into a chair in the back row beside Rankin. He shakes his head when he sees me and hands me his tobacco pouch. I take out a paper and a pinch of tobacco.

I scope out the room. Expressions range from excitement to forced nonchalance to barely concealed dread. I know what this is. This is the fucking captain's doing. Somewhere deep down in the thick of my brain, a cluster of cells tells me not to go through with his plan.

And what I'm seeing here today in this tent is the start of it. There's no question. The captain sits up front, right next to the lieutenant. When he catches my eye, he lowers his sunglasses a notch and winks. No doubt something they taught him back in spy school.

"This will only be a probe," Sergeant Oliphant says. "General Pett wants us to get a feel for their size and readiness. Satellite photos show very little enemy concentration up there. HQ believes the insurgents in each camp number less than ten. Some of us think different. Only three small encampments have been spotted. Here, here, and here. HQ calls them shepherd camps." Several people in the room grumble about this. He ignores them, pointing to the green boxes with his marker. "We plan to hit this one, the one nearest the base, because it's probably the group responsible for the latest attacks."

Sergeant Oliphant goes on to explain that a single squad, led by himself, will head up into the Noses for an early morning mission. The exact time has not yet been decided upon, but it will most likely go down in the next day or two. He stresses once more that this is only a probing mission.

The sergeant finishes by telling us, "We're not trying to sweep every last one of these assholes out of the Noses. We're not manned or equipped for a real fight right now." This, his expression implies, may come later. "But with the right info, HQ might. . . ." He leaves it at that. The tent is silent. We all know this could be a big one, no matter what he says. Sergeant Oliphant looks from man to man, making brief, intense eye contact. Before I can find a suitable hiding place for my eyes, he catches me. His look is hard, but I can't read it, and he pins me with it for an uncomfortable length of time.

Someone up front groans. Another soldier, probably Boyette, says "But I want to kill me some hajjis." Boyette means it. He wants to spill some blood on the sand. Preferably gallons. Sergeant Oliphant himself doesn't look all that happy about the rules of engagement either. The sergeant tells us to pipe the fuck down and explains that our roster has been shaken up over the last week, something we are all too aware of already. Because of this, the lieutenant has instructed him to try something new. He asks for volunteers. The room goes silent again. This is completely unexpected. Never in my entire time over here have I heard a call for volunteers for a mission force like this. It just isn't done. I can only believe there's an ulterior motive at work here, some kind of officer maneuvering. No doubt involving the captain. I keep my hand firmly pressed against my leg. The first rule of the infantryman: never volunteer for anything.

Boyette's arm shoots up right away, no big surprise there, as do those of two or three others. After a moment, Rankin raises his hand. I look over at him and he shrugs. I raise my arm. I do my best to avoid looking at the captain. The tent fills with subdued murmurs. Sergeant Oliphant writes the names of the volunteers on the board. When he sees my hand, I swear I spot a smile crinkle up the corners of his eyes, even if his mouth stays tight and grim, and then he glances back at the lieutenant. Something passes between them, but it's impossible to interpret. The sergeant writes out more names, mine and Rankin among them, then tells us about the new water-rationing system. We have to reduce our consumption yet again. The whole tent groans. Despite the danger of the mission, I'm relieved. I didn't realize how much the captain's plan bothered me until now that I'm out of it.

But, of course, I don't get out of it that easily. As I'm stepping through the flaps of the tent, someone yanks my elbow. It's the captain.

"You little prick," he hisses. "What was all that about?" The captain takes a quick look around before going on. Near the end of the tent, a group of guys are joking. Salis has a squirming scorpion impaled at the end of a broken plastic spork and he's waving it around in someone's face and giggling. The captain frowns and hooks a thumb over his shoulder. We take a walk. He doesn't speak for fifty yards.

"We had a deal," he whispers between gritted teeth, barely opening his mouth. The captain grabs the meaty part of my bicep and squeezes hard. His fingers feel like pliers.

I take a deep breath. Here goes. "It would of looked suspicious if I didn't volunteer after Rankin did. We always work together."

The captain stares at me. I can't see his eyes behind the sunglasses, just two tiny Durrant heads reflected in the lenses. These Durrant heads look unhappy and tense. The sunlight feels like hot wax poured over my neck and shoulders. A handful of very hard seconds tick by. He looks at me; I look at my heads. Just when I've decided I'm done for, the four deep grooves in his forehead flatten out and relax. He actually smiles. "Not bad," he says, "you're thinking on your feet. Now I'll fix it."

He turns and stomps back toward the common tent. As I'm rolling a smoke, the tent flap opens and Rankin calls for me to come back inside.

48

"**You're staying on** base for this one, Durrant," Sergeant Oliphant says. "We need you here."

I look over at Sergeant Guzman for support. He holds out his palms and shrugs. The unlit cigar jammed in the corner of his mouth bobs as he moves his shoulders. He looks seriously annoyed. Maybe it's the mission itself, or their refusal to let me take part, I don't know which. He chews at his cigar. I turn back to Sergeant Oliphant.

"But, sir," I say, "Rankin and I always go on mis—"

"That's an order, Private. Let it go, how about?"

The lieutenant glances away from the laptop. He scratches his scalp with a pencil. And then, as though it takes a huge amount of energy and patience, he turns to me. "Where were you earlier, Durrant? It shouldn't have taken you that long to burn the shit barrels. Not by half."

I explain about the fuel and the siphoning. The story doesn't sound very convincing. Even the true parts sound flimsy.

"I'm surprised you got the diesel to catch at all," Lopez says. "You can throw a lit cigarette on that stuff and it won't burn."

I ignore him.

"That's what we've always used to burn it, Lopez. But if you're so interested to see how it works, I can easily arrange for you to get some firsthand experience." Sergeant Oliphant gives him the stink-eye. Lopez wisely shuts up. Then, in the silence that follows, Lopez kneels beside the lieutenant's table. He seems to be examining the man's boots. Is he about to give them a spit-polish? Jesus. Then he plucks something off the ground between the lieutenant's feet. It looks like an unspent M16 cartridge.

"What are you doing, Lopez?" the lieutenant asks, his voice tight with irritation. "Get up off the floor."

Lopez jumps back as though slapped.

Edging sideways into the lieutenant's field of vision to try another tack, I say, "Can I ask why, sir?" The sand scrapes loudly beneath my boots and the lieutenant flinches. "I—"

"Are you questioning an order, Private?" Sergeant Oliphant says.

"No, Sergeant." I straighten my spine and look at the lieutenant. "I'm sorry, sir. It's just that I really want a go at those assholes. After what happened with Gerling and Studdie, I—"

"We're all angry about what happened," the lieutenant says.

"I'll take his place," Lopez says. His voice sounds strange and high-pitched. Rehearsed.

"I have something else I need you to take care of, Lopez," the lieutenant says. "We'll discuss it later."

Lopez fights to keep his expression calm, but I can see he's angry. I make a point of smiling at him.

"The rest of you, out," Sergeant Oliphant yells, pointing at Lopez and me.

Lopez knocks against my shoulder as we leave.

Once we're outside, I grab his sleeve. He pulls away and keeps walking.

"I don't care if you're promoted to sergeant next week. You do that again, Lopez, and you'll regret it."

"You won't be around next week," Lopez says without turning around. As he walks off, he mumbles something else I can't quite make out.

49

Rankin wakes me up to say good-bye before he leaves the wire to go downrange. It's just after 0300. His face is smeared yellow with greasepaint. On each cheek he's drawn twin chevrons in black. I flinch. He looks like a bad dream.

"Thought you saw the bogeyman, huh?" He bares his teeth and screws up his eyes. "Just wait until those hajjis catch an eyeful of me. They'll need to use those turbans for diapers."

"Yeah," I say, knuckling sleep from my eyes, "they'll think you're the bassist from Kiss and go running for their earplugs."

Rankin plays a little air bass and sings about how he intends to spend his nights rocking and rolling and his days partying. Each and every one of them.

"Why the hell are they making you wear that shit?" I ask. My heart still pounds from the start he gave me.

Rankin doesn't answer me at first, and I think I've annoyed him. He's bent over my locker. My head is still fuzzy from sleep, but I don't want Rankin going off on a weird half-baked mission like this one angry at me. When I sit up, I see he's written Blood for Oil on the trunk at the end of my bed with greasepaint. He waggles his eyebrows. I'm relieved.

"I'm so black, I stand out against the desert. I got to lighten myself up with this shit so they don't spot me," he tells me.

We laugh, but I can tell he's wound up and on edge. Maybe not too happy about going into battle with a bright yellow face.

"I'm sorry," I say, "I wish I was going with—"

"Don't sweat it, D." He holds up his hand. His right palm looks like it's been smeared with mustard. "All that shit last night was a show. Lopez knew he wasn't going. Why the hell else would he have come into the tent when his name wasn't called? He was playing you. All an act."

"You think?" I say.

"I know it, man." His nostrils flare. "Lopez and the lieutenant had their heads knocking together like a couple of sissies. They were whispering and shit before they sent me off to get you."

"I'm not sure. I wondered about that too, but Lopez looked pretty hacked off about not being able to go." I swing my legs to the floor. "Who's taking my place?"

"Doc Greer." Rankin sits at the end of my cot and wipes his hand on the ragged boxer shorts we use for polishing boots. "Listen to me. I'm serious, D. Something's going down. He's laying for you, so watch your ass. Don't be doing none of your disappearing-act shit today. Lopez is just waiting for you to screw up. If he found out about you going to that factory, he'd piss himself with joy."

"He's all talk." I wanted to believe this.

"No, man. He's looking to ambush you. Watch your shit."

We knock fists. He gives me a worried look, as if I'm the one going up into the Noses.

"Shake one out of the tree for me, Gene Simmons," I say.

Rankin snickers and does a little jazz hands number. For some reason this really gets me laughing. I think we've both got a case of the nerves. He breaks into a bit of a softshoe routine and sings, "I want to lock and load all night and shoot them hajjis all day." He taps out Shave and a Haircut with his desert boots and slips under the tent flap.

"Two bits," I try to say, but I'm laughing too hard to get it out in time.

I don't even try to go back to sleep.

50

All day I've been worrying about Rankin, wondering what he's up against out there. I can't take three steps without thinking about it. My dread comes from knowing I'm partly responsible if anything happens. It's even worse when I'm back at the tent staring at his gear, so I head over to the latrine to read in privacy. A Harry Crews novel about snake-handlers and dogfights. The sand beneath one corner of the latrine has blown away, and now the whole ramshackle structure is off balance. Each time I shift my weight, the plywood wobbles. The latrine is a two-seater, but thankfully someone rigged up a bit of oily canvas around and between the two holes. The sand hisses against the heavy cotton fabric. Motes of dust sift in from above and make the beam of my flashlight look as though you could pick it up and swing it. It's still too dark to read, so I crack a couple of chemical sticks. Someone has written on the tarp with a red Sharpie: *To come in here it takes guts, to shit so high I can rest my nuts.* Soldiers over here talk about the consistency of their bowel movements the way people back home might discuss the weather.

I open my book. A bodybuilder in southern Georgia is taking perverse liberties with an ex-baton twirler. Harry Crews goes into great detail. Just as I'm really getting into it, letting the story shoulder aside all those thoughts about Rankin and the rest of the heavy shit that's cluttering up my head, something scratches against the big sheet of plywood behind me, the only solid wall. The other three sides would be open to the air if not for the ragged curtain of canvas.

Another scratch. It sounds like a cat. Has a jackal gotten onto the base again? We sometimes catch them slinking in at night to paw through the kitchen scraps.

"Go sniff around somebody else's ass," I shout, laying the book on my knee.

"Shut up, Durrant." The voice is muffled but familiar.

"Who is that?"

"Lower your voice, for Christ's sake." It's the captain.

"What?" I say, knowing exactly what. "I'm conducting serious business in here, sir."

"Don't be a smartass, Durrant. Stop waxing your knob and listen to me. We've got plans to make."

"But the lieutenant didn't go on the probe." When the captain laid it out for me the first time, this was a crucial aspect of his plan.

He makes an irritated throat-clearing sound. "Right, which is why we need to set up a little distraction for him. A controlled explosive event."

"A what?"

"I've got a timer set on a grenade over near the gate."

"Jesus," I say, "what if someone accidentally walks by?"

"It's safe," he says, using the old *and you call yourself a soldier* tone of voice. The three most annoying Army expressions are: "Yo," "Hooah," and "And you call yourself a soldier."

"And?" I say, rubbing my eyes and yawning. The past few days have worn me down. I feel like a steak knife that's been used to chop bricks.

"At 0900 tomorrow, I want you to position yourself somewhere near the lieutenant's trailer. When you hear the blast, wait three minutes and go in."

"What if it's locked?"

I hear a thump followed by a soft, metallic scrape. A key drops in through a hole in the canvas. It bounces once on my knee, hits the plywood seat and nearly goes skittering between my legs and into the hole. I snatch it up just before it slides into the barrel and put it in my cargo pocket.

"Half an inch to the right, Captain, and it would have been down the hole."

"Yeah, Private, and you would have been down there right after it."

I can't see my way clear of this shit any more. There's no room to maneuver. All I have are delaying tactics, and if I try another of these, he's bound to get suspicious. The captain actually chuckles. He's literally got me over a barrel with my pants down. And he enjoys it. This shouldn't surprise me. The government paid good money to train him to do this.

"Where's it supposed to be, this Goddamn box?" I ask. "Sir."

"I've looked all over Saunders's old trailer and I can't find it. The only other person who knew about the box is Blankenship." The captain's breath becomes raspy and uneven. "I know he still must have it. He hasn't left the base since the IED attack on the highway. Saunders told me Blankenship hides his important shit in a hollow place beside his window AC unit, so that's where it'll be." He coughs, a dry, nervous hack.

"Captain?" I say.

"That's all you need to know," he says quietly. "Rap on the wall around the AC until you find a hollow space."

"What happens when he discovers it's missing?"

"Let me take care of that. I promise you this: when I get that box, he'll be the one with something to worry about."

"What's in it, sir?"

"Oh-nine-double oh, Durrant. 0900. This is your *second* chance. Don't fuck it up."

51

I station myself in the doorway of the Comm Trailer around 0900. It's empty for once, but I pretend like I'm waiting in line to use the phone. The captain and Lieutenant Blankenship go into the office trailer together a few minutes later. I tilt my watch back and forth, trying to read the minute hand. I can't. Even though it's almost useless, I can't seem to bring myself to throw the thing away.

When the controlled explosive event finally goes off, the ground shakes. That sure as hell wasn't any grenade. I wonder if the captain rigged up an artillery shell. I'm far enough away that the sound isn't painful, but it's still loud enough to make me wince. Someone in the motor pool yells. The captain and the lieutenant come running out of the office trailer. Sergeant Guzman jogs across the parade ground. There's a cluster of men down by the gate. I look around to make sure anyone who might see me is otherwise occupied, then duck behind the Comm Trailer.

I count out the seconds. After a hundred and eighty, I run behind the Conex units, sprinting when I hit the gaps between them. The windows of the lieutenant's trailer have blinds. The AC unit wheezes away. My uniform is drenched in sweat and the key feels greasy in my fingers. A last look around, then I dash up the steps. When I lean against the door to unlock the bolt, it opens on its own. Frosty air slips out. If he left the door unlocked and the AC on, it must mean he plans to come back soon. I step inside and close the door behind me.

I've never been in one of the officers' trailers before. Back home, this would be a small, shabby place to live. Here in the sandbox, it's a palace. On the left is a tiny kitchen separated from the rest of the room by a counter and two barstools. The linoleum is yellow with a pattern of green squares, peeling in the corners. In the center of the living room is a card table with three folding chairs. An orange couch and a yellow easy chair fill the remainder of the space. On the wall above the couch, someone has hung a framed photo of President Bush, the official one you find in federal offices where he's wearing a false half-smile like you sometimes see in wedding group shots. Something about his face in this picture has always reminded me of the TV puppet Howdy Doody. He looks smug, as though the inside of this trailer amuses him but not very much.

Other than this, the walls are bare. A narrow hallway leads to the other end of the trailer. I check to make sure all the window blinds are drawn before going on. This is a two-man trailer, but the lieutenant has it to himself for now. That never would have happened before they split the base. I try the first of three doors. Empty, except for a steel bedframe and a mattress with a brown heart-shaped stain. In the closet, a bent wire hanger sags from the rod. The next door leads to an extremely clean bathroom. The whole trailer feels abandoned, like a motel room after the guest has checked out.

The last room is his bedroom. A dresser, bare, and a bed so tightly made you could crack an egg on it. The AC unit whistles. As the sweat cools, my skin gets clammy. It can't be less than 75 degrees in here, but compared to the temperature outside it feels like a refrigerator. I try and remember what the captain said. A hollow space in the wall beside the AC. I thump at the fake wood paneling. The entire wall sounds hollow. Maybe what I'm looking for is a full place. Just below the unit, I get a solid thunk when I tap on the press board. I run my hands along the base of the wall, trying to find a crack. It might just be a stud. But no, there's a bit of splintering where two pieces of paneling come together. I pull out my Gerber knife and try to pry it open.

Not two yards outside the window, I hear Hazel calling someone a stupid asshole. At least it sounds like Hazel. I freeze and listen for a moment. Sweat drips from my chin. Was that the sound of a boot on the steps? Where can I go if the lieutenant comes back? In the closet? Under the bed? I feel like an adulterer in a bad romantic comedy.

As I shift my weight to look around, I bump my knee against the wall and something inside clicks. When I step back, a panel the size of a folded newspaper swings open. The hinge is sprung, so the little door pops free if you apply pressure in the right place. It's very neatly done. The pressure point is no larger than a dime. I could have thumped the wall all day and never found it. The lieutenant must have fixed this himself. It strikes me as unlikely he just stumbled upon it while adjusting the AC. Handiwork like this has always impressed me, probably because I can't do it myself. A dull green metal box is lodged between two load-bearing studs. A very tight fit. Resting on top is a photo album covered in desert camouflage material. It falls open when I pull the lockbox out. A child's birthday party. A little girl in a bathing suit standing in a wading pool holding a hose. The water gushing out sparkles in the sunlight. A dog drinking from a toilet. I flip through it. Some wedding pictures, but not the lieutenant's. A photo of an attractive blond woman standing on tiptoes to kiss the lieutenant on the forehead. Sister? Girlfriend? Wife? I try to remember if the lieutenant wears a wedding ring. This is the only personal item of his I've seen. I flip back to the beginning of the book to give it a closer look. Outside, Sergeant Guzman shouts my name, and I start so badly I nearly drop the book. What the hell am I doing messing around like this? Stay alert. Keep on task. Remain frosty.

I yank out the lockbox and put the album back. The box is heavy and secured by a combination lock with four tumblers. Something solid slides around inside. I give it a little shake. There's also a light fluttering of paper. It sounds like it could be loose bills. The panel snaps easily into place when I push it closed. The woodwork is so good the seams vanish. I wipe the sweat off my forehead. It drips onto the carpet. I'm sopping wet.

A shadow passes by the windows at a trot; the sound makes my stomach cramp. I dig a booney hat and some sunglasses out of my cargo pocket and make sure my hair is tucked up inside and that it's pulled way down over my eyes. Using my knuckles, I worry a roll of masking tape out of my other pocket and tear off a piece to cover the name tape on my shirt. Someone fires a triple burst with an M4, fairly close. Seconds later, they fire another. And another. I pause at the door to draw a deep breath, so I can stuff the lockbox into the waistband of my pants. The fabric pulls very tight and cuts into my back. I exhale and turn the doorknob. The last thing I notice is a small plastic figurine of the Little Mermaid lying sideways on the armrest of the couch. Go, I tell myself. And I do.

52

I hear the shout as soon as I reach the corner of the trailer. It's Lopez. His boots come crunching over the gravel at a quick clip. I break into a run. Flat out, as fast as I can go. I head behind the line of trailers, head ducked low. I found the booney hat I'm wearing in Common Tent 2 last night. It's an extra-large one so the brim covers the upper part of my face fairly well, but if Lopez gets closer, he'll recognize me. Even if he doesn't, I'm sure he'll think it's me. He'll want it to be. I don't intend to let him prove it. When I hear him following me, I cut between the Comm and office trailers and sprint across the parade ground. I only spent a few minutes in the lieutenant's trailer, five minutes tops, so most people are still down by the blast site. As far as I can tell, no one else notices me running. Lopez shouts again.

I duck inside the bay doors of the motor pool. No one's here. The door leading down into the lower levels is ajar. The steps go down quite a long way, and there are several different possible exits from the building if I take this route, but this is the direction he'll expect me to head. An old plastic mayonnaise jar filled with screwdrivers sits beside the door. At the far end of the bay, Cox has stacked truck tires. I'm pretty sure I could squeeze behind them. Lopez yells something that sounds disturbingly similar to my name. I give the jar a kick and send it bouncing down the stairs and then I run for the tires. The one at the top nearly tips as I scrape behind the sloppy pile, but I steady it with my hand and crouch behind the stacks. I can see a slice of the room between them. Lopez comes sliding across the sandy concrete and almost falls. He's panting and wheezing. After a few raspy breaths, he jerks his head to one side. It's my mayonnaise jar, still rattling down the steps. Bless you, little jar. Lopez smiles. A tight, mean pursing of the lips. And then he's off.

I slip out one of the side doors. The lockbox digs into my ribs as I move. It feels alive and dangerous, a little metal mammal that wants to burrow into my chest. I follow the crumbling wall, walking quickly, until I spot a small pile of rocks about fifty yards behind the mess hall. There's no way I'm bringing this time bomb back to my tent. If they suspect me, that's the very first place they'll look. I use a thin flat rock to dig. I bury the box just deep enough to stay covered if the wind comes up again in the night. Every inch of my uniform is drenched in sweat and my face is crusted with grime by the time I pat the sand smooth. I mark the spot by impaling the Marlboro box the captain gave me on the sharp tip of a broken radio antenna.

I wish I could take a cool shower, but with water rationed, that's impossible until next week. I consider going back to my tent and using the last of my Wet-Naps. Instead, I jog over to the back entrance to the kitchen tent. It's empty. I peek into the buckets lining the tent wall. All empty. One of the deep steel sinks is half full of dingy water. It smells like rotten onions, but I smell worse. With a metal cup, I pour it over my head. Never in my life could I have imagined how refreshing a bath in dirty dishwater would be.

The kitchen clock reads 0912. Only twelve minutes. A criminal's life must feel ten times as long as the honest man's.

53

The old woman comes at dusk. She drives a wooden cart mounted on two mismatched car tires, pulled by a donkey. The back is filled with empty rice sacks and ruined clothes. No one bothers to poke through it. The cloth has a sour smell, like the dregs of a beer bottle left out overnight. Strong winds and billowing dust follow her off the plain. She's wrapped in several layers of heavy black cloth and from a distance looks like a pile of laundry. The sentry doesn't know what to do with her. He and Sergeant Guzman look her over and let her in. Soon after, the lieutenant sends for me.

When I get to Common Tent 2, I find Ahmed standing by the flap, staring up at the Noses. In the late afternoon light, they are the dark purple color of a deep muscle bruise. Cox told me Ahmed would be gone for the next few days because of a religious holiday. He doesn't hear me coming and jumps when I say his name.

"Ahmed, what are you doing here?" I ask.

He shrugs his shoulders and tries to bum a cigarette. I shake my head, even though I have a sack of tobacco and papers in my cargo pocket. Ahmed seems distracted, worried even. He follows me into the tent.

The lieutenant sits across a card table from the old woman. He pulls absently at the hair behind his ear. A glass of water sits untouched beside her hands. They turn as we come in. When the woman sees Ahmed, she looks down.

Before I have time to salute, the lieutenant says, "Find out what she wants. I can't get a word out of her."

I attempt to ask her this in my halting Arabic. She doesn't respond. I look over at Ahmed.

"Furdu," he says, spittle coming out with the word. "Nasty."

"How do you know?" I say. She looks like every other old woman I've seen since coming here.

He whirls a hand around his head and mumbles something about hats. She's not wearing a hat, just a piece of dark cloth wrapped around her hair and face. It's of an indeterminate color that could be black faded by the sun or discolored by years of grime.

"Ask her what she wants," the lieutenant says impatiently.

Ahmed says something in a sharp voice and the old woman responds slowly, never once looking up at him. I catch something about Allah and demons.

"She's come for the body of her brother and of her sister's daughter's son."

"How did she know they were dead?" the lieutenant asks. "For that matter, how did she know they were here?"

Ahmed asks. The old woman looks down at her feet and points to the ceiling.

"She says God told her in a . . ." Ahmed bites his lip in frustration. "In a sleep movie." He closes his eyes and puts his hands against his ear in a pantomime of sleeping. "Lies. The God isn't speaking to nasty peoples like this."

"What did we do with them, Durrant?" the lieutenant says. He speaks quickly and with distaste.

"We put them in body bags and Ahmed buried them behind the cement factory building."

"We did?" He seems surprised, although he was the one to give the order. The lieutenant turns to Ahmed. "Tell her we'll get them. But first she needs to tell us how many of her people have turned against us and gone to the Noses."

Ahmed frowns and starts to complain. The lieutenant shuts him down with a loud, "Do it." Ahmed salutes in his sloppy way and reluctantly turns back to the old woman. She appears startled by the question and answers at some length. When she stops, Ahmed stares at the table, rubbing his hands together. It should be obvious to everyone he's trying to formulate a lie of some kind.

"So?" the lieutenant asks.

"It is all old-woman talk. She is telling make-up stories."

"Just tell us what she said," I say.

Ahmed sighs and rolls his eyes. The lieutenant clenches and unclenches his hands. The old woman tells her beads, which appear in her hands suddenly, like a dove from a magician's sleeve. The small dry clicks sound very loud. Ahmed squints at them with disgust.

"She is saying her peoples are leaving." He continues to stare at the old woman's beads as he speaks, as though he would like to tear them from her hands. "But not to the Noses. They go south. To Inmar. These are lies. I know lies. Every word a fat and juicy lie."

I wonder where he got this fat and juicy business. Probably Cox.

"Just translate," the lieutenant says.

"She is saying she came back to make a noise. A big noise for the bad men to hear so her peoples can get away. She is alone and old. No childrens left. She is saying it doesn't matter what happens to her." Ahmed looks at the old woman again. She whispers something so softly it sounds like radio static. He scrapes at a tooth with his thumbnail and blinks. An odd expression passes across his face. He almost looks scared for a moment, but then he pushes whatever troubles him aside and smiles a smile so large and false that even the lieutenant looks alarmed by it. "She is saying you must go too."

"We must go? *Must*?" The lieutenant snorts and tugs at the hair behind his ear. "Tell her we're safe here. There's nothing for us to worry about."

I wonder if the lieutenant actually believes this.

Ahmed tells the old woman something. God only knows what. I try and decide for the hundredth time if it's really possible for us to communicate this way. It's hard enough to have a conversation with someone who speaks your language, much less to talk through an untrustworthy and incompetent translator to someone who doesn't know a single English word. I wondered the same thing when we tried to interrogate the old man. Even if he had spoken to me man to man, would I have understood him? Probably not. I doubt the captured boy could really express what he thought either. I'm pretty sure he made an earnest go at it, but—but what we got in the end was just a crude approximation that essentially transformed what he said into a well-meaning lie. One jump is hard enough, but two must be almost impossible. From thought into word and then from one language to another. Drawing pictures might be better.

The old woman makes a low monotone humming sound and rocks back and forth, clicking her prayer beads. Then, suddenly, she stops and stares into the lieutenant's eyes. Her voice is husky with excitement as she speaks.

Ahmed shakes his head. "She is telling to you, no one is safe. Not any more."

The woman continues, even louder now. Suddenly, Ahmed makes an angry guttural sound and lunges across the table. She screams and spits at him. The lieutenant and I grab Ahmed's arms, pulling him up just before the flimsy card table collapses. The old woman darts forward and pinches the top of Ahmed's hand with her fingernails. They have the color and texture of a cow's hoof and it isn't easy to pry them away from Ahmed's skin. He squeals.

When we finally manage pull them apart, his hand is swelling from a burst blood vessel. The old woman examines her work with great satisfaction. Just behind his knuckles is a purple mark the size of a cat's tongue.

"Guzman!" the lieutenant shouts.

The sergeant appears almost immediately.

"Take this woman outside."

"Yes, sir."

Once she's gone, the lieutenant starts to shout again. "What the hell was that, Ahmed? She's an old lady!"

"No, she is a trash on the road. Nasty dead pork woman."

"What did she say?" the lieutenant asks.

"Lies."

"I don't care to hear your interpretation," he says. "Just tell me what the fuck she said."

"She is lying that many thousands men go to Noses. Not her men. Others. She sees them walk on roads. She is hearing them pray for Allah to put strong in their arms and put more red on their hearts. This praying means they are almost coming soon. That is why her peoples go south. She is saying before the moon of Ramadan they come and kill all of your things. Trucks and houses and papers and clothes. They kill even the rocks." Ahmed's voice rises, as though this possible destruction pleases him a great deal. The way his eyes shine makes me want to punch them shut, but the lieutenant seems fascinated, somehow both excited and worried. "They kick your heads open like melons and make a tasty kind of soup out of your hearts and put many spices in the pot after it bubbles and then they are eating heart soup. Bowls and bowls and bowls. It puts the strong in their arms. Then they feed your sexes to dogs. These are the lies she is saying."

"Heart soup?" I ask.

The lieutenant looks intently at the empty chair where the old woman sat a minute ago. He is out of breath, as though Ahmed's rant was something heavy he had to lift. I have the disturbing feeling this information connects in some way with other things he knows. In the murky light of the tent, Ahmed's eyes gleam like two wet prune pits.

"This is all a bunch of hokum," the lieutenant says finally, but without much conviction. His face is red and splotchy and he plucks at the back of his head in a fast, uneven rhythm, like he's tapping out a message in Morse code. "Peasant crap."

"Yes, yes, pleasant crap." Ahmed looks triumphant. "Lies, I am telling you. Fat and juicy lies. Now you see. She is a nasty dead pork woman."

"Take Ahmed and dig up those bodies, Durrant." The lieutenant sounds tired. "Then get her out of here."

"Lies," Ahmed says again and pumps his fist in the air. He only seems to pick up Cox's most irritating affectations. It baffles me.

54

I try to stay behind for a moment so I can speak with the lieutenant about the Ahmed situation, but he orders me to leave. He takes off his steel-rimmed glasses and presses the heel of his hand against his forehead. I pause at the tent flap, hoping he'll change his mind. When he bows his head, I notice a raw patch of scalp just behind his left ear. It's a bald spot the size of an M16 bullet casing. I open my mouth to say something, but he shouts "Out!"

Ahmed waits outside with shovels. If I killed him, I'd probably be hauled up in front of a court-martial for murder, but I have no doubt he's the most dangerous person on base. We walk to the burial place without speaking. The old woman hisses at us as we pass. Sergeant Guzman laughs.

"Durrant, your girlfriend here's jealous of the little chickpea chicky who gave you that stuffed animal."

Ahmed stares at me, puzzled. Then, something in his face changes. His eyebrows bunch up and his eyes narrow. He looks as though he's doing long division in his head. When the answer finally comes, it arrives with a gruesome smile. "You have hajji girlfriend, Mr. Toby?"

I decide to ignore him.

"Who told you that?" I ask Sergeant Guzman with maybe just a tad too much anxiety in my voice. I immediately regret saying anything at all. I should have told him I do have a hajji girl and that she's smoking-hot and puts out like a nickel slot machine. Then he'd think I was full of shit and forget the whole thing five minutes later. But no, I have to be a dumbass and act freaked out about it. Worst of all, Ahmed is standing here taking notes.

"Boyette." Sergeant Guzman's grin grows an inch wider. "He thinks you've got a girlfriend in town. Says she gave you an ugly stuffed dinosaur."

It's an elebear.

"Yeah, right," I say, only now getting the tone right, when it's too late to do any good. "Sure, Sarge, I've got a girlfriend in town. A real looker."

"Maybe it is not girl," Ahmed says with a sly and deeply repulsive grin. "Maybe it is little boy."

My heart seizes up and stops completely.

"Don't ask, don't tell, Ahmed," the sergeant says with fake sternness.

I cough up the obligatory laugh. Ahmed blinks at him and attempts to work out the joke.

Sergeant Guzman tries to help him. "Faggotry, little man, you hear me? I'm talking about ass-spelunking, cock-smoking, moustache rides."

Ahmed looks lost, so the sergeant continues.

"Fudge-packing. Rectum-wrecking. Nutsack-nuzzling. Wiener—"

"I think he's got the picture, Sergeant." Jesus, what is it with soldiers and fag jokes? Nothing tickles a grunt's funny bone faster than cracking wise about two men touching wee-wees.

"Nope," Sergeant Guzman says, "look at him. I don't think he does."

Sure enough, Ahmed's face could be an illustration of befuddlement.

"What is all this?" he asks me.

"Should I draw him a picture?" I say. "In the sand with a stick?"

For some reason this makes Sergeant Guzman break up laughing. Throughout this entire episode, the old woman glares at us from under her stained head wrap. I'd almost forgotten about her there for a mike. Thank God she doesn't speak English. Ahmed laughs along in a polite but insincere way. His expression indicates that fake laughter gives him a feeling similar to a mild earache.

As we walk off, the old woman points at us and hisses something.

I look over at Ahmed for an explanation. He shakes his head furiously.

"She tells us not to bother the dead peoples with our sex parts."

Maybe she does understand English.

55

When the old woman drives her mule cart out through the gates, Ahmed tells me he needs to go back to the village. I see his purpose in his eyes. He wants the old woman. I'm filled with a rage so sudden and intense that I very nearly hit him with my shovel. Ahmed senses something and takes a few steps back.

"First," I say, "let's put away the shovels."

I lead him to the storage area behind the garage. Wind whips sand across the parade ground. Somewhere a door creaks back and forth. This gives me an idea. When we step inside, I direct him to the small room where we store tools and extra uniforms. A few weeks ago, Cox had got stuck in here when the door closed behind him and locked. It was Ahmed who found him. I hand Ahmed my shovel.

"Watch out for the door," I tell him.

He smiles warily. "Yes, the bad door."

"Put them on the shelf at the very back," I say. "I need to ask the sergeant something. Meet me at the gate and I'll give you a ride into the village."

"Yes," he says, "I do not need ride."

As soon as he disappears inside the storage room, I nudge the door with my foot. It creaks closed very slowly and locks.

56

I am the only one in line for the telephone.

"Did you get my letter?" Clarissa asks. She doesn't even say hello. Her voice is tight and she speaks very quickly. The line hums and crackles. There's a half-second delay that drives me crazy. I'm tempted to hang up and call back. Our phone connection seems to get a little worse each time.

"No," I say, "we haven't gotten any mail in a while."

"Damn," she says, "I thought you would have gotten it by now. Why don't you have e-mail any more?"

"I don't know. It's a crappy posting. We don't have anything."

"Damn," she says again.

"Well, just tell me. I don't mind reading it again."

"Damn."

"Whoa," I say, "what's going on, honey?"

"I'm seeing someone else." The words tumble out of her mouth, almost on top of each other.

These are perhaps the worst words any soldier can hear from a loved one back home. It's like hearing of a death in the family. Each of us with a girlfriend or wife worries over the possibility constantly. We listen for clues in the anecdotes of home life they tell. We read and re-read the letters they send looking for meaningful absences, small slips. We talk about the stories we've heard of soldiers back home seducing other soldier's wives. Jody stories. And although most men will tell you the worst possible thing one soldier can do to another is steal their girl while they're stationed overseas, it is almost always another soldier who is responsible.

"What?" I say. "I don't understand." I don't want to understand. I want to believe it's a mistake, that I misheard.

"I met someone, Toby. It's hard. I can't—"

"Who?" I sound breathless, as though someone has just punched me in the gut, and that's exactly what it feels like.

"Jack, from work."

"But Clarissa—"

"I can't do this any more, Toby. It's not fair to either of us."

"What can't you do any more? Keep a guilty secret?" I can't seem to get enough air into my lungs. "Was this a one-time thing, and it's making you miserable keeping it from me? What is this? Do you mean you went on a date with him? Kissed him? What are we talking about here? Clarissa—"

"Stop," she yells, her voice distorted by the earpiece. It's too much emotion for the satellite to process, so it breaks it down into digital chunks. "Listen. I think we should end it, Toby. It was a bad idea. The whole thing. I'm too young. You're too young. I can't even remember why I liked you in the first place. We hardly know each other."

"That's not true," I say. "It isn't true. You know it."

"It *is* true. You don't really know me. I mean, *really* know me. At all. I've changed a lot. Look, Toby. It was a fun little thing, but we took it way too far too fast. I should have known better. It seemed romantic. *Romantic.* I actually remember thinking, I'm getting married to a soldier. La, la, la. Now I know what a load of bullshit that is."

"Clarissa—" The muscles in my legs twitch and quiver.

"This stupid fucking war. If it wasn't for you leaving to go over there, I would have thought it out more clearly. I'm not blaming you, Toby. I should have known better. *I* should have known. I should have—"

"Hold on, baby. Wait, wait, wait. Let's not do something drastic. It's this distance. It's hard to talk. I couldn't explain how it feels to be here even if I wanted to. I admit, it's changed me some, too. That's probably why you feel like you don't know me any more. So when I get back, we'll get to know each other all—"

"That's not what I mean. You've got it backwards. Like always. Listen to me, Toby, I—"

"—over again, but I'm still basically the same guy you met that day in the nature preserve. And when I get back, we can pretend like we're meeting up for the first time. I know what this is. I understand. I do, baby, I do. I'm lonely. I know you're lonely. So you went on a date with some guy. So what? I don't like it. I don't like it all. But I can deal with it. Just tell him it's over. It's done with. We won't talk about it again. Maybe you need to hang out with your family a little more. If not your parents, then Sarah. Go and see your sister—"

"You're not listening to me, Toby. Stop. This is exactly what I'm talking about. It's like you don't hear what I'm saying."

"I hear what you're saying. I just think you're lonely and stressed out. You've got a baby coming. You're not thinking straight. I forgive you, but—"

"I don't want you to forgive me!" Clarissa shrieks. I pull the phone from my ear.

"What the hell was that?" I say.

"I can't do it."

"You've barely given it a chance. I'll be back in a few months, and we can work this shit out. Baby. Honey. Come on. This will kill me. I'm not joking. You and the baby are all I have to come home to, to plan for—"

"No, Toby, no."

"What about the baby?" I'm trying to maintain, but my anger slips away from me. "What about the fucking baby?"

"Don't curse at me."

"Sorry, but the baby is—"

"I don't know, Toby. Okay? I don't know."

"There's nothing to know. We have a baby coming. It deserves to have a mom and a dad."

"That's just it." She sighs, filling the earpiece with a sound like an ocean storm. I think about the time we drank a jug of wine and spent the entire night on the beach at Tybee Island. The tide came in and woke us up. "I don't know. I'm not sure I can have it."

That yanks me back. My eyes throb. They feel very dry.

"Don't do this," I tell her. I want to go down on my knees. "You can't do this."

"I don't think it's a good idea. Jack says—"

"I don't care what fucking Jack says. I'll raise the baby. If you don't think it's a good idea, then *I'll* raise it. My grandpa raised me by himself."

"No, Toby, that's different. You were older and—"

"I won't let you do it. No fucking way. No one else is going to raise my child."

"I'm not talking about adoption, Toby," she says softly.

A strange sound comes out of my mouth.

"It's *my* body," she says.

"It's half my child. If I could take it out of you and put it in me, I would. Or put a fucking lock on there and—"

"Don't be stupid, Toby. You can't lock up my womb like a safe. It's not even a baby yet. It's not much more than a clump of goo, a tablespoon of Goddamn jelly."

"No," I say, "no, no, *no*." My voice gets louder with each word.

"It's not your choice."

"Don't you fucking do this."

"Read the letter," she says, and hangs up.

"Fuck, fuck, fuck," I scream at the wall. Then I kick it.

Sergeant Guzman comes out of the office. "Don't abuse my fucking trailer, Joe. I don't care what Jody did to your girl. Go outside and kick a Goddamn rock if you want to break your foot on something."

I give him a look. It must be a pretty ugly one, because he tenses up and squares his shoulders.

"Don't do something stupid, Durrant." He says this very quietly.

I close my eyes and shout, "Fuck."

"You're right about that, Joe," Sergeant Guzman says. "That's where all the trouble comes from. Hold up a sec." He ducks into his office. When he comes back out, he tosses me something. It's a cigar. "Cuban," he says. "I bought it in the capital a couple of months ago. I was saving it for I don't know the hell what. But. You need it more than me. Go take a walk around the wall. Blow some smoke."

"Thanks," I say.

I leave before something bad happens.

57

The cigar is good. It tastes like a better life. One I might have had if my parents had taken a left instead of a right, if I had said no instead of yes, if I had kept my eyes on the ball, if I had cleaned my plate, brushed my teeth, and said my prayers. It tastes so good I can barely smoke it. The better life makes me choke a little.

58

The convoy rolls in at four that morning. I wake to the sound of excited shouting. From this distance, it's impossible to tell if this is good or bad. I jump into some pants and sprint to the mobilization point. A sharp wind whips dust across the base. The stars are so bright they bleed together. They left in two Humvees; they come back in one and a half. The lead vehicle is missing a bumper and two side windows. The doors are peppered with bullet holes. The armor kit seems to have worked, but just barely. The second Humvee's windshield is demolished. There's a hole the size of a basketball in the center and the rest of the glass is only held together by the sheet of plastic shatter-proofing. It sags.

I look around for Rankin. He's not with the rest of them. The men look tired but relatively unharmed. Sergeant Oliphant has blood on his cheeks, but I can't make out where it's coming from. Boyette, Rankin, and Nevada are missing. I grab Doc Greer by the sleeve.

"Where is he? Where's Rankin?"

Doc Greer stares at me, eyes blank. After a while he says, "Go look in the back. Your girlfriend's sleeping like a baby."

The relief is physical. Like when an abscess bursts and the pain melts away. For a moment, I was almost certain Rankin was dead.

"It was a close thing." Doc Greer shakes his head and looks weary. "A cunt hair away from buying the ranch. If it wasn't for the old woman, you wouldn't be talking to me. I just fucking wish—"

"Old woman?"

But Sergeant Guzman pulls Greer away before he can answer me. "Come on, Doc. You can't quit yet. Somebody still needs stitches."

"What that *some*body needs is a halo," Doc Greer mumbles as they walk off together.

Both Humvees are empty. The second one is splashed with gore. Blood covers everything. The muscles in my neck and shoulders contract. It's too much blood. A human can't lose this much blood and survive. In the starlight it looks like chocolate syrup. The back windows are smudged with bloody handprints. A puddle of blood thickens between the seats. Wads of bloody field-dressing pads cover the sandbags on the floor. Behind me someone shouts. And then howls. Thousands of brass shell casings glitter on the dashboard. Even these are smeared with blood. I don't want to know. I really don't. I want to stay here and hold this moment when I don't know.

59

Hazel sits Indian-style in the sand outside Common Tent 1 with his head in hands. His shoulders shake, vibrate. But he doesn't make a sound. Either he doesn't notice me or he doesn't want to. Inside the tent, men shout. It's impossible to make out who's yelling at who. Or what about. I take a knee in the sand beside him and put my hand on his shoulder. He jerks away. Like I prodded him with a hot rifle barrel.

"Hazel?" I say.

He keeps his face in his hands.

"Hazel?" I reach over and try to pull his hands away, but they stay stuck to his face. "Come on, man. What happened?"

Hazel makes a wet growling sound like an injured dog.

"Guy, come on. What's going on?"

"Boyette," he mumbles through his fingers. A string of drool hangs from his chin.

Understanding comes fast and hard. A load of wet sand dropped on my head. "Not—"

Hazel jumps up and whirls around. He kicks the tent's guy wire. He kicks sand. Rocks fly. He kicks me in the leg. He kicks and kicks and kicks. All the while, he covers his face with his hands. He goes around and around in this jerky, angry dance.

"Shit!" he shouts. Spit and snot and tears drip from his fingers. "Shit, fuck, shit, shit, shit, motherfucking shit fuck shit!"

"Do you want—"

"Get the fuck away from me or I'll kick your fucking ass!"

I step away. I feel like someone's wrapped a rope around my neck and is slowly pulling it tight. Air whistles in my throat. I don't know what to do with my hands. I don't what to do.

Hazel stops spinning and drops to the ground face-first like he's been shot by a sniper. His boots continue to kick at the sand. He makes that wet growling sound again. Boyette gave Hazel constant shit, but they were rarely apart. Once I even saw Boyette cutting Hazel's hair with a battery-powered razor. Way out in the sand behind the mess tent. Just the two of them. Hazel in a chair and Boyette stepping around him with the razor. Laughing their heads off about something.

My thoughts are all jammed up in a tight knot. All I can think to do is go look for Rankin. Rankin. He'll know what the fuck.

60

Nobody goes to bed. As tired as they are, nobody's sleeping until they get the story out of their system. It's always this way after a shitstorm. After any kind of fight, actually. We tell ourselves the story over and over again. Tonight we sit around in Common Tent 2, wishing we had beer, wishing we had whiskey. Wishing. Sergeants Guzman and Oliphant are off somewhere else. The rest of us have piled into the tent. Even Ahmed's here. He sits in the corner with his hands in his lap and watches us, like a wasting disease that will eventually kill us all. When I tell Lopez to get rid of him, Ahmed glares at me.

"Somebody locked the guy in a closet, Durrant," Lopez says.

I shrug.

Nevada's starting the story when I sit down in the circle. His voice is the only sound in the room. It sounds hollow and fragile, like he's talking through a cardboard tube. "We got pretty far with the Humvees. Further than I thought we'd get. Shit, I didn't think we'd get a klick away from the base before we'd have to start humping. Oliphant has us stop at the bottom of a trail. We can see it stretching up the side of the hill—"

"And smoke," Greer says. He hasn't washed. His face is black with ash. Rusty bits of dried blood flake away from his cheeks when he scratches them.

"Yeah, and we see this itty-bitty little dribble of smoke coming up in the distance. This makes Oli happy."

"Small smoke, small force." Rankin usually does a pretty good Sergeant Oliphant imitation, but there's something missing from this one.

"So our man Rankin here is on point. He's lugging that big M249 right on down the trail. Has that SAW up on his shoulder like it was just a little stick. The man's got rounds wrapped every which way. A regular Mexican bandit." Nevada looks over at him and smiles. A tired smile but a real one. Shit, I think, when did this start? They're making eyes at each other now, like teenagers on the way to the prom. It takes me a moment to realize I'm jealous of their shared experience, bad as it might be. It's an ugly reaction and it irritates me to realize I'm having it. Nevada takes a drag off his cigarette, blows a thick blue spurt of smoke at the ceiling, then continues the story. "He takes us all the way up the hill. How many klicks you think, Mr. R?"

"Ten maybe," Rankin says.

"That's right, y'all, that's right." He sings this to us like a sad song. "Ten klicks straight up the Nose. Up there at the top, when we're getting closer to the smoke, Oli tells us to get ready, we're leaving the trail. We're going up and over. So get on your bellies. We crawl through them rocks like lizards. The sun's sucking the sweat right out of us. It's hot, man. I mean pizza-oven hot."

"Pizza-oven," Hazel repeats, as though it's a word he's never heard. This is the first thing he's said in almost an hour.

"Big bad Rankin here, he's on point and when he gets to the top, he's like—" Nevada holds up his fist, sign language for stop. "Oli creeps up there beside him and glasses something with his bee-nocks. The rest of us, our cheese is melting, bubbling."

"They were holding a conference up there," Doc Greer adds.

Rankin frowns. His eyes are pink and glassy. If he shut them, he'd be asleep before he hit the floor. If I didn't know better, I'd think he'd just smoked a J. But I know better. Battle fatigue can be a sort of intoxication.

"Oli comes back and tells us to shut the fuck up. We're too loud. They must have heard us coming, 'cause they've skipped. We follow him over the ridge. There, in a little flat spot carved out of the side of the hill, is a tiny, baby camp. Ain't hardly nothing. A pile of dirty filthy clothes. A boot with holes. A blanket that smells like Greer's meemaw's nookie."

"Hey, my granny's got a washcloth," Doc Greer says and tries to smile. But that smile is about something else. It's a look of pure relief. I'm not dead, this half-smile says, I'm not dead.

"Then I notice they left behind their dinner. A big old pot of stew boiling over the fire. And I'll tell you what. It smelled good. Real good. Ain't that right, Salis?"

"It did. I'm thinking it was goat." Salis's hair is mashed down and matted with yellow dirt. The patchy growth on his cheeks looks like mildew. He listens with a clenched fist on either knee, nodding like an autistic child.

"Well, I grab the stirring spoon off a rock and dip me up a bite. We hadn't stopped to eat for a long, long time. Right before we hit the trail I had one of them chicken MREs. You know the kind. No flavor, just a block of tough old meat."

"I like them," Salis says, surprised to hear someone else might not.

"You would," Greer says.

"My stomach's growling and fussing. I need some fuel. This here's a snack, I tell myself, just to hold me over till supper. Right as I'm fixing to pop it in my mouth, Rankin comes by and swipes it out of my hand. Goddamn, I told him, what the fuck? I was fixing to pop him one."

Everyone looks over to see what Rankin thinks about this. He stares at the tent wall like he can see right through it. I'm not even sure he's listening.

But Nevada doesn't stop. "Rankin says, 'Could be something's wrong with it.' 'Nah,' I say, 'they just left a second ago. It's their dinner. What'd be wrong with it? They don't know we're coming to lunch. Looky here,' I tell him, 'that cat's eating it and it looks fine.'"

The men who made up the fire team all laugh. A raucous angry laugh. A hellish in-joke. They bare their teeth like rabid dogs. The rest of us look around, feeling left out and maybe glad to be that way.

Rankin winks at me and mouths the words, *Fucking Nevada*. Then he falls back into his head. His eyes go as blank as hard-boiled eggs.

"Well, I leave it at that. No time to fuss over it. 'Cause here comes Uncle Oli telling us he's spotted the hajjis running off on the far hill. We got to hustle. Here's our chance to get the assholes who've been shooting up our base this week."

Salis says, "I was looking to fuck somebody up bad."

"I know you were, baby. I know you were." Nevada thumps him on the shoulder. "Well, we take off after them."

"Booking it," Cox says.

"Flat out," Salis agrees.

"We must a chased them two more klicks. Right down into this shallow wash. Even though we're being careful, traveling overwatch and moving from cover to cover, Oli, he tries to stop us with a raised fist and says, 'Whoa, this here ain't right.' I'll admit I heard the man, but we were close on them. Close enough to smell their dirty towels. Too close to stop. And these two, they needed killing bad."

Salis laughs his agreement. It's an awful sound.

"I didn't even hear him," Rankin says, perking up for a moment.

"Me neither," Doc Greer says.

"Well, here's where it gets hairy. Whoa, man, I mean hairy. Like a gorilla. Starts to look like Durrant's ass."

A laugh comes out of my mouth. I don't think about it, but all of a sudden there it is. In a sense, Nevada saying this about me is a compliment. He's putting me in the story even though I wasn't really there.

"Rankin and me, we're popping off some rounds now. He's got that heavy 240 and it's louder than shit in this little canyon. I'm feeding in the rounds. The muzzle blast's blowing the sweat off my face. And then—" Nevada snaps his fingers. "—they're gone. Vanished. So Rankin and me, we screech to a stop. Look around. Doc Greer and Boyette come slowpoking along." He takes a breath after this. The sound of this name casts a spell on the room. We all look down at our feet. "And then, and then—" Nevada's voice gets squeaky and high.

"Cox, doing his—" Nevada bounces his shoulders, pulling his chin down tight against his chest. "—his monkey march."

Nevada waits for the laugh. Nothing. Cox has his eyes closed. He might be asleep. A couple of guys smile. This would have brought down the house last week. But last week was a month ago.

"Oli shouts, 'Back. Get the fuck back.' And then the air fills up with lead. This wash we're in ends about fifty yards away in a pile of boulders. A dead-end. And waiting behind them rocks are about thirty fuckers with their heads wrapped up in dishrags throwing lead at us. Thank God almighty they can't aim for shit. Spray and pray is all the training these kids got. Still, we are smack up against a shitload of hajjis. That bunch in front, and then a handful up on the hill trying to flank us."

We're all leaning in to hear what comes next. The ones who went and the ones who stayed. We're all in this story now. We hear the guns. We feel that hot, greasy metal. We smell the cordite. We smell the fear in our sweat. All of us here have lived this story. We might have known different actors and different settings, but the plot is just the same. There is only one war story. And we all know the ending.

"Oli pulls us back behind a couple of big rocks. There's a kind of overhang in the side of this wash that gives us a little bit of cover. They can't get at us, but we ain't going nowhere neither. Shit, man, it looked bad. I was saying my prayers."

"All one of them," Lopez says.

"Yeah," Nevada says, "but I was saying it as many times as I could."

"I know that prayer," I say. "Please God, save my ass."

This gets a couple of smiles.

"That's the one." Nevada forces his lips into a smile, but the rest of his face stays blank.

"We were goners," Salis says.

"No doubt." Nevada leans in, his storyteller face back on. Wide eyes, serious brows, and a tight, crafty mouth. "Oli looks around with that badass expression he's got. They must teach you that shit at sergeant school. I can see them all lined up in a classroom, 'All right, you all, give me your fight face.'"

Rankin returns from his head to do a pretty good imitation of Sergeant Oliphant's mean look and we laugh, but quietly, like we're all still trapped behind that rock until Nevada brings us out and away, back to the base. Back to our little lockbox, our safe little mud-brick womb. Ollie, ollie, oxen free.

"He looks at us, face to face to face, and says, 'What we got to do here, men, is set up a diversion.'" Nevada whispers this, the way the sergeant must have done while they were behind those rocks.

Rankin chimes in. "And I said, 'What the fuck with, boss?' I thought he was out of his fucking mind." He is inside the story now, telling it like it's happening again. I can almost see the scene playing out across his pupils, upside down and tiny, like looking in the lens of a movie projector.

"I couldn't believe it," Doc Greer says, squeezing his knees and shaking his head back and forth. "I thought he was shitting us."

"And then it gets crazier," Nevada says.

Hazel lets out a soft groan.

"He says to us—" Nevada looks around the room, catching every eye.

And then every one of the men who went on this mission shouts, "Tighten up your bootlaces!" Busting up with laughter once they're done. The first honest laughs I've heard all morning.

"What?" I say, confounded like the rest of us shut-ins.

"Nobody asked, 'What,' D," Cox tells me. His face looks as serious as a knife blade. I see he misunderstands my question, which was just a sound of surprise. "We didn't say shit. It looked that bad."

Nevada waves this away. "He has us give him all our smoke grenades and star clusters, and he lines them up on a rock. I had a feeling I knew what he was going to do then, but I kept my mouth shut. Then good old Uncle Oli says, 'I'm going to give you all some covering fire. And when I say "get," you get the hell out of here. Hear me?' Then Rankin says to him, 'What about you?' Oli, he just spits. 'Let me fucking worry about me. You worry about your own ass. I'm going to throw out some smoke and set up behind that rock up there where I can lay down some suppressive fire.' He points to a big white boulder about ten yards ahead of us that's split in two like somebody'd chopped it with a great big ax. He gives us all a hard look and says, 'When I run, you got to give me a big blast of covering fire, I mean big. Then once I'm in place up there, I want you all to let loose with the rest of them smoke grenades on my signal. Every Goddamn one of them. Fire off a couple of star clusters too. Once we got this wash good and choked with smoke, it's time for you to get the fuck out of here. Don't wait too long. I'll put down as much cover as I can, but then you all got to run. Don't slow down till you get back to that little camp.'" Nevada closes his eyes and shakes his head. His voice sounds suddenly gruff. "I tried to ask him what he was going to do, but he don't give me a chance. 'On the count of three,' he says, before we can think too much about what we're about to do. 'One, two, three.' He chucks out two blue smokes and sprints to the rock. Every last one of us lets go of a clip. The wash ain't that wide, maybe fifteen feet across. Tops. We can hear those fuckers jabbering back there at the other end, probably thinking we blown ourselves up. One of them laughed."

Cox shivers. "I heard that. I heard that." From the way he says it, I don't think he'll ever be able to get it out of his head.

"We all heard it, Collie," Rankin says softly.

"It didn't sound like a person," Cox says. "No real person could make that sound."

Without warning, Nevada points to the tent flap and shouts, "Go, go, go."

All of us jump. Ahmed gets out of his chair and starts to run. We laugh at him and jeer. The tent sounds like a kennel. After a second, Ahmed sees it's just part of the story and stops, but he makes it all the way to the tent flap before he notices he's the only one running. His face turns red, but he doesn't say a word. Nobody really cares. We want the story.

"That's all he says to us. He don't shout it. Somehow, though, it felt loud. And believe me, every last swinging dick of us is on the move.

When it comes time for us all to cut out of there, Oli, he ain't moving. 'What about you?' I yelled over at him, 'cause I had a feeling this was going to happen. I yell this at him just before we throw out the rest of the grenades. 'I'll meet you,' he says. And that's it. That's all he says. I think right then, he's dead. He's killing himself for us."

Greer makes a grumbling sound deep in his throat. His eyes are bright and wet. Dyson punches him softly on the leg.

"We run. Shit, do we run. Back through the smoke and up out of that fucking death wash. Bullets were winging off rocks all around us. I caught one—" Nevada bends down so we can see the top of his head. His hair is short, cropped down to about half an inch, but running from ear to ear, there is a crease. I bend in to see it and get a whiff of burnt hair. "Those fucking helmets ain't worth a shit. That bullet went right on through. Knocked me on my ass and made my eyes cross. I was out cold for a second. Rankin, he yanks me up, and then him and Boyette had to drag my ass on up the hill. Like to of carried me for some of the way." He gives Rankin one of these new looks of theirs. No smile this time. But now I think I see where this new thing between them came from. Nevada turns back to the rest of us. "And this whole time I'm hearing Boy firing off bursts and shouting, 'Get some. Get some. Get some.' That fucking Boyette. He could do some shit. In a tight spot, you wanted him on your team."

"Get some," Hazel says very quietly, almost as if he's not aware he's doing it. It sort of slips out of him. He watches Nevada's mouth with glazed, pink eyes.

"Get some. Seemed like an inch from my ear. Get some." Nevada chuckles in a dispirited way and shakes his head. "Like the man's feeding hogs. My head still fucking hurts."

"Look here, look here," Salis says, standing up and showing us the holes in his pant leg just above his right knee. We see how the bullet caught a bit of extra fabric and passed right on through without so much as brushing a hair on his leg. "You ain't the only one who dodged one. A few inches higher and my dangler wouldn't dangle."

"I don't know how we got out of that wash," Doc Greer says. "It felt like magic."

"So, so, so," Nevada says, yanking us back into the story. "We ran toward them pretty fast, but we flew on the way back, grew wings and took off flying. I saw smoke coming off of Doc Greer's boots. My lungs were whistling and burning."

"Tell them about the cat," Salis says, swaying back and forth in his chair. His face is intent and greasy with sweat.

Nevada looks down. It's hard to read the expression on his face. When his head comes back up, his eyes are slits. "The fucking thing was dead. Rankin was right. The whole Goddamn thing was a trap. They knew we were coming. And that's the shit of this whole Goddamn thing. How the fuck did they know we were coming? Boyette didn't have a fucking chance. That Goddamn cracker. I mean, what the fuck? What was that shit? How did they know? How did they *know*?"

"Fucking right. They didn't just see us coming up the hill. Somebody set that shit up." Doc Greer starts to stand, then sits again.

I look at Ahmed. He's glancing off, unconcerned, bored even. This isn't his story, his attitude suggests, but I strongly suspect otherwise. I watch as he knits and squeezes his fingers together. My cheeks are hot with blood. He says a word, I tell myself, and I'm going to pound him. No, I'm going to fucking shoot his ass. And then I notice Lopez, drilling my head with one of his glares. I don't look away. You fuckwit, I think. You can't really believe I'm the one who did this, that I'd sell my buddies out.

"Jesus, Lopez," Rankin says, "the way you look, you'd think it was you got ambushed."

Lopez starts, as though caught out doing something he shouldn't, like picking his nose and eating it or playing with himself in public.

"Well," Nevada says, catching us all with his eyes once again and reeling us back, "we slow down after the poison camp. Walking and jogging. Walking and jogging. We start talking about Oli. Like maybe we should go back and get him. Boyette's all for it. But Boyette—" He makes a deranged face. We all know how Boyette was. "That boy wanted to get a range named after him, win him a medal of honor, some shit like that. Well, he got it. That asshole. Goddamn. After a bugout like that, there's no going back. There ain't nothing left for us to get, I try to tell him. Nobody could of gotten out of that shitstorm. I guarantee, I told the Boy, it was over in a couple of mikes. Maybe we can come back later with a bigger force and get, well, you know, but not now. No way. And it's coming on night now too. We'd been humping along for a good while. We hadn't eaten hardly a bite for hours and our CamelBaks were running dry." Nevada wipes his forehead on his sleeve, as though just the memory of this march exhausts him, which it probably does.

"It's always longer coming back," I say.

"It took about three days," Salis says.

The whole team nods. Hell has a very flexible chronology and its own special measurement of time.

"Just when we're coming down the last long stretch of the trail, we hear it. Pop, pop, pop. What the hell? we say. Somebody's firing off the Ma Deuce on the back of our Humvee, but they ain't firing it at us. They're firing in the other direction. By now it's boogie dark. All you can see are green and red tracers zipping back and forth through the night. We hustle down to the trailhead, and shit if it ain't fucking Oli on the back of that Humvee. We got the vehicles all parked facing downhill at the very end of the road where there's this open space large enough for a turnaround. Oli's up in the lead vehicle, working the .50-cal, so I can just barely make him out. Damn, I think, is it a ghost? Sarge, somebody yelled out." Nevada cups his hands around his mouth and makes like it's happening right then. "That you down there?"

"It was Boyette yelling that," Doc Greer says, grimacing.

"How'd Sarge get back to the Humvees before you?" I ask. It doesn't seem possible.

"That's what I asked," Salis says. "I asked him, what'd you fly on, Sarge, a magic carpet?"

"He never did tell us," Rankin says, "but I figure he must of come straight across, right down the cliff."

"See, the trail we took curved back and forth across the hill. The slope was real steep." Nevada tilts his hand. "If you went straight across, as the bird flies, it might be like, what?" He turns to Rankin. "A fourth the distance of the trail we took."

"About that," Rankin says. "Maybe less."

"Is that what he did?" I ask. "Go straight down the cliff? Did he have rope and gear?"

"Nope," Nevada says, "he didn't have none of that shit."

"He never told us how he did it," Doc Greer says. "And don't think we didn't ask. He just spit and looked away. You know the way he does."

"But then, but then," Salis says, bouncing in his chair like a kid with the answer to a math problem. "Tell about the old—"

"I'm getting there," Nevada says, holding up a finger. "The road right there by the trailhead is pinched up. Two cars can just barely get by. It's tight. Just as we reach the Humvees, we see what Oli's firing at. This beat-up Toyota truck's coming up the road with a bed full of dirty towels. Maybe half a dozen of them. And they've got a heavy gun in the back."

"And pistons with bad timing," Cox adds. "These people can't tune an engine for shit."

"We get through everything—death canyon, poison stew, all of it—and now we got this shit. It was enough to make a man give up, wave a white flag and give in." He pauses and gives us an evil grin. "Except we all know they hate Americans. I believe I'd rather die with a gun in my hand."

"And take a few of them with me," Salis says. "Shit."

Ahmed laughs at this and we all turn to look at him. This quiets him down right away. What the hell is he doing in here anyway? Why isn't he back in the village? Because he's a fucking spy, I tell myself, that's why.

"And then. Oh, man, I couldn't believe it," Cox says. He looks like his stomach hurts.

"Shit," Rankin says, studying his thumb. "He should of known better."

"He just wanted to help Sarge. That's all. It looked pretty bad, remember? That truck coming and him all alone in the back of the Humvee. It looked bad," Doc Greer says.

"Boyette jumps up and runs," Nevada says. "Rankin tried to grab him. Tracers were coming every which way. We were moving from cover to cover. But Boyette breaks loose of Rankin and runs straight into it, unloading a clip as he goes."

"Sarge said if Boy hadn't of hit the gunner on the back of that truck, then he would of been a goner for sure. He saved Sarge's life," Cox says. He keeps rubbing his thumb and forefinger around his mouth. It's the only clean part of his face now, a circle of white skin around his lips.

"Boy looked like he was going to make it. He got right up to the second Humvee. Then a piece-of-shit hajji stitched him right across the middle with that big Russian machine gun. About cut him in two. Boy didn't have a chance after that."

"The poor fuck had just about bled out by the time we finally got him in the Humvee," Doc Greer says. "I tried, but—shit. Goddamn."

Hazel hyperventilates, holding his throat and wheezing.

"Are you having an asthma attack, Tim?" Doc Greer asks him.

Hazel doesn't answer. Instead he jumps up, jogs to the corner of the tent, and stands with his face against the canvas, making choking sounds. I get up and start toward him, but Doc Greer puts a hand across my chest. He shakes his head and motions for me to bend down.

"He'll punch you," he whispers. "It happened earlier. Cox touched him on the arm and Hazel socked him one. I don't know what he needs, but it's best to leave him alone. After a while he'll tie it down or let it out, one."

Nevada keeps glancing over his shoulder at Hazel, chewing on his cheek. He inhales and holds his breath.

"Go on, Nevada," Doc Greer says, "tell them the rest. Tell them about the miracle."

This seems to revive him somewhat. He shakes his head and goes on with the story. His voice is gruffer now, but his shoulders are straight and his chin is up. "And now comes the strangest part of a strange fucking day. Maybe the strangest thing I've seen in this man's Army. An old woman, looks like a witch, she comes riding up behind them fucking hajjis in this Wild West wagon. Horse and all. I shit you not." He crosses his heart with his hand. "It looked to me like she was going faster than the truck. She don't stop when she sees those guns going off. Hell, no. She just keeps right on coming, standing up on the seat and whacking that horse with the reins. I expect she freaked those hajjis out same as she did us, because they stopped firing and braked. We don't stop. Hell, no! Every one of us keeps running till we reach the vehicles. Rankin and the doc pulled Boyette in and the rest of us prepared to get the fuck out of there. This lady rides her Wild West wagon right on up to their truck. There ain't a single sound in the nighttime. Nothing."

"Half a mike goes by and nobody does a damn thing. Not one Goddamn thing," Doc Greer says.

"Nah, a little something was happening," Cox says. "I got the engine started in the lead vehicle. We were easing forward. They were still about forty yards away."

"Still," Doc Greer says.

"And then that witch woman, she makes this sound. Like nothing I ever heard before," Nevada says in a quiet voice. "I can't even imitate it."

"Me neither," Rankin says.

"It was like a wildcat," Cox says.

"Worse than that," Nevada says, although I seriously doubt either one of them has ever heard a wildcat scream.

"Like bloody murder," Salis says.

"Nah," Nevada says, shaking his head, "there ain't a word for this sound. It's still in my head, bouncing around, but I don't have any words for it."

"It *was* a word," Cox says. "It meant something. I know it. I wish I knew what it was she yelled."

"Fuck you?" Salis suggests, seriously.

"Whatever it was," Doc Greer says, "she got the last word."

Nevada clenches his fists into one big ball. "Boom." And then stretches out his fingers.

"What?" I ask, leaning in toward him. All of a sudden I get a very strange idea. I look over at Ahmed. He's listening closely now too. And he's thinking the same thing I am. I know it. This is the same old lady who came to the base for the bodies.

"Old lady go boom. I mean a big boom. It cracked the windshield on the Humvee. A piece of their truck went flying and knocked a big old hole in it. Sliced up Oli's arm pretty good, too. But shit, whatever it was that old biddy set off, it tore their Toyota *all* up. Hajjis went flying every which way. Killed them all. To a fucking man."

"So the old lady came to save you?" Lopez asks. He's been quiet all this time, leaning forward and listening with his whole body.

"No," Rankin tells him, "there ain't no way she'd of known we were up there."

"Our vehicles were parked at the turnaround all day," Nevada says. "Unless the same ones who told the hajjis about us told her too."

"She had to of been chasing after those hajjis in the truck." Rankin stares down at his hands, squeezing his fists one at a time as he considers this. "No, her blowing them up didn't have nothing to do with us. It looked to me like she had a score to settle. Like she'd been following this bunch for a while. I don't think these hajjis were the same as the ones in the wash. They might have been together in this shit, but they were coming from a different place. I don't know, like maybe the plan was to smash us from both sides. They were probably waiting further down the hill. When they saw Sarge reach the Humvee, they came up the road looking to pick a fight. The old lady must of seen them a while before this and followed them. Only way it could be."

"However it was, I'll tell you what, that was one damn big blast," Nevada says. "It was a shitload bigger than that IED that got us on the way to Inmar. What do you think it was, Cox?"

He thinks for a moment, tapping his chin with a thumb.

Salis gives us a serious nod. "A granny scorned."

This gets a big laugh. The only one that's felt right all day. But that's not saying much. Salis smiles, not sure what to make of it. And over in the corner of the tent, Hazel begins to sob.

61

The captain catches me as I'm heading toward the front gate for sentry duty and asks what I did with the lockbox. He keeps looking over his shoulder, and speaks in a gruff whisper even though we're alone. When I tell him where I buried it, he seems to relax a little. He wants to know if I've looked inside, and just as I'm telling him about the combination lock, Cox comes stumbling past. The captain makes a loud show of commiserating with me over Boyette's death and then strides off before I can say another word.

Cox looks like a puddle of dog puke. I'm not sure he even sees me until I call his name. If he had his arms stretched out in front of him, he could be a B-movie zombie, lurching and drooling and rolling his eyes. Once I get his attention, I ask him why Ahmed's still on base, because Cox talks with him more than anyone else. The reason Ahmed originally got the job was because of his so-called mechanical ability. The lieutenant put him in the garage to help Cox, and the two of them still work together when he's not out with me on the shit-burning detail. I didn't like seeing Ahmed lurking in Common Tent 2 when weapons squad got back this morning. It has me on edge. Baba hardly ever spent time in the tents with us. It doesn't make sense. Ahmed must have known he wasn't wanted. Especially after what happened to Boyette. I'm surprised someone didn't beat the shit out of him. I'm surprised *I* didn't. Ahmed's like a pimple that's sprouted up between my shoulder blades, irritating but impossible to reach and pop. Cox tells me Ahmed's living in Baba's old room in the back of the fort. We're standing outside the mess tent. Every few seconds his eyes flutter closed, his bony shoulders sag, and I think he's fallen asleep on his feet. It's not as uncommon as you might imagine. But then he jerks upright and his long, thin fingers flutter up to his face to give his cheeks a light slap. He's the only one from the squad who hasn't racked out.

"But why?" I ask him. "I thought he didn't want to live on base."

"Lopez set it up." He yawns hugely. It seems to come up from the soles of his feet. "Ask him."

"Lopez?" I say, louder than I should.

Cox flinches and steps back.

"Sorry, man. I just have a bad feeling about Ahmed. And about that ambush. How they knew you were coming long enough to set up a fake camp."

"Nah," he says, yawning again, "Ahmed ain't such a bad guy. He wouldn't do something like that."

"Maybe not," I say, but I know he is. I just haven't worked out the how and when.

Cox closes his eyes and slowly tilts to one side. I steady him with a hand. He leans against my fingers, and even through his shirt, I can feel how bony his arms have become. We stand like this for a moment. His eyes twitch beneath their lids and he begins to snore. I feel bad about waking him up, so I decide to stand there and let him snooze a bit. With each breath, the snores get louder and louder, until finally, they get so loud they wake him up again. He starts and looks around with a desperate, frightened expression. When he realizes where he is, the muscles in his face relax a bit.

"Have you eaten anything, Collie?"

"I forced down an MRE energy bar." He makes it sound like he rammed it down his throat whole. "A cherry one." He smiles at the memory.

I tell Cox he should really get some rack time in. If he keeps on like this, he won't be much use to anybody. Cox nods and mumbles something about a work detail. I'm not entirely sure he heard me.

He stares off at something in the mid-distance that only he can see. I wonder if I should walk him back to his tent. When I suggest this, he waves it away. Suddenly, he's all business, as alert as I am.

"You sure?" I say. I'm afraid he's going to sleepwalk into something dangerous.

"I tried to rack out a while ago, but—" His eyes have got that absent look again.

"Dreams?" I ask.

"Yeah," he says, trying to focus on me. "You know what I'm talking about."

"Sure," I say, and I do. Sometimes sleeping can be more exhausting than staying awake. During the daytime, I can keep the cigar box at the back of my head tightly closed.

"Hey," Cox says as I'm walking off, "don't sweat the Ahmed thing, man. If we start turning on each other, this place will fall apart in a week."

62

Sergeant Guzman doesn't want to let me see the lieutenant. And it's not because he's naked. We stand near the cab of the water truck and speak in whispers. The sergeant carries a clipboard and a thick sheaf of requisition forms. The wind has risen again. The truck rocks back and forth on its shock absorbers like a small ship. When the wind gusts, it makes a low humming sound as it passes over the roof, a single deep note like the lower register of a pipe organ. Sometimes I catch a quick glimpse of the lieutenant between the cab and the tanker hooked up behind it, scrubbing himself with a soapy rag. Water splashes in the bucket and the lieutenant hums something tuneless. I try to step around the sergeant, but he's too quick for me. Behind him, I notice three different sets of muddy prints, two entering and one leaving the spout we use to collect our bi-weekly allotment of bathing water. Today is not one of the usual allotment dispersal days.

"It's very important, Sarge. Time is an issue." I've said this same thing before in several different ways.

"Then tell me," he says, examining my face as though it were a situation report full of dubious facts. "We have a chain of command in the Army, remember? You talk to the NCO and the NCO, you'll like this part, the NCO, he talks to the lieutenant. And up it goes. Right on up to the president."

"It's sensitive, Sarge."

"And you don't trust me? Is that what you're saying?" The sergeant attempts a comic grimace. Each time I shift my body weight, he shifts along with me. Nevada once told me the sergeant wrestled on a scholarship at some big midwestern university. Watching him now, I believe it. When Sergeant Guzman sits or stands still, he looks oafish and clumsy, but he blocks each of my attempts to dart past him as deftly as a bantamweight boxer slipping punches. For such a large man, he has very dainty feet. I bet he's a good dancer.

"It's about the ambush, sir. I believe I know who's responsible."

"From what I understand," the sergeant says, narrowing his eyes, "the lieutenant's already got a theory about who's responsible for the ambush."

This startles me and then, after a moment of thought, worries me. The last time I saw Lopez, he was toting a dripping plastic jug. I glance over at the muddy footprints again.

"What do you want, Private Durrant?" It's the lieutenant. He steps around the front of the truck wearing only green flip-flops. Sudsy water drips from his crotch. He puts his hands on his hips and frowns, as if he was in full uniform. "Don't think I can't hear you pussyfooting around out here."

"I need to speak with you, sir." I find his pale skin and water-shrunken genitals very distracting. "About the probing mission."

"Fine," the lieutenant says in a voice that suggests he'd rather be having a cavity filled than deal with Private Durrant this afternoon.

Sergeant Guzman shakes his head, but he lets me pass. I follow the lieutenant around to the other side of the truck, where he continues to sponge himself with dingy gray water from the bucket.

"Have you heard any word about the supply drop, Guzman?" he asks.

"They're saying 0700 hours tomorrow, sir," the sergeant calls out from the other side.

"So," the lieutenant says, bending over to scrub a foot. "What the hell do you want?"

"I believe I know who's leaking info and how." This is overstating the case a bit, but—

"Who?"

"Ahmed."

The lieutenant looks at me for the first time. Then he twists to wash the other foot, and I'm forced to look at the three large pimples on his ass. Tendrils of blue cigar smoke drift around the cab of the truck.

"Funny you should come along with this information just now." He glances over his shoulder at the purple evening shadows. The sun sets so quickly you can almost see it move. "At this time."

"Why is that, sir?"

"Not thirty minutes ago someone else came by to see me with the same claim. A fairly plausible one."

My heart tries to climb up my ribcage and out of my mouth.

"About Ahmed?" I ask, barely able to respond. "Sir."

The lieutenant laughs. It is a dry sound. A jackal barking in the winter dark.

"No, Private Durrant," he says, wearing his smile like a crooked necktie, "and, I might add, I find it somewhat disingenuous of you to suggest it."

"I don't understand, sir."

"Of course not." He stops rinsing his legs for a moment, so he can study my face. "And how, Private Durrant, did you arrive at this conclusion? Ahmed hasn't left the base for the past two days. I had Sergeant Guzman check the sentry logs. Then how did he warn the insurgents? Smoke signals? Did he fly?"

"No, sir, he went through a door in the perimeter wall."

This surprises the lieutenant in a very satisfying way. His hand pauses midway between bucket and leg. Water dribbles from his fingers. I fight to keep the smile off my face.

"Explain."

I tell him about the night I saw Ahmed leaving the motor pool and exiting the base through a door in the wall. And what I think it means.

"A magic door?" He purses his lips together.

"No, sir, a normal door disguised to seem like part of the wall. It looked very old. If you don't believe me, it would be simple to show you."

The lieutenant grabs my wrist to examine my watch and grunts with irritation when he sees that it's unreadable.

"If you're wrong, Durrant—" The lieutenant leaves it at that.

63

We take a Humvee. A very skeptical Sergeant Guzman drives. I sit alone in the back. The wind blows just hard enough to fill the air with dust, lowering the visibility to about ten feet. The locals call this wind a *dourma*, which is their word for coffee dust. A *dourma* lifts up only the smallest particles of dirt and sand, turning the air into a thick soup. It is worse in some ways than a hard wind, because the dust doesn't blow away. It just hangs there, suspended. I ask the sergeant to drive along the wall. In the dark, it's a good deal harder than I thought it would be to pick out the spot where I left the cigarette butt. I hadn't expected the lieutenant to want to look tonight. But here we are.

"It's going to be a bit tricky to find with all this sand blowing around," I suggest.

"Already starting with the excuses?" The lieutenant smirks.

Sergeant Guzman laughs. This irritates me more than it should. The men consider Sergeant Oliphant a brass-licker, but I always figured Guzman to be on the side of the enlisted. I feel betrayed.

"No, sir," I say, worrying now, "it's just that it might take a while. I marked it with a cigarette butt."

"A very distinctive marker. And just when was it that you saw this magic door? Last night? I heard you locked Ahmed in a closet last night."

"No, sir." This won't sound good. "It was several nights ago."

"What?" The lieutenant nearly yells this. Even Sergeant Guzman looks around in surprise. "If that's true, why in the hell did you wait so long?"

"I'm not sure, sir." Which is true. "I wanted to make sure that—"

"You waited for three days after finding an enemy breach in the perimeter?"

We pass a section of the wall that's faced with purple stone instead of mud bricks. I ask for the sergeant to slow down. This looks like it might be the right part of the wall, but it could be anywhere along this hundred-yard section. A terrible apprehension perches on the crown of my head like a large, ungainly bird. I have them stop the vehicle so I can get out. The sergeant turns on the floodlight attached to his outer rearview mirror. I raise my hand to thank him. The wall stretches on and on with an awful sameness. A cigarette butt! What the hell was I thinking? I trudge along for some time, feeling the stones with both hands and straining my eyes for any sign of the metal keyhole or the cigarette butt. It's impossible.

The lieutenant sits in the Humvee and watches this for thirty minutes. Once I hear his muffled laughter. The wind scours my right cheek and fills my ear with dust. Every few minutes I stop and knock the side of my head with the heel of my hand the way I would to clear my ear of water. I wish I had a scrap of paper I could use to block it up. My tongue feels like it's coated with thick, grainy paste. I berate myself in rhythm with my steps. A cigarette butt? You are a worthless son of a bitch. A fucking cigarette butt. I don't hear the horn at first. I'm too busy searching for my phantom cigarette butt.

"Private," Sergeant Guzman shouts, "get your ass in the vehicle."

I run a list of excuses through my head as I drag ass back to the Humvee. None of them sound too good, especially after the way I acted back at the water truck. I'm fucked, but good. No one speaks on the drive back. Five minutes seem like five hours. They drop me at my tent.

"Report to Common Tent 1 tomorrow morning at 0630." Sergeant Guzman barks this out like a parade drill call. It almost sounds as though he's been practicing it. Maybe he has.

"Yes, Sarge," I say.

The truth, I think, is not setting me free.

64

A dark figure slips out of the left latrine. The wind is rising. Larger grains of sand now whip across the open space between the trailers. This blowing sand has turned the moon to mud. I yell over at the person who just came out. He either doesn't hear me calling or doesn't want to respond. I shout again. "Hey, guy, slow up." But he hunches over and runs off in the direction of the motor pool, quickly disappearing in the murky night.

OUT OF SERVICE. One of the two holes has this sign pinned to the canvas curtain. It flutters and flaps in the wind, and I have to grab the paper to read it. The handwriting is a jerky scrawl, the penmanship that of a spastic second-grader. It takes a few seconds for me to puzzle out the words. I don't know how in the hell a hole over a fuel drum can be out of service. It seems unlikely they'd be full already. I emptied both yesterday. Great, I get to kiss butts with whoever it was that just left. I duck inside and give the plywood seat a quick inspection. Taking a shit is not the primary reason soldiers use these latrines, and it only takes one sticky surprise to make you forever diligent. The tarp flaps violently in the wind. Thankfully, it also blows off some of the stink from the barrels.

After a few mikes, I hear a noise that tugs at my attention. A sort of fizzing sound. I stand up and flash my light around. Something isn't right, but I can't quite place it. I tilt my head and listen. The fuel drum explodes. A hollow boom. I'm instantly covered in liquid shit. The smell chokes me. Putrid brown gunk drips from my face and hands.

My hair is soaked with it. I'm still not sure what just happened to me. I tear open the tarp and step into the wind. Within seconds I'm coated with grit. I kick off my pants and pop a button pulling off my shirt. The wind catches it and sucks it away into the dark.

I look around for the perpetrator. Was this supposed to be a joke? I shout at the sky like an angry dog. The moon is the same color as the gunk on my arms. I take off at a run toward the water truck. I'm washing this off me, water ration or not. The parade ground is empty. Just as well. Had I seen even a hint of a smile on anyone's face, even the lieutenant's, I would have attacked him. Instead, I take out my rage on the water nozzle's flimsy lock. I hit it with a rock so hard, I nearly knock the toggle switch clean off.

65

"An MRE bomb," Rankin says, knocking his flip-flops against the stack of tires he's sitting on. "Got to be."

Rankin sniffs when he thinks I'm not looking. At least he tries to hide it. He can see where my head is at tonight. An eggshell filled with nitroglycerin. I walked back from the water truck naked but for my boots. The rest I threw away. I would have thrown my boots away too if I thought I could get some new ones. Rankin wouldn't let me back into the tent until he was sure I'd cleaned myself off completely, so he gathered up all my antibiotic cream and the germ-killing gel Clarissa sent me, and we moved operations over to the motor pool's garage. Rankin sits a short distance away and watches me rub hand gel over my entire body. A single fluorescent tube lights the room, making my shadow look gawky and frantic. At least the smell of dirty oil and spilled diesel cancel out some of my stink.

"MRE bomb. No, man, it—" I try to explain, but Rankin won't let me.

"You're still able to sit on that skinny ass of yours, ain't you? Well, then, it couldn't of been all that big of an explosion."

"It was big enough." I stretch my arm out and rub gel in as hard as I can. Rankin watches, disgruntled.

"You ever seen one go off?" he asks.

"Of course, man. I've made one myself. It's just a tiny—" I make a little pop sound with my mouth.

"Listen here, if you take the powder out of a few of those plastic sacks and pour it into a two-liter emergency water bottle and then you put glow-stick juice in there, those fuckers are loud. What did this one sound like?" He picks at a rubber nub on the tire and thinks this over.

"Big, Rankin. Big." I splash myself with cloudy black water from the bucket where Cox washes his hands after work. "If I hadn't of gotten up to look for the sound, it would have knocked me off the seat."

"Shit," he says, solemn and insincere, "that's big."

I pace around the room. My arms are raw from scrubbing, and now they sting from the alcohol in the gel. My face hurts. Back at the water truck, I didn't have any soap, so I scoured my body with sand. It took off plenty of skin, but it didn't do a whole hell of a lot about the smell.

"Why'd you get up off the pot?" Using a broken strip of an aluminum measuring tape that he'd picked up off the floor when we first came in, Rankin points to a place I missed on the back of my neck. The man's not touching me for anything, not even with a two-foot piece of metal. I rub in more gel.

"I heard something in there."

"Like what? Make the sound."

I make a little hissing noise by blowing air through the gap between my front teeth. "That ain't quite it, but—"

Rankin chucks the tape across the room like a wobbly spear. It hits a stack of worn engine belts and they tumble onto the floor. Something about this makes him grin. "You're right. That don't sound like an MRE bomb. Let me marinate on it a bit."

"Marinate?" I say. Rankin has two words that drive me crazy, and he knows it. Marinate and conversate. He attended college. He knows. He just doesn't care. Let me express myself in the manner I choose, he usually says to me when I mention it. Always in his most proper voice.

He ignores this. "Maybe Cox would know. I think he took a demolition course. He wanted to be a sapper."

"Think we should tell him about this?" Wind whistles in through a broken window on the other side of the garage. I shiver. My legs are covered with goose bumps and starting to turn purple. I want to go to bed.

"Maybe you're right: after all, someone did try to. . . ." He doesn't even want to say it. He stares off into space

I walk back and forth, rubbing my arms for warmth. The plastic gel bottle is empty, so I squirt a little antibiotic cream into my hand and work that onto my legs. "What I don't understand is how they knew I'd be there. Maybe it wasn't for me. I don't know. Am I being paranoid? I did see someone come out just before I got there."

Rankin laughs quietly. I glare at him.

"No." He jumps down from his stack of tires and picks up the measuring tape again. "I'm laughing because anyone who's spent a week around you would have known." He pokes my ass cheek with it and I jump. "Your ass is like a cuckoo clock. 2100 hours. On the nose. Every night."

"Is that right?" I say. This surprises me. I think about it for a moment and decide it's true.

"Whoever did this set it up for *you*. The little sign. The time. All for you, D."

"Lopez?" The obvious choice.

"No, man, this ain't his style. He's a dick, but he ain't vicious, at least not like this. Besides, he's too fussy to fuck around in a field latrine. The problem is a hajji wouldn't know about your alarm-clock asshole."

"This is true."

I'm out of medicinal cream of any sort. Rankin watches me try to squeeze out the last little blob from the tube. "You ain't done yet. I can still smell you." He digs through his knapsack for a few seconds. When he finds what he's looking for, he grins and tosses me an aerosol can. It's jock-itch spray. As I'm spraying it onto my back, I realize I need to tell him about Ahmed. The whole story. Including the hidden door. So I clear my throat and spill it all. When I finish, he squints at me for a long time.

"We need to fix this shit," he says. "And soon."

66

I stand at attention and stare at the wall of Common Tent 1.

"We have reports," Sergeant Oliphant says, "of you driving off into the desert after your shit-burning detail."

The sergeant's about as angry as I've ever seen him. And, believe me, this means something. This is a man I once saw tear in two a weapons manual the thickness of a small-town phone book with his bare hands during a monumental rage over proper rifle maintenance. Today his neck, which usually looks like the bottom half of a broad pyramid, has flexed and widened so far that his head appears to sprout right out of his lungs. The thumb-thick blood vessels on either side of it pulse and throb. Every word he shouts is wet with spit. For some reason this morning's anger seems personal, and for the life of me I can't figure out why.

We've been here in Common Tent 1 all morning. Lieutenant Blankenship, the captain, Sergeant Oliphant. Sergeant Guzman even popped his head in a couple of times, and now who should arrive but Lopez.

It is 1100 hours. I haven't eaten anything since dinner and my head is pounding. The AC unit in the tent keeps sputtering out. The air is hot and thick as engine oil. A bit of grit got into my right eye last night, either while searching the perimeter wall for the door, or more likely when the latrine exploded, and now it's swollen shut. During the last couple of hours, Sergeant Oliphant has gone over the log books from the sentry box for the last three weeks day by day and discussed every detail I've been a part of for the same time period.

"Where the fuck did you go, soldier?" Sergeant Oliphant pushes his face right up into mine. I find it difficult not to eyeball him back.

"Who told you that, Sarge?" I say, looking over at Lopez. He doesn't meet my eye.

"Just answer the Goddamn question," Sergeant Oliphant shouts. He clutches the legal pad in his hand so tightly the cardboard backing tears away. "Is something wrong with you? Having trouble understanding basic English this morning?"

Sergeant Oliphant rolls the pad up into a tube and whips it back over his shoulder like he's going to smack me with it. Instead, he taps me lightly on the nose. A drop of sweat drips down from my sideburn to the tip of my chin. The itchy tickle it causes makes me want to yell.

"No, Sergeant," I say. What can they prove? Nothing. If they had a witness, then they'd have said so by now. Never volunteer anything.

"No, what?" Sergeant Oliphant yells.

For whatever reason, the lieutenant has allowed Sergeant Oliphant to do all of the questioning up until this point. He and the captain sit and watch the proceedings in silence. The captain has not acknowledged my presence at all. This hearing is about a lot more than just me.

"No, I did not drive out into the desert after the burn detail, Sergeant."

The lieutenant leans forward and looks at me, hard. "Do you have any idea how much trouble you're in, son?"

Son? *Son?* This man is a good two years younger than me. God, I wish we were back home in some bar, any bar, both of us dressed in civvies. I take a deep breath. I'm afraid of what I'll say if I don't cool down for a second.

"No, sir, because I don't know what any of this is about."

The captain laughs. We all look over at him and wait, but he says nothing.

"I find that very hard to believe," the lieutenant says.

"What about the day you were late to the mission briefing? What about that?" Sergeant Oliphant asks.

"I explained it to you that morning."

"Well, explain it again, Private. That's why we're here."

"Yes, Sergeant. We did not have a sufficient amount of fuel to do the burn. I considered all of my options and decided to siphon some fuel from the truck. This took some time. Ahmed had difficulty accomplishing the task. If you don't believe me, then ask him."

"We did," the sergeant says, "and he told us you dropped him off an hour and a half before you arrived at the base."

"That's a lie, sir. First, Ahmed does not own a watch, and secondly, he was visibly ill from swallowing fuel. I doubt he knew what time it was for the rest of the day."

"What possible reason would Ahmed have for lying to us?" the lieutenant asks in a mild voice.

I want to pull out my hair and scream. "Every reason, sir. He's spying on us for the insurgents."

He gives me a blank look and lets out a long sigh.

"Lopez," he says in a bored voice, "why don't you explain your suspicions about Private Durrant's behavior."

Lopez reels off a series of places and dates, never once looking me in the eye. He's made this speech before, maybe even this morning. I wonder if he's been coached.

He starts with an incident I'd totally forgotten about. Several months ago while working a traffic patrol on the highway at the edge of Kurkbil, I tripped on a rock while waving a car through the road block and bumped into an elderly man. He was on his way to the village with a basket of eggs, and when I stumbled into him, I knocked it out of his hands. All of the eggs broke. Yolk dripped from his pants. The poor man was frightened and angry. I felt terrible about spoiling what was probably his family's only source of income for the next few weeks, so I pressed a wad of bills into his hand, far more than the eggs were actually worth, and apologized several times. Lopez leaves out the part about the eggs, but he goes into great detail about the money and triples the amount of time I spoke with the man. When I attempt to explain, Sergeant Oliphant screams at me. Lopez goes on to describe several other times he's seen me speaking with village men. Once, he tells them, he even saw me writing a message in Arabic for a man at the town café. In actuality, I'd been trying to learn how to write my name in script. The café's owner, a man I'd become friendly with during my area patrols, was kind enough to correct it for me. Another time, Lopez says he observed me speaking to a young man at the FOB's main gate for over an hour while I was on sentry duty. It's true that I pointed out something inside the base and then talked with him for a while about it, but it sure as hell hadn't lasted for an hour. Twenty minutes, more like. I remember that day clearly. The young man had come looking for a job. I explained that we already had all the employees we needed for the time being, but I'd speak to my CO. I did. In fact, Sergeant Oliphant had been there when I talked this over with Sergeant Guzman.

Again, I try to explain. "You were there when I told Sergeant Guzman about that. Don't you remember, Sergeant Oli—"

"Shut the fuck up, Durrant," Sergeant Oliphant says. "If I have to tell you again, I'll put you in restraints and gag you."

Lopez then tells them about his suspicions regarding the IED and my dash into the toy factory immediately afterward. I notice both the lieutenant and Sergeant Oliphant perk up at his mention of the factory. Lopez thinks this is a dead drop where I leave information for the insurgents. He believes I've been directing the mortar fire during the past week, that I allowed a small group of insurgents to enter the base in order to blow up the Humvees, then helped them to escape. Somehow, he isn't sure how, he admits, since I didn't leave the base during this time, I signaled our intent to mount a movement-to-contact mission into the Noses. The list goes on. Many of the things he tells them are so insignificant as to be laughable, but no one in the room is laughing. Throughout it all, I grit my teeth and bunch my fists. It takes every bit of self-control I have left to keep from running across the room and pounding him. Then he adds that Ahmed came to him unbidden and said he also suspected me of trafficking with the enemy. Ahmed told him I went off into the desert after our burn details, somewhere in the direction of the toy factory, and also that I'd spoken in secret with the boy prisoner. In a somewhat melodramatic conclusion, Lopez tells them I probably have a pirate radio stashed away somewhere in my tent. This, he says with an odd flourish of his hand, is his best guess as to how I've been directing mortar fire and leaking mission intel.

I don't know whether to shout, shit, or go blind. There's no way they can take this seriously. No way. But when I look around the tent, I see Lopez's little speech has made quite an impact. The lieutenant looks absolutely furious. Sergeant Oliphant's face has turned the color of Tabasco sauce.

I'm fucked.

"Excuse me, sir," I say to the lieutenant after a moment. "May I defend myself against these ridiculous charges?"

"No," Sergeant Oliphant barks, "you had your chance."

My chance? I think. What chance?

"Let him talk," the captain says in a hoarse voice. He coughs a couple times and clears his throat, as though he intends to say something more.

We all turn to look at him, waiting for him to go on, but he doesn't. Finally, the lieutenant nods, but from the way he clenches his jaw, I can tell he'd just as soon I shut up.

I go through Lopez's accusations point by point, explaining how he's held a grudge against me since the moment I arrived. I tell them the story of how I punched his half-brother, Sergeant Reyes. That he has a motive. The captain laughs at this, masking it with a cough. Sergeant Oliphant gives Lopez a puzzled look. I explain that Ahmed is only trying to cover his ass, that this whole thing has been turned upside down. It doesn't make any sense. What motive would I have for giving up my friends? I even volunteered to go on the probe mission. The lieutenant stirs uncomfortably after this comment, so I push it a bit further. Then I mention the door in the wall. But only in passing.

I know it doesn't sound very reasonable after the snafu last night. Finally, I urge them to search my tent. I tell them they won't find any contraband items. No girlie mags, no liquor, and especially no pirate radio. Christ, I hope nothing's been planted.

"We do not need permission to search your tent, Private," Sergeant Oliphant says.

"If you're looking for a reason for all this, the obvious person to speak to is Ahmed, Sergeant. It seems—" I almost say insane. "—like he has a motive and a means for doing all of this. I've been trying to tell you about him for a long—"

The lieutenant holds up his hand. "All right, you've said your piece." He looks at the inner flap of the tent. "Sergeant Guzman, bring him in."

Sergeant Guzman and Ahmed duck through the flap. They've been just outside. Ahmed heard my entire speech, I'm sure of it. He catches my eye and holds it until he passes me where I stand at attention. At least he has the balls to face me.

"Guzman," the lieutenant says, pointing at me. "I want you to take this man to his tent and go through all of his belongings in his presence. Search everything. If it has a lock, make him produce the key. Pay careful attention to anything that looks like a radio or looks like it could store one. Police the surrounding area for recently disturbed ground."

"Sir," he says and salutes.

The lieutenant and I look at each other. He's making a decision. That much is obvious. About what isn't quite so clear. Maybe it's only a matter of degree. How severely he's going to punish me

"We'll discuss this further, Durrant." The lieutenant crosses his legs, making sure not to spoil the sharp crease of his pants. "This isn't over. Not even close. If you do anything, and I mean *anything*, that could be considered suspicious, I will put you in a cell until I can have you shipped back to HQ for a court-martial. Do not leave the base. Do not use the telephone. Do not even go near the perimeter. Is that understood?"

"Yes, sir."

"Dismissed," Sergeant Oliphant shouts.

I salute.

The captain folds his arms and snorts.

67

Sergeant Guzman puts on purple latex gloves and searches my tent. He works slowly and methodically. Rankin and I watch from outside, silent, along with the two newbies Howley and McCrae, who had arrived on a helicopter earlier in the morning. We ignore their questions. They make a wager about whether the sergeant will find booze or spank mags. I can see this task makes the sergeant uncomfortable. His mouth is grim. I'm sure something has been planted in the tent. The only question is what. When Sergeant Guzman emerges with a hard look in his eyes, I'm certain he's found something.

But he says, "You're clean. I knew that bit about the radio was bullshit."

"Thanks," I say. My relief is enormous.

Sergeant Guzman walks away without responding.

Rankin flicks my arm and points. A group of men have assembled near the mess tent. I immediately assume the worst. My eyeballs throb, as though someone is squeezing them between a thumb and finger. I follow Rankin across the parade ground and inside the tent. It's only Hazel, passing out the mail that arrived on the helicopter. This is the first time I've heard him speak since the night Boyette died. He curls a finger at me as we enter the tent.

"Durrant."

I trudge over, expecting him to fuck with me. Somehow the latrine bomb incident has gotten out. Rankin swears he didn't say a word. I believe him. And this makes it all the more difficult to figure out who might have been involved. My eye was swollen at breakfast and so the whole base has taken to calling me Stink-Eye. Hazel's lips make a sad, strange smile shape, and I get ready for whatever feeble joke Private Brokedick here has been working up in his head all morning. Instead, he tosses me an envelope. It's pale blue and thin. Something small and heavy shifts inside when I shake it. I know what it is. I know who it's from. I know without reading the address. Rankin questions me with a look. I wave it off and leave.

The sky is the color of skim milk and the air is still and hot. In the desert, diffuse light hurts your eyes more than bright sunlight. I squint behind my new designer sunglasses and look for a quiet place. The whole base shimmers in the early afternoon heat. I sit down in the shade of the motor-pool wall, turn the envelope in my hands, and smell it. I consider burning it. I'm not sure I want to read it. Not right now, not today. Maybe not at all. Shit. I tear it open anyway.

The engagement ring is wrapped in pink tissue paper and tied with white ribbon. I drop it in my shirt pocket and chew on my lip. What I really want to do is shout at the top of my lungs. I want to hit somebody. I want to level the whole base with a bulldozer. She sends the engagement ring here. *Here.* She couldn't even wait a few months. Damn Clarissa. I roll a cigarette and light it. Something in the tobacco smells like burnt hair. Even so, I suck in as much smoke as my lungs will hold. My fingers make damp marks on the thick violet stationery she likes to use. The paper has a very faint smell. Mandarin oranges. I unfold it. Two pages. Back and front. Big looping letters in green ink. Her handwriting makes me angry, and I haven't even started to read the letter.

Dear Toby:

I hope you're doing alright. I hope things are going OK. Ugh. I might as well get to it. I've tried to write this six times and the first few sentences always sound like bullshit. I hate starting letters. Especially this one. Look Toby, don't get me wrong, I like you. I like you a lot. We had some good times. When I look at your picture, I still want to kiss you, make love to you. That's all fine. That's good. But it isn't something to get married over. When I got knocked up, it seemed like we didn't have any other choice. I mean, that's what people do, right? You get knocked up and you get married. At least in Savannah. At least in my family. My parents hate you. You know that. And even they agreed we'd have to go through with it. But that's not what this is all about. Not all of it.

When you left, everything changed. The whole thing seemed different. You know, **US.** *Our relationship. It didn't change right away, but pretty soon after. I started thinking about what getting married and having a baby meant. I haven't had a chance to do shit with my life. If all this had happened later, then maybe it would have worked. Maybe if I was old, like 27 or 28. But right now I don't know who the hell I am or what I want to do with my life, so how the hell could you? I'm not the same person you knew at all.*

I know this will hurt you. It's shitty, I know, to lay this kind of stuff on you while you're off fighting a war. It's all fucked up. But I can't pretend like nothing's wrong, that we're all peachy. I tried to tell you on the phone, Toby, but it's so hard to talk that way. Sometimes when we talk on the phone I'm thinking is that really him? Is that really his voice? Oh Toby, I really do miss you. I really do like you. I know I said I loved you before you left, but now I've been thinking about it, I'm not all that sure it's true. But I do like you. I like you a hell of a lot. I just don't love you. Not marriage love, not baby love. I know this is going to hurt you. You have every right to hate me. I probably would if I were in your place. I'm sorry. Please believe me. I can't be a mom. I can't. I really, really, really can't. Can you understand that? Or are you too much of a man to get it? All you have to do is pay the dinner check, squirt and go to sleep. I've got to drag this thing around inside me for nine months and then squeeze it out like the biggest shit of my life. I'm not ready. I don't want to be a mom. I don't want to live in a crappy apartment and wait for you to come home from some shitty job you have to take because we have to have money for diapers and milk. I'm so sorry, Toby. I'm so sorry, but I just can't keep the baby.

The other thing is I met somebody. He isn't THE one, but he's a nice guy and smart. I work with him. It's probably hard for you to understand this too, *but I can't deal with all this shit alone. I have my friends, and Sarah, of course, but it's not the same. I thought about keeping all this about the new guy to myself. It'll just make Toby feel worse, I thought, but then, and maybe this is selfish, but then the guilty feeling I had kept coming up and up and up. It wouldn't be fair if I didn't tell you. So I did, and now you can shout, Fuck You, and tear up the letter. I know I would.*

Most of all I'm sorry about the baby. By the time you get this, it will all be done with. I've already made an appointment at the clinic for next Tuesday. I didn't want to tell you over the phone because I knew you'd try and talk me out of it and I just can't deal with that right now. I just can't. I'm really sorry Toby and I do like you even though it might not seem like it to you right now.

Keep your head down,
Clarissa

P.S. I sent a mix CD in another envelope.

68

I read the letter five times. Then I go inside the broken building and puke. That fucking bitch.

69

In the garage I wash my face and rinse my mouth with stale water from a CamelBak. Somewhere at the far end of the motor pool, a Humvee engine revs and revs. A mix CD? I think. What the hell? I stumble outside and lean my forehead against the wall, close my eyes, thump Clarissa's letter against my thigh. My mind isn't working right. I can't even remember what my duties are this afternoon. I can barely remember my name. Someone crunches up behind me. I wipe the water off my face with a sleeve and turn around. It's Lopez. He has an odd look on his face. Not smug. Confused maybe. I can't read it. We square off and face each other. Lopez looks down at my hand. He points to the letter.

"Bad news?" he asks.

I hit him in the eye.

70

Sergeant Oliphant kicks my cot, and I jerk awake. He shines a flashlight in my face. I sit up, cover my eyes. Not a word from the sergeant, just the light. Rankin doesn't wake up. It must be about 0430. Sergeant Oliphant looks me over with disgust, thumps my leg with the flashlight, and points to my fatigues. I get dressed and follow him outside. We walk toward the office trailers. Frozen condensation sparkles on tent flaps. A night's worth of snoring, turned solid. My head feels muddled. I can't stop shivering. When I ask where we're going, he tells me to shut up. Somewhere in the direction of the village a jackal yips three times. Otherwise the night has no sound. The world looks clean and dry and cold in the antiseptic moonlight. A landscape of silver and brown. Sergeant Oliphant turns around when we reach the mess tent.

"You remember your old duties?" he asks.

"Yes, Sarge, I remember." Sentry, traffic patrols, guard-tower rotations.

"Well, forget them." He hands me a sheet of paper. "Here's your new life."

At the top of the list are three KP shifts—breakfast, lunch, and dinner. Nobody gets three shifts of fucking kitchen patrol. The first shift starts at 0500, which means I'll have to report for duty at 0445. In the Army you always have to be fifteen minutes early, so you can stand around and wait.

"What are you waiting for, Private? Mommy to give you a kiss and a pat on the ass? Get moving," Sergeant Oliphant shouts. "Your first shift starts in five mikes."

"Yes, Sarge."

71

Last KP shift of the day. I'm alone. My new commander, Private Foster Harrison, set me to work scrubbing pots and then went back to his tent to sleep. Before this, I'd hardly spoken to the guy. Everyone calls him Foss. Foss Harrison is a classic fobbit. Almost never leaves the base. Hates to be around weapons. Used to pay Boyette in tobacco to clean his M16. He'll take any job, no matter how menial or dull, as long as he can remain on base. He's short and plump and generally cheerful, with a round head about the size of a soccer ball and squinty eyes pressed back deep in his doughy face like raisins in an oatmeal cookie. So now Foss is giving me orders. The lieutenant has made his point very clear. I am officially at the bottom of the chain of command.

The kitchen tent has become my entire world. I come to work before the sun rises and I leave well past dark. It's about the size of a two-car garage, but it's packed end to end with cooking equipment and boxes of food. Big jute sacks of flour and rice and gallon jugs of ranch dressing and cheese sauce. Foss has created little pathways from sink to grill, to supplies area, to mess tent. It feels like a crowded little market.

The problem with dishwashing isn't the nastiness of half-congealed food or the monotony of scrubbing what seems like the same dish over and over again: it's the time it gives me to think. I can't stop thinking about the mistakes I've made in the last week. If, if, if. There's nothing here to distract me from myself. Not this Goddamn pan, anyway.

Whenever I'm not cursing Clarissa and worrying about what she might have done, my thoughts keep coming back to that lockbox, what it means, what will happen if the captain gets it, what kind of awful shit will fly out when he opens it. I'm stuck between him and the lieutenant, and they're crushing me into goo. I tap a dirty spoon against the sink and turn all this over in my head, and then suddenly I see what I have to do: move the lockbox. That will delay things for a day or two. It's not very long, but maybe it'll be enough. I grab an empty plastic bleach bottle and head out. It only takes a few seconds to dig the box up again. The metal still retains the warmth of the day.

72

A single-vehicle night patrol rolls across the parade ground. The deep thump of a hip-hop bass line rumbles in my chest as it approaches. Someone on the passenger side is playing with the searchlight on the Humvee's door, flashing it around the tents. An arm extends from the flap of one of the nearby tents and flips them the bird. The Humvee stops about ten yards away and then shines the light in my face. It's bright enough to hurt. I cover my eyes with a hand.

"Come take a ride, D." It's Rankin.

I jump in back. Nevada drives. He catches my eye in the rearview and smiles, making his gold-capped dog tooth flash. Nevada told me once that his mom gave it to him on his fifteenth birthday as a reward for passing all his classes. If he'd been able to go a year without getting suspended, she would have paid for one on the other side too. He slams us into gear and the Humvee leaps forward, leaving a wake of sprayed sand. The engine whines. Over the iPod-rigged sound system, a man sings his apology to Miss Jackson, explaining he's for real. Nevada powers us across the base. When we reach the outer wall, he slows down and eases back into patrol speed.

"I've been thinking on this, D," Rankin says, his voice flat and low, serious. "And we got a problem."

"Ahmed." Nevada pronounces it like Ah-mad. "Ahmed the A-rab."

We pass under a perimeter flood and it fills the car with a light as thick and yellow as melted butter. Nevada sings along with the song's chorus, thumping out the rhythm with his hands. Otherwise he keeps quiet. I lean forward and wait to hear what comes next. The soft light of the instrument panel makes their heads look as shiny and smooth as oiled wood. Just after the bugout, the two of them had shaved off all their hair. Rankin never explained this. I didn't ask.

"But—" I point my chin at Nevada.

"We need to bring somebody else in. We can't do this on our own. And besides, it concerns all of us, D. Today it's you, but tomorrow it could be any of us. Right now, we got to be careful who we tell. I don't trust the spook, and I don't trust Oliphant neither. Guzman's a good guy, but I have a feeling Oliphant has some dirt on him."

"Like what?" I ask. This is news to me.

"Could be anything. But Guzman sucks up to the man something awful."

"Makes me sick," Nevada adds.

"Ever strike you as odd that they don't argue? Never even seen it happen once. The man don't disagree with him. Ever."

"That just ain't natural," Nevada says.

"What I'm saying here is we got to be careful. Even someone we trust may be a liability. Somebody like Hazel, say, might slip up and let them know. Not on purpose, just—" He holds out his hands. "Nevada here, now he can keep his lips together."

"Listen, yo, I can keep a secret. I've got practice." Nevada says all this in a soft voice, as though we could be overheard even here. "This Ahmed shit has grown some serious legs. I been watching this game you and Lopez be playing, D. The man's an asshole, no doubt, but he's straight. I don't believe he'd do this shit he's doing if he didn't believe and believe hard. I've thought it over."

"Dyson said something funny to me today. I don't think he even realized it himself," Rankin says. "He told me he was talking to Lopez the day you popped him—"

Nevada snickers. "That's quite a shiner you gave him, D."

"I couldn't help it," I say.

"Well." Rankin waves this off. "Lopez told Dyson he waited till he was absolutely sure before he made this big fuss about you. But here's the funny part: he said someone asked him to keep an eye on you. And this was some time back. They been keeping tabs on you a while now. Waiting for something. I don't like it. It feels all wrong."

"You mean—"

"Tell him," Rankin says, grim.

"Somebody's playing Lopez." Nevada glances back at me in the rearview.

"Like who?" I ask, already lining up my own answer.

Rankin ignores this. The shadows on his face flicker as we pass beneath the floodlights. "Lopez has got real suction with the El-Tee. That makes him even more dangerous."

"Who's the guy that's playing Lopez?" I ask again.

"Guys," Rankin says.

"What?" I say.

"Let me go back a bit. I've been putting some shit together all day. Shit I didn't think about at the time, but now it all connects. First, Cox told me he overheard the El-Tee and Lopez talking in the Comm Trailer one night. This was right after the last IED, mind you. He said to Lopez, we need to make a note of everything he does. I want you to think back and make a list of every time you saw him doing it. But Cox doesn't hear who the *him* is. At the time, Cox thought they might be talking about *him*, selling Cassandra whiskey, so he stayed and listened. When Lopez asked why, the El-Tee told him he'd had his suspicions about this person a while now. And not just him. Lieutenant Saunders mentioned it too, he says. Then he asked Lopez to tell him if he saw this guy doing anything. Cox got freaked out and tried to leave and Blankenship saw him, so that's all he heard. Now you know how Cox is, so this ain't word for word, but I expect it's pretty close."

"Man," I say, "I always thought it was Lopez who first brought it to the lieutenant."

"Puts it in a different light, huh?" Rankin says.

"Shit. I don't know what to think now." I sit back in the seat.

"I seen Ahmed and Lopez talking a bunch of times," Nevada says, looking over his shoulder and catching my eye. "How's it a man'll trust a hajji over a person? That shit ain't right."

"Nevada," I say, "how much did Rankin tell you about all this? The whole Ahmed thing."

Rankin nods, says, "Go on," so I tell Nevada about the hidden door. Why the hell not? I figure. If he's in, he's in. And Rankin trusts him. So I go ahead and tell him about what the captured kid said and explain about the old insurgent's death. I tell him about everything except the green lockbox. That's a whole different soap opera, best kept on its own separate channel.

"Damn," he says, squeezing the steering wheel. "I didn't think about the old man. But you're right, D. He was just a little guy. No way he could of done himself like that."

"So what are we going to do?" I ask, sliding down in the vinyl seat until all I can see are the shiny tops of their heads.

They exchange a look.

"We chewed it over some," Nevada says.

"And we agreed we got to do something real about this Ahmed situation. Get rid of him." Rankin turns and searches for my eyes in the darkness.

"Kill him?" I ask, not sure how I feel about this, not sure at all.

"How often do people go down under the old fort, Nevada?" Rankin asks. I'm thrown a bit by the subject change. "The part under the garage where we kept the old guy."

"Only time I ever did was with him."

Rankin looks at me.

"Never," I say. "Not before and not since the old guy."

"Here's what I'm thinking," Rankin says. "We snatch Ahmed and bag his head before he gets a look at us and then put him down there in one of them cells. Lock him up tight. Give him some water and a slop bucket. A little food."

"Seal him up like a bumblebee in a tuna can." Nevada sings this.

"How long?" I ask.

Rankin shrugs. "Everybody'll be looking for him. Their guys, our guys. We might just learn a couple things, seeing how people take it."

"Okay," I say. I'm impressed. These two have a strategy. They've promoted themselves a game plan.

"Give the tree a shake," Rankin says, flashing me a smile big enough to show all his teeth, "and see what falls out."

"Or who," Nevada says.

We pass beneath a floodlight and both of their heads flash like windshields on a sunny day. The Humvee comes back around the gate, and Nevada wheels us through the parade ground. Our conversation took exactly one lap of the base. Just before they drop me at the kitchen tent, a sizzle of orange sparks draws a line across the base. It looks like someone lobbed a burning softball. Before I can even say "Oh, shit," it hits an empty patch of sand beside the tent Rankin and I share. The Humvee rocks back on its shocks. A spout of sand rises twenty feet. Little stones patter against the roof and hood. I tighten my shoulders and duck. Our tent flips over and flies several feet. It lands, wobbles for a moment, hangs there like an enormous box kite, then deflates. Canvas smolders. Something inside burns with a soft, orange flame.

The next tent down looks like it got hit by some shrapnel. The new guy, Howley, tumbles out half-naked and shouting. Blood is spattered across his chest. Rankin is out of the car, running, before I can wrap my head around what's just happened.

"That's hard, D," Nevada says, opening the door and jumping down. "They thumped your crib."

73

Cox got hit. A piece of metal the size of a molar ripped into his chest and he bled out in minutes, spraying his life on everything around him. Another went in through his eye. He never even woke up. Nevada drove Cox and Howley to the clinic. Rankin sat in back with them. I'm not sure how much of the blood on Howley was his own and how much came from Cox, but he could talk and walk around, all right. The inside of their tent was a dripping mess. I still can't make myself believe it. Cox and I had eaten together a few hours before. He waited till I finished in the kitchen, so I wouldn't have to eat alone. We played tabletop football with a folded triangle of paper, the way we used to in junior high. I gave him a lot of shit tonight about his bug collection. I don't know why the fuck I didn't just keep my mouth shut. He didn't need that. He gets it enough from everybody else. Got. I told him he had a head like a grasshopper. With big alien eyes. Jesus. And now the asshole's dead. Just like that. Dead.

Salis stumbles over, puffy-eyed, red lines from his pillow pressed deep in his cheeks. He and Hazel pour sand on what's left of the wooden pallet we used as a floor. I can only watch. The two of them manage to save most of our gear, but the tent and all but one of my books are a total loss. I can't seem to move. If they weren't here, I would have just stood and stared as it all burned away.

The siren goes off, but it's a complete afterthought. Everyone's already out of their tents. Sergeant Oliphant shouts. We jump.

"Listen, asshole, you don't have the luxury of sitting around feeling sad," he yells at me. "So move your ass."

Somebody up in tower four turns on a searchlight and sends a bright dot bouncing along the ridgetops just beyond the base. Once the tent fire is contained, I pull on my battle gear and lock my rifle, but that's the only rocket-propelled grenade that lands. By now everyone's wide awake and keyed up. Salis paces back and forth between the tents, shouting "Hooah." He's not the only one who feels let down by the lack of action. It's disappointing not to have a target to fire your weapon at after something like this. I want to kill someone. I would gladly do it with my hands. Salis fires his rifle in the air, probably just getting it out of his system. Sergeant Oliphant screams at him, "Stop acting like a fucking hajji!"

I arrange our salvaged belongings into little stacks. When Rankin gets back from the clinic, he stomps a sort of angry war dance around the piles. His forehead is tight and wrinkled and his uniform is splotched with blood. Occasionally he tells the moon to fuck off. Shouts it up at the sky. I've never seen him quite so mad as this. The lieutenant puts Howley in Lopez's tent. It's probably not a good idea for him to sleep alone for a while, he says. After Doc Dyson cleaned him up, it turned out he hadn't been hit at all. All that blood was from Cox. The lieutenant tells me and Rankin he's sorry we lost our shit and that we can stay in an empty officer's trailer tonight.

"Shit luck," the lieutenant says. "A bad business all around."

"That wasn't just a lucky hit, sir," Rankin tells him, pushing his face up just a little too close to the lieutenant's and speaking just a bit too loudly.

The lieutenant takes it well. He steps back and puts a hand on Rankin's shoulder. "I know it can seem that way, soldier, but they're after all of us, not just you."

"It ain't me they're after, sir." Rankin points to me. "It's him."

"They're happy when they hit any of us. And we're Goddamned lucky it was just one rocket."

"Look," Rankin says, ignoring this completely, "that rocket came in low. We watched it. It came in too low to be from outside." He traces the route of the rocket with his hand. "Just like this."

Behind me comes the click, click, click sound of metal on metal. Nevada sits on the bumper of the Humvee and snaps bullets into a spare magazine for his rifle. His movements are steady and unhurried, but his jaw is set, his eyes flat and mean. When he's finished, Nevada nods at me and walks off.

"That's impossible," Lieutenant Blankenship says.

"No, sir, it isn't." Rankin points toward the south wall again. "I know you don't believe it, but there has to be a door in the wall. There's no other way this could happen. The same door they used when they blew up the Humvees. We got to do something about it, sir. Or it'll happen again."

"If there's a door, Rankin," the lieutenant says, his voice sharper now, "why didn't they just rush in tonight and take the whole base?"

"I don't know, sir."

"If they made a well-coordinated night attack, they could get us all in twenty minutes." He snaps his fingers. "Like that."

"Maybe they're waiting, sir." Rankin's face is expressionless and his voice is even, but his eyes scream fuck you. "For the right moment."

As the lieutenant walks off, I shake out a ready-made from a pack Salis gave me after we put out the fire and ask Rankin if he really thinks tonight's RPG came from inside the wire.

"Sure as sure." He sucks down the cigarette as though he'll suffocate without it. "No other way. Had to be."

"Ahmed?" I light my cigarette and cough immediately. How long has Salis been saving these? They taste like sawdust.

"Or one of his pals who came in through the door. Probably that. But it had to be Ahmed who told him where to point the fucking thing. It ain't a coincidence it hit *our* tent. I know it. You know it. We got to move on this, D. Now. If the El-Tee won't do it, we got to make good on this ourselves."

"Want me to go get Nevada?" I ask him.

"I'd say tonight, but it's past that now. Too late. And what I've got in mind won't work during the day. I got a nasty feeling, D. Something bad's coming down. You take us to that door tomorrow and the three of us'll stake it out from dusk on. Catch him coming or going, one."

"Check," I say.

"Something bad's coming down," Rankin says again, flicking his cigarette onto the remains of our tent. It draws a bright orange arc in the dark air. "Every now and then I get a whiff of it. Smells like rotten fish."

74

Tap, tap, tap. I look up from the dishes I'm scrubbing with a ragged puck of steel wool. Tap, tap, tap. What the hell is that? Foss is out front busing dishes. I spin around. The captain stands in the back doorway, the one we keep open for the breeze that never comes. There's no need to use an oven back here: the kitchen is the oven. The captain shakes up a smoke from a brand-new pack and points outside with his chin. I follow. A knot of dread ties up my intestines. The cellophane wrapper from his cigarettes flits past my face, caressing me on the cheek as it goes by.

"Sorry about your tent, bud. Tough luck. And your pal."

"Right," I say, "luck."

"Oh, yeah, I forgot. The secret door. You didn't really expect Blankenship to believe that, did you? And marking it with a cigarette butt?" He clucks his tongue at me like a kindergarten teacher. "Even if it was true, that's pretty half-assed, to say the least. And to think I was considering you for Intel training."

There's nothing to say to this.

"I hope you didn't lose our little item when the hand grenade hit. Those boxes are pretty solid, but I don't think it'd survive a direct hit."

"Rocket-propelled grenade, sir."

"Whatever," he says, exhaling smoke with his words. "So?"

"What are you talking about, sir?"

"Don't be dense, Private. The lockbox you located for me." He laughs quietly, almost to himself. "The lieutenant's just about shit himself with worry. He's accused me of taking it ten times now."

"You did, sir."

"No, Private." He points his cigarette at me. "*You* did. And you'll do well to remember that, especially the way things stand vis-à-vis you and Blanky. Now tell me what happened after that grenade hit."

"I didn't keep the box in my tent, sir. I told you. So when the rocket hit, it was somewhere else, safe."

"Oh. Well, that's good. That's very fucking good." He digs a hole in the sand with the toe of his boot and spits into it. "If it's not in your burned-up tent, then where the hell is it? Because I've checked. It's not where you said it would be. I hope for your sake you've—"

"I moved it."

The afternoon sun is low in the sky. A small breeze ruffles the legs of my fatigues and makes the long purple shadow of the mess tent shudder. I shade my eyes and look around. Rankin should be here soon, and I'm hoping the captain will finish this quickly.

"Well, how about you take me out to the new spot now?" He kicks sand into his spit hole and looks over at me. "A helicopter is coming in sometime tomorrow or the next day, depending on the weather, to take me back to HQ. The box is coming with me. I'll risk it from here on."

I take him out to the small grove of date palms that grow in a muddy seep behind the ruined old fort. Baba told me once that this was a true oasis, the main reason the fort was built here in the first place, but the spring has clogged with sand after years of neglect. No one cares about it any longer. And soon it will be hidden again. It is the only natural shade on the base. Six trees grow in a circle around a muddy puddle. They arch slightly to the west, like unstrung bows. The tree furthest from the spring appears to have died. Its dry branches rattle like insect wings when the wind blows. Dead fronds crunch beneath our boots. I spot the bleach bottle and stop.

"Right under the bottle, sir," I say, nudging it with my foot.

"How deep?"

"Just a few inches."

"Stand in front of me. Block the view from the parade ground."

The captain takes one last drag on his cigarette and tosses it away. More than half of it is left. This waste irritates me. I stand at parade rest. A Humvee skitters across the sand in the far northeast corner of the base.

"Vehicle," I say.

He glances around quickly and then kneels and digs, fast, frantic strokes. He looks like a dog, throwing out dirt through its hind legs. He digs deeper and deeper. Could I have buried it this far down? No. A new worry arises, worse than the first.

"Sir," I say, "it wasn't that deep."

"What do you mean?"

"You should have found it already."

"Then get down here and dig, Goddamn it."

I kneel beside him and dig. We excavate a five-by-three foot area. The lockbox simply isn't here. The captain's digging becomes faster, wilder; sand goes flying everywhere. I see something in his eyes. Just a quick flash and it's gone, but I see it all the same. A couple of months in Six Zone and you'll know that look for the rest of your life.

Fear.

So the captain has a Lopez of his own. Instead of gloating about it, this realization worries me. No matter what happens with that lockbox, it will be bad. If this deal goes south, what's going to be the result? I heard a rumor when I was back in the States about a remote forward operating base like the Corn Cob or maybe a coalition operating post, somewhere up in the northern mountains. It just up and vanished like the Lost Colony in North Carolina. A convoy of supply trucks came in and found the place deserted. They'd had radio contact with the base that morning, but when they arrived, nothing. Not a trace of anyone, anywhere. Food on the tables, Stars and Stripes waving on its pole, clothes folded neatly in their lockers, weapons and ammo still locked up in the dump. No bodies, and no sign of a fight. And I seem to recall there was some mention of MI in that story too, just a hint of it.

When the captain finally stops digging, sweat has soaked through his uniform in large circles beneath each arm. His cheeks are coated with sand. Dust cakes the rims of his nostrils. He blows out a breath, brushes the dirt off his hands.

"What the fuck did you do with it?" He pants between the words.

"It was here last night."

"Don't dick me around, Private. I can make you wish you'd never been born."

"I wouldn't do that, sir. I told you, I moved it last night."

"Did you see anyone? Did anyone see you?"

"The only person I saw was the mechanic, Cox, but he couldn't have seen me. I went down on my belly as soon as I heard him and kept flat until he went into his tent. And anyway, we can't ask him about—" The words die in my mouth.

"What? We can't what?" He scratches his cheek, leaving behind a smudge of yellow dirt.

"Cox died last night."

The captain stares at me for a very long moment.

"Who else could have seen you?" he says, finally.

I don't know. Maybe somebody else who was lying flat. Someone who followed me. My brain is broken. Foss?

"Think, Goddamn it." The captain doesn't have enough breath to shout. It comes out as an angry wheeze.

"The last person I saw before Cox was Foss."

"That fat fuck in the kitchen?"

"Yes, sir."

"You keep digging." The captain points to the ground, as though I might have forgotten.

"What if someone asks what I'm—"

"Refer them to me." He jogs toward the kitchen. After a few steps, he turns. "If you've lost that box, son, understand this—I will be the one to personally nail your balls to the wall."

I am well and truly fucked.

75

Ahmed leans in the back doorway of the garage and smokes the stubby butt of a cigar. Probably picked up one of Guzman's castoffs. His yellow-checked scarf is wrapped around his face. Each time he takes a drag, he pulls it down an inch and then exhales through the cloth. He's scrounged up a pair of old Wayfarer sunglasses with scratched lenses. When he sees me, he blows a long stream of smoke from his nostrils and smiles. Wait until tonight, I tell myself.

"You lose your keys, Private Toby?" he asks.

I walk past on my way to the mess tent. My throat sticks shut each time I swallow. I have a demon of a headache and I'm in no mood for banter with this creepy fucker. He must spot something in my expression because he stands up straight.

"What?" I say, my voice hoarse.

"You dig and so I am thinking maybe Private Toby he drop his keys. You want, I can help."

"No, Ahmed," I say, "I got my keys right here." I pull them out and jangle them. The sun catches the metal and throws off sparks.

"Ah," he says, trying to French-inhale through his scarf, "that is good. You find the buried thing."

I grunt and walk on by. Suddenly, something shitty occurs to me.

"What did you just say, Ahmed?"

Ahmed smiles. I step closer. A dusty-looking Durrant is reflected in each lens of his glasses. I notice that this Durrant looks pretty pissed-off. Homicidal, in fact. I give smiling a try. The reflections show a spectacular failure.

"You find your buried thing." He fidgets with his inch of cigar, rolls it between his fingers. He looks like he wonders whether or not he should regret this last comment.

"How'd you know we buried something there?"

"I see you dig." He shrugs.

"Uh-huh," I say. "You ever do any digging out there, Ahmed?"

"I do nothing to you. Why you say I bad to the sirs? What I do?"

"Next time you fire an RPG," I tell him, quietly, trying to control myself, "you better not miss."

Ten yards away, I realize I'm holding my breath again, and I let it out. What an irritating habit. Sometimes I find myself doing it even when there's nothing wrong. I wonder if I'll keep doing this when I go home, holding my breath until it feels like my head will burst. Stop, I tell myself, angry to discover I'm following this train of thought. It chugged past, and I stepped right on board. You have to police your head, Durrant. You can't let trash like this collect. This is not the time to worry about it. You'll have plenty of time when you get home. One task at a time. One Goddamn task at a time. Just before I reach the end of the motor pool, Ahmed says my name. I'm so caught up in berating myself that I turn without thinking. He flashes me an ugly grin.

"I know about your girl, Private Toby." He stretches out the vowel sound of the E after B. In his mouth, my name sounds like a dirty word. "The little brown bird you play with. You make nest for her in factory, yes?"

"What are you saying, Ahmed? Cough it out." I grit my teeth and sprint toward him. "You want, I can help you get it out with my Gerber knife."

Fast, much faster than I'd ever have believed possible, Ahmed is gone. He runs into the garage and out some rear door. I give chase. Blood pounds at the back of my eyeballs. Adrenaline makes my tongue taste like I've been sucking on a nickel. I'm going to get that fucker, and when I do, I'm going to make him show me the door and then I'll—and then I'll nothing. He's gone.

The complex chain of half-collapsed rooms behind the motor pool is a dangerous place to run blind. There are plenty of dark corners, bad spots to be surprised in. I stand in the doorway and peer down the murky hallway. Somewhere up ahead, the soles of his shoes flap against the stone floor. The dust is scuffed and smeared here. This is the way he went. I could follow him if I wanted. The question is whether it's worth it. I chew my lip. Somewhere in the dark, Ahmed coughs. Loud theatrical coughs. He *wants* me to chase him.

I'm struck by a sudden fear: he's going after Herman. We can't let him leave the base. We've got to get him tonight.

76

"You ain't still going on about that kid in the factory, are you? Don't pay no attention to Ahmed's bullshit, man. He just heard you talking about it somewhere and wants to freak you out. That's all, D. If you get all worked up about this thing, then he's playing you. He'll be getting what he wants. You won't be thinking straight. See?" Rankin barely looks at me while he talks. Occasionally his eyes gaze over in my direction, but they never settle anywhere for long. His mind is somewhere else. Laid out on his new bunk in the trailer are two 9-mm Glocks and a .38 revolver.

"Sure, right," I say, "forget about Herm—"

Rankin looks me full in the face for the first time and frowns.

"—the kid, I mean." I shrug. "The point is, I think Ahmed's going to rabbit on us. You're right. You're right. He's trying to distract me. I think he wants for me to go out and check on her, so I'll lose sight of what he's up to. That's why I'm telling you this. We can't let him leave the base. I don't think he's coming back after this. We're almost positive those are his guys up in the Noses, so—"

"Hey, see? You're getting worked up. Stay frosty," Rankin says, patting the bunk beside him. "Sit down. Level out. You got to get yourself correct before we move on him tonight. Check this out."

Rankin pulls a roll of duct tape and two sixteen-ounce plastic Coke bottles out of his duffle. I sit down on the bed beside him. He puts the barrel of one of the 9-mms into the bottle and tapes it tight. He whistles an old Public Enemy song as he works, sometimes singing under his breath about how we shouldn't believe the hype. I can see that this thing he's building pleases him. His lips are a tight line broken only by a cigarette, but he smiles at me with his eyes. He's already prepared the bottles in some way, washed and stuffed them with something, maybe punctured them. When he's done taping the barrel up, he hands the Glock over to me and starts on the next one.

"Doesn't really work so well on this snubnose .38. Barrel's too short. We'll just have to save this to use as a last resort if things get hairy."

"What the hell is this?" I ask, setting the gun between us. With the bottle taped onto the barrel, it looks silly and harmless. Something a kid might whip together in his garage on a dull day in July.

"Ghetto silencer."

"Does it really work?"

"Shit, yeah. It's not as good as a fitted steel compressor, but it'll keep the noise down," Rankin says, jiggling the bottle on the second gun to check if it's tight enough.

"You never lived in the ghetto," I protest.

"I saw it in a movie. Then tried it out on my own."

We laugh.

"But it works," he says.

"I thought we were going to put him in a cell."

"We are, D. We are. But as my meemaw always told me—" Rankin puts a high waver into his voice, hunches his shoulders, and looks up from under his eyebrows with a suspicious squint. "—don't get caught with your pants down if you ain't got on clean drawers."

I laugh again. "I have no idea what the hell that means. You just made that up."

"I ain't joking, D. What I'm saying, you got to take precautions. I thought you were a Boy Scout. Be prepared, baby."

"Where in the hell did you get this mean little bastard from?" I heft the revolver in my hand, then offer it to him, grip first.

"Good old .38 Special." He knocks it open and checks the load before flipping it shut.

"Nice."

"Bought it right outside the gate of the base we stayed at when we first come here. In the capital. They were selling all manner of shit. Smutty DVDs. Chronic. Said it was chronic anyway. Smelled like oregano. I didn't try it."

"It's weird I've never seen this before," I say.

"I keep it buried next to a support beam over in the cement factory." He winks.

"So, I've been thinking. What if Ahmed tries to rabbit on us during the day? Before we can catch him. Maybe tries to slip out through the gate on the sly. If he makes a run for it in broad daylight, how are we going to stop him? Hell, he may *already* be gone." I peel a strip of dead skin off my chapped lower lip with my teeth. "What if he got away after he ducked into the old fort?"

"Don't sweat it, D." He punches me lightly on the arm. "Nevada's got sentry duty until 1800. I told Salis to keep an eye out, too. He's pulling duty in the tower near where you said the door is. I'm telling you, D. It's cool. We've got the man covered. You put big bad Rankin on the job and Goddamn if it don't get done."

"Now you sound like Nevada." I give him a curious look. "What happened there? Since the bugout, you two have been pretty cozy."

"Yeah, well, we rectified our shit up there on the mountain. He was grateful for the heads-up about the poison stew." Rankin sniffs and holds out his hands in a gesture that says, what else could I do? He nods and sniffs again. "And I realized I was being kind of tough on the boy. Something he said brought me up hard and made me think."

"What's that?"

"While we're running back to the Humvees, Nevada says to me, see, 'I ain't all that bad for a boy who grew up eating government cheese.'"

I laugh at this but cut it short when I see Rankin's reaction. "Government cheese?" I ask.

"Families on assistance used to get these big wheels of government cheese. Pretty good, actually. When I was a kid, I had a friend from school that grew up rough. I was small, too small to really see the difference money made. I must of been about five or six. When I told Meemaw about that cheese, told her we should get some next time we're over at the store making groceries, her face got all pinched. 'I don't want you playing over there any more, you hear me?' That's all she said. Not that I couldn't play with him. Just, not over *there*. Even when you're five, you know when something rubs the adults wrong. So I figured something was wrong with the boy. After that, I stayed away from him. And for the longest time, I thought it had something to do with eating cheese. Like that made a person nasty." He laughs and digs around in the duffel bag until he finds a roll of blue friction tape.

I hold out my hands and he chucks it over. He knows I have a thing about wrapping my grip. My hands sweat. "So, what then? Him saying that made you think about your friend?"

"Yeah, well, it came to me I was doing wrong by Nevada. I tried to think what it was that made me start hating him to begin with, and I couldn't remember what it was. I just didn't like him."

"That happens to everybody, Rankin. Bad chemistry."

"Nah, D. I couldn't see past the gangbanger attitude Nevada throws around. I should of known better, because that's exactly what it is—it's just a front. And we all got one."

"True," I say.

"All of a sudden, while we're running for our lives, I see it for what it is. I ain't got no reason to hate him like that."

"Yeah," I say, because I can't think of anything better.

Rankin nods, but I can see his thoughts have raced on without me. I'm not even sure he heard me. He picks at a scab on his cracked upper lip. From the expression on his face, I imagine he's back in Sandfly, his old neighborhood in Savannah, sitting with his meemaw on the porch. We work quietly for about five minutes, the only sound in the room the tearing of tape, and then suddenly Rankin comes back from Sandfly with a message. He puts down the 9-mm and looks at me.

"Watching how Nevada acted when the shit came down on us got me to thinking about it differently. Up there on the mountain, we were just two black men fighting for our lives. And I was thinking, why can't I take this with me when I come back down from the mountain?" He experiments with a smile, but what forms is closer to a wince, like he accidentally pressed too hard on a bruise. "Why hold on to all the old bullshit? You know?"

"Yeah," I say, and I think I do.

"Mmm-hmm," Rankin says, but his eyes look bleary and distant. He's gone off again to some other place.

"But what I don't get about this new thing of yours with Nevada is the shaved heads." I pick up a sock and make like I'm polishing his head with it. "What's that all about?"

"Hey, get that nasty thing off me. Damn, man, your feet be smelling like old cheese. Shit."

"So how come?"

"It's just a thing, man. Something people used to do back when he was a kid in New Orleans after two guys settled a beef without killing each other."

"Sounds like blood brothers. Is it a gangbang thing? A cellblock thing?"

"Something like that." He picks up the sock and pops it at me. "Ain't nothing but a haircut. Don't make a case out of it. You want, you can shave yours too."

Outside the trailer window, someone whistles three quick chirps and thumps on the wall of the trailer. This must be the sign Rankin has been waiting for, because he's up off the bed before I can turn to look for the source of the sound. He goes over and lifts the blinds just a crack. I stand. Damn, I think, he's really taken this thing over. But I don't mind. Rankin has always had a better head for details and logistics. I may be good at coming up with the occasional plan, but he's better at working out the kinks and putting it into action. He flashes a victory sign at the person outside. Another three whistles and a slap. Rankin smiles at the sunlight pouring in and lets the blinds slide to the sill with a whoosh and thump.

"You're right, D. He's having a go at the front gate. You stay here. We don't want him to know you're on to him."

"Sure," I say, somewhat disappointed.

Rankin slips the revolver under his shirt into the back of his waistband. He smoothes down his missing hair, gives me a salute, and opens the door. Just as he's stepping into the hall, he thinks of something. He spins around and smiles.

"You're my partner, right?" He speaks quickly, the words bumping into each other.

"Yeah," I say; "fuck, yeah. More family than family, right?"

"Don't let this shit with Nevada mess with you, then." He gives me a funny smile, shy almost. "The mope's got a right to look up to the man who saved his life, don't he?"

"Sure," I say.

"Then how 'bout we let Baldy Joe play with the big boys this once." He absently checks the position of his gun. "It don't change nothing."

"Nah, man," I say, embarrassed now, but grateful too, "I didn't mean—"

"Well, shit, then." He steps forward and makes a fist. "Let's us bring this motherfucker down."

We knock fists. He spins on a heel and leaves so quick, his smile hangs in the hallway for a second. The front door slams behind him. In the front room, I sit on the beat-up old couch. A framed picture of the president hangs above two battered folding chairs. All the officers' trailers must come with these things. The president and I exchange smiles.

"How do you like your war now, Mr. President?"

He doesn't answer. I'm not sure he's listening.

77

The moon is a hairline crack in the heavens, just a rumor in the sky behind the Noses. A steady wind blows across the base. It is cold and sharp and makes my hands feel numb and clumsy. I lie beneath a sand-covered tarp about fifty yards behind the kitchen tent. After an ungodly amount of finagling and forty perfectly rolled cigarettes, I got Foss to cover for me tonight.

I glass the open space between guard tower four and tower six with a new pair of night-vision goggles Hazel snagged for me from supply. The goggles make the stars look green and bleary. Every thirty mikes or so, Hazel and Greer lap my position in their Humvee. They're on perimeter patrol tonight and have no idea we're out here. Nevada's waiting in a collapsed room at the very back of the old fort. About two hundred yards from the wall, Rankin crouches in a spiderhole. The two of us dug it while Nevada kept Ahmed occupied with a game of craps. He had to lose a few bucks to keep Ahmed there. I asked how you can make yourself lose at craps, but he wouldn't tell me.

Every little sound sets me off. I swear I hear footsteps about fifteen yards behind me, but no one walks past. I lie very still. If I get up to have a look, I risk my camouflage. An hour passes. And then another. I don't know for sure, but I'm guessing it's almost midnight. My left leg keeps cramping up on me, and my arms feel like they're full of rusty nails. I'd never make it as a sniper.

Again, that same sound behind me. The scrape of rubber on sand. I'm still not sure it's footsteps. The wind is blowing. It could be a loose piece of cardboard rolling across the ground, but I doubt it. Maybe Ahmed's too jumpy to use the hidden door tonight. I wonder if he's walking back and forth behind me, waiting for a signal. Come on, Ahmed. Move.

There it is again. A soft crunch. And then another. Adrenaline makes my fingers twitch. The crunch has two parts, like the rolling pressure of a heel and a toe. Whoever it is, they're moving with purpose and determination. It's got to be Ahmed. The sounds get closer. And closer. And then a foot lands right near my face. Sand showers my left cheek and gets in my goggles. My bad eye is still so swollen from the latrine explosion that my vision is narrowed to a slit. In this condition, I can't even make out the person's legs. All I see is a large green blur that steps back, moving somewhere just behind me. A few more inches to the right and this guy will trip over my head. But thankfully, the footsteps move off to the left, away from the hidden door. Rankin and I agreed not to come out of our positions until Ahmed reached a spot somewhere midway between us. I wait for the figure to move again. What happens next takes me off guard.

The hidden door opens inwards. Not all the way, but wide enough for a dark space to form in the wall at ground level. Then a second man comes jogging past me, about ten steps to my right. I know he's someone different because he's barefoot and the sound his feet make in the sand is more of a swish than a crunch. The first guy, the one who nearly stepped on my head, was wearing combat boots. As soon as this second man passes, I see the yellow-checked scarf wrapped around his head. It's got to be Ahmed. But if so, who was the guy in the boots? I take a deep breath and push up and out. I tear off the tarp and sprint toward him. Out of the corner of my eye, I spot Nevada. He's cooking along about thirty yards to my left. And then Rankin leaps up out of the spiderhole, startling the hell out of Ahmed, who trips, picks himself up, and makes for the door. I still can't see who opened it.

I'm closing in on Ahmed, but Rankin gets to him first. With a flying tackle, he takes him down. Ahmed goes sprawling and flings something toward the door. It pops open and papers flutter all over the place.

"Hey, gosh darn it. Stop!" someone just behind me shouts. The owner of the first footsteps. I recognize the voice, but I don't want to believe it's true. Lopez. Rankin and I saw him pass a couple of times earlier while we were digging our hidey holes, but it was nearly dark, and besides, there's always someone digging holes on the base.

Ahmed and Rankin wrestle in the gravel. Just before I reach them, Rankin yells. Ahmed springs up like a frog and snatches a handful of the papers that fell from the package he was carrying. It has to be the lockbox. I'm not going to catch Ahmed: he has too much of a lead. I'm tempted to pull out the pistol and lay into him, but with Lopez added to the equation, I'm afraid to risk it. Then I get a better idea. A couple yards ahead of me in the sand is a rock about the size of a baseball. I slide to a stop and grab it. Lopez runs past me toward Rankin. I heft the rock once to get a feel for it.

"Ahmed," I shout.

He hesitates a moment but doesn't stop. I hurl that rock as hard as I can. It sails over Lopez and Rankin in a beautiful arc. Ahmed is almost to the door. But there's Nevada right behind him, galloping and leaping like a white-tailed deer in flight. From here it's impossible to tell who'll get there first. Just ahead of me Lopez reaches Rankin; he tries to stop short but ends up sliding on the loose gravel. He loses his balance and tumbles.

Ahmed makes the mistake of taking one last backward glance. For a moment, our eyes connect. And then he swings around, but not before my beautiful throw catches him high on the cheekbone. It's a glancing blow but hard enough to drop him. I let out a cheer and start to run again. Nevada looks as though he's got our man. He's only about ten yards behind him. But then the figure in the doorway reaches under Ahmed's armpits and pulls him up and in. The door begins to close.

Nevada leaps, twisting sideways, like a runner sliding into home base, and hits the bottom of the door with both feet. The sudden impact makes the stones screech. Ahmed's rescuer steps forward and kicks Nevada in the leg, hard because I can hear him grunt from here. With one hand, Nevada grabs the man's pant leg and pulls, and with the other he fumbles for his gun. The man pivots and kicks him full in the chest. Nevada loses his balance and pitches backward, dropping his gun but keeping a grip on the man's pants. Two booms. They sound like someone pounding on an empty metal trash can but much, much louder.

I reach the door just as it grinds shut. Nevada lies on his back in the sand. "Motherfucker!" he shouts. The sound carries.

"Hey," I say, "you all right, man?"

"He just clipped me. It ain't nothing," Nevada wheezes. "It don't even hurt much."

Blood darkens the sand beneath his right shoulder. Behind me, Rankin shouts my name. Lopez scrambles about, snatching up the fallen papers. Rankin lies on his side in the sand.

"I'll be all right," Nevada says. He closes his eyes and mumbles. "Go get that asshole."

"You sure?"

"Mmm-hmm."

I'm breathing hard; but, even so, I run again, hoping to reach Lopez before he gets everything back in the box. I notice a piece of blue cellophane stuck to a dead shrub. I grab for it, but Lopez beats me, slipping it into the box and snapping it shut. It's only then that I get a good look at what he's holding. It's definitely the lockbox. Green and battered and covered with dust.

"Gimme that," Rankin says to him. "That ain't your shit."

Lopez doesn't answer. He looks back and forth between us, a hand on the holster clipped to his waist. Rankin sits up, clutching his arm, and eyes Lopez's gun very carefully. His own gun lies beside him on the ground in two pieces. It must have smashed on a rock during the tussle with Ahmed. I crouch down next to him to get a better look at his arm. His sleeve is slit and soaked in blood. This isn't a tear. Something sharp cut through and into him. Nevada shouts in the dark behind us. Something about chickpeas and bitches.

"You all right?" I ask Rankin. "Nevada got winged but says he's okay."

He grumbles something unintelligible. All his attention is focused on Lopez, his gun, and the box.

"Hand it over, motherfucker," Rankin says, spitting. "Just let leave of it and move your sorry ass on back, unless you want me to kick it home for you."

Lopez holds up the lockbox. It's barely visible in this miserly moonlight, but I can see a glint here and there in those places where scraped-off paint reveals metal.

"You saying this is yours, then?" Lopez shakes the box at us. Something shifts inside. Once again I think of loose bills. "This yours, Durrant?"

"I know it ain't yours," I say, careful now. He's leading us into something.

"Darn right it's not." His voice quavers. "This is the lieutenant's lockbox. It's been missing for several days."

"So what, we get a reward?" Rankin says.

Lopez shakes his head in an exaggerated display of disgust.

"Well," I tell him, "at least you've got proof we didn't take it. We were, in fact, in the process of recovering it."

"Sure you were," Lopez says.

Rankin frowns at me and then looks over at the box. I can see him wondering if I know anything about it. "What are you doing out here anyway, man?" he asks Lopez.

The blood drips from his fingers into the sand. A lot of it. This worries me. I kneel closer to inspect the wound more carefully, but all I see is blood-soaked cloth. There isn't near enough light. Rankin grunts when I move his arm. I glance back at Nevada. He hasn't moved.

"Ahmed told me you—" He points to me. "—were up to something this afternoon. He said you were burying something out here, so I came by to check and I saw you two digging. I checked the duty roster and there wasn't any digging on it. Then I came back to see what would happen. Ahmed said he thought you might try—" He pauses, looking back and forth between me and Rankin. "—something. And he was right." Lopez takes a step toward us, keeping one hand near the holster on his belt, and peers at Rankin's arm. "So you're in on this too, Rankin?"

Rankin clears his throat and spits.

"It's a shame you came out here tonight," I say. "It really is. We almost caught him but for you. And now—" I heft the .38 in my hand. I honestly don't even remember pulling it out. I just suddenly find it in my hand. I'm careful, however, not to point it at him.

Lopez stiffens and jerks back, face rigid.

"So what's your game? Are you going to try and make it look like an accident? If I shout, they'll probably hear me in the guard tower. You think about that, Durrant?"

"What are you talking about, fool?" Rankin says.

"My murder."

Rankin laughs. I don't. I wonder what Lopez saw in my face to make him say that.

"So it's just a laugh to you, that it?" Lopez glances from face to face. His eyes are wild. "A man's life. A fellow soldier. You won't get away with this, Durrant. The lieutenant knows what you've been doing."

"Shit, Lopez," Rankin says, "I might not like you, but I ain't going to kill you 'cause of it."

None of us notice the patrol vehicle bouncing along the perimeter road until it's right on top of us. When its headlights sweep across this sorry scene, it stops. Doc Greer, who can smell blood from a mile off, jumps out with his ever-ready bag and runs over. Lopez takes a step back, and then another. I wonder if he really believes we were going to do him in. He strides off toward the officers' trailers. Well, I think, there go my balls.

"What happened here?" Doc Greer asks.

The two of us exchange looks.

"Did you get in a knife fight with Lopez?" He drops his bag in the sand.

"No, man," Rankin says in a cheerful voice, "he'd be dead if that were the case and—" He stops short and looks around. "Where's Nevada?"

"He told me a bullet winged him. He's lying over there." I turn and point at the dark shape on the sand. "Hey, Nevada."

He doesn't answer.

"Fucking fuck," Rankin says, pushing himself up with a grunt. I have to help him to stand.

The three of us sprint across the sand. Doc Greer gets there first and takes a knee.

"Nevada," Rankin says, his voice ragged and hoarse and shrill. "Get your ass up. You best not be fucking with us."

Doc Greer presses his fingers against Nevada's neck. Even in the shadow of the wall, I can see his face looks wrong. I fall on my knees beside him and touch Nevada on the shoulder. Doc Greer turns away and starts to cough. Rankin eases down into the loose sand. "Nevada," he says.

"Dead," Doc Greer croaks.

Rankin punches the sand with his good arm. Each time he hits the ground, he shouts "Fuck!" He yells the word so loud, it stops being a word. Just an angry sound. I touch him on the arm and he punches me in the chest, knocking the wind out of me. I fall onto my back. I can't make my brain work. There isn't a thought in it. The sky is huge and black and very cold.

78

I don't sleep much. Maybe an hour. After a while I say "Fuck it" and get up. As soon as all the excitement died down, two thoughts remained in my head. Nevada's dead. Because Ahmed killed him. He knows about Herman. And now that asshole's out. I roll up every flake of tobacco I can find and stack the cigarettes one after another on the table beside Rankin's bunk. There isn't anything to say about what happened, so I'm giving him these. I imagine each cigarette as a prayer. One by one, as I finish them, I say to myself, "Take me, save the kid." White and perfectly rolled and heaven-bound. Each breath of smoke will lift my message up into the sky. I take the last one onto the steps of the trailer. Venus rises over the Noses.

79

I look for Rankin all morning. In the mess. On the parade ground. In the trailer. I left for KP duty before he woke up. When I got back after breakfast, he'd disappeared. Finally, just before I have to start the lunch shift, I find Rankin outside the motor pool, cleaning Nevada's blood out of the Humvee. Because we have so little water to spare, he's spraying the back seat with disinfectant foam. The blood has dried, but as he wipes at the vinyl with a moistened rag, the brown flakes turn bright red again.

"Can I talk to you about something?" I yell over to him. "I want to ask your advice about that kid in—"

"I don't want to hear about it," Rankin says. "I know what you want, and I'll make it simple for you—no. All I care about is making those fuckers pay. That's it."

"Rankin," I say.

"Nevada's dead." He turns around and shakes the bloody rag in my face. "And you're seeing ghosts, D."

"That kid's real, Rankin. I swear."

Rankin rattles the aerosol can. I can see he's worried I'm losing my shit. One of the reasons I haven't told him about Clarissa's letter, though I carry it in my pocket everywhere. He'll think there's some connection.

And there probably is. Just not the one he'll make.

"I don't care about doing the time," I say, sitting down on a wooden crate just beyond the bay door. "Or whatever it is that happens after I do this. Listen to me here, man. I feel like I've messed up every other part of my life. If I let that fucker kill the kid, it will drive me crazy. I won't be able to forget it as long as—"

Rankin holds up his hand and breaks in. Blood has gotten under his fingernails. He hasn't shaved and his neck is caked with yellow grit. "If you go out there on your own, they're liable to shoot your ass. I'm talking blindfold, cigarette, up-against-the-wall shit, D." He throws the bloody rag into the old diesel barrel we use for burning trash.

"Five minutes. That's all it'll take. I'm not asking you to come with me. I don't want to drag you into this shit too. Just lend me the keys. I'll be out and back in thirty minutes tops." I hand him a new rag from a pile near the crates. It's a piece torn from the pant leg of an old BDU, a battle dress uniform. I wonder briefly whose it was.

"Yeah, and then I'll be cleaning your blood out of this thing."

The base is strangely quiet. Not even a breeze to move the dust. Down the long sandy strip between the tents, I don't see anyone moving. It feels like we're the last ones left. "Listen, last night after we took Nevada to the clinic, Guzman dragged me over to the armory and asked me to explain what the hell happened," I say.

"Yeah," Rankin says. He doesn't turn around. He keeps rubbing down the seats. "He talked to me too. So what?"

"He said Lopez told him he saw Ahmed leave the base yesterday afternoon."

"That's bullshit. Nevada was on sentry until 1900. Played craps with the asshole." Rankin swings his hand back and forth across the seat. The vinyl's clean, but he keeps wiping, like the mechanical arm in a carwash.

"I told him that. And that's when this totally depressing idea came to me. Could Lopez be doing the shit he's accusing *me* of? I don't want to believe it, but it sure makes sense." I move around to the other side of the car so I can face Rankin as he works and maybe catch his eye. He doesn't look up.

"What are you getting at?"

"You want to get the fuckers who killed Nevada. So do I. Lopez is one of them."

"Sorry, D, I don't buy it. Lopez might be a nosy busybody, and he might of fucked things up last night, but I don't think he did it on purpose."

"I'm just saying."

"Well, go say it to somebody else." Rankin picks at something on the seat with his fingernail.

"Why can't we kill two birds with one stone?" As soon as I say it, I cringe inside. I'm talking like the captain. "I know you don't believe there's a kid in the factory, but Ahmed does. I'm positive he's headed out there to kill him. He as good as told me. We can lie in wait for him and get him when he arrives."

"I know what you're doing, D. It ain't going to work." And then, suddenly, Rankin stops scrubbing, and for the first time this morning, he looks me in the eye. "This business with you going out and saving some kid has to do with Clarissa, don't it?"

Sometimes Rankin's ability to read my mind scares the shit out of me. I light a cigarette and close my eyes. There are times when it takes all of your energy to keep from flying apart, when you have to focus and concentrate just to avoid having your cells spin off and explode. This is one of those times.

There's nothing to it but to show him. I dig into my cargo pocket and get out the letter and the ring. He watches without saying a word. But he must see it, whatever it is, smeared all over my face.

"Man, I don't want this." He tries to push it away. "This is your private shit. Your woman."

"Just read it," I say. "You asked."

He does. The paper crinkles softly in his hands as he flips over the page. In my head, I read along with him. Without meaning to, without wanting to, I know each word of the letter by heart. Finally, he looks at the ring and inhales so fast it whistles. Rankin knows Clarissa. He's met her half a dozen times. Liked her, I think. Rankin stares through the hole in the ring for some time before he folds it up in the letter and hands it back to me. On the corner of the top page, he's left behind a smudge of Nevada's blood. I take it without a word and stuff it back into my pocket. Neither of us says anything for a bit.

"I. . . ." He runs a hand over his newly shaved head.

Whatever he decides will affect both of us for a long time to come. I've pushed hard enough. Now he has to make his own choice. Rankin takes one of the cigarettes I rolled him last night from his tobacco pouch. He has yet to say a word about them. I toss him my lighter.

"Listen to me, D." He walks around the Humvee and sits beside me on the wooden crate, a trail of smoke in his wake. "You listening?"

I nod.

"This is it. The last time. No more of this shit. We get back to base and it's over. Then we get the one who started all this."

"Ahmed?" I ask. "Lopez?"

Rankin doesn't answer.

80

"Five minutes," **Rankin** says quietly. He hasn't spoken since we left the base. I ducked down on the floorboards and he told the sentry the lieutenant wanted him to run a package into the village. "If you ain't back in five minutes, I'm leaving your ass. Hear me?"

"Five minutes," I say and jump down into the dust.

It's Tuesday. A hundred and ten degrees Fahrenheit. Eleven forty-four hours by the clock on the dash. I should be back at the mess tent, dishing out sloppy joes.

As I climb the steps to the factory door, I whistle the chorus to "Muskrat Love." But I stop short in the doorway. If the place had been trashed before, now it's destroyed. The piles of wood have been kicked around the room. Barrels of trash are strewn from one side of the factory floor to the other. Bullet holes splinter the wood on the office door. The bodies of shredded toy bears smolder everywhere. I smell piss and shit and sour smoke. Goddamn. I drop the MREs I brought along and run for the factory office where Herman made his little nest.

"Herman," I shout. "Herman."

No answer.

The office looks as though it has been hit by several grenades. The desks are twisted scraps of blackened metal. Little bits of shredded paper cover the floor. Something dull and green catches my eye. A small oval portrait of Ben Franklin. Then I see the others. There must be fifty or so of them. All neatly torn away from their original bills. Another of Herman's little art projects?

The grown and greedy men who stumbled across these must have gone insane over the loss. At my feet I see at least several thousand dollars' worth of useless heads. I stuff one of the hateful heads into my pocket. Herman's bed is gone. In its place is a blackened crater in the concrete floor. The first outfit I saw him in, a robe of purple knotted teddy-bear skins, hangs from a nail on the wall and smokes like roasted meat.

"Fuck," I shout at the mess, at Ahmed, at my own stupidity.

The smoke in here is relatively fresh. If fucking Rankin would have made up his mind a little bit faster then—I cut this off before it goes any further. If it's anyone's fault, it's mine. I step back into the factory and look for Herman's remains. I can only hope it was over quickly. Possibilities flick through my brain like stills from a horror movie. I put Herman's face on the young girl killed by stray bullets I saw in the capital, the child hit by the IED in an Inmar marketplace, the elderly woman shot at a checkpoint when her brakes failed and she drove through the warning shots. I can't seem to stop these images from invading my head. My little cigar box isn't big enough to hold this much awfulness. The seams are tearing and the rubber bands won't stretch any farther.

A bird whistles. The one innocent witness to this shitty business. Some small brown bird.

But it isn't a bird.

It's Herman. He climbs down the stack of empty oil drums on the other side of the room and comes skipping across the mess in his rubber tube shoes, a strip of blue cellophane wrapped around his neck like a scarf. I find myself laughing. The relief is physical. My heart nearly explodes with it. The last time I felt something even close to this was the second time I saw Clarissa, a few days after we got back from the state park. She met me at a BBQ place for dinner, and as soon as she walked in the door, I knew right away that the adventure we'd had out in the forest would be something more than just a single night between strangers.

I sing to him. The song I tried to teach him the last time I was here.

The Sesame Street song. I know I should be worried about Ahmed or whoever tore this place up coming back, but for the moment, I'm simply happy to see Herman alive.

"Sunny day," I sing.

When he gets closer, I notice he's wearing a new outfit. Another of his paper dresses. I suppose all the rest of his clothes got burned up. This one looks peculiar from a distance, colorful and shiny, and becomes stranger the closer he gets. He's fashioned an odd shift out of pages from glossy magazines and black electrical tape. All of the photographs are of women. Some are modeling hats, some modeling shoes, some applying lipstick. In the very center of his chest, there is a photograph of a reclining nude model. It shames me a bit when I recognize it. This came from the same copy of *Jugs* that was circulating the base a couple of weeks ago. The issue that disappeared the same day Baba did. Surely it can't be the same magazine. I want to tear it off and burn it.

For a moment, I think he's going to throw his arms around me, but at the last second he stops short, sliding on the broken glass. He smiles. I smile back. Herman nods and points to a smoldering teddy bear on the concrete in front of him. He nudges it with his foot. Look at this crazy shit, his gesture seems to say. I walk us over to the MREs, which are scattered where I dropped them. Herman squats and stacks them into a neat pile.

I don't mean to say it. It just slips out. "Ahmed," I say.

The boy freezes. His entire body goes rigid. He makes a low, guttural growl. I can't think of anyone else who might have done this, except maybe the owners of the cash. And who the hell would they be? I want to reach over and touch him, comfort him, but I'm afraid the gesture will be mistaken and he'll flee. I speak to him in simple, ungrammatical Arabic. I make sure to keep a quiet, even tone. I tell him it's no longer safe here. The man who did this will come back. You need to find a new place to stay. Herman continues to stare at the floor.

I try again to think of a way I could bring him back to the base. The worst the lieutenant could do is force him to leave again. The only real worry I have is that Herman might be even more vulnerable to Ahmed on the base. Fuck it. It's better than leaving him out here and worrying.

"Herman," I say.

He looks up. I explain to him in my halting and probably useless Arabic that I have a friend outside in the Humvee. No doubt Herman's already scoped this out. He's a pretty cautious kid. There's a reason he's still alive. I tell him I'm going to bring my friend in here and see if I can convince this friend to take him back to the base with us.

"All right?" I ask finally, using the local word.

Maybe I imagine it, but I could swear the boy nods, almost imperceptibly. I take this as a sign he understands at least some of what I've said. I point to our vehicle and then motion for him to stay put. My head feels light, as though pumped up with helium. I jog outside. Rankin watches from the Humvee. I can see from his expression that he's anxious about the way I'm acting. Manic, no doubt. From his perspective, crazed.

"Rankin," I say through the window, "come inside a mike. Ahmed was here. I told you he'd come after the kid. The place is still smoking. I want to bring the boy back to the base. We'll say—"

"Ah, ah, ah," Rankin says, frowning.

"I'll say he came to the gate. Come on. If we leave him, Ahmed will kill him, and probably do worse before that. I can't leave the poor kid for Ahmed to fuck with. I mean, shit."

Half a dozen expressions flit across Rankin's face.

"This is on you," he says finally.

Reluctantly he walks into the factory. He wrinkles his nose and looks around in distaste. Herman is gone. Damn. We spooked him. Rankin's eyes widen, his expression saying, And? He kicks at a half-melted elephant.

"He was just here, damn it. I swear it, Rankin. I swear to God I was just talking to him."

"Okay," Rankin says, but it's plain he doesn't believe me.

"Why else would the place be shot up like this? They chucked a few grenades into the office where the kid sleeps."

"Maybe," Rankin says, "or maybe Ahmed thought there was someone here since he heard you talking about him. When he didn't find no one, he opened up on the place."

"But look," I plead. "The kid took the MREs I brought."

"Okay," Rankin says, expressionless.

"You don't believe me."

"Let's just go. You got your five minutes."

"Herman," I yell, trying to sound cheerful. "Come out, pal. We're going to take you out of this place."

Rankin adjusts the strap of his M16. I can see it's hurting his wounded arm. I motion for him to give it to me, but he shakes his head and starts for the door. I kick a piece of wood, and it tumbles across the floor and smacks into a large pile of trash. We both watch it. After it hits, something shakes loose in the pile and comes skittering over the concrete in our direction.

"Damn," Rankin whispers.

Grenade! Rankin swings around and leaps to cover it with his helmet. If it goes off, it'll kill him, but he'll have protected me from the blast. He reacts in less time than it takes me to identify the problem. While I'm tensing for the explosion, he begins to laugh. Rankin lifts his K-pot and nudges the object toward me. A pair of wind-up joke teeth. Bright red gums and enormous horse teeth.

"It's laughing at you, D," Rankin says. I can't read his tone.

We walk back to the Humvee, Rankin alert and wary, with a tight grip on his rifle. I let him move ahead so I can look through the factory door one last time. It's empty. Of course. When Herman heard the commotion we made over the teeth, he'd have taken off running as fast as he could. Even so, I doubt myself for a moment. From the doorway, I can just make out the smoking knot of fake furs hanging in the office. No, I didn't imagine this. I consider pointing out Herman's clothes to Rankin, but then I think better of it. If he doesn't believe Herman is real, this will only make me look worse, like I've been in here making doll clothes for my imaginary friend.

Something sticks to the bottom of my boot. I try to scrape it off on the Humvee's step, but it won't come off. I sit down on the running board to pick it off.

"D," Rankin says. "We don't have time for this—"

I pick it out of my tread. A bit of silver metal with a pin. It's all bent and twisted. One side is fire-blackened. It looks a hell of a lot like a first lieutenant's pin. I hold it up in the sunlight. This could have been here an hour or six months. It could be anyone's. Even so, it gives me a very bad feeling.

"What's this look like to you?" I toss it over to Rankin after I climb up onto the seat.

"A piece of junk." He throws it back.

"A first lieutenant's pin?"

I hold it up for him to see again. He shrugs. What difference does it make? his expression says. He's right. I chuck it out the window and strap in. Rankin turns the ignition and the motor clears its throat and comes to life. I'm angry, but I'm not quite sure who at.

As we pull out of the factory yard, Rankin nudges me with his elbow.

"Sorry, D," he says.

"What for?"

"I shouldn't have said that about the teeth laughing at you."

"Well," I tell him, watching the factory shrink in the rear window, "it's probably true. They *were* laughing at me."

The hard-sprung shocks creak as we crash through the potholes. From out here on the plain, FOB Cornucopia looks like a giant brown lockbox. Or a prison. I'd just as soon keep driving. All the way to the ocean. Put as much space as I can between me and all of this accumulating shit. This feeling I have is almost physical, like a vicious hangover or a migraine. It fills my head like ink.

"Now," Rankin says, glancing over at me and then back at the road, "you best start thinking of ways to cover your ass."

81

Hazel apologizes five times. Once as he's putting the bracelets on me, twice during the walk to the old fort, once as we go down the dark stairs, and a last time as he shuts the door to the cell. The same one we used to hold the old man. Even Hazel must see the sour irony in this; but if he does, he keeps it to himself. Salis doesn't say anything until we get to the cell.

"What the hell were you doing out there, man?" He makes an unhappy face at Hazel, as though it's his fault I'm here. Hazel takes a cautious step back. Salis's been known to give people a quick smack for no reason but simple meanness. It builds inside him until it has to find an outlet. And then, pop, whoever's closest gets it. "I mean, damn." He shakes his head hard, the way boys will sometimes after they take a tumble and see stars. "I know you ain't no traitor, but still, I mean what the fuck, man?"

"There's a kid living out in the abandoned factory. I thought Ahmed was going to kill him."

"Did he?"

"No," I say, "but he tried."

"You could of made a good soldier, Durrant." This is his highest compliment. He gives me an appraising look and works his lips into a makeshift smile. "Those are some hard boys up in Leavenworth, but you'll make do. Look me up once you're out. We'll go to my grandpa's farm and shoot us some white-tail. What say, D?"

"Sure," I say. We've talked many times about going hunting together after we get back. I wonder if he really believes this will happen.

Hazel looks like he might burst into tears.

It had come down on us much faster than I expected. They stopped Rankin and me at the gate coming back. Sergeant Oliphant stood in the middle of the road with his hands on his hips and glared at us. I wondered how long he'd been waiting. We weren't gone but an hour. Less. The first words out of my mouth were, "It ain't Rankin's fault. I tricked him into it."

The lieutenant was nowhere to be seen, which surprised me. Lopez watched from the sentry gate. They pulled Rankin out of the cab and Sergeant Oliphant marched him off toward the trailers, Lopez a few steps behind. Hazel and Salis got stuck dragging my ass off to the clink.

"You ain't going to fight us, are you?" Salis asked me as I climbed down from the Humvee.

"Nah," I told him, "I don't want to hurt you."

"Shit," he said, grinning, "I was looking forward to shooting your ass."

Hazel looked over in alarm.

"He's kidding," I told him. Hazel didn't look reassured.

The lieutenant visits the cell a couple of hours later. Boots scrape the concrete outside the door and I know someone's peeking in through the Judas hole. The scrutiny causes the same shivery disgust I feel when a fly crawls on my face. He waits out there for a long time before he opens up the door. I'm surprised to see he's alone. He shakes his head at me like a disappointed Sunday-school teacher.

"You really dug yourself a deep one this time, Durrant."

"Yes, sir," I say.

"I don't think you understand the trouble you're in."

"All of it," I say. "Every last code in the seven-dash-eight."

"Still joking." He lets out a choppy, uneven breath. "Lopez has it that you go to that factory to confer with the enemy. That you've been going out there after shit-burning runs and that after that dust-up last night you went and reported what happened to the enemy. He's been after me about this for some time. I'm starting to believe him. Is that what's going on, Durrant?"

"No, sir."

"Is that all you've got to say for yourself? 'No, sir'? We've lost three good men in the last week."

"I know, sir. They were my friends, but I'm not sure what else to tell you. It seems you've made your mind up."

"You leave my mind to me. Mind your own mind."

I smile, unable to help myself.

"Damn, Durrant." He shakes his head again. Everyone's shaking their heads at me today. He takes a breath, lets it out, rubs his eyes. Lord knows what he's got weighing on his shoulders. If the captain's right, it goes far beyond my problems.

"What would you like me to tell you, sir?" I ask, surprised to find myself feeling sorrier for him than I do for myself. I don't, in fact, feel all that bad. I feel something closer to relief, relief that all this shit is coming to a close. That it's out of my hands. Not the end I would have picked for myself, but a finish all the same. I no longer have a say in the matter, which can sometimes be a comfort. At least to me. Right now.

"How about the truth, Private?"

"You won't believe me, sir. You haven't believed me before."

"Try me," he says.

So I try him.

I tell him the story again. Beginning to end. Even the parts he's already heard. Especially the parts he's already heard. I tell him about Herman. I tell him about Ahmed. I even tell him about the captain. I tell him about taking the box and about the bind the captain put me in. This, it gratifies me to report, makes him frown. The only part I leave out are my problems with Clarissa and my unborn child. The lieutenant nods throughout, watching my eyes, and toward the end, pulls at the hair just behind his ear. He does this rhythmically, as though keeping time with a song in his head. I don't imagine he has much hair left back there by now. When I finish, we sit in silence for a good mike. I feel emptied out: cleansed, almost. The lieutenant does not. My story's had the opposite effect on him. He looks up at the ceiling, up *through* the ceiling. He sees something there. Then he stands up and takes a deep breath. His right hand flits from his mouth to his nose, to that place behind his ear.

"I think I might have been wrong about a few things, but I don't know there's a whole lot I can do about this now," he says finally. "Even if I had a mind to. There are a lot of people involved. Too many to just brush this under the rug. When you and Rankin and the Humvee went missing, I had to radio in a sitrep to HQ in Inmar. Standard operating procedure."

"Yes, sir," I say. "I didn't expect that you could do much. I knew what would happen when I went out there."

He inspects me carefully. "I guess you did."

"I know you'll have to ship me back to HQ, but do you think you could pick up that kid at the factory? I know it's not reg, but I'm worried Ahmed's going to kill him. I'd feel a lot better if I knew he was safe." I beg him with my eyes, with the set of my mouth. "He could work in the—"

"No." He shakes his head, smiling apologetically. "But I promise you this. I will take care of that fucking factory," he says to the ceiling.

I attempt a smile. At least I tried to save the kid. He's lasted this long, maybe he'll make it on his own. I want to believe it. I try to picture him grown up and living his life, but the image won't form. His face blurs. None of this will happen.

"I'm not sure if this FOB will be around much longer anyway," the lieutenant says, but I'm not really listening. He says something about "clear and control." Something about native police training. But already I'm wondering how long I'll have to stay in prison. Will the court-martial be in-country or back in the States? I get so caught up in my thoughts that I don't hear what he says next. He has to repeat it.

"Did you say the captain no longer has the lockbox?"

"He does not, sir. Lopez had it last, but Ahmed got a handful of the papers. I'm not sure how many. But no more than a half dozen, if that."

This stops him cold. He stares at me for a good while. "Ahmed?"

"Yes, sir."

"Did you see the pictures, Durrant?"

"Pictures?" I ask, confused.

"Pictures, papers. Whatever they were." His face is the color of wet newsprint.

"I did not, sir," I say, relishing the alarm I've caused.

Again, the lieutenant pulls at his hair. If anything, he does it twice as hard as before. Then he walks from wall to wall. Toe to heel, as though he's measuring the length of the cell. He does this four times, and then he takes another long, raggedy breath. I watch him. Finally he stops and opens his mouth to speak. But after a moment, he clamps his lips shut and starts walking again. He measures off the length of the cell two more times. When he stops this time, he's facing the door.

"I told him. I told the general we should have destroyed that cell phone," the lieutenant says quietly, staring up at the ceiling again. At times like this, I wonder if he recognizes enlisted men as humans. Who is he talking to? Because it sure as hell isn't me. "He didn't believe me, but I told him. Instead, he just confiscates the damn thing. He says we might have a use for it some day. A little insurance. *Insurance.* Jesus, Mary. Once those pictures are out in the world, you'll never be able to stuff them back in the box. I told him, but—God, I hope it hasn't come to—" The lieutenant turns and looks at me as if he only just now realizes I'm in the room.

I don't understand, and I tell him so.

"You can thank the Lord that you don't. I wish to God I didn't."

Before he leaves, I call out to him one last time. Something bothers me and I want to set it straight, at least in my own mind, especially in my own mind.

"Do you believe me, sir?"

He steps into the hall. "I wish I didn't," he says and then shuts the door behind him. The lock turns.

82

Hours pass. I sing to keep myself company. Hank Williams and Kool and the Gang and Donna Summers. I'm working through the final verse of "You Are My Sunshine" when the door shrieks open on its crooked hinges. It's Sergeant Guzman. An unlit cigar wobbles between his lips. He looks me over grimly.

"You've got this whole damn base turned upside down. I bet you're proud of yourself, too."

"You overestimate me, Sarge."

"Want something to eat?"

I hadn't thought about it until now, but food seems like a very good idea. As if in answer, my stomach growls. I smile at it, give it a pat. I'm astonished by my unnatural cheerfulness. Sergeant Guzman seems mystified as well. The muscles in his face shift from expression to expression, never quite settling. It reminds me of how Rankin looked in the Humvee this morning. Like he didn't like what he thought or know what he wanted to believe.

"All right," he says, "well." He passes the cigar from one corner of his mouth to the other. "Foss said you like the Salisbury steak and mashed potatoes."

"That I do."

"Good, 'cause that's what you're getting." He steps back into the hall and picks up a tray. "I also brought you a Coke."

"I thought we were out of Coke."

"There's one or two still sitting around. Tucked here and there." He pulls the can from a cargo pocket. "It's warm as dog piss."

"Your own private stash?"

The sergeant is known to be a dedicated lover of colas. I've even seen him drinking the local brand, which is similar in texture to carbonated pancake syrup. But this is the real thing. Coca-Cola. He cracks the top and sets it by the meal tray.

I raise the can in toast.

"God bless America."

The sergeant rolls his eyes. "Shut up, Durrant, and eat your food."

I pick up the plastic fork and eat with an appetite that amazes us both. If he handed me another tray of food, I could down that too, no problem. Sergeant Guzman leans against the doorjamb, arms folded. Watching me eat seems to satisfy him in some way, as though he'd cooked it himself.

"He's not what you think," Sergeant Guzman says, after I swallow the last bite of mashed potatoes. Foss has swamped them in so much gravy, it's more like eating soup. I'm impressed and—yes, I'll admit it—touched that Foss paid such close attention to the way I like my food.

"Who?" I ask. "The lieutenant?"

"No," he says, dead serious. "Lopez."

"How do you mean?"

"He takes all that Stars-and-Stripes stuff seriously. Howley told me he says the pledge of allegiance each morning after he does his prayer and push-ups."

"Prayer and push-ups?" I lick the last drops of gravy off the tray. "You've got to be shitting me."

"He's just trying to be a good soldier."

"A little too hard."

"Maybe," Sergeant Guzman says. "You see, he don't understand that you can tell a joke every once in a while and still be a good soldier. For him it's just yes or no. Nothing in between. No gray."

"And it's just my tough luck he decided I was a 'no,' is that what you're saying?"

Sergeant Guzman frowns. "Hey, look buddy, don't tell me you didn't know what you were doing, going out there like that."

"No, Sarge," I say, "you're right. I take full responsibility. I'm just saying, he's a little bit tough on the boy is all. That's it. I'm not laying blame. All this shit is on me. But what happens next?"

"There's a chopper coming tomorrow at 0600. It's taking you back to HQ."

"Is that the same one the MI guy is taking out?" I stand and stretch. A belch comes rippling out of me. "Excuse me," I say.

"I don't know nothing about that." But I see something pass across his face, a sort of anxious recognition. He chews on his cigar.

"Do you think they'll let me make a call home?"

"Doubt it. Who you want to call?" He takes the cigar out of his mouth, looks at the wet black stump, and sticks it back in.

"Fiancée." Or whatever she is now.

"H'mm."

I hand him my tray, and he steps into the hall. I point to the Coke can.

"Thanks," I say.

The rush of air when he shuts the door makes the cobwebs in the corner flutter like streamers. I stare at the dark Judas hole, listening. A lizard darts across the mildewed stone above the door and disappears into a hole in the corner. Its feet make no sound. The sergeant's footsteps are swallowed by an enormous gray silence.

83

An hour later, Sergeant Guzman comes back. He glances behind him and steps in.

"Make a fist," he says quietly, holding out his own.

I do.

"Same stakes?" I ask.

He holds my gaze for a spell before saying, "Nope. You'll be gone. Just give me that book you're always reading."

"Sure."

"One, two, three," he says, knocking his fist against mine.

I hold out paper. He holds out a rock.

"You got five minutes. No more." His expression is as blank as an Easter Island head. You can say whatever else you want about Sergeant Guzman, but he's not a poor sport.

"Thank you, Sergeant, thank you." I walk toward the door. He grabs me by my shirt front and pulls me back.

"If you get me caught, I'll personally pound your head out your asshole."

"Yes, Sarge," I say, cheerfully. "I wouldn't expect any less."

And I don't.

84

The phone rings six times and then the answering machine picks up. I prepare a message in my head as I listen to the recording. This is the worst connection I've ever had. Her voice bobs on a sea of static. I can barely make out what she's saying. If it were any other fucking day, I'd just hang up and have Sergeant Guzman give it another shot. But I'm afraid to ask and have him tell me I got my one chance. The answering machine beeps, I say hello, and then, miraculously she answers. For a moment, I'm actually disappointed. I didn't know how hard this was going to be until she picked up the phone.

"Clarissa," I say.

Now, with a bad line, this will be extra hard. My words have a full second delay. Static blows along the line. Dead dust drifting between stars. I try to picture her face. I get an earlobe, a wisp of hair, a tooth. She refuses to be summoned. Without meaning to, I make a soft sound.

"Oh, shit, if it isn't old Toby, calling for his pound of flesh. Not five minutes after my sister."

"Clarissa, come on. Don't let's start. I haven't even said hello."

"I knew you'd do this. I knew it."

"Do what?"

She puffs in a disgusted way.

"I need to talk to you. I only have a few minutes." I glance over at the office. Sarge fiddles with something on the desk.

"Well, whatever load of guilt you planned to lay on me, just let it go. I don't need it. It's over. The whole shitty thing is over and done with. So if that's why you're calling, then you can just go—"

"Wait, Clarissa, slow down."

She clears her throat. "You got the letter, right?"

"Yeah, but—"

"Then that's all you need to know." Her voice rises in pitch again. "It's all in the letter. Read it again if you have to, but leave me alone. I don't want to go through this whole thing again, especially not now and not with you."

"Why are you so angry at me? I've barely said a word. I don't understand what—"

"Because every time you call it's always me, me, me. Why would I think today would be any different?" Her words distort as they get louder. "You think because you're over there you're the only one with problems. Well, you're not. Try being alone, pregnant, not sure if the father of your child will live to raise it, working a shitty job for sixty hours a week. So if you're calling to tell me how bad my letter made you feel and what a bad person I am for having an abortion, then go to the back of the line after Mom, Dad, my sister, Dr. Andrews, Pastor fucking Keebles, the Goddamn mailman—"

"Stop," I say, louder than I meant to. "I read the letter. That's not why I'm calling."

"What?" This seems to take her aback.

"I need to talk to you about something else. I—"

"What do you mean, that's not why you're calling? I don't fucking believe you. You're just waiting until I'm not expecting it, and then you'll lay into me. Just like everybody else."

"Why are you cursing so much, Clarissa? I thought you hated when—"

"Why the fuck do you think?" She says something else, but I can't understand it because she's speaking through sobs. Huge gulping sobs. I imagine her bent over her knees on the cracked leather couch I found for her on a sidewalk up on 61st Street and Abercorn, shoulders shaking, long hair sticking to her wet cheeks.

"You're talking like I know what's going on, but I don't." I feel oddly detached, as though I'm looking down on some other version of myself, a very confused one. Who is this guy? What does he think he's trying to do?

"I had a Goddamn abortion. What the fuck do you think is going on? My head hurts, my belly aches, I'm bleeding more than—" She goes on, but her voice becomes garbled, a series of digital bleeps. Even so, the anger carries through the noise.

"I mean, why are you—wait, Clarissa." I press my forehead against the trailer's fake wood paneling. "I thought that's what you wanted."

"That doesn't mean it was easy. That doesn't mean I liked it. Do you know what happens to you when you have an abortion? What actually happens? What they do after you go into the clinic and put on the robe and they clamp your feet into those Goddamn stirrups?"

"I don't want—"

"I didn't fucking well think so. Why don't I let you in on a little secret, then? Just between us girls."

"Why are you shouting at me? I never wanted you to do it in the first place."

"No, but you had to tell them about it, didn't you? You had to go and spill the fucking beans. I thought I could trust you at least that much. What did you think was going to happen when you told them? Did you think you could reach them before I went to the clinic? Maybe the sheriff would gallop in on horseback, scoop me up and save me. Tough fucking luck there, Toby."

"I don't have any idea what you're talking about. Whatever it is you think I've done, you're wrong. I live in a tent in the middle of the desert. I'm sure you're having problems over there. I never thought you weren't, but guess what? Over here people are shooting at me." My eyes throb. My mouth tastes like blood. At some point I bit my chapped lip so hard it started bleeding. Stop, I tell myself. Remember why you're calling. You've got, like, a minute left.

The line clears briefly. Somewhere far in the background, I can almost swear I hear an ice cream truck. A jangling version of "Pop

Goes the Weasel." The sudden jolt of homesickness this sound causes takes me completely by surprise.

"Did you hear me?" I ask. "I don't know what you think I've done."

A lighter scratches. She inhales, exhales. "Well, when you *didn't* call and tell my parents I was having an abortion, they somehow magically appeared at my apartment an hour after I got back from the clinic. My dad said—get this, you'll love it—he said, 'The next time I talk to you, Clarissa, it'll be in hell, unless God has mercy on my soul for killing that little shit who started all this.' In case you wondering, you're the little shit he meant. After he stormed out of the apartment, my mom said, 'Let's hope for all our sakes some little brown man gets to Toby first. It would be a mercy.' And then, just in case I wasn't feeling bad enough, she gave me the little white caps she'd knitted for baby. Seven of them."

"Jesus."

I see her father then, another uninvited guest in my head, certainly an unwanted one. I see him standing in the doorway of Clarissa's new apartment on the day I left. Filling up the entire space. A thick neck and eyes the loud artificial blue of Kool-Aid. Smiling at the shabby furniture like he had a stomachache. Dressed in his Saturday uniform. A short-sleeved button-down shirt and gray polyester slacks. Clarissa's mom stood behind him, literally in his shadow. A pink smudge of color on her lips. Mousy, in a brown dress and thick-soled nurses' shoes. Each time I caught her eye, she winced in an odd, apologetic way.

"And the fucker who paid for the operation," Clarissa says, speaking faster with every word, "the one who told me I should just clean the slate and start over—that's what he actually said, clean the slate—where do you think he's gone?"

"Jack?"

"I knew you wouldn't forget *that* name. Well, then, you'll be pleased to hear this next installment of *Days of Clarissa's Life*."

"I didn't mean it like—"

"Oh, you never mean shit, do you? Shut up and listen for a second. After Jack's check to the clinic bounced, so did he, along with all two of my credit cards, my grandma's cameo brooch, and, let's see, what else did he take? Oh, yeah, right, my fucking car!" She takes another pull on her cigarette and speaks as she exhales. "Don't worry. They found it in a rest stop outside Jacksonville. Just to set the record straight, the police told me his name isn't really Jack. It's Frederick Vander-something or other. They told me I'm lucky. The last woman he did this to got a broken arm in the bargain."

"Jesus, Clarissa, I'm sorry."

"Sorry, sorry, sorry, sorry, sorry, sorry," she says. "Sorry doesn't count for shit."

Neither of us speaks for a while. As if to make up for the awkward silence, the phone fills with a rolling hiss of static that sounds like breath exhaled between teeth. Please don't let me get knocked off the line now. Please.

When the line clears again, Clarissa's voice sounds calm, steady. "It's odd. We're talking right now, but you could be anyone. We're basically strangers. You know that? What's the longest time we spent together? A week? Two weeks? All right, you've told me what you *haven't* called about; so what the hell *do* you want, then?"

"Want?"

"If you didn't want something, you wouldn't have called. What is it?"

"I'm in trouble."

"You're in trouble?" She laughs, an ugly brittle sound. "What'd you do? Punch somebody again?"

"No, it's not like that."

"Hey, if you're lucky, maybe they'll send you home. God knows the Army hates violent men. But don't come sniffing around here if they do. No drunken midnight booty calls. No surprise Sunday visits. I don't want this any more. I don't want any of it."

Sergeant Guzman chooses this moment to step out of the office. As he passes, he taps his watch. "Forty-eight seconds." His cigar trails a thin stream of blue smoke. He cracks the front door and peeks out. If he's surprised by what's being said on my end of this phone call, it doesn't show on his face.

"Maybe I shouldn't have called," I say.

"*Now* you decide this." She's right. I don't know her. This isn't any Clarissa I've spoken to before. This is some new person who shares her name. Even her voice sounds different today, somehow lower and raspier. "Just go ahead and spit it out, Toby, whatever it is."

"I'm being accused of treason."

"Oh, poor Toby."

"It's all a mistake."

"It usually is."

"I mean it. I've been set up. It's all a very, very complicated mistake. They're making me out to be the fall guy."

"Why would anyone bother to set up a lowly private fuckup like you?"

"Because I am a lowly private."

"Well, if someone *is* setting you up, it's only a mistake to the one taking the fall." She lets out a breath, probably thick with smoke. "In this case, *you*."

"Jesus, Clarissa, why are acting like I'm your worst enemy? You sound like you hate me. Even your voice sounds awful. I barely recognize it."

"Gee, thanks."

"All I wanted to do was see if you were all right and tell you what was happening. I thought maybe—"

"You thought maybe, what? You could win me back by telling me you've become a traitor? Or maybe I'm supposed to feel so sorry for you that I'll rush back into your arms when they let you out of prison twenty years from now? Or is treason a firing-squad offense?"

"I just didn't want you to think what they're saying about me is true. Believe it or not, I still care what you think. Listen, I might of broken some rules, but—"

Again, that terrible new laugh. A wave of white noise crashes. Somewhere in the whoosh of static I hear another conversation. A woman speaks rapidly in Spanish. *Pendejo, pendejo, pendejo*, she yells. A man makes consoling sounds. And then they're gone. Some other trouble, some other place. Misery is in the air all around us.

When these other voices fade away, I go on, but my voice sounds weak and pathetic, guilty, even to myself. "But I'm not a traitor."

"Okay, you convinced me. You're not a traitor. Is that it? Have you said everything you wanted to say?"

"I guess so." I'm no longer sure why I called. What was it I wanted to happen? Was I really expecting her to pat my head and tell me everything would be all right?

"Well, I guess I'll be seeing you on CNN sometime soon. Or will anybody care about this?"

I'm more than a little surprised to find that this doesn't make me angry. Anger seems beside the point. All the words I'd saved up over the past few days to tell her, shiny and hard and mean, polished to a high gleam with spite, seem unnecessary now, ridiculous. I needed them then, but they've outlived their usefulness. I wish she could set her own anger aside for ten seconds or so, just long enough for me to say good-bye. I doubt I'll ever see her again. I didn't know this until I heard her voice.

"You don't want to talk to me," I say finally. "I get it. That's fine. I'm almost out of time anyway. Let me tell you one last thing, even though it's probably stupid to say it at this point. I am sorry about all this shit you're going through, everything. I wish there was some way I could make it right, and—"

"Here's how you can make it right: say good-bye and mean it. Whatever point there was to—"

"—and, listen, for whatever it's worth, I love you."

"I'm sorry to hear it." She takes a ferocious drag on her cigarette. "That must suck."

"Yeah, it does."

Hard. Guttural. Fast. Final. And that's that. We're all through. My battered old organ stops thumping altogether. The blood drains. The tissue dries. The cells blow away. I'm left with a dry pink cave between my lungs. But for some reason, I keep on talking anyway. Longing moves the muscles in my mouth much the same way that, after you've run it down with your car, a dead deer's leg will continue to twitch.

"I doubt if I'll see you. . . ." I say, and then can think of nothing more.

Clarissa's voice softens. "I did warn you. Remember that day when you were driving me home after our little adventure in the woods? I told you, 'My life's a slow-motion car wreck, but it's usually the other passengers that get hurt.' And you probably thought I was only joking." She sniffs and clears her throat. When she speaks again, her voice sounds even lower. "I didn't mean what I said about the firing squad. I'm sorry about that. I'm sure all this will—"

A shrill buzz blots out the rest. Buried somewhere in the squall of sound, Clarissa says something about a change of heart, or maybe she says "heart transplant"; but before I can ask her what she means, the line goes completely crazy. Bleeps, gurgles, squeaks. I think I hear Clarissa's voice, tiny and sharp, yelling, "I'm sorry, you're right, it's just that I need you near me now." Maybe I don't hear this. Probably what she said was, "I'm sorry you have to hear this, it's just that I don't need you now." But then again maybe I don't hear that either. Maybe it's not even Clarissa speaking. It could be some other soldier's girl telling some other soldier the end has come. The earpiece gushes so loudly that I have to pull it away, and then the line is dead.

When Sergeant Guzman sees me tapping the phone against the wall, he steps out of the office and takes it from me. I avoid his eye. He gives a sad little nod and hooks his thumb in the direction of the office trailer, where the lieutenant and Sergeant Oliphant and the captain and all the rest of the shit that will soon be raining down upon my head await.

85

Outside, Sergeant Guzman jams a cover onto my head and smears a finger or two of greasepaint under each of my eyes. "It's my ass if they catch you out of that cell," he says, wiping his sticky, brown fingers on my neck.

The base looks exactly the same as it did when I went into the Comm Trailer, but it's not. Tent canvas flutters in the wind, the American flag flaps on its splintered pole, sandbags still surround the office trailers, the old fort continues to crumble bit by bit into the desert floor; but nothing is the same as it was before, and it never will be again.

The evening feels heavy, dense. As warm as unspilled blood. A physical thing that weighs on my shoulders and head. As Sergeant Guzman walks me back to my cell, an explosion rumbles in the distance somewhere north of the base. Both of us look off toward the Noses. Neither of us says it, but I'm sure we're both thinking it. HQ has finally decided to give us air support. Sergeant Guzman smiles. A splash of water hits me on the cheek. I look around to see where it came from. We're still about fifteen yards from the fort's bay doors. Sergeant Guzman hustles me across the parade ground, pushing the center of my back with his palm. Another drop of water. I look up, and when I do, the heavens crack open and an ocean comes down all at once. A storm the likes of which I haven't seen since the summer I left Savannah. Lightning forks the plain. Water falls in thick sheets. The rain is so heavy that within seconds, the motor pool disappears behind a curtain of gray. I turn my face up and drink it in. Sergeant Guzman grabs me by the crook of my arm and pulls me into the entrance to the old fort.

86

A couple of hours go by. I mark the time by counting off the seconds
between falling mortars. At first I thought it was thunder, but then
one landed close, maybe even hit the old fort, and I knew they were
shells. From the sound of it, we're really getting hit hard. I wonder
what the guys are doing, if they're all right. I hope we're giving them
hell up there. It pisses me off that I'm not fighting beside them. I try
to sleep, but it's no good: I'm too keyed up.

"Hey." Someone raps a hand on metal. "Hey."

The door opens. Rankin gives me a strange look. About an hour
ago, I heard Rankin relieve Sergeant Guzman of guard duty, but
this is the first I've seen of him. If they weren't so shorthanded and
Rankin wasn't injured, there's no way they'd let him watch my cell.
Even now, it strikes me as odd. The lieutenant must be desperate.
He steps aside and in comes Lopez behind him, dripping water on
the floor. Rankin winks at me over Lopez's head and shuts the door.
I notice that the Judas hole is open now, but it is eyeless. A mortar
round lands nearby. It shakes centuries-old grit loose from the
ceiling. Lopez puts a hand on the wall to steady himself. I haven't
really gotten a good look at him since the night of the fuckup by the
wall. And that night it was too dark to see him clearly. One side of
his face has swollen up where I popped him. The skin around his
eye is purple with splotches of green and murky yellow. He notices
me looking at it and touches his face gingerly. I offer an apologetic
smile.

"You don't look much better," Lopez says, but there isn't any heat in his voice.

"Probably not," I say. "But I bet old Ahmed's sporting a shiner himself. And a pretty good headache, I hope. I beaned him in the face with a nice-sized rock before he got away."

Lopez shifts from foot to foot, jangling something metallic in his pocket. It makes a hollow clank, like a handful of spent cartridges. I can't for the life of me figure out what he's doing here. So I ask him. He stares down in a dazed sort of way, tightening the muscle in his injured cheek, then letting it go slack.

"I need to talk to you," Lopez says. The swollen eye makes him appear to be squinting, as though he's trying to make do after losing his glasses. "I think I might have made a mistake. A big mistake."

When I'd thought about Lopez over the last couple of days, I imagined that a scene like this would bring me immense satisfaction. But I don't feel much of anything. Lopez looks as though he hasn't slept in days. Dark stubble has sprouted on his chin and jaw. His boots are scuffed and his fatigues are wrinkled. I've never seen him like this. A brown splotch that looks like Salisbury steak gravy covers the bottom half of his shirt pocket. The whites of his eyes are a mess of painful-looking blood vessels. He rubs his upper lip in the place his moustache used to be.

I don't say a word.

"I got the lockbox that night, right? But I didn't give it to the lieutenant. I meant to, but I didn't. Something you said bothered me."

I nod.

"I looked at that darn thing and I looked at it. Something, I don't know what, just wasn't right. So I prayed on it. I couldn't stop thinking about the stupid thing. Something about this felt very wrong. Finally, I couldn't—I mean, well, I had to know."

"You opened it."

"Yeah, I did." He continues to stare at the ground.

"What'd you jimmy it open with? A screwdriver? Ahmed already had it open somehow. Did he bust the lock?"

"No, I don't know how he got it open. I used the combination."

"How'd you get the combination?" I'm amazed. Does Lopez have safe-cracking skills?

"I've gotten to know the lieutenant pretty well. I even know the year he graduated from West Point. He should really have used random digits."

"I would of used a hammer," I say.

"Of course you would." He unbuttons the top button of his shirt, thinks about it, and then buttons it up again. This is getting weird.

"So?" I ask.

"When the lieutenant told me to go look for it, he said he'd taken it from Lieutenant Saunders. He said that's the real reason we were going to Inmar the day we got hit."

I say, "I thought the meet with the sheikhs was an excuse for *Saunders* to take the box to Six Zone HQ. Lieutenant Blankenship was supposed to think the real reason for the trip was to talk with the sheikhs. A hearts-and-minds thing. The rest of us were going to try and shake loose some supplies and video—"

"Wait, wait, what did you just say? Back up a second." Lopez reaches for my arm; but when he realizes what he's doing, he pulls away again. "Who told you that about taking the box to HQ?"

Oh, shit. There's nothing for it now but to tell him. What difference does it make at this point? "The MI guy, that new captain."

"The captain?"

"He was planning to leave tomorrow with the box," I tell him.

"How do you know?"

"I stole it from the lieutenant for him." I run a hand through my hair. Here we go. I explain how the captain had me backed into a corner, that I could either steal the box and get his help or not do it and have him lie and say I did all those things Lopez thought I was doing. When I tell Lopez how Ahmed stole it from me after seeing me bury it, he gnaws at his lip. I continue: "The captain went batshit. But I wasn't positive Ahmed had it, until we went after him last night. Nevada and Rankin didn't know anything about the box. We wanted Ahmed for other reasons."

Lopez frowns and fidgets. I'm not sure how to read this.

"I know you don't believe me," I say, "but that's the way it was."

"I believe you. I just don't know what to do," Lopez says. "Right is right and wrong is wrong. But this, I don't know any more."

"Have you told the lieutenant that you have it?"

"No."

"Well, he knows now."

"Did you—" Lopez jerks back like I'm fixing to smack him one.

"I'm sorry." And I am, although I'm not sure why. He doesn't deserve it. "I didn't think it mattered any more. I was sure you'd already given it to him, and he didn't say otherwise."

He shrugs.

"I'm surprised you didn't—"

"I opened it." Lopez examines my face. "And now I'm all mixed up about what—" His voice falters and then trails off.

"What'd you find?"

"Pictures mostly, and some other stuff, stuff I don't quite understand. Or I think I *do*, but if it's what I think it is, then—"

"What kind of pictures?"

"They're strange. I didn't get what the big deal was at first, but then I recognized some of the—" Lopez seems to be trying to make up his mind about something. "—people."

"And?"

The photos, he says, are of a bunch of locals around a table. Two of them are leaders of militia groups. They're the ones who've been causing most of the trouble up in the capital. He recognized them from CNN. They've been in the news for months. The third is a religious leader who is supposedly hiding out in Iran or Pakistan now. He heard about it on Army radio just last week. As he tells me this, his voice becomes odd and contorted.

"I don't follow," I say.

"There's a big-shot U.S. Army general in the pictures too. One of the main leaders of ground forces during the initial invasion. He's sitting across from them, smiling."

"Are you telling me the general was a traitor?" I ask.

"No, not really. I don't know." He looks completely lost. "In the pictures, there's money on the table. Lots of it. It looks like they're negotiating something. In one of them, a man on the general's staff is pointing to photos of machine guns. But I don't think they were selling them to the militia. It didn't look that way. One of the photos was of a Chinese-made AK. I got the feeling they were giving these guys advice. But that doesn't make much sense either. I don't know. It's—I don't know why I'm telling *you* this. I don't know why I'm talking to you at all. Ahmed, or whoever went through that door in the wall last night—"

"It was Ahmed."

"Well, Ahmed got some of the pictures. I don't understand *exactly* what they mean, but I do know one thing. If these get out, the whole Army will be disgraced."

"Like now we're fighting guys who have weapons we helped them buy?"

"Here, I'll just show you one of them. The one that's got me feeling—" He pulls a sour, disgusted face.

Lopez unbuttons his shirt and pulls out a manila envelope. We sit down on the cot. He fusses with the red string that closes the flap for such a long time I take it from him and finish unwinding it.

"Dump it out." He squeezes his hands together, staring at them as though they are someone else's. "Please."

A fancy cell phone rolls onto the cot. Lopez picks it up and cradles it in his hands. And then a piece of blue cellophane slides out along with a brown paper money wrapper with "$10,000" marked on it in green, an old highway map produced by the former regime, and a piece of typing paper covered with hand-printed lists of some sort. At the bottom is a stack of photos held together with a yellow rubber band.

Lopez fumbles through the photos; he can barely keep the pictures from falling. He finds the one he's looking for and gives it to me. "Look at this one first."

I do. It shows a florid-faced general I recognize from TV news reports early on in the war. He's grinning and shaking hands with the famous cleric-turned-militia-commander. The one Lopez says left the country. In the background of the shot, there's a stack of blurry green. Behind the general, two other soldiers stoop over the table. Something strikes me as familiar about the one next to the general. Lopez jabs the photo with his finger.

"Look," he says, "right there. Who does that look like?"

The man's face is difficult to see. But I'm sure I've seen him before. It's like trying to remember a dream later in the day, though. You reach and you reach, but you can't quite pull it up.

"All right," I say. "I give up. Who the fuck are these people?"

"That guy," Lopez jabs at the photo with his finger. "Look closer. See that scar on his cheek? Doesn't that look like Sergeant Oliphant to you?"

Oh, God, I hope he's wrong. Many, many unhappy possibilities fill my head.

"Look really closely."

I bring the photo closer to my face, tilt it back and forth. I'm trying to find anything that might prove him wrong. But he's right: now that the name is in the air, I see it. It's him. I decide to play it carefully. This is still Lopez, after all. "Now that you say it, he does look similar. But there's no way you could prove it."

"I don't care about proving it. I just want to know if you see it too." He shuffles through a couple more. "And this one. Doesn't this man's head look like the lieutenant's?"

In the foreground of the shot, an officer points at an enlarged photo of a rocket-propelled grenade launcher with a pen laser. Lopez taps the head of the person next to him, a young man in dress uniform with only a small section of his face turned toward the camera. His pin shows he's a first lieutenant, but the hair and the neck, they could be anyone. I tell him this.

"That mole, right there. Lieutenant Blankenship has one just like it."

"So, what are you saying?" I ask him.

"With the proper equipment, they could enhance these photos. Then there'd be no doubt. And there are others saved on the phone."

I wonder if I look as freaked out about this as he does. Tiny beads of sweat have formed on his nose. His pupils look enormous. He studies my face, trying to make a decision. Finally, he purses his lips and picks up the road map. Yellow dust spills onto the cot. When he unfolds it, I see someone has circled three spots in the desert just south of Kurkbil, maybe fifty or so klicks from our base. A completely uninhabited zone. Next to each circle there's a number: 9,000,000, 18,000,000, 8,500,000. Below this, another circle and a date from a couple of months ago. I look closer. It's the toy factory. Before I can wrap my head around this, he takes the sheet of paper and reads a series of dates and grid coordinates and physical markers. A truck tire painted blue, a waist-high pile of white stones, a circle of green cinderblocks.

"Okay," I say, "I've got it. Grid coordinates."

"And this." He holds out the 10-K money wrapper.

"And this." I point to the cellophane. It suddenly comes to me. I've got it now. It's something Doc Greer told me the day after the IED attack that makes me realize.

"That I don't get." Lopez crinkles it in his hand. "A piece of trash? I was going to throw it out, but—"

"The American ambassador, brilliant asshole that he is, shipped some fifteen billion dollars in cash into the country a year or so ago. Flew it in on troop carriers. Most of it is now unaccounted for. Vanished. It came in ten-thousand-dollar blocks. They wrapped it in—"

"Blue cellophane."

"Right," I say.

"Holy crud. I thought Greer was just making that stuff up."

And then the last tumbler falls into place and the lock opens. This is really fucking big. Colossal. No wonder the captain got so exercised. Lopez has the same lightbulb going on above his head. His breath hisses out between his teeth. Then I remember something else. The last time I saw Herman, he had a bit of that cellophane wrapped around his neck.

"Now," he says slowly, "I get what he said."

"Who?"

"The captain. He said he'd go in on it with me if I handed the box over. I thought he was talking about blackmail. This is bigger. This is—"

"How did the captain know you had it?" I asked.

Above us, three mortars land in quick succession. The lightbulb in the ceiling jiggles, making our shadows twitch.

"I don't think he did for certain. He was just sounding me out. Like a fool, I admitted it."

"But what about the cell phone?"

"That's what they used to take the photos. I went through it this morning after you got back." Lopez picks the cell phone up and hefts it in his hand. "I guess it's like keeping negatives."

"Why the fuck would they do something stupid like that? Why not just break the thing?"

"I wondered about that too." He flicks through the stack of photos again. "Now I think I get it. Look at this one." He hands me another picture. It's crumpled, probably from the rough handling it got last night, but the image is clearer than some of the rest. In it, the ambassador himself hands one of the sheiks a blue block of bills. Both men grin.

"It's rotten," Lopez says. "The whole darn thing. Top to bottom. I bet the general just wanted to cover his butt if all this went wrong. 'I can take you down, too' sort of thing, I guess. It makes me want to cry." And for a moment there, it actually looks as though he might. We're quiet, but down deep in his chest I swear I hear something creak and smash to bits. I'm familiar with the sound.

"You better watch yourself, Lopez. People die for a lot less money than this. What are you going to do?"

"I don't, I don't—" He rubs his good eye with the heel of his hand.

"Listen, you need to take this stuff to someone up the line."

He looks at me in alarm.

"Not the lieutenant," I say. "If that's him, he's in on it too."

"I know."

"Even more reason for you to get the hell out of here, now that they know you know."

"Go AWOL?" he says.

"Not quite. Just take a little trip. Now you know about this, you've got to cover your ass."

I watch the implications of this sink in. In the dim light of the cell, his cheeks look shiny and dark, almost purple. His lips twitch, and he licks them. Once, twice. He stares at the floor like there's a Bible verse printed on it.

"But how?" he says helplessly. This goes against all his training. Like a divine command to kill his son. "I can't just leave."

"Yes, you can. Get in a Humvee and go. They'll go apeshit, but when the chain of command sees what you've got, I think they'll forgive you. Take it to Colonel Marquart in Inmar. Just make sure you've got plenty of witnesses around when you do it. Who the fuck knows how deep this goes."

"What do you think they'd do with the photos?" he asks me.

"Bury them. Destroy them, maybe. They ain't going to let this shit go public. No way."

He looks stricken, as though he's just received news of a horrible death. And I suppose he has—the death of his hero, the lieutenant.

"What would *you* do?" he asks.

I look at him in surprise.

"What I just told you," I say.

"That's it?"

Rankin raps on the door. "Somebody's coming. You got to go, Lopez. I'll put you in this other cell. Move."

Lopez scrambles to stuff everything back in the envelope and tuck it into his shirt. Rankin opens the door. He catches my eye. Of course he was listening. So would I. I touch Lopez on the arm before he steps out.

"Hold back a few of the photos. For your own insurance, if nothing else. This is going to get hairy."

Lopez stands in the doorway, his back to me. Rankin's nostrils flare. Lopez spins back around and thrusts out his hand. For a moment I think he intends to punch me in the stomach with it. His whole arm quivers from the elbow down. I stare at his thin, olive-colored fingers for a few seconds, unsure what he means by this gesture.

"Won't even shake my hand, huh?" he says.

"Sorry," I say. "You surprised me, is all."

It feels like squeezing a toad.

"No, *I'm* sorry," he says, looking for all the world as if he means it. I wonder if he does. "I had you figured wrong. You're something—" Lopez eyes me cautiously. "—I don't know what, but you're not a traitor."

87

Mumble, mumble, mumble. A mortar blast. Mumble, mumble, mumble.

"I have orders. I can not do that, Captain, sir." Rankin shouts this out, Basic Training style. Loud, with emphasis on the "sir."

Thanks, Rankin, I think. At least this visit won't come as a complete surprise. I'm a popular man tonight. The bolt on the door clanks open and I turn around. I try and control my breathing. When the door opens, I'm sitting on my cot, legs crossed, smiling.

Rankin whispers "Bohica." Which, in this man's Army, means bend over, here it comes again.

The captain shoulders him out of the way and steps into the gloom of the cell. He makes a face like something smells off, which it probably does, but I've been in here so long that I don't notice it any more. The captain steps around the place where the old man's body made a damp imprint on the packed-clay floor and stops just in front of me. I clasp my hands in my lap. The perfect Sunday-school student. Before the captain shuts the door, he tells Rankin to close the Judas hole. No flies on this guy.

"You're late, sir," I say, "visiting hours ended an hour ago."

"Shut the fuck up, shitbird."

Wow, I think, he's getting nervous. I'm not sure if this should make me feel better or worse.

The captain inspects my face like it's a flat tire he needs to fix. I stare right back.

He kicks me in the shin, hard.

"Pay attention," he says. "Your girlfriend Lopez has the box."

"So I heard," I say with more bravado than I feel. Those dollar amounts keep reverberating in my head. Ten, eight, nineteen million. Money enough to kill a few people over. Leavenworth suddenly feels like a happy outcome to this situation.

"You're pretty well informed for a prisoner. Who told you?"

"I overheard someone talking about it in the hall." I point to the door. "Out there. But I couldn't make out who it was."

The captain appears dubious.

"Ahmed got away with half the photos," I say. "I saw him snatch them."

"I'm not worried about that."

I'll bet, I think.

"Maybe you should be," I say.

"It's not *my* ass that will get kicked over this. And frankly, it'd be just one more scandal in a string of them. These days, the media loses its hard-on for a story after a cycle or two." He swings his foot back and I cringe, expecting another kick. Instead, he taps me very lightly on the leg. "What I need you to do, partner, is help me persuade Lopez to hand the box over."

"He hates me. You know that, sir."

"Even better. That makes you more trustworthy."

His logic escapes me. "Maybe you can make a trail of pages torn out of the seven-dash-eight leading into a big trap. That ought to get him, sir." I fight to keep my voice steady. Given the choice right now, I'd much rather be out in a big hairy firefight.

"Shut up, Durrant. This is fucking serious." He thumps the side of my head with the back of his hand. My ears ring. "Listen to me." The captain crouches so we're eye to eye. He takes his sunglasses off. "Are you listening? You are going to persuade Lopez to—"

"No way, sir." I blurt this out as fast as I can before I lose my nerve. Without quite meaning to, I find myself backing away from him. My head bumps against the wall. "I'm out."

"That's an order."

"I'm locked in a cell, sir."

"We'll get you out soon enough." The captain frowns at the walls of the cell as though they'd been constructed just to irritate him.

"The lieutenant said he confiscated those photos from Lieutenant Saunders."

"Of course he would." He smiles. His right eyetooth is several shades whiter than the rest, like it's plastic. "He'd say almost anything to get out of this. Not that it will do him any good if and when the right people see those snaps."

"Have you seen them?"

"What do you think?"

"Lopez said you'd split the money with him, sir. What's that mean?"

"Split? Hah." He sputters and coughs. It takes me a moment to realize that he's laughing. "So, what else did Lopez say?"

I suddenly realize my mistake. Jesus, I'm a fool. Why do I let this asshole intimidate me? "What do you mean?"

"Did he tell you about what he found in the lockbox?" The captain coughs. Harder and harder. His face turns the same color as those grape jelly packets in MREs. When it finally stops, the captain stands again, pulls a dark yellow handkerchief from his pants pocket and spits into it. He examines this closely, then stuffs it back into his pocket.

I don't say anything.

"What else?" The captain tries to shout, but his voice is hoarse and the effort seems to wear him out.

"Nothing, sir. It had a bunch of photos of brass tucking money in turbans. A map with some circles. A sheet with strange numbers. Where's the money in that, sir?" I examine the dirt lodged under my fingernails.

"I said nothing to him about money," the captain says, moving his head so close to mine that I can feel his breath on my cheek. "Have I said anything to you about money?"

"No, sir," I say, "but I never looked in the box."

"Lopez is confused."

"So am I, sir. What do you want with those pictures? They—"

"The lieutenant is a corrupt man. He needs to be relieved of command."

"Who else is in those pictures, sir?"

The captain grins. It is an unpleasant thing to watch.

"Somebody big, huh?" I say, hoping I'm not pushing this too far. "How much money are you going to ask him for, sir?"

The captain kicks me in the other shin. Harder this time. I try not to yell and end up choking. He takes a step back and examines me from boots to buzz cut like an induction doctor. I wonder what he sees. When he speaks again, his voice is calm and his speech measured.

"You've got a head for this business, Durrant. You're a quick study. It's a pity about all the trouble you've been having. You'd have made a good intelligence officer. If you can get me that box, you may still have a chance to make a go of it. How does intelligence school out in sunny Arizona sound?"

Despite myself, I'm flattered. This quickly gives way to disgust.

"Even if I wanted to, Captain, I really can't help you." I gesture to the cell around me. "But maybe if you told me what all this is about, then I'd have a better idea of how to go about it. Lopez had a few ideas."

"I'll bet he did." The captain eyes me, sucking at his cheek and chewing it. "You've already got the general picture. That's enough."

"No," I say, "sir." I'm startled to find myself really angry.

"We'll see." The captain sits beside me on the cot and taps his foot. I consider jumping him and making a dash for it; but to where?

"Did Lopez mention where he's put the contents of the lockbox?" the captain says, prodding me in the side with his elbow.

"Come on, sir." I edge away. "He may be an uptight asshole, but the boy ain't stupid."

"No, of course not. At least we've established that you've spoken to him about it. That's a good first step." He picks something from his tongue and wipes his finger on my pants. "I'll give you a general outline. I have a feeling Lopez will come back. You're the only one he can talk to about this. A guy like him, shit, he'll be worrying over this all night. He's going to explode if he can't talk about it. I'll be keeping an eye out, and when he makes his move, I'll be waiting. If he won't tell you, we might have to find some other way of getting the information out of him. If you're nice, I might even let you help. You could get out some of that famous rage of yours. I'll bet you'd like that, wouldn't you?"

For weeks I'd been daydreaming about punching Lopez, and then I did, and it felt shitty. This offer to do something worse makes me squirm. Not because it disgusts me, but because I've already considered it. A part of me still wants to. After all, Lopez is the reason I'm locked up down here. God, this man frightens me. He knows just how to release my inner asshole.

"All right," I lie, "I'll do my best to convince him you're the man to set this straight." Lopez isn't coming back here, I think. If he has any smarts at all, he's lying low until daylight. "But first you have to tell me what this is really all about."

The captain looks at me, then down at his clasped hands. Finally, he lets out a sigh, as though it's been quite a struggle, but now he's giving in. I don't buy this crap for a second. Whatever he's about to tell me is bound to be at least half bullshit.

"No," he says.

"Fine," I say. "If Lopez comes back, I'll tell him to burn all of it."

"There are other copies of those pictures."

"Yeah, Ahmed has them. But it's the grid coordinates you really want, isn't it?"

"I don't see what difference it makes to you, Private. If you think you can use any of this against me, think again. Nothing about any of this implicates me. My interest in this matter has nothing to do with self-preservation, unlike your lieutenant."

"Then what difference will it make if you tell me?" I wait for him to hit me again.

"Of course, it makes no difference to me," he says, toying with a button on his sleeve, "but it might make *all* the difference to you. Still, you're right, why shouldn't you know? You've seen the evidence. You're up to your neck in it now anyway. Along with the rest of us."

"Not quite."

"Don't be a child, Durrant. Knowledge means guilt to these people, and they can really put the hurt on you if they think you're a liability. Nor are they as easily fooled as the empty-headed grunts and peasants you spend your days with." The captain presses his hands together, as if to pray, and taps the end of my knee. He becomes solemn and fatherly, hoarse with false sincerity. This, his expression seems to say, is our come-to-Jesus moment. "Before I go on, let me make something clear: once you know, some will say there's only one way for you to forget. And all sorts of accidents can happen between here and there. Are you sure you want to hear this?"

I nod.

"All right, but don't blame me when the other shoe drops on your head and you want your cherry back," the captain says. He moves even closer, placing a hand on my arm and squeezing hard enough to make marks.

I shake him off. "Fine. I get it."

"At the start of the invasion, Lieutenant Blankenship was assigned as adjutant on a certain general's staff." The captain puts on a bedtime-story voice, and shit, what a story he tells.

"It began at the end of the initial fighting. Once we'd taken the capital and rounded up most of the regime's ministers, the ambassador worked with the State Department to airlift in a large quantity of cash, dollars, ostensibly for use in development and reconstruction. At the time, the Army was short on manpower and the natives were getting restless. There really should have been twice as many troops as we'd sent. Some of the brass were starting to get an inkling of the shit to come. The idea was to arm some friendlies. We couldn't train an entire national police force fast enough to take care of the problems that were arising, and there weren't enough boots on the ground to do it ourselves. One of the fears at the time was that rogue elements of the former regime, trained combatants, were regrouping across the border. True, as it turned out, and even worse than they imagined. I remember seeing this shit on TV. It was a fucking mess.

"A chunk of the money the ambassador shipped over was secretly earmarked to arm the friendlies. This was not info for general consumption, but the word got out to a group of like-minded people inside Intel. Read: crooks. Instead of giving these militias American-made arms, which could be traced back to us if the thing went tits-up, we gave them cash and introduced them to independent contractors from Russia who could get them the weapons. Cheap plastic Chinese AKs and RPGs. That was the first mistake."

I must be giving the captain an odd look as he tells me this, because he coughs and blinks and begins to seem uncomfortable. For a moment, it would appear he's thought better of giving me the rest of this history lesson, but maybe that's just more bullshit, a way to misdirect me from some lie at the center of his story. Even so, I give him an encouraging look.

"Right away," he says, wiping his mouth with the yellow handkerchief, "the whole thing went bad."

It seems that even before the Army could finish handing out all that money, some of these groups started using the weapons to hit our own convoys. The captain isn't sure if this was spontaneous anger on their part or if they'd planned it all along. Maybe it was simple greed. They could resell the supplies from those hijacked trucks for quite a bit. He says he's heard of MREs off those trucks turning up in markets as far away as Pakistan and Kenya.

"And then that fucking ambassador decides to—Jesus—" A cigarette appears in the captain's hand, and he lights it with a wooden match. I give that cig a hungry stare, but he doesn't seem to notice. When he goes on, his voice sounds worn out and his face looks drawn and haggard.

The general, it seems, still had millions and millions of dollars on his hands. He didn't want to give it back. You never want to admit to the bureaucrats that they've given you too much money. But he didn't want to keep it in his pocket either. Big piles of cash like that draw flies like fresh shit. You can only keep it quiet for so long. So the general took aside his most trusted junior officer and an experienced older sergeant and told them to hide the cash someplace nobody would look for it. They decided on *this* pile of rocks. It was out in the middle of nowhere and had been quiet for a while. Once the two of them arrived, the first thing the general did was pull out half the men on base. The fewer eyeballs, the fewer problems. Even so, the lieutenant worried about keeping the money on-base. They decided to cache it in the old toy factory.

"The one you've been poking around in," the captain says. "I imagine you scared the hell out of those two. You were fucked the moment you set foot in that place. Jesus, and you wonder why the lieutenant's been suspicious. When did you get to this base?"

I tell him.

"Then you probably pulled duty guarding that factory."

I hadn't, but I remember Rankin doing some. Suddenly, a few more things make sense. At the time, none of the guys could figure out why the hell we were protecting a shell of a factory. After a month, we stopped. One day it's important, the next day it's not. We forgot about the place in a week. In the Army, this kind of random shit happens all the time.

"But there's still some money there," I say, pulling out my crumpled portrait of Ben. "I found dozens of these."

He snatches it out of my hand and holds it up to the light. "Shit. It's got the Coalition stamp. It's real. So those two were holding back a little for themselves. Where—"

Above us, a mortar lands somewhere close. The light in the hall becomes dim, goes out and returns.

"Why did you cut it up?" he asks.

"One of the local children tore out the heads," I say.

"Maybe the child you've been blabbing on about. That was stupid, by the way. Did you find any whole bills?"

"I didn't have time, but they must be there." I'm not sure why I tell him this. Maybe so he'll fuck with the lieutenant. Or worse, some perverse part of me wants to impress him.

"It certainly bears looking into." He studies the head a moment longer and then crumples it into a pellet and throws it at me. It bounces off of my cheek and onto my lap. I slip it back into my pocket. The two of us sit in silence for a spell.

"So," I say, "I don't know. Maybe I'm wrong. Maybe they only left a few bills by mistake."

"No," he says, thinking hard, but not about this. "I'll bet there's still a small stash."

"So?" I say. "What happened to the rest of it?"

The captain can't help himself. This story of someone else's fuckup is too good to keep to himself. He tells me the lieutenant started having the same worries the general did: someone's going to find it and blab. Soldiers are like little boys—when they're bored, they poke around and get themselves into trouble. There's nothing to it but for him and the old sarge to go bury it out in the desert. Four or five night drops.

"They did it by themselves?" I ask. This is starting to smack of coulda-woulda. I get a whiff of something stale.

"I don't fucking know," he says. "The second big mistake the general made, and this, this I really—" Whatever it is, it cracks him up something fierce. He takes out his handkerchief and wipes his face. When he's finished, he looks over at me with a wet-lipped smirk.

He tells me the joke. The general let someone take pictures of the cash hand-overs. With the camera on their cell phone. Pictures of smiling officers and sheikhs. Even the Goddamned ambassador. The captain thinks that maybe the general didn't see it happening at the time, but he sure as hell knew about those photos later. Then, instead of making the smart move and destroying the phone and all the prints, he keeps them. Probably thought he could use it as political capital later on. The captain says the ambassador is famous for being slow-witted, but he pulls a lot of weight back in Washington, and apparently the general has a few political ambitions of his own. Most of this was an open secret. The turning point came when the captain found the cell phone.

"But we didn't know where the money was. No one did. It took a little work, but Saunders and I found it." Again the ugly smile.

"How?"

The captain shakes his head. "If you make it into Intel, maybe I'll show you a few tricks. A little of the famous razzle-dazzle."

"Thanks," I say.

He keeps on talking. It's almost as though he can't help himself. He has to tell the rest of the story. When you are the keeper of so many secrets, it must be a pleasure of sorts to disclose a few—or just simply a relief to unload them onto someone else.

He and Saunders knew where the base was, but not the actual cash dump. It took a little finagling and some forging of documents, but after a while he managed to get Saunders posted out here. Saunders brought the phone and a few prints with him, but the photos were all backed up on a computer somewhere else. Here their game got tricky. Saunders had to move carefully. The captain wouldn't go into the dirty details, but somehow Saunders got Lieutenant Blankenship to agree to give him grid numbers for the drop sites in exchange for the phone and the prints. This was the real reason we'd been going to Inmar that day. Saunders had planned a meet with the captain in Inmar because Lieutenant Blankenship, who was working with Sarge for the general, believed the captain was the one who had the photos. And that's where he told Lieutenant Blankenship he'd hand them over.

"And, well, you don't need to know the rest." He snorts. "Suffice it to say, your lieutenant, he bought it. Swallowed the whole salty load. And he agreed to give us the details and a map. He showed Saunders the map, but he wouldn't give him the GPS numbers until he had the photos and phone in hand. And now I find out the crafty little bastard was holding out on us. Well, believe me, he won't for long."

The captain stretches and moves around the room. He kicks the wall. Mildewed chunks of concrete break away and drop to the floor. "And then, imagine this. On the way to Inmar, there just happens to be an IED attack."

The captain studies my face, waiting for me to get the picture.

Whatever he sees must satisfy him, because he smiles again. His teeth look wet and sticky.

"Shit," I say, genuinely shocked, "you don't really think he *planned* it. I mean, how, sir? I interviewed the prisoners."

"Yeah," he says, "and what did they tell you?"

I must look completely dumbfounded. He smirks at me like I'm a complete and utter dumbass. And maybe I am.

"Exactly," he says. "I bet they told you the story about their long tribal battle with the Gashtus, right? Well, guess what? Their tribe, the Furdus, just happens to be one of the few friendly groups that *didn't* go sour on us."

Something else becomes clear to me. Something awful. Something else awful.

I speak too quickly, before I really think it all the way through. "But weren't the prisoners killed by Ahmed?"

"Oh, right." He rolls his eyes. "*Sure* they were."

"The hinges on the cell were taken off. Why would the lieutenant do that if he had the key?"

The reason is so obvious he just waits for it to come to me.

"Why do you think he chose you to interrogate them? Why didn't he do it himself? Do you really believe you're the one on this base most qualified to conduct interrogations? He needed a fucking patsy, someone just smart enough to notice things like scratched hinges." The captain takes two brisk steps across the room, so he can jab me in the sternum. "You. He had to make a report. He had to make it look good. If you talked with them, he wouldn't leave his fingerprints. And then, once he thought you were getting too close to the money, he found a way to put you down here. Just before that kangaroo court the other day, he told me he suspected *you* of killing the prisoners. Pretty neat backup plan, huh? I was impressed. But that was back when he still had the phone and the photos."

"No one will believe that, sir." I'm speaking too quickly, my voice shrill. "There's no proof to—"

"When you tell them your sad little story during the court-martial," he says, not unkindly, "tell me, who do *you* think they're going to believe?"

I take a breath. And then another. I need to calm the fuck down. "I don't know, sir. This all sounds too crazy. I can't believe the lieutenant would sacrifice soldiers. Two soldiers. The prisoners, maybe, but I mean, come on—"

The captain looks at me like I'm pitiful, a rube. "Expendable."

"Oh." It's the only sound I can manage to get out.

"It's all piss under the bridge now. Forget about it."

Right.

"How much of that story is true, sir?" I ask him.

"Oh." He taps his chin with a knuckle. "Say, about ninety-five percent."

"What the hell does that mean?"

"Sir," he says, cuffing me on the head.

"Sir," I say.

"It means take it or leave it. You wanted to know. And now you do. Like I said before, knowledge is guilt in this game. You're in it with the rest of us now." He lights another cigarette. This time he gives me one. "Talk to Lopez. That's the only thing that can save you. All that matters now is that we get the shit back."

We, he says. Sure. I must look pretty stupid.

"I can do it more quickly if you get me out of here."

"Listen, Durrant. You do this for me, and I'll arrange it so the charges are dropped and you're out of here by morning. I'll figure out what to do with you when I get to Inmar. Get the stuff and I'll make sure your records are cleansed. We'll take the same chopper out of this dump."

I imagine a quick shove out of the helicopter door and the long fall to the desert below. I see now how deep I'm into this. I'll be lucky to come out of it with my head still attached.

"I want you to have some alone time. To think. You're not out of the soup yet, and without my help you'll drown in it."

The captain raps twice on the cell door.

"Where are you going now, sir?"

"To have a frank discussion with your lieutenant."

Rankin holds up a finger behind the captain's back and mouths the word, "Wait," before he closes the door. I don't know whether to believe all of the captain's story, part, or none. Ninety-five percent, my ass. It sounds too clever by half. Nothing that happens in this war adds up quite so neatly. I walk back and forth. From one wall to the other. One, two, three, four, five. One, two, three, four, five. The numbers add up to the same sum every time. Nothing else in this place does.

88

After the captain leaves, Rankin comes to the doorway to talk with me.

"Lieutenant's sending a team out to blow the factory in the morning." Even as Rankin tells me this, I can see him starting to regret it. A narrow-eyed cautiousness.

"What?" I shout.

"Damn, man. There ain't nothing you can do." He holds out his palms as if to stop me from moving, even though I'm sitting on the cot. "You've done enough, D."

"Why are they doing it?" I pick at a loose string in the cot's fabric. When I tug on it, a line of green thread pulls away from one end to the other and then back again. If I sat and did this long enough, the whole cot would come apart in my hands. A big pile of olive-colored string. A big pile of nothing.

"Lopez has him thinking there's insurgents holed up in there." Rankin puts his hands on either side of the doorjamb and leans into the cell, but he's yet to take a step inside.

"But Lopez told me he doesn't believe that any more."

Rankin gives me a skeptical look. "He said exactly that?"

"Well, not exactly *that*, but close enough. We had a heart-to-heart."

"I heard. Heartwarming."

"You listen in?"

"I might of heard a word or two."

"Or a number or two?"

Rankin smiles.

"You get those GPS numbers?"

Rankin keeps on smiling, but now maybe a touch wider. He taps his head.

I know he knows what I'm thinking. It's there on his face. Why can't we take the money instead? Why let them have it?

"No," he says, his smile becoming wary now.

"Why not?"

"Aw, shit, man," he says. "There ain't no way we could get that money back to the States with us, even if we did get it before they did."

He drums the very top of his skull with three fingers like he's fingering a trumpet.

"It sure would be nice, though," Rankin says, probably imagining everything he could do with money like that. From the expression on his face, it looks like he can think of quite a few things.

"We could open up a Bubba shrimp franchise," I say. "I hear they do really well in the malls."

"Bubba shrimp. Shit." He moves his chin from side to side very slowly. "Your ass is locked up anyway, D. You can't be serious."

"Listen, Rankin—"

He sees something he doesn't like in my expression. Somehow he always knows which direction my thoughts are moving before I do.

"Oh, no," he says, before I can spit out the rest, "I know where you're going with this, and—"

"No, wait, hear me out."

"You are joking." He looks at me and tries to decide. The shit of it is, I'm not too sure myself. "I really hope you're joking."

"I can't let that kid die." About this, I'm absolutely sure.

"I believe you said that the last time. I believed you last time and now I really, truly, believe you. See, the problem is that my ass is on the line here too."

"The last time we didn't know about fifty million dollars sitting under a truck tire in the desert."

"No, more like thirty-three and a half million. Split between three different spots."

"Damn, you do have good ears."

"I can't do it, D. Something bad's going to happen. I can feel it."

"Yeah, well, something awful's going to happen if I don't. A dead kid."

"Oh, man, D. There ain't no fucking kid and you know it. You tried to show me, remember? All I saw was some joke teeth." Rankin turns his hand into chattering joke teeth, tapping the heel of his palm with his fingers. His pink-nubbed pinkie wiggles like a little tongue.

"Rankin, please, I'm begging you." I get down on my knees and clasp my hands together.

"I ain't listening to any more of this bullshit."

"Come on, Rankin, come on."

Rankin shuts the door. I can't say that I blame him. I shouldn't. But damn if I don't.

89

I don't sleep.

90

A door slams. Someone shouts. But at first when I hear Rankin's voice, I think he's talking to me through the Judas hole. Then I hear the second voice. It's high-pitched and breathless.

"I have to, Rankin. It's important." Lopez is back.

"You already seen him, man. Once is enough. They find you down here, they're going to throw both our asses in these cells. You already wound his chain up. Leave him be." His voice moves closer, as though he's physically blocking the door to my cell.

What comes next is confusing. Another voice yells from the far end of the hallway. The echoes make it impossible to understand the words or recognize the voice. Lopez and Rankin shout back at the same time. There's a brief silence. And then a rifle locks.

"I don't have it," Lopez shouts. "I gave it to him last night. It's too late."

"Put that thing away, sir," Rankin says, his voice tight and tense. "There ain't no call for that."

I press myself against the door and listen. I hold my breath.

The first gunshot is so loud, the door rattles in its frame. My ears ring. Two three-burst shots follow that are even louder. Boots pound the floor. Another shout. Another gunshot. A cry of pain. Just outside the door, Lopez mutters. His voice is very low and guttural, and he speaks so quickly that the words run together.

"Rankin!" I shout. "What the hell is going on?"

Footsteps move away and return. The door opens. Outside, the hallway is completely black. I step back and instinctively look for cover. There's nothing. The light from my cell cuts away a slice of the darkness. Just enough to make out a figure.

"Rankin?" I say, clenching my fists.

The figure makes a choking sound and steps forward. It's Lopez. There is a bright red mark on his chin the size and shape of a strawberry. His good eye is wide and its iris is rimmed with white. He glances quickly over his shoulder, then steps closer. The spot on his chin is a perfect bloody thumbprint.

"What—" I start to ask even before I know the question.

"He shot him." Lopez grinds his teeth and makes a strange, high-pitched humming sound.

"The lieutenant? Rankin? What are you talking about?"

"The captain."

"But I don't—"

"The captain killed him." He speaks faster now. His words tumble over each other. My ears still buzz and it's hard to understand him. "I came back to tell you I would do it. I would take the stuff to Inmar. I didn't know he was following me. I swear it. I didn't know. Rankin didn't want to let me in, and then the captain came and—"

"Rankin is dead?" One part of me stays and asks Lopez this question, and another floats up and watches from the ceiling of the cell. My hands go numb and my right leg starts to shake and spasm. I try and hold it still with my useless hands. It is right then that I stop believing in the world, the same way I stopped believing in God when I was seven. The morning after my parents' funeral when I woke up in my grandpa's house. Bright white light and the rumble of his voice: "You'll be staying with me now, Toby."

Lopez nods.

I have to hold it together. I have to hold it together.

"Are you sure, Lopez? Are you sure?"

He glances over his shoulder into the dark hallway and then back again at me, clicking his rifle's safety on and off, on and off.

"Where's the captain?"

"I don't know. He just—" He makes an odd little gesture with his hands, as though trying to form a shadow puppet. "—ran away. I think I hit him once. At least once. Maybe twice. Then the light went out. I heard him running." He points to the ceiling. "Up."

"All right, all right." I take a deep breath and let it out. "We got to go. You and me. We'll both go to Inmar."

"But what about. . . ." He grimaces.

"None of that matters any more. If we stay here, we're both dead."

Lopez looks down at his rifle. "I shot an officer. I, I. . . ." His voice wanders off and his eyes lose focus. He goes blank.

I snap my fingers. "Lopez, Lopez, stick with me here. We don't have time for this kind of shit now. Pack it away. Think about it later. Come on."

"Uh." This is all he can get out.

I grab Lopez by the sleeve and pull him into the hall. He follows without resisting. Before I take three steps, I stumble into something. I kneel, my leg pressing against Rankin's side. Immediately, blood soaks through my pants. I feel for his neck. He's still warm, but his heart has stopped. Even if it weren't dark, I wouldn't be able to see. My eyes burn and blear. A tear drips off my chin. Fucking Rankin. I'm sorry I got you into this shit. You must be so pissed off at me right now. Rankin.

"How will we get away?" Lopez asks. His voice sounds tiny in the darkness, but it brings me back to the here-and-now. "The keys for the Humvees are locked away, and—"

"Are they still firing mortars?" I stand and thumb away the moisture from my eyes. "Are we still fighting?"

"No," Lopez says, "it all stopped a couple of hours ago. I left my post at the sentry gate to come here."

"Who else was there with you?" I'm thinking as fast as I can.

"I replaced Howley. It's just that other new guy, uh, what's his name? McCrae, I think."

"Perfect," I say. "Come on."

"But what about—"

"Trust me," I say.

I feel around in the darkness for Rankin's rifle. It's wet and tacky. Lopez and I bump heads as I stand. Purple stars whiz through darkness. I grab his sleeve and pull him behind me down the hall. On the second step of the stairway, I slip on something wet, and I fall. It smells like rusty nails. Lopez stops. He won't move even when I yank on his shirt.

"Trust me," I say again. "There's no other way."

Lopez doesn't answer, but he moves when I pull.

91

I hand Lopez the keys. He looks at them as though he's never seen such things before. I guide his hand to the ignition and turn. The truck grumbles to life on the first try. It's the one Ahmed and I take on shit-burning runs. The bed in back is full of charred oil barrels. Lopez hasn't spoken a word since I pulled him up the stairs. It took us forty-five minutes to find our way out. Every time we turned a corner, I expected the captain to appear with a rifle in his hands. We saw no one until the motor pool. Just before we got the bay door open, Salis came jogging by, dragging a large plastic tub. I ducked into the building. Salis shouted something I couldn't make out, but he didn't see me. "Ammo," Lopez said in response to whatever it was he asked.

And that is it until we reach the gate and the newbie named McCrae stops us. I'm hunched down on the floorboard sandbags, trying to make myself disappear. All I can see is the top of his helmet.

"Why'd you take off on me like that?" he asks Lopez. His voice rises into a whine. "I've been hearing gunfire all over the place since you left. Where are you going? It's not even light out yet."

Lopez's face looks pale green in the light from the dash. He hasn't turned on the truck's headlights. For a few seconds, the only sound I hear is the uneven chug of the diesel engine. He must be choking up, losing his shit. I'm not sure how to get him going again. If we don't move now, then—

Without turning his head, Lopez says, "Mind your own fucking business. I'm under orders."

"Sorry," the new guy sputters, "sorry, I just—"

Lopez jams the truck into gear, and we lurch ahead into purple-streaked morning.

92

Lopez parks the truck behind a boulder on the far side of the factory. The sun nudges itself up to the edge of the horizon. The world is purple. I check the magazine on Rankin's rifle and sling it over my shoulder.

"You can't go in there," Lopez sputters. "What if it blows?"

"At this point. . . ." I shrug. "Just keep the engine running. If someone comes, gun it. Take off without me."

He shakes his head. "I thought all that stuff about the kid in the factory was nonsense. I was sure you'd just made it up. Not as an excuse to meet insurgents, now I know that was wrong, but for something. Goofing off. I don't know."

"The kid's really there. Or at least he *was* there."

"Are you sure about this? There wasn't anyone in the factory a few days ago."

"What?" I say, squeezing the stock of the rifle until the joint on my thumb cracks. "What do you mean, a few days ago?"

"The lieutenant and me and Sergeant Oliphant came down here with a squad to check it out after your first hearing. We put up a perimeter and they went inside. Believe me, I would have known if they found someone."

"Did you go inside?"

"No." When he opens his mouth to speak, it smells as though there's a small dead animal inside. The skin beneath his good eye is dark and wrinkled, his cheeks caked with grime.

Somewhere from the north comes the distinct thudding sound of a Kiowa helicopter. At first, I can't see anything, and then, drifting up from the base, I spot its running lights, weaving slightly as it rises into the air.

"Oh, shit," I say. My voice cracks. "The captain's helicopter. Did you see it when we left?"

"It must have come when we were lost under the fort. I didn't think we were down there that long, but—"

"We've got to move. If he gets to Inmar before you, then you're—"

"There's no way I can beat a helicopter in this piece of junk."

"You're right." I think for a moment. "You'll have to go north. There's a huge base where the highway meets the river. FOB Wounded Knee."

Lopez nods reluctantly.

"He can't call every base around here. There's too many places you could go. When you don't show up in Inmar after five hours, that's when he'll start looking. By then you'll be fine. There's no way he'll be able to fuck with you after you give them this stuff. And then a few of these assholes will be the ones doing the explaining."

Lopez winces, and for a moment I wonder if he's ill. His good eye looks bleary and wet.

"What about you?" His throat sounds damaged, raw.

"What about me? Keep the truck running for five minutes and then go if I don't come out. And in the meantime, you better move this truck in case—"

"—you get your stupid butt blown off." He grimaces. The cab of the truck feels very hot and only now do I notice the dirty sweet smell of liquid shit. It's going to get a lot worse when the sun comes up, I think. Lopez will have something nice to remember me by.

As I open the door, an assault pack starts to slip out and I catch it before it falls. I must have left this after one of the shit-burning runs. Inside are a half-full canteen and two red flares. Whenever a soldier leaves the wire, they're required to bring at least two flares in case of emergency. It can't hurt, I think, and swing it onto my back.

"Remember," I tell him, "hold back a few of the better prints just in case."

He gives me a sad, imploring smile. "Come on, Durrant, don't do this. I need your help. Besides, it's not worth it. This folder is more important than—"

But I don't hear the rest, because I'm already out and running toward the factory.

93

I hide behind the far wall until I get my bearings. Even at this hour, the desert is warming up fast. Sweat drips down my rib cage. I move from bush to bush and rock to rock. As the sun breaks free from the horizon, it burns the sky. First purple, then red, then pink. The massive desert vista takes on the color of chewed-up bubblegum. The desert itself seems an odd color as well. The world becomes visible in small increments. And then I suddenly see what's caused this. All across the plains, small green sprouts are breaking through the muddy sand. It looks like a field of Georgia clover in April. The desert has sprung to life.

I stop at the factory gate and scope out the area as best as I can. As always, it looks completely deserted. I glance back over my shoulder at the highway and see the shit truck's dust trail moving north and away. Good luck, Lopez. The base seems tiny from here, a collection of gray blocks, like something a child could knock over with his fist. Usually it's just a dark smear below the hills, but the air is clear enough today to see for miles. The storm has washed the sky clean. I race around the wall and into the factory grounds. I don't have much time.

I wait to whistle until I get inside. Something strikes me as odd, the air smells strange, so I wait. On the other side of the factory, people are speaking. I creep across broken glass, crouch below a window. American voices.

"All right, fucko, let's get her done."

"I hate that guy, that cable guy. He ain't funny," another voice says.

"Shut up."

"Why you think the El-Tee wanted that kid anyway?"

"Hell if I know."

"Did you see how fast that little bugger ran?"

"Will you please shut the fuck up, please?"

"I'm just saying. It must of hurt when she kicked you."

"Shut up."

Salis and Hazel. So they're already here. If the lieutenant has these two out looking for Herman, that must mean the captain has spoken with the lieutenant about the money I found here. Probably just before he killed Rankin. It takes everything I have not to pop up and ask Hazel if he's seen the captain. The Goddamn captain dogs me like a guilty conscience. I wish Lopez had shot him in the heart. We didn't hear any radio chatter on the way over here, but the radio in the shit truck doesn't always work right. I pull myself up to the edge of the windowsill. They're just below. If I'd peeked any sooner they'd have seen me. Salis and Hazel crunch across the factory yard, playing out wire from a big plastic spool as they go. They must have been inside when Lopez and I pulled up or they'd have come out to meet us.

"I couldn't believe it," Hazel says, chattering away as happy as can be. He sounds like a five-year-old on the way to the zoo. "I had to laugh when I see that little kid kick you like that. Tell me now, for real, you ever see a kid run that fast before? The El-Tee's got every swinging dick doing—"

That means Herman's still around here somewhere.

"Hazel?"

"Yeah?"

"Shut up a sec." Salis twists Hazel's earlobe until he yelps. "You're cluttering up my head. Just wait till we get this done, and then you can babble all you please."

"Jesus, Sal." His face falls. "Sorry."

"You set one under the support in the middle like I told you?"

I can't hear Hazel's answer. The two of them climb over the twisted iron gates and leave the yard. An engine turns over. A moment later their Humvee edges past the gate. Hazel sits in back with the door open. He's got the fuse spool in his lap. It clatters as the wire unrolls. The Humvee crawls over the gravel toward the highway. As soon as I think they're out of earshot, I start calling for the kid.

"Herman, Herman, you hear me? You've got to get out. Now!"

I rush through the factory, yelling and whistling. Presidential heads are scattered all across the factory floor from the office to the main entrance. There are hundreds and hundreds of them. I can imagine the reception this got. What on earth did Herman think he was doing? He's not in the office. He's not in the warehouse. I kick through the rolls of rotten fabric. I run through the old sewing rooms. At the back of the last sewing room is a door I haven't seen before. A heavy metal door painted sky-blue. I shove it open and hurry in without looking, tripping over an injection mold of some sort almost immediately. The floor is sticky and warm. There's a heavy chemical smell in the air, like burning plastic.

"Herman!"

Goddamn it. I'm going to get my own ass blown up if I don't find him soon. I make one more circuit of the factory, shouting as loud as I can. It isn't until I stop to breathe for a moment that I wonder if Hazel and Salis have heard the racket I'm making. Out of habit, I glance down at my watch. It's sand-scoured and unreadable. I throw it against the wall. There's nothing I can do. I've got to get out.

I make for the door, sprinting as fast as I can. As I'm rounding the factory gate, my foot catches on a piece of rebar sticking out of cement block and I go down. Hard. I land with my knee turned in and I hear it pop. The pain races from my knee to my head and back again. It fills me up entirely. I try to stand, but it's no good. I fall before I can put any weight on my leg. Shit. I drag myself as best as I can across the highway and into the ditch across the way. The sound of the explosion is so loud I can't hear it. The sky turns white and then orange and then black.

94

I wake to the sound of humming. The *Sesame Street* theme. My ears ring so loudly I can barely hear it. It sounds as though it's coming from a klick away. Something pets my head. Fingers trace the top of my skull from forehead to neck. I try to move and find I can't. My body's numb, except my left arm, which is filled with pins and needles. My twisted leg doesn't hurt, which is good. And then I realize it's bad. The gentle hand strokes my cheek.

Herman's huge black eyes look down at me. His head fills the sky. He smiles. I try to smile back, but I'm not sure my lips are moving the way they're supposed to move. Somewhere in the far distance I hear a faint popping sound, and I wonder if it's coming from inside my own head. Herman stops humming for a moment and squints at something, puzzled. I want to ask him what he sees, but I don't have the breath for it. He looks down at my face. It dawns on me then. He's got my head in his lap.

"Sunny day," Herman sings, a little off-key, "chasing clouds away."

I don't know how long we sit like this, but it feels like all day. I have absolutely no desire to move. I stare up at this child's face and wonder again whether Herman is a boy or a girl. Something about the shape of his cheekbones strikes me as distinctly feminine from this angle. Who are you, Herman? As trivial as this may seem, my frustration amounts almost to a rage. They've stolen everything from you, Herman, haven't they? Even your gender.

The popping noises start up again. Herman frowns at whatever is making this sound. He notices me watching him and points. I try to push myself up with my left arm and fail. Herman puts his hands in my armpits and tugs until I'm slumped against his chest. Nothing hurts, and I know it should. This frightens me, but not as much as I would have expected. Rough cloth chafes the side of my neck, and I notice that the assault pack I found on the floorboard of the shit truck is still strapped to my back. At least I'll have a bit of water to drink. Herman points again, still humming that song. I feel it vibrate on my cheek. It takes a while for me to get my bearings. I'm on the far side of the highway across from the factory. Something drips from my chin. My nose is bleeding.

Herman points again. This time more emphatically. The factory is a smoldering ruin. Mounds of broken cinderblocks and huge twisted steel girders. Small dark wisps flutter across the burnt rock. But this is not what he wants me to see. He turns my head with his cold little fingers. The air above the Noses has filled with thick, black smoke. I follow it down to its source, and what I see knocks the breath out of me. The base is on fire. Worse: every few seconds, artillery shells burst, sending fountains of rock and sand hundreds of feet above the base. It seems louder now that I know what it is and can see where it's coming from. The larger explosions vibrate the ground beneath us even here, and the smaller ones cause orange spurts of flame to bloom inside the torrents of smoke. The hills seem to be moving. That can't be right. But it is. And then, suddenly, helplessly, I understand. Hundreds and hundreds of men pour down from the hills. There is a roar just above our heads. Three jets pass at very low altitude. Their cannons pepper the hillside. Several rockets burst at the edge of the base. I can't imagine what it must be like inside. Has anyone survived? I think of Rankin and see his face so clearly he could be sitting next to me. I find it very hard to breathe.

And then I notice motion in the smoke above the base. A Kiowa comes thudding up and away. It can't be the captain's helicopter. He's already left. I should be riding along with him, wearing restraints. The helicopter flies low and fast, buzzing over the landscape like a dragonfly. It passes directly overhead. So close I feel the rotor wash in my hair. Then it continues on. If they saw us, then they've decided not to stop. I find I don't mind too much. I just want to rest here for a while.

Herman hums louder. He has something tucked behind his ear. Something pink. A tiny flower bud. All around us the desert floor is covered in miniature flowers desperate to take advantage of their brief moment of life after the sudden rain. Pale pink and cream, blue and lavender—that rosy lavender the sky sometimes turns just before the sun disappears. The jets circle back and shoot off several more rockets. The explosions blossom white and red and angry orange. Their sound rumbles through my chest. They are beautiful to watch—brief, unnatural, and bright, like flowers in the desert. The smoke drifts east, pulled along by the long, dry suck of the desert wind. Then I notice what I should have seen before. The rockets those jets fired weren't aimed toward the hills outside the base. They're exploding inside the base. American planes. American base. American dead. I can't work it out for a moment. My head is a broken clock. And then I understand. They've decided to sweep the board clean. Maybe the captain called it in; or maybe when the lieutenant reported the insurgents' surprise attack, someone higher up decided to use this as an excuse to end it all. They could easily blame the destruction of the base on the insurgents. Ultimately, we are all expendable. I want to feel something about this. Anything. But that part of me has stopped working. Herman takes the bud from behind his ear and strokes my nose with it. His face seems like one more blossom. I close my eyes. Somewhere in the distance I hear the soft thud of rotor blades. They're coming closer. They're coming back. Herman hums a little more, but the song has come unraveled in his mouth and these are only random notes.

"Herman," I say, when my battered brain finally works out what this means. I jerk my head toward the factory. "Go! You need to go. If they find you here with me, they'll kill you too."

He only smiles. I tell him to leave again. Louder this time. I point with my left hand, make clumsy shooing gestures. Herman looks around, maybe thinking I see something he doesn't, but he stays put. Finally, though it makes my heart sick to do it, I shout, "Get the fuck out of here, you dumbass! Go! Now! They're going to fucking kill you!"

Herman frowns at me, confused by this outburst.

"Please," I say, "go." My eyes blur and I blink frantically to clear them. After all this, I can't let Herman die too. I won't. "Why the fuck can't you understand?"

He strokes my nose with his flower and murmurs something. Of course now, when he finally speaks to me, it's useless.

"I'll be damned if I'm going to let Ahmed win," I say, as much to myself as to Herman. At the mention of Ahmed's name, he straightens up and scans the rubble around us, clutching the collar of my uniform so hard he crushes the flower.

"Ahmed's coming, kid," I tell him. "You've got to go before he gets here."

The skin on his forehead bunches up. He wriggles out from under me and props my back against the cinderblocks. We are surrounded by a broken chunk of the factory's outer wall on one side. On the other is a crumpled piece of steel from the gate. Herman crouches behind it and shades his eyes, scanning the area. God, what more do I need to do to get him moving and away, safe?

"Ahmed, Ahmed, Ahmed!" I shout as loud as I can.

Herman whispers something, his face now pale and pasty. The sounds mean nothing to me. When I don't respond, he puts his hands under my armpits and tugs, but I'm much too heavy or he's worn out from supporting me. We barely go an inch. His cheeks redden from the effort. A small vein above his temple pulses. Finally, he sits beside me, pats my shoulder, and shrugs.

Somewhere in the valley behind us, the helicopter's rotors throb. From the sound of it, they're sweeping back and forth across the flat country, looking for stragglers. Or maybe me. The crew must not have spotted us on the first pass, but it won't be much longer before they're back. Herman needs to run now before he's in their sights.

Door gunners love a moving target. I've seen it before. Stationary targets are boring. If they see him running, they'll mow him down.

I have no other choice. Please forgive me for this, Herman. I slap him as hard as my limp left hand can manage, which isn't much. The expression on his face makes me feel ill. Tears stream down his cheeks. I make another shooing motion.

"Go," I tell him softly.

And this time he does, scampering out between the warped metal gate and the chunks of broken concrete. After a few seconds, it's as if he'd never been here at all. With all the strength I can muster, I push myself a little higher against the concrete blocks. Now I can see Herman again. He dashes from rock to rock like a squirrel, pausing behind the larger mounds and peeking out before moving on to the next. The relief doesn't last long.

They're coming now, and that will be the end of it. And what will that mean? A bright jolt of pain and then nothing. That's not so bad, is it? If the gunner's a good shot, maybe there won't even be any pain. Everything I've ever seen will seep right out the back of my head. Everything I've touched or loved or hated. The scaly calluses on the pads of Grandpa's thumbs, my mom twisting her wedding band as she scolds me, the mirror reflection of Clarissa's toes flexing as we make love, the white-hot flash of the IED vaporizing Lieutenant Saunders on the highway, the muscles bunching up in Rankin's jaw as he cleans the blood from the Humvee's seats, Herman singing about sunny days like a deaf-mute. Everything. And then a whole lot of nothing.

None of this has turned out how I expected. Not a single minute of it. If you asked me two weeks ago, I couldn't have told you this story. Hell, a year ago I couldn't even have imagined it. I think that must be true of everybody who comes to find themselves in a spot like this, maybe even those who meet their end in a warm bed with clean sheets and a loving someone sitting beside them, patting their hand as they die. No one expects what they get, even if they expect it. But this much we all have in common: there's nobody there but you when the dark comes to swallow you up.

Maybe the story was simply meant to end this way. If I'd stayed in the cell, not much would be different. My corpse would simply be a mile away. And who knows, if I'd gone with Lopez, they might have tracked us down and hit us on the highway. This very thing might be happening now. You try and try, and still it turns out the way it's going to turn out. It is what it is. And then you die in the desert. Try and put that in your stupid cigar box.

It's not so much the dying that scares me now. I just don't want to leave yet. I'm not fucking finished. Twenty-four years? My grandfather got nearly three times that. And I wasted most of what I had. If I could have ten more years, that would be enough. Even five. Even one. Jesus, I'd be happy to see the sun rise tomorrow. What a Goddamn waste. I grit my teeth. Sand crunches. Is this what my life adds up to? There isn't any point thinking like this. It's almost over. Think of something sweet. A long jump from a tall cliff. The upward rush of air. The nerves in my belly jangling in happy terror. And then the pop of the silk chute and the fast, hard jerk of the harness catching my fall. After that, it's all softness and gliding.

More fire on the mountain. Across the highway, something in the factory grounds explodes with a dull thud. Gravel patters across the smoking rubble. Small dark bits of cloth or doll-stuffing flutter up into the air and drift across the rocks. Some of them twirl high into the hard blue sky. Dark green butterflies. Thousands of them. I know it can't be true, but that's exactly what it looks like—like someone dropped a butterfly bomb. And then I understand. The dirty green butterflies drifting across the crumbled concrete have numbers on their wings. Fifty-dollar butterflies. Hundred-dollar butterflies. A wind whips down from the Noses, filling the air with dust. It also sucks thousands of bills up into the air. An impossible amount of cash, a huge green cloud of money. The helicopter pilot must see the money cloud too and wonder what it means. The thudding of the rotors gets closer, but they continue sweeping back and forth behind me. They won't spot me until they're directly overhead.

Herman chooses this moment to make a dash across the highway. I crane my neck and watch the Kiowa wheel around and come this way. The helicopter pilot has seen Herman as well. He flies straight ahead, no longer swinging back and forth above the valley. I have thrown everything away for this small child. If I do not succeed in this, I have not succeeded in anything. I cannot let them get him. No matter what that means.

Once I decide what I'm going to do, it only takes a moment to set it all in place. I wrestle one of the flares out of my assault pack, pop off the cap and screw it onto the detonator. I rest the flare on my stomach and feel for a rock big enough to bang it on. Herman seems to realize what the sound in the air behind him means. He runs faster, jumping over the mounds of rubble, his skinny legs a blur. All the speed in the world won't do him any good when that Kiowa swoops down behind him. But I don't intend to let that happen. I twist around and try to get a read on how fast the helicopter is moving. With the rock lodged between my legs and the flare's tube tilted at the correct angle, I should be able to hit it. Even if I don't bring it down, it might just distract the pilot long enough for Herman to escape, because if the Kiowa does stay in the air, it'll come hunting me instead. The Kiowa's shadow races almost half a kilometer ahead of it. I need to pop the flare just as its shadow crosses the highway.

The rotors pound the air. Each thud seems impossibly slow. The helicopter's purple twin glides across my useless legs, blotting out the sun for a moment. I hold my breath. Sweat makes a puddle of my face. I wonder briefly about the possibility that they're coming back to rescue me. What if I'm making a terrible mistake? And then it's too late. Its shadow kisses the asphalt, and I pound that flare as hard as I can. It shoots off with a beautiful whoosh of sparks. When the flare bursts, the Kiowa wobbles. Black smoke mixes with the red. I'm not certain what the flare hit, if it hit anything, but the helicopter's engine sounds unsteady. The door gunner fires wildly, unsure where his target is. The rounds ricochet off the twisted steel around me, making it gong and ping, but none of them hit me. Brass shell casings glitter as they drop to the ground.

Twelve klicks away, a dust devil swirls across the valley floor. The world seems to have abandoned me some time ago, or me it, and now it's flying past so quickly I can't keep a grip on it, can't even keep my feet on solid ground. From this vantage, upside down from the rest of my life, the world looks a different place altogether from the one I've always thought it to be. Using my left arm, I grab on to the cinderblocks and pull. This effort makes the blood from my nose drip faster. Behind the twisted metal of the gate, there is a small space that might provide some shelter from the door gunner's bullets. They thump into the sand all around me, ricocheting off the steel and concrete. It's a small chance, but so were all the rest. I doubt I'll see the sun rise tomorrow, but I'm not dead yet.